# SHADOW

*- of the -*

# KNIFE

## Richard Ayre

Burning Chair Limited, Trading As Burning Chair Publishing
61 Bridge Street, Kington HR5 3DJ

www.burningchairpublishing.com

By Richard Ayre
Edited by Simon Finnie and Peter Oxley
Cover by Burning Chair Publishing

First published by Burning Chair Publishing, 2021

ISBN: 978-1-912946-20-4

This book is dedicated to my ever-growing brood of grandchildren:

Miles, Samantha and Theo (when he gets here)

# Chapter One

## The Discovery

The night was greasy with sulphur. The coal smoke allied itself with the cold fog and formed into a thick, yellow mist that swirled and undulated over the slimy, discoloured bricks of the alleyways and back yards. Everywhere stank of rotten eggs and dank vegetation. It reeked of desperation. It had only stopped raining an hour before, and the storm had released the stench of the rotting food and the animal droppings and the dead vermin that dotted and lay around on the pavement. The fog—a ghostly, vaporous shroud—shifted and twisted and formed nebulous, momentary shapes, becoming opaque as the yellow light passed through it.

The light shone from the Bull's Eye Lantern of Metropolitan Police Constable John Wellingby; and it was needed on this, the last day of August 1890, for, as usual, many of the streetlamps had failed. The policeman walked amongst the misty shadows like a wraith, his cape dampened and beaded with moisture from the dewiness of the coal smog.

It was very quiet. Far away, muted by the smog and by distance, Big Ben struck 2am. A dog barked once, before yelping as someone clouted it into silence. Wellingby's footsteps clumped hollowly on the pavement as he followed the path of his regular beat.

Up ahead he spied a couple of women crouching under the illusory protection of one of the few working streetlamps. Prostitutes, by the looks of them, guzzling from a bottle of gin like there was no tomorrow.

Wellingby paused opposite them. They were both incredibly ugly women: blousy and ragged. He could smell them from across the street. One of them scratched vigorously at her crotch, staring blearily at the constable.

Wellingby forced a smile onto his face. He thought of himself as a good Christian, but these spectres of the East End night always disturbed him. They seemed to be the very epitome of sin and degradation, although he was more than experienced enough to know that there were a legion of reasons why they may have ended up as they had. Whitechapel had long ago taken them in, chewed them up and spat them out onto its unforgiving streets. Any youthful dreams they may have once harboured about how their lives would turn out had been destroyed many times over. His smile softened at these thoughts.

'Get yourself home, girls,' he called. 'Not safe to be out here at this time of night.'

The first woman laughed at this advice, but Wellingby could swear he saw tears in her eyes.

''Ow are we supposed to get fucked if we do that?' she asked, sadly.

There was a pause and then they both cackled again, raucously, and Wellingby turned away from them with a sigh, shaking his head. They never learned.

He left the still laughing women holding each other up, and turned left into Buck's Row, glancing up at the small, uncurtained windows above. No light shone from any of them; the alley seemed impenetrably black.

Wellingby hated that part of his beat. Two years ago, he had been called to something there that he had no wish to remember, but did so every time he passed through the place.

A momentary flash of memory brought to his mind a white face: mouth twisted into a grimace, eyes staring unseeingly into the night. And the throat. Christ, the throat.

Wellingby quickened his pace. He wanted to get past as swiftly as possible. That night still haunted his dreams. It was not just what had been discovered by his mate John Neil that night. It was what that discovery had led to over the autumn of 1888. It was the fear. The stultifying fear he had felt when he had been called to the scene.

Wellingby had been a copper in the East End for over ten years. He had experienced things no one would believe; things that the gentry, up in their big houses in the West End could never even imagine. He had stepped into knife fights between brutal thugs where the blood had frothed and foamed like a river over the filth-strewn cobbled streets. He had hefted up broken, inebriated prostitutes from cholera-wet puddles of their own waste and had watched them as they cursed him for his temerity, straightened their lice-infested dresses and wandered off to find their next penny knee-trembler. He had seen everything a man could see. He had become inured to humanity, and often believed he was watching the fall of civilisation as he walked the cold, hard lanes and alleys of Whitechapel.

However, the corpse discovered in Buck's Row that night had terrified him. Not because he was a coward or had never seen a corpse before, but rather because what had happened to that woman was just not *normal*. There had been a restrained savagery about the wounds inflicted upon her that had turned his blood to ice. Wellingby had seen many, many dead bodies, but the corpse of Mary "Polly" Nichols had been an obscenity. That was what it had been. An obscenity.

He continued on his beat, forcing himself to slow down. After all those years, he knew exactly where he should have been at any given time. There was no use hurrying, as much as he wanted to; he would only be returning later, just as his route demanded.

He almost did not discover the corpse. He had passed the gate of a fishmongers, and it was only an errant gust of wind that swirled its way through the fog and swung the gate, causing it to creak. The noise made Wellingby halt. He knew that no fishmonger worth his salt would leave his gate unlocked. Not around here. His stock would have disappeared in half a minute.

Realising that his heart was beating faster, and with the ghostly memory of Polly Nichols screaming in his face, Wellingby pushed the gate open further and shone his lamp around the yard.

Everything seemed normal. There were the usual fishmonger's wares lying around the walled area; ranks of wooden barrels, coils of rope, and reams of tarpaulin, ready for the next morning's work. The yard stank of salt and rotten fish and it was completely still. A sudden noise caused Wellingby to quickly swing his lamp around to a particular pile of tarpaulin, his heart jumping into his mouth, but it was only a rat knocking against a discarded tin cup as it scurried away from his presence. He released his pent-up breath, which disturbed the fog in front of his face, momentarily giving the yard a ghost-like luminosity. There was no one there. Everything seemed to be fine.

Until the gate he had pushed open bumped softly against something to the side of it. Something inside the yard.

With a wet swallow, Wellingby forced himself to step inside the dark yard, drawing his truncheon as he did so. It could be anything. Probably nothing more than another pile of tarpaulin. He took another step. Shadows stretched everywhere. Far away, sounding like it was coming from the mouth of Hell, he heard the two prostitutes he had passed cackle manically again. He swung his lamp around the gate.

The woman lay on her back, and he immediately knew that she was not just another drunken dollymop. This woman lay like a discarded sack.

Despite his trepidation, Wellingby hunkered down beside the body, his lamp peeling away the shadows. He swallowed again, hard.

Her arms were crossed over her chest, the fingers entwined, as if she were simply sleeping, but her legs were spread wide and drawn up, and her dress was pulled up above her waist. When Wellingby saw her abdomen he turned quickly away, gasping, memories once again heaving inside him. He sat like that for a second or two, averting his gaze; then, regaining his breath, he licked his lips, and slowly turned back to the corpse. He stared in horror at the woman's stomach.

Her abdomen had been sliced open and, if that was not awful enough, to add to the constable's horror he saw that her intestines were lying neatly by her side. Despite his revulsion, Wellingby noticed that they were still steaming, indicating that she had not been dead for long.

'Good God Almighty,' he breathed.

Steeling himself for more horror, he moved his lamp slowly up the woman's body, and eventually forced himself to look upon the throat he knew would be as open as the abdomen.

He was right.

The throat gaped at him, just as the bone-white face of the dead woman gaped at him. Blood, resembling a black funeral shroud in the night, had stiffened the woman's clothes, but there seemed little evidence of it anywhere else in the yard. The corpse grinned at him, stupidly, as if mocking him for his horror.

Despite the shock he naturally felt, and even though he knew it was a wasted effort, Wellingby felt for a pulse, but all he managed to do was get sticky blood on his fingers, which he hastily wiped on his trousers.

He stood suddenly and staggered out of the gates, leaning with his back against the outside wall and gasping in the dank air for a few moments. Then he managed to raise his whistle to his lips and blew for assistance.

\*

Inspector Jonas Handy was a strange looking fellow. Sergeant Frank Callow thought that it was a good job he was a copper, otherwise he would be getting his collar felt every time he stepped outside of his house. Handy looked like a proper criminal.

He was short and broad, with close-cropped brown hair and mutton-chop side-whiskers. His face was a strange mix of ugly and likeable, with a large round nose and prominent eyebrows. He looked, thought Callow with a smile, like a shaved chimpanzee in a cheap check suit. The bowler hat he wore perched on his large head simply made him look even more incongruous.

Handy sauntered up to him and nodded.

'Morning, guv,' said Callow.

Handy looked at him expectantly, and Callow found himself staring into eyes so blue they did not seem to be of this world. That was what made Handy stand out. His face might have looked like a blacksmith's bench, but those eyes, those clear, ice-blue eyes, spoke of an intelligence far higher than the average man would ever acquire. That was why Handy was so good at his job. It was also why he was so good with the women. He was as ugly as a workhouse slop bin, but those eyes, and his attention to detail, had turned up the temperature of many a girl that more handsome faces had failed to heat.

'Morning, Frank,' said Handy in his soft, East End voice. 'What we got here then?'

Callow pointed him towards the gate of the fishmongers with a turn of his head, giving Handy all the information they had as they walked. Standing around them in the early daylight, a crowd had naturally gathered, and they stared curiously. Handy nodded at a couple of people who were being kept away by the local bobbies. They smiled back at him; they knew him and trusted him as far as anyone in those parts could trust a jack. He was from their manor. He was one of them.

'Dead woman, about thirty years of age. No identification yet. Throat cut, abdomen opened.'

Callow got the expected glance from Handy as this information was received.

'We're not jumping to any conclusions, are we sergeant?'

Callow smiled at the mild rebuke.

''Course not, sir.'

They stopped by the gate and a constable let them in. Handy recognised him.

'Morning, Wellies,' he said to Wellingby, who smiled wanly at him.

'Morning, Mr Handy.'

'You found her then?'

Wellingby nodded and began to give his report.

Handy stopped him by holding up his hand.

'You finished your shift?'

Wellingby rubbed a hand across his chin. He was deathly pale and looked done in.

'Finished it about three hours ago, sir.'

Handy nodded.

'Right, off you go. Get home and get some sleep. I'll talk to you when you've done that. But write everything down before you do.'

'Already done that, sir,' said Wellingby, unpocketing his notebook.

Handy smiled at him.

'Good man. Go on, get back to that wife of yours.'

He took the notebook and shoved it in his pocket as Wellingby left into the newly dawning day. Then he turned to the corpse.

*Christ alive*, he thought. *Another one gone to meet their maker, another wasted life over far too soon.* As he stared down at the woman's face, a face that had been ravaged and haggard long before she had met her sad end, he couldn't help but feel that she had been perhaps set free from the misery of her poor existence, rather than been murdered.

He half listened as Callow went through what had been discovered so far, which was precious little.

'You do get the importance of the date, guv?' asked Callow.

'What?' Handy had been thinking about his mother for some reason, and the dark, flea-infested midden he had been dragged up in.

'The date. And place.' Callow stared at him, pointedly. 'Bucks Row. August thirty-first.'

Handy nodded.

'Yes, sergeant,' he said, heavily. 'I thought about that when I first got the call.'

7

Callow nodded, staying silent. He knew better than to interrupt the Inspector's train of thought.

Handy stood and took off his hat, rubbing his head roughly before replacing it.

'I don't want anything about the bloody Ripper mentioned,' he said, staring hard at Callow. He swept his gaze around the half-dozen coppers who were crowded into the yard. 'By anyone.'

He waited until each one of the constables quavered under his gaze and nodded at the order. They knew that, if they did say anything, Handy would come down on them like a ton of bricks.

Not that it would make any difference, thought the Inspector, as he spied a familiar and unwanted face in the crowd outside.

Edward Ely. Edward bloody Ely. That was all he needed.

He ignored the reporter as the man gestured at him with a raised pencil to try and gain his attention, and instead turned back to Callow.

'Right, Frank. Any witness accounts, anything on the body that might tell us who she was. You know what to do. And don't touch anything until we get photographs of the entire area. You know the mistakes made the last time.'

Callow nodded and took control, organising the constables to their various tasks. He knew what his boss meant. The early Ripper scenes had been made useless by the size tens of the coppers who had trampled all over them, even moving some of the bodies before every avenue of investigation had been studied. He wasn't going to be responsible for that sort of amateurish behaviour this time.

Callow watched Handy push roughly past Ely the reporter and climb into the hansom cab he had appeared in, then his gaze turned back to the dead woman.

*Not again,* he thought. *Christ, not again.*

# Chapter Two

## Jigsaw

'It's all in the wrist, Gresham. All in the wrist.'

Gresham smiled as Doctor Carter Jarman briefly flourished the scalpel in his hand.

'You demure, surely,' he responded. 'Your modesty does you great credit, Jarman, but I believe there was more to it than that.' What he had just witnessed in the operating theatre of the London Hospital was, in his opinion, nothing short of miraculous.

'That young boy should have lost his leg,' he continued as Jarman carefully packed the scalpel back into his bag. 'What was it? Fractured femur? And in how many places?'

'Oh, several,' said Jarman.

'Exactly. *And* his tibia. *And* his fibula, as well as all those torn arteries. It's a wonder they managed to get him into the hospital alive at all.'

'He was indeed a lucky young man,' said Jarman, closing his bag with a snap. 'If the accident hadn't happened just outside the hospital doors, I do believe that would have been the end of him.'

*Not to mention the fact you were here*, thought Gresham.

He and Jarman had been alerted to the young boy's plight by the screaming of a woman. They had been in Dr Gresham's office, which was just down the corridor from the public waiting room, sharing a bottle of port after a long day. They both groaned when they heard the screams. No doubt another drunken pauper looking for a free place to kip for the night and starting a fight when they couldn't find it. The waiting room resembled a dosshouse on some occasions, as the ranks of the homeless and feckless used the benches and the floor to shelter from the cold nights. Drunkenness and brawls were commonplace: hence the brawny "assistants" the hospital employed, all of them armed with short truncheons used either for self-defence or to encourage the rougher sorts to vacate the premises when they became too vocal or too rowdy.

They had sauntered into the waiting room to see a ragged woman carrying what looked to be a blood-soaked sack in her arms. She was screaming like a banshee. The assistants were already moving in to intercept her.

'A child,' Gresham had said, sadly. 'Dead, by the looks of it.'

Jarman had left his side and went to the woman, and Gresham watched as he gently prised the child away from the woman whom he assumed was the mother. Jarman talked to her, softly, smiling encouragingly. Then his face changed as he realised that the child, a boy of about seven years old, was still alive. The boy's face was like alabaster, but Jarman had found a pulse.

'Gresham!' he had shouted. 'Organise the theatre. Now!'

They had rushed the child to the theatre, both of them stripping off their coats and rolling up their sleeves.

The boy's leg was in a terrible state. It was tattered and ripped, the flesh torn completely away in some places, and blood had almost completely enveloped the child. They discovered later that the boy had been dragged under the wheels of a dustman's cart and the leg was mangled and twisted. In Gresham's opinion, amputation was the only option if the boy was to survive.

Jarman, however, had thought differently. He operated for over three hours, fighting to keep the boy alive. Gresham, acting as anaesthetist, had watched, agog, as skin and muscles were repaired and stitched backed together, as arteries and veins were sutured, as bones were re-set. The boy was eventually carted off to a ward upstairs.

Jarman had calmly washed, made sure he was presentable, and had then gone out to the mother. He had talked to her softly, showing her a compassion and a respect that would have been worthy of the highest-ranking duchess. The fact that the mother was a ragged, dirty dressmaker from Turner Street meant nothing to him. Gresham watched as the woman all but collapsed at his feet when he told her the boy lived and that his leg had been saved.

'God bless you, sir, God bless you, sir,' she wept, over and over. The grimy, stinking throng in the waiting room watched in dead-eyed silence as the emotional scene was acted out in front of them.

Jarman gave instructions to the assistants that the woman was allowed to stay for as long as she wanted and ordered soup for her. He then smiled at an old drunk he recognised who lay half propped-up on one of the benches. The drunkard waved back at him, happily. He re-joined Gresham.

'Should we finish that rather superior port?' he asked.

Gresham followed him back to the office, where Jarman finished packing his surgical bag. He picked up the glass of port and sprawled into a leather armchair, drinking deeply and closing his eyes.

'It's little wonder they call you "Jigsaw",' Gresham finally said, and Jarman smiled softly, his eyes still closed.

'That boy's leg would be burning in the incinerator right now if you had not been here tonight,' Gresham added.

'I'm always here,' murmured Jarman, his eyes still closed.

He suddenly looked incredibly tired, and Gresham realised what the operation had taken out of him. Jarman *cared* about the people of the East End. He really cared about them. They were the dregs of society; a huge, heaving mass of alcoholism and disease and crime that terrified those who were lucky enough to only rarely encounter them. But they were people to the surgeon, not the homogenous lump of inhumanity that most of the London elite believed them to be. Some of these elite even visited the slums from time to time, to stand in silent, staring groups, pointing their fingers and telling their children how lucky they were not to live in such squalid deprivation. To Jarman however, they were sentient, individual people. Gresham shook his head at the surgeon. The man was an enigma.

Jarman was thirty-five years old; tall and lean. His black hair, just beginning to show some grey at the temples, was long enough to brush his collar and he had acquired a habit of pushing it away from his face so that it lay flat over his head. He was clean-shaven and his eyes were a dark, liquid brown-imbued with a sense of sparkling intelligence. He wore black trousers that matched the frock coat hanging from the hook behind the office door and the Homburg hat that sat on the desk, but his waistcoat was a warm, mulberry red, giving a splash of colour to his rather sombre appearance. He sat with his long legs stretched out in front of him, his ankles crossed, and Gresham noticed that his expensive boots were scuffed and scarred under a recent coat of bootblack. This seemed typical of Jarman. He had money, but he seemed to care little about it. It seemed he used it only as a tool to study medicine and indulge in his other main interest in life: criminology. These two things took up all his time.

Gresham knew Jarman had been married once but was married no longer. He had never plucked up the courage to ask his colleague why that was. Although Jarman was usually a very affable fellow, there was something a little dark about him at times. It was not that he was standoffish, rather that he was a singularly private man who possessed an incredible gift for life, but who was fascinated with the dark side of that life. Truth be told, Gresham was a little afraid of Jarman. He had never asked his colleague about his private life because he had never wanted to know about that side of him. He believed that if he did, it might prove to be something truly awful.

Jarman suddenly opened his eyes and he seemed to scrutinise Gresham for a second, before the usual, lazy smile spread over his face as he repeated, 'I am always here.' He held out his glass and Gresham filled it.

'You *are* always here,' responded Gresham. 'And actually, that's why I asked you to come and see me today.'

Jarman continued to stare at him, his dark eyes unfathomable. 'Go on,' he said, eventually.

Gresham shifted uncomfortably under that dark stare. It seemed to suggest that Jarman knew what he was going to say, and perhaps he did. He had probably heard of the mutterings coming from the hospital administrator's office.

'I'm speaking now in my capacity as secretary of the hospital,' he said. 'We think you should have a small sabbatical. You have been here, in this hospital, nearly every single day for the last four or five years. You have never taken a holiday as far as I'm aware, and I fear it is playing on your nerves. We don't want to lose you to nervous exhaustion, Jarman; you're too good a surgeon for us to risk that. What you just did tonight proves that very fact. But the reality is, things have been noticed. The hospital has noticed. You're at the end of your tether, Jarman, and I have been asked to tell you that the hospital authorities want you to have a rest. For your own good. It is an order. Not a request.'

Jarman continued to stare at him, a strange nervousness in his eyes now. He seemed to be unsure as to how to answer Gresham.

He eventually stood and placed his glass on the desk, smoothing back his long, dark hair. He turned back to Gresham.

'I take it this order is unanimous with the board?'

Gresham turned his eyes to his own glass under that gaze.

'It is,' he said. When Jarman failed to respond, he sighed and then continued. 'Jarman, you are the best surgeon I, or anyone else at this hospital, has ever seen. We do not want to lose you. But we feel we will if you continue to push yourself as hard as you do. You spend all day, every day here at the hospital and then sit up half the night working on your criminal investigations. Something has to break at some point and we do not want that to happen. The hospital has said that they want you to take at least a month off. Go and have a holiday. The coast is very good for recuperation of the soul.'

He smiled, encouragingly.

'Go to Brighton,' he suggested. 'Take in the sea air. Relax, man. You need to relax. You've been like a coiled spring for years now. If you're not careful, something will snap, and we do not want that to not happen. You are too important to us here to lose you.'

Jarman turned and stared out of the window at the darkening street outside. The thought of not going into work seemed to freeze his heart for a moment, but when he turned again to look at Gresham, he saw the man would not be moved. A sudden feeling of calmness told him that a part of him was grateful for what Gresham had said to him, and he knew the man was right. He was on edge. He had been on edge ever since Mary.

He pushed that thought away and shot a lop-sided smile at Gresham, taking in his new situation in his customary easy way. The decision was made. There was nothing he could do about it. And, to be honest, now that it was being taken out of his hands, he was surprised he felt a form of relief beginning to wash through him. A little time off may, indeed, be good for him. He smiled at Gresham, nodding his acquiescence to the order.

'Well, I suppose I could use some time to catch up on my reading,' he muttered. 'Why don't we have another sherry to celebrate.'

Gresham happily concurred, pleased that he had agreed, and they had just finished the sherry when a porter knocked on the office door to let them know that Jarman's man had come and was waiting to pick him up.

'He don't seem very happy, Mr Jarman,' said the porter as they made towards the hospital entrance. 'He's been a-moaning and a-groaning and he says he's been waiting around for you for hours.'

'Curmudgeon is never happy, Grover,' replied Jarman, slipping on his gloves and hat. 'Being miserable is his *raison d'être*.'

Grover frowned at the unfamiliar phrase as he held the door open.

'Night, sir,' he said.

'Goodnight, Grover.'

Jarman stepped out into the noisy throng of Whitechapel Road. It was beginning to get dark, but dog carts and hansoms and horses still clattered up and down the street, almost completely obscuring the shop fronts opposite where the shop keepers were packing up for the day. The noise of the iron-shod cartwheels on the road and the general chatter of the crowded street was terrific after the relative quiet of the hospital.

He searched around and soon spied Curmudgeon, sitting atop Jarman's brougham, parked up by the kerb. Grover was right; he didn't look happy. He sat with his arms crossed, one eye half-closed as he regarded Jarman, sourly.

'Took your bloody time,' he growled as Jarman reached him. His North East accent was as strong now as when he had left his native Northumberland fifteen years before.

If Jarman was annoyed by the tone in his manservant's voice, he didn't show it. He was long used to it by now.

'I was involved in a little emergency, Curmudgeon. I hadn't time to let you know.'

Curmudgeon just harrumphed at this and leant down to open the door of the brougham, tutting when Jarman didn't instantly transport himself into the carriage.

Jarman had just closed the door when Curmudgeon slapped the reins and Dusty, the mare in the harness, jerked forward into the traffic.

Jarman shook his head to himself as he sat up and straightened his hat. He stared out of the window of his rich man's transportation at the real life of the East End of London.

Whitechapel Road hid its denizens of the night quite well. It was only when one ventured further into its dark warrens that the true East End truly showed itself. There, the tavern rats and the tanners and the drunkards and prostitutes leaned about on every street corner, ragged and wasteful and violent. Domestic crime was commonplace, muggings and rape the norm. Murder was definitely not an uncommon event. The alleyways and dark back lanes stank of sewage and filth and bodies that had never seen a bar of soap. The faces of those who peopled its dangerous labyrinths were brown with ingrained dirt. They were the uneducated, the illiterate. They lived from day to day—indeed, from hour to hour—only to obtain their next poor meal or quart of gin.

The workhouses, usually so feared, had queues half a mile long every morning, the line of ragged hopelessness desperate to perform the menial, repetitive tasks in return for a plate of greasy mutton fat and a burned potato. The dosshouses, lice-infested and stinking, held doubles and singles for anyone who could afford the *4d* or *8d* needed for their dubious embrace. Women who could not pay the price would often accept a trade of casual sex for the chance of a night's sleep in one of the thin, lumpy mattresses. For those who could afford neither was the two-penny hangover: a length of rope to lean over to try and grab a few hours of blissful unconsciousness from their blighted existence.

Jarman sighed quietly to himself as the brougham slowly made its way down Whitechapel Road and into Aldgate High Street. He did not really know why he cared so much about these people. They were alien to his own middle-class upbringing in Richmond. Most of them had seen nothing of the world outside their raucous streets, whereas he had travelled over a great part of the world. The people they met were all like themselves, even though a lot of them were immigrants from all over Eastern Europe. Jarman had mixed with a veritable melting pot of civilisations and cultures. He had been privileged enough to be able to afford travel and education, at least up until everything had changed, and he had seen more than his fair share of adventure during his time in the army. But the people of Whitechapel? They didn't know anything outside their own blighted existences, and they didn't seem to care, and this was probably why he liked their company. That and the guilt, of course. The never-ending guilt. The East Enders had a refreshing frankness and almost child-like gullibility that made him want to help them. To help them from what, however, he still did not know. Perhaps themselves.

After a journey broken only by the muffled curses of Curmudgeon at anyone who had the temerity to be in his way, the brougham eventually clattered down the quieter, more genteel, shop-fronted scenery of Bond Street and so to his bachelor maisonette, situated above a well-to-do jeweller: Garretts.

Curmudgeon drove the brougham into the yard at the rear of the building to deposit Dusty in her stable house to feed. Jarman opened the front door and jogged up the stairs.

He went straight into the sitting room and poured himself a sherry, taking it over to the window and staring down at the street below, allowing the stillness of the room to comfort him.

It was very quiet; the clock on the wall ticked and tocked. Mary tried to push herself into his thoughts, but he gently pushed her back. Later, perhaps. But not now. Not now. It seemed that he would have plenty of time in the near future to think of her.

He sat in his favourite wing-backed chair by the fireplace, his face suddenly looking tired and drawn. He sighed, as he always sighed when he returned home from Whitechapel. It was a sigh of sadness as well as comfort.

The door downstairs slammed and Curmudgeon appeared, slapping his cap on his thigh to rid it of the London soot.

'Help yourself, Curmudgeon,' muttered Jarman.

Curmudgeon, who had been eying the various bottles on the occasional table, did not need asking twice. He strode across to the decanters and poured himself a large whisky, gulping half of it down immediately. When he saw that Jarman had his eyes closed, he quickly refilled the glass, not noticing the smile that appeared on his employer's face at the small noises he made.

'Did the boy survive?' Curmudgeon asked, eventually.

Jarman opened his eyes, and the smile became broader.

'He did, Curmudgeon, he did. Now it's in God's hands if he makes a full recovery. I've done all I can.'

'More than anyone else could have,' said Curmudgeon, quietly, then seemed a little embarrassed at the praise.

Jarman looked at him for a while until Curmudgeon's face, naturally the colour of boiled ham, reddened even more.

'Thank you, Curmudgeon.'

Curmudgeon suddenly straightened to his full height, which was well over six feet.

'Aye, well…'

The clock ticked and tocked once more.

'I'll make your evening meal,' he continued. He downed the whisky and went into the kitchen.

Jarman spied the evening newspaper lying on the table and settled down to read it. He frowned when he saw the headline.

'*THE RETURN OF THE RIPPER?*' it screamed. '*DESPICABLE MURDER IN THE DARK STREETS OF WHITECHAPEL.*'

He quickly scanned it, his eyes pausing when he saw where the murder had taken place two days before. He remembered the body he had seen in '88. Ripped, torn. Kelly, he believed the victim's name had been. God alive. That had been horrific.

He read the rest of the report, noting that it was an Inspector Handy who was leading the investigation. Jarman had never met the man, but he had heard good things about him. Hopefully there would be no more killings; but for some reason, Jarman doubted that.

He closed his eyes again, just for a second, and was awakened by Curmudgeon calling him for his dinner an hour later. Sitting down to eat, he told Curmudgeon what the hospital board had decided.

'You do need a break,' agreed Curmudgeon. 'More than anyone, you do.'

'Well, it seems I must,' said Jarman. 'For everyone keeps telling me.'

Curmudgeon took his own food to his room next to the kitchen whilst Jarman dined alone. He finished with a brandy, and then, glancing at the clock, he made ready for bed.

As usual, Mary awaited him.

# Chapter Three

## The Escalation

### London, 1864

*The man sauntered through the rough, gas-lit, reeking streets. He was dressed in a fine frock coat and top hat, and he carried an ivory-handled cane. He could feel the eyes of the street-people glaring at him as he passed them in the dank, damp corners they squatted in, and he knew just how much he looked like a target. Any one of these creatures could attack him and take from him what they could grab, and there was little he could do about it. No one would come to his aid. But they seemed to shrink from his presence as he passed them by. They watched him silently: the filthy, half-naked and shoeless urchins, the grimy, worn-down women, the ragged, slack-faced men. They watched him stroll by, carrying enough wealth about his body to keep them in beds for a year, and they did nothing.*

*They feared him. This was the strange thing the young man had discovered when he had first started walking those streets the year before. They feared his wealth, they feared his health. They feared his class. They would happily beat and kick and stab each other over a few coins to drown themselves in a quart of the cheapest gin, yet they shrank away from his obvious riches. Something about his presence made them crouch like wild animals that had sniffed the scent of a predator in the air. They waited for his presence to pass them by. Behind him, he would hear them start talking again, hear the organ grinders start their discordant music once more; but, as he passed them, they were silent and still. He grinned into the night at the feeling of power he had over them, and his face was white in the gaslight.*

*He came across a bright, noisy pub. The original blue paint was peeling and faded, and all around, at every corner, the cobbles were wet with urine as men and women toileted in public. The smell was abysmal, but the dark man breathed it in, ecstatically, still grinning his white-faced grin.*

*Up ahead, in the shadows created by the nearby gas lamp, he spied what he was looking for. The shape was huddled, and it staggered and swayed as it tried to lean itself upright against the wall.*

*He approached the figure and eventually saw that it was a woman. Her hair was in disarray and her right eye was blackened and half-closed from a recent beating. She wore a faded red dress that was stained with old sweat under the arms. The hem, once white, was now a dingy grey.*

*The woman grinned at him, and he saw that a few of her teeth were missing. Her breath stank of gin and her clothes smelled revolting. She was perfect.*

*'Hello deary,' she slurred, when she became aware of his presence. 'Are you looking for me?' She giggled to herself, but her eyes showed the falsehood of her bravado.*

*'I may well be,' he replied, looking around. There seemed to be no one nearer than twenty feet from them and they all stood in the yellow light cast from the windows of the pub. He and the woman would be nothing more than dark shapes to them. Even the raucous noise from the pub seemed to be beaten into submission by the blackness surrounding them.*

*The woman giggled again and limped towards him. He noticed that the stocking of her right leg was torn at the knee and the skin underneath was scraped and bleeding, probably from a drunken fall. Or maybe from her position with her last customer. The thought of that and the sight of the blood made the young man's heart beat faster.*

*He leaned towards her ear and whispered something into it.*

*She recoiled and was about to rebuff him when he held out the note in front of her.*

*'It will be worth your time. You'll recover very quickly. And think of what you could buy with this.'*

*The five-pound note hovered in front of the woman's blood-shot eyes.*

*She looked into his grinning face, then nodded, still uncertain. She took him into the dark recess of a doorway just beside where she had been standing.*

*'Not too much,' she whispered, fearfully. 'Just a couple of scratches. Like you said.'*

*'Absolutely, my dear,' whispered the dark man. 'Just a few scratches. You have my promise.'*

*He took one of the woman's hands and placed it on his crotch, groaning in pleasure at the touch. His left hand reached up and began tugging lightly at the woman's hair.*

*His right hand brought out a small blade, and he grinned as she whimpered.*

*And in the shadows, across from the doorway, another figure watched the man and the woman. The figure's breathing became heavier and more excited as it watched the two people in the doorway, and then it grinned itself at what it saw.*

*And the grin split the darkness like a knife.*

\*

It was Sergeant Callow who had discovered the identity of the victim. Another end-of-the-line prostitute: washed up, broken down and drunken. He had scoured the area, asking anyone if they knew of a missing woman, until he had found two of her brethren hawking for trade outside a grimy pub. They told him that a woman called Eliza Cotton had not returned to the dosshouse they had shared whenever they had the money. This was not unusual, but it had given him a lead. He went to the dosshouse dwelling they had spoken of.

The place was filthy. It was a large, rectangular room, poorly ventilated, and the fetid air was thick with the old, familiar smells of dirt, sweat, sewage and seminal fluid. Almost every square inch was taken over by single or small double beds, and the outrageous stench emanating from the stained and yellow sheets and crusty mattresses encouraged Callow to breathe through his mouth. Separated from the beds by a narrow walkway and lying on the floor against the far wall of the room, were ranks of numbered, wooden "four-penny coffins" which afforded some comparative luxury to the stinking beds. The man in charge of the place, a greasy individual with a face like a jackdaw, said he knew Eliza, and the leer he gave Callow suggested to the sergeant that this "knowing" was very much in the biblical sense. She had probably used her thin, grimy body to pay for a bed for the night whenever she didn't have the money.

The deputy told him that Eliza had not returned to the dosshouse on the night she was murdered, even though she had told him earlier in the day that she had wanted a bed that night because she was "shagged out". Callow had taken the man to the hospital where the body lay and he had confirmed, in hushed tones as he stared at her white face, that this was indeed Eliza Cotton. Enquiries were now underway to try and find out where she had gone that night, and who she may have talked to.

Later that day, Handy watched as the body of Eliza was dissected, quickly and efficiently, in front of him. It was not his first post-mortem and it would not be his last, but he never enjoyed them.

Before the surgeon had started, he had pointed out to Handy the injuries the woman had sustained. They were familiar, yet strangely different to the Inspector, who had studied the Ripper case carefully over the last couple of years.

The throat had been cut right down to the spine. The trachea and the muscles of the neck were sliced cleanly through. The surgeon could only make out one cut, which was different to what Handy knew of the cases two years previously, where there had usually been at least two slices.

The abdomen had been cut open in a diagonal line, from just

below the woman's left ribs down to her right hip. Then it looked as if the wound had been pulled apart: 'ripped', the surgeon said. The intestines had been taken out, but not cut; simply laid by the corpse in that dirty backyard to sit, steaming, beside her. From the direction of the cuts on both her throat and her abdomen, the surgeon thought they were looking for a right-handed man.

The poor woman lying on the cold slab had also been mutilated horribly around her inner thighs and in between her legs. It must have been a heavy-duty knife that had done this sadistic work: sharp, but also very strong, with a wicked point to it. There were several incisions around this area, but none of them too deep.

'It's as if whoever did it was just…prodding at her,' said the surgeon, William Shafto. 'And I think it happened post-mortem; there was very little blood on her underwear.'

Handy grimaced and nodded, writing in his notebook. He remembered some of the women his mother knew when he was a child. They had all been as rough as the roads, but they had always been kind to him. None of them deserved to end up with the lives they'd had to endure, and he had no doubt that the woman before him had not deserved it either. No one deserved that. The surgeon then commenced with the autopsy.

There was nothing missing from the corpse. In the previous Ripper cases, body parts had sometimes been cut from the cadavers, but all the woman's organs were where they were supposed to be; apart from the intestines, of course, which had been scooped out of the corpse. Under Handy's instructions, the stomach was opened and they discovered some half-digested mush that may or may not have been eels. Whatever it was, it stank to high heaven. Handy again wrote some details into his notebook, taking a couple of steps backwards as he did so.

He left the room when the surgeon began sewing the woman back up again with thick, ugly catgut. He stepped outside the building and took a deep breath before lighting a cigarette, leaning against the wall of the workhouse morgue and closing his eyes momentarily, trying to unsee what he had just witnessed.

'Afternoon, Jonas,' said a quiet voice in his ear. 'Nice day for it.'

It took a second for Handy to recognise who had spoken, but then he smiled and held out his hand.

'Hello, Fred. What's the Yard doing slumming it around here?'

Inspector First Class Frederick Abberline smiled back and shook the proffered hand.

'Old haunting ground,' he replied, looking around him at the throng of people moving backwards and forwards on Whitechapel Road, just outside the workhouse gates. The carters and tanners and merchants, the brewers and the fishmongers. And, of course, the never-ending procession of faded prostitutes. They all went about their everyday business through the dirty, brick-walled streets.

'I heard about the woman. Do you think it's him?' he asked after a while.

Handy shrugged. 'I don't know, Fred. But it's very similar. I think it might be.'

Abberline nodded, several times. Then he held out his hand. 'Do you mind if I cast my eye over it?'

Handy hesitated. Abberline had no business being here. He worked from Scotland Yard now. However, he reasoned that the man who had hunted the Ripper in the first place might have something to add that may be useful. He handed his notebook over.

He slowly finished his cigarette, and then had another as Abberline went methodically through the notes.

'Nothing missing?' asked Abberline eventually.

Handy shook his head.

Abberline nodded again. He was a very quiet man, was Frederick Abberline. Quiet and thorough. Handy waited.

'The stab wounds,' said Abberline, and Handy smiled. He knew he would come to those.

'Like the ones on Martha Tabram and the two other girls?'

Abberline sniffed suddenly and gave the notebook back to Handy.

'I never really thought that Polly was the first one,' he said. He was referring to Mary Anne Nichols. "Polly" was the name she often went by. Handy nodded, waiting.

'All the murders, they got worse over time,' continued Abberline. 'Until we got to Mary Kelly.' He stroked his moustache slowly, his eyes unfocused, perhaps seeing that savaged monstrosity in Miller's Court two years before. Handy had seen the photographs of that case. They alone had been enough to haunt his dreams for months afterwards.

'I always felt he was leading up to something big,' continued Abberline. 'And I always thought that Kelly wasn't it. He was working up to something even worse, if that's possible.'

'How could anything be worse than that?' asked Handy, lighting yet another cigarette and offering one to Abberline. 'I didn't see her, but I've seen the photographs. Nothing could be worse than what he did to that woman.'

Abberline smoked silently for a while, watching the street scenes. A young urchin across the road tried to nick an apple from a fruit stall and got a smack across the head for his trouble. The lad ran off, whimpering, holding a hand to his red cheek.

'It's just a theory,' Abberline said, eventually. 'And it wasn't just me who thought it. We had someone helping us on the last case. A surgeon, although we got him involved because of his knowledge of criminal behaviour. He's done a lot of research over the years into what he calls "serial" killers.'

'Cereal killers? Like barley?'

'Serial. As in they commit a series of killings. He believed that Jack was always trying to out-do himself in the horror stakes. That he got a thrill out of the mess he made of those girls. And he told me, that night in Miller's Court: "Inspector", he said, "This man will not stop until we stop him. He is indefatigable." That's what he called him. Indefatigable. But it seemed he was wrong, because then of course the murders did stop. At least until now.'

'Who was this surgeon then?'

Abberline smiled at him.

'I thought you'd never ask. His name is Dr Carter "Jigsaw"

25

Jarman.'

'Jigsaw?'

Abberline nodded, smiling.

'On account of his ability to reconstruct broken bones. But he's one of the cleverest men I've ever met, Jonas. His knowledge of the East End underworld is about the best you could ask for. He's studied murders all over the world. He's about the greatest living expert on why men kill and how to stop them killing.'

Abberline gave Handy a card with Jarman's name on it.

'He gave me this at the time,' he said. 'I can't tell you what to do, Jonas, but if I were you and if the Ripper is truly back, then I would get in touch with this man as soon as possible. He might just be the only thing between you and a morgue-full of new killings.'

Abberline stood on his cigarette and shook Handy's hand before looking out the gates at the street again.

'I do miss it,' he said, wistfully to himself. Then he sauntered away, disappearing through the gates and out into the grimy crowds.

Handy looked down at the card and noted the address. Then he placed it in his pocket and re-entered the hospital building.

Callow had returned by this time and was standing in the white-tiled corridor outside the morgue, waiting for him.

'Anything?' asked Handy.

'Nothing new,' replied the sergeant. 'We know she left the dosshouse in Pelham Street at about eight-thirty. She said she had some business, which the dolly she was talking to seemed to think was an appointment with a client.'

'Did she say anything about this client?'

Callow shook his head.

'A pie seller on the corner of New Street said a woman matching her description bought a meal off him at about ten. Said she was three sheets to the wind and could hardly stand up straight. She didn't say anything other than to order her stewed eels. He said she stumbled off towards Whitechapel Road. No one saw anything else of her until Wellies came across her at two the next morning.'

Handy sighed and rubbed a hand across his stubbled chin.

'Right. Let's get back to the station. I need a shave and a cuppa.' He handed Callow the card Abberline had given him. 'Give this to one of the lads and tell them to ask this Jarman fellow to give me a call when he has time, will you?'

Callow looked at the name.

'A lead?'

'Don't know what he is. But I'd like to have a chat with him.'

Callow nodded and they exited the workhouse, making their way back through the thronged streets to the station.

*

Molly Harnath grunted as the man struck her hard in the face, but she was determined to hang on to the scuffed and faded bag he was trying to wrestle from her grasp.

'Let go, you bitch,' the man wheezed. His breath stank of cheap gin and halitosis. From what Molly could make out in the gas-lit shadows, most of his front teeth were missing.

Molly didn't answer but simply tugged harder, wrenching the bag back from him. The man staggered and Molly saw her chance. With as much strength as she could muster, she swung back her foot and kicked him in the balls and he sagged, the fight immediately going from him, drool sliding from his mouth. He collapsed to the cobbles, flattening a pile of old horseshit as he did so.

'Bitch,' he mumbled again, but his eyes were already closing. Within seconds, he was snoring gently into the manure. A couple of ragged men across the street watched for a moment longer, but it seemed the entertainment was over. Molly pulled her dress straight and dabbed at her greasy hair, tucking an errant strand back behind her ear.

She walked with her head held high past the two men who had watched her predicament with the attempted theft, but who had done nothing to help her. One of them said something to the other and they both laughed. Molly spun around and glared at them, and then, grasping the hem of her dress, she hoisted it high and bared her dirty arse at them. They laughed even harder at this and she grinned to herself, rubbing her already blackening eye. Just another night for a Whitechapel prostitute.

She walked through the thronged alleyways. Everywhere was filth, everywhere was decay, but Molly noticed none of it. She had lived in those streets for the whole of her twenty-six years, and the rats and the shit and the stench and the violence were as familiar to her as her own face. Molly had moved from being an abused child at the hands of her father—before the bastard had died, of course—to abused wife at the hands of her husband—before *that* bastard had died, too—to abused prostitute at the hands of many more bastards. She had never known love. She had never known comfort. If Molly ever thought about why she had been forced to survive by sharing her body for money, the reasons were enough to make her weep. Therefore, she tried never to think about it. It was simply the way of the world and Molly had learned to take one day at a time and not dwell on her blasted past or where her future might take her. Molly was a victim of life and there was nothing she could do about it. As she walked, she thought again about the message she had received, and a small frown crossed her brow. Then she seemed to shrug to herself, continuing on her way. What would be, would be.

Up ahead, she spied the yellowish glow from the windows of her local pub *The Barrel*, and the jaunty plonking of an out-of-tune piano seemed to lighten her mood. A nice stout would go down well before her rendezvous.

She entered the smoky pub and saw two of her brethren at a table in the corner, quaffing gin. She sat beside them.

'Evening, ladies,' she said with a smile. 'How are we tonight?'

The other two prostitutes didn't smile back, although they moved their stools to let her sit with them. They were both a little jealous of Molly. She still had her looks, and she was relatively young. They were both in their forties and riddled with disease and alcohol. They seemed to represent the future existence of Molly

Harnath, but even as Molly contemplated this sobering thought, she pushed it away. Nothing she could do about it. One of the women, Connie Myers, coughed raucously into her hand and then wiped the specks of blood from her palm onto her knee. She did not yet know that she had tuberculosis and would be dead before the year was out. Or if she did, she was trying not to think about it.

The other woman, Janey Swann, stared at Molly.

'You're looking pleased with yourself tonight, despite your face,' she said.

Molly grinned, showing teeth that, although yellowing, were at least all in place. 'Some old tosser tried to nick me purse,' she replied. 'Got a kick in the tallywag for his troubles.' They all laughed. 'No. Got myself a customer for later on tonight,' she continued. 'All sorted. He says he's going to pay me five English pounds for the pleasure of my company. Five pounds!'

The other women scoffed.

'Who's this customer then?' wheezed Connie. 'The Duke of York?'

She and Janey laughed again, until Connie collapsed into another coughing fit. Janey slapped her back until the hacking had subsided and Connie had wiped her hand on her dress again.

'Proper gentleman he is,' replied Molly, catching the eye of the landlord and holding up a few coppers. He brought over a bottle of stout and a glass, which she filled.

'Where did you meet a proper gentleman around here?' asked Janey, scathingly.

'Wasn't here. It was up town,' responded Molly, taking a long draught of her beer. 'I went for a lovely walk through the park and this gentleman's servant came up and started talking to me. That was a while ago, of course. I've known him for a while. When we first met, he said it was a pleasure knowing me.'

'Pleasure of knowing your Cock Lane, more like,' said Connie and the two women laughed again. This time, Molly joined in.

'He can have me cock lane and me dairies for a fiver,' she said, drinking deeply. 'In fact, for a fiver, he can have all of me.'

The women all laughed again, although Molly suddenly seemed unsure of herself.

'I've known him for a while now,' she repeated. 'Him and his friends. I don't know what he wants tonight. I thought I was finished with him.'

She shuddered suddenly and sipped her stout to cover the feeling of unease she felt.

'But for a fiver…'

She left the sentence unfinished, and the three women finished their drinks and parted ways outside *The Barrel*: Connie and Janey to stalk the dark alleyways for their next cully and Molly to meet her gentleman. He had said he would be at the corner of Church Street. The note, handed in at the dosshouse, had said he just wanted to talk. To explain what had previously happened to her.

Molly didn't really know what he wanted, but she needed the money. She always needed the money, which had been the only reason she had allowed what had happened to her before. She shuddered again as she walked. Bunch of horrible mad bastards.

She continued on her walk from Brick Lane into Church Street, squinting into the gloom of the shadows cast by the imposing structure of Christ Church itself. Nothing moved except a cat, which slinked along the pavement towards her. The cat was black, and Molly moved out of its way so it wouldn't cross her path and give her bad luck. It presented her with an aloof, yellow-eyed stare as it stalked past her and disappeared into the darkness.

Molly walked further into the street, her footsteps sounding very loud in the quietness of the narrow ally. Water dripped from a broken gutter somewhere, sounding alien in the stillness.

She stopped. Something was wrong. She suddenly knew. Something was very wrong. The note from that man. Why would he have sent that? What was she to him? He could have whomever he wanted. Why would he choose to meet a prossie from Whitechapel when so many other girls were easier, and closer, for him and his friends?

Molly belatedly realised that whatever the reason for the note and the promise of the astronomical sum of money had been, it was for nothing good. She turned, glimpsing the brighter lights of Brick Lane, less than twenty feet away. But she was already far too late.

A hand appeared from the shadowy cloister beside her and grabbed her by the throat. Her own hands instinctively grasped the wrist but, as she did so, she felt a booted foot crash into her thigh and a huge pain welled up, her leg giving way beneath her. She was dragged, still struggling but unable to scream because of the pressure around her throat, into the darkness.

She was slammed to the wet flagstones of the church entrance portico and a knee slammed into her stomach, the weight of her attacker pressing down on her. Another hand joined the fingers around her throat, and they squeezed.

Sparks began to flash in front of Molly's eyes as the pressure around her throat cut off her breathing. She tried to pull the hands from her neck, but she may as well have been trying to lift a carthorse. The attacker was just too strong.

One of the hands released its pressure and Molly had a fleeting glimpse of reprieve, but then she saw what that hand was now grasping, and she tried, again to no avail, to scream murder. The huge blade flashed down, just above the other hand still around her throat, and suddenly Molly was choking on something even worse than the attacker's hands. She coughed, harshly, as the blood from her severed neck rushed down her throat.

She was still not yet dead when she felt that cold, cold steel cutting—*slicing*—into her stomach, but she could not move. The shadows were gathering; the pain, the intense, unbelievable pain she had first felt, was lessening.

In the fading seconds of Molly's life, she recognised the white face grinning down at her, and she realised what a fool she had been. She should have known. This was where her broken life had finally led her.

Her own stupidity had killed her.

# Chapter Four

## The Second Body

The constable who called on Jarman the next morning was new to the job: a slightly built, downy-faced youngster with red hair and a face full of freckles. He quailed under the glowering stare of the huge man who opened the door to him.

'Well?' asked the man, frowning down at the lad.

The constable, whose name was Rose, squared his shoulders under that fierce stare, but his eyes blinked too much, and he eventually lowered them to the step the huge fellow stood on.

'Compliments of Inspector Handy, CID. Is Dr Jarman in?' He eventually looked up again into the man's pale grey eyes.

The man standing there on the doorstep was massive. His sandy hair was short-cropped, and his face was very scarred. Everything about his face was bent: the nose, the mouth, even his eyebrows were out of line. One long scar— thick and raised and ugly— cut his left eyebrow in half and ran up his forehead to disappear into the hairline. His whole visage was the colour of boiled ham. He wore knee length boots, black trousers, a grey waistcoat and a shirt with an open collar. The one hand that Rose could see curled around the door was enormous, and the fingers were as scarred and as gnarled as the man's face.

'Got a card?' asked Curmudgeon, and Rose handed over the card that Callow had given him. Curmudgeon squinted at it.

'This is Jarman's own card,' he growled.

If Rose thought it was odd that a servant should call his master by their surname like this, he did not show it.

'I don't know what it is,' he said, his voice a little higher than he liked the sound of. He cleared his throat and tried again. 'Look. Is your master in, or not?'

'I have no master,' said Curmudgeon. 'But Jarman is in. Wait here.'

He shut the door in Rose's face and the constable heard heavy footsteps ascending the stairs inside. Feeling self-conscious, he stared around the busy street, touching a finger to his police helmet as a respectable-looking couple wandered by, then blushing when the woman smiled back at him.

The door opened and that horrible man was there again.

'He says he'll see you.'

Leaving the door open, Curmudgeon preceded Rose up the stairs. The constable frowned again at his manners and closed the door behind him. He jumped when Curmudgeon barked at him from the landing: 'Wipe your feet!'

He quickly did as he was told and ascended the stairs, finding himself in a smart sitting room.

It could be best described as frugal. There was a comfy-looking leather chair by the empty fire, a settee and a large, ornate work desk, books and papers piled neatly on the corners. Apart from a few lamps and a couple of nick-nacks, that was virtually it as far as furnishings went, but every wall was lined with bookcases: leather-bound tomes stacked side by side. Rose had never seen so many books in one place outside a library and the sight impressed him. The doctor must have been a very fine fellow indeed to own so many works. Then he glanced at Curmudgeon who stood by the door, scowling at him. He could do better in the servant department, though.

After another disdainful glance in his direction, Curmudgeon wandered off, presumably to fetch Dr Jarman, and Rose was left alone, with only the ticking and tocking of a wall clock to keep him company.

He had wandered over to the fireplace and was staring intently at a statuette of a half-naked nymph on the mantlepiece when a voice spoke behind him.

'Constable. What can I do for you?'

Rose turned, his face once again reddening from staring at the breasts of the statuette, and saluted Dr Carter Jarman.

'Compliments of Inspector Handy of H Division, sir,' he said, repeating the words he had practised on the way there. 'But could you call, at your earliest convenience, to Leman Street Station? For a chat, he said.'

Jarman stared at the constable for a second.

'Inspector Jonas Handy, yes?'

'Yes, sir.'

Jarman nodded. 'I've heard of him.'

If he seemed surprised at the invitation, he did not show it. It was almost as if he had been expecting it. He already wore his coat, and his hat was in his hand.

'Kindly inform Inspector Handy I will be there forthwith, constable.' He smiled at Rose, and the smile made the constable feel much more at ease.

'Curmudgeon will see you out,' the doctor continued.

'Yes, sir,' repeated Rose, following Curmudgeon who indicated at him with his head.

Outside, the constable turned to the other man and tried to inject a sense of authority into his voice.

'Well, thank you, Curmudgeon, is it? An unusual...' he started.

Curmudgeon slammed the door in his face.

*

Jarman and Curmudgeon arrived at the station an hour later. Curmudgeon waited outside: 'To stop these thieving bastards from stealing the horse for their dinner,' he muttered, glaring around him. Jarman made his way inside into what seemed to be mayhem.

Policemen were running around in all directions and bumping

into one another, most of them were carrying files or papers and looked like they didn't really know what they were doing.

Jarman strolled calmly through the havoc to the counter, where a harassed looking desk sergeant stood. He was berating Rose, the young constable who had called on Jarman.

'Well, you should have gone there first, shouldn't you!' shouted the sergeant.

Rose looked offended.

'Well, how was I supposed to know, sarge?' he complained. 'Sergeant Callow sent me up town on a message.'

The sergeant scoffed.

'Message,' he repeated, scathingly. 'You wouldn't know police work if it sat in your lap and bit your cock, would you, lad.'

Rose was downcast.

'No, sarge,' he said, miserably.

The sergeant seemed to take pity on him. He sighed. 'Well, you're here now,' he growled. 'Get yourself over to Church Street and see if you can perform any worthwhile duties when you get there.'

'Yes, sarge,' said the young lad, and turned to leave. Jarman smiled and nodded at him as he passed.

'What can I do for you, sir?' asked the sergeant as the constable left.

Jarman told him his name and a look of surprise fell across the sergeant's face.

'Rose!' he roared, and Rose stopped and turned, looking even more miserable.

'Take this gentleman with you. Inspector Handy left word that if he turned up, he should go straight to Church Street. Well done, constable. You did something right for a change.'

The sergeant smiled at the effect the words of praise had on Rose's young face. The constable came running up to Jarman.

'This way, sir,' he said, indicating to the door.

'Mr Handy's compliments, sir,' said the sergeant to a bemused-looking Jarman. 'But something has occurred, and he said that, if you showed up, we were to send you straight there.'

Jarman could guess what that meant. He nodded to the sergeant and turned to the constable.

'Come along, Rose. We'll use my brougham. We'll get there faster.'

Rose looked just about ready to explode with excitement at the prospect of riding in the fancy carriage.

The two of them left the station, climbed in, and made their way to Church Street.

*

Curmudgeon parked on the corner of Osborn Street and the three men walked past the ragged crowds and the bobbies trying to hold them back. At the top of Church Street, they ducked into the church portico and saw what was lying there. Rose immediately ran to one side and deposited his breakfast on the grass of the churchyard.

A short, squat figure approached them, taking off a bowler hat.

'Dr Jarman?' he asked with an East End accent.

Jarman nodded. They shook hands and Handy introduced himself.

'You can see why I asked you to come,' he said, softly.

They both stared at the remains of what had once been a human being.

The old dress the woman had worn was in tatters, and it was soaked in blood that had congealed to a brown crust. The corpse lay with its legs spread wide, the arms by its side.

The abdomen had been sliced open from the ribs to the hips; it looked like more than just one cut. A slippery coil of what could only be intestines was piled up beside the dead body and, without them there, the abdomen seemed empty. For all intents and purposes, it looked as if someone had used a spoon to scoop out the woman's entrails, leaving only a huge, gaping hole. A quick glance told Jarman that most of the organs left in there had been savagely attacked.

Even standing where he was, it was obvious to Jarman that the body had been stabbed several times, as well as been mutilated. The muscles of her stomach were flayed and sliced—*carved* would have been a better word—and the bloodied remains hung in tatters of skin and yellowish fat.

But it was the face that drew the men's attention in grotesque fascination.

The tip of the nose had been sliced off and the lips were gone, revealing teeth that seemed to grin at the men surveying her sad carcass. But worst of all, the head looked like it had been partially scalped, leaving half a blood-streaked skull open to the air. The sodden mass of black hair and skin lay crumpled around the corpses head.

'Christ, alive,' whispered Curmudgeon, over and over. 'Christ, alive.'

Jarman turned to Handy, and the Inspector saw the horror on his face, mixed with what looked like a steely rage. Over by the graves Rose was on his knees, gulping in fresh air, his face ashen.

'Curmudgeon,' said Jarman, quietly. 'Attend to that constable, would you? Sit him down somewhere away from here.'

Curmudgeon heard the barely contained anger in his voice and simply nodded, taking the lad away. 'Come on, son,' he said, softly.

Handy indicated with a turn of his head for Jarman to follow him back out into Church Street.

They stared at each other whilst Handy lit a cigarette, offering one to Jarman who accepted, gratefully.

'I have seen many things in my life,' murmured Jarman. 'But I have rarely seen anything even close to this. Except two years ago, at Millers Court.'

Handy inhaled and closed his eyes for a second, then held Jarman's own with his piercing stare.

'That's why I asked you to come here,' he said. 'This is the second murder like this in three nights. Except that the other wasn't half as bad as what's been done to this poor sod.' He indicated to the corpse with his cigarette.

'Inspector Abberline said I should call you,' he continued. 'He said you were very useful the… The last time we had things like this going on.'

Jarman turned and stared at the dismembered horror inside the portico. For some reason, Mary reared in his thoughts and he quickly shut her out. He had no wish for her to be associated with this awfulness. He nodded at Handy.

'Of course, Inspector. Strangely enough, I suddenly find myself with some spare time. I'll do everything I can to help find the person who did this.'

'I'm not even sure it is a person,' said Handy. 'How could a human do this to another?'

'Human beings are capable of such atrocities as you would not believe, Inspector. The mind of a lunatic can manifest itself in the most outrageous horror. If this is the same man we were looking for two years ago, I believe that we may yet see what that horror is. Unless we catch him, I believe we shall witness hell on earth.'

He crushed the cigarette under his worn boots.

'I'll get to work,' he said.

Around the corner, in the weak but warming morning sun, and with birds singing in the background, Curmudgeon sat on a bench next to Constable Rose.

As he stared at the young lad's pale profile, Curmudgeon had a sudden, vivid memory: heat, blood on dust, gunfire, screaming, and a young boy lying, dying in his arms.

*'Tell me mam I love her, sarge,'* he was gasping, over and over again. *'Tell me mam I love her.'*

Curmudgeon pushed the thoughts away. He sat silently as Rose got himself back under some sort of control.

'Who the hell could do something like that?' asked Rose, eventually. 'Why would someone do something like that?'

Curmudgeon contemplated the lad, then reached into the folds of his old army greatcoat and pulled out a hipflask. He sipped some of its contents and then handed it over.

'Have a pull on that,' he said. 'It'll make you feel better.'

The young man tipped it down and coughed harshly, but some colour returned to his cheeks.

Curmudgeon had another pull then put the flask away.

'I don't know who or what did it,' he said, 'but I do know that, if we're going to catch them, then there's none better than Jigsaw Jarman to do it.'

'Jigsaw?' asked Rose, confused.

Curmudgeon smiled, and the smile transformed his grim face. He indicated to the huge scar on his forehead.

'On account of his surgical skills. Too many years ago to remember now, in a land a long way from here, my head was broken open by an Afghan fighter. It was in pieces, and they left me to die outside a broken-down hut that called itself a hospital. Jarman found me, and cut my head open and put it all back together again. He never gave up on me, even as all the others left him to work alone 'cos they said it was a useless cause.'

Curmudgeon grinned at Rose.

'That man saved my life. And he did it because he's a tenacious bastard. He's like a terrier. He never gives up. He is the cleverest man I've ever known, and all he does, apart from fixing up hopeless cases like me, is study the minds of killers.' Curmudgeon's eyes seemed to stare into the past for a second. 'It's all he has left, I suppose.'

He pulled out his hip flask again and the two men shared another, by now quite companionable, drink.

'If your Inspector Handy has any sense,' Curmudgeon continued, 'then he'll give Jarman whatever he asks for. Any help he needs. If he does that, believe you me, he'll find whoever did that around there. And when he does, the bastard better hope he gets the rope for it. Because if Jarman ever gets his hands on him, he'll wish he was dead a thousand times over.'

They were interrupted by Handy, who sauntered over to them.

'You all right, son?' he asked Rose, and Curmudgeon was surprised to see genuine concern on the Inspector's ugly face.

Rose nodded and stood. 'Absolutely, sir. Sorry about the mess.' He indicated to the vomit in the distance.

Handy smiled at the lad, then told him to get back to the station. He turned to Curmudgeon, who stood. The two men stared at each other, eyeing each other up. They both seemed to come to the same conclusion about each other at the same time.

'Dr Jarman says he'd like your help.'

Curmudgeon grimaced.

'He always does,' he said.

He watched Rose walk away and sighed. When his face turned back to Handy, it was as ill-disposed and morose as usual.

The two of them returned to Jarman.

And that mangled corpse.

# Chapter Five

## A Surprising Turn of Events

The body lay under flickering gas lamps on the slab at the mortuary. It was a terrible sight to behold; it looked barely human. To the unfortunate morgue attendant who was given the job of cleaning it up ready for Jarman's autopsy, it looked like one of the props decorating the outside of the travelling freak shows he had visited as a lad. It seemed devoid of anything that could be described as "human". When he had finished preparing the body, the attendant had washed his hands over and over again. He wanted no trace of it left on him.

Jarman had performed the autopsy with a close attentiveness, making sure Handy wrote everything down in detail in his notebook.

'The throat was cut when she was still alive,' said Jarman as he was washing his hands. 'Everything else, all the other mutilations, including the scalping of her head, were done when she was dead, although I have a feeling they were started while she was still breathing her last, the poor woman.'

'But the blood from the throat…' Handy began, and Jarman nodded.

'Indeed. You remember I showed you the arterial spray on Church Street? The way it spread both sides of the body? I believe the murderer must have been on top of her when that happened, and it must have hit him straight in the face. He would have been completely enveloped in her blood. How he managed to wander around after that is a question we have to add to all the others we need to ask.'

Jarman then indicated at the corpse.

'Look at these marks,' he said. Handy squinted down at the body. On the arms and legs, were what looked like scars: short, thin scars.

'There are more of them on her breasts,' said Jarman.

'You, know, I believe I saw a few marks like that on Eliza Cotton's body,' said Handy. 'Only a few, though, if I remember correctly. What do you think caused them? They look quite old.'

Jarman nodded.

'I think they are anything up to a year old. I have known patients in the past who will cut themselves in similar ways. It seems to be a psychological need for them to do so. A sort of "self-harm"; the results of hopelessness and lack of self-worth. Perhaps this poor woman felt the same. However, the marks I have witnessed in the past were always on the arms, sometimes the legs. I have never seen them on the breasts.' He threw the towel over a hook and pulled on his frock coat.

'It may be something or nothing. God knows what sort of life she's led to gain those scars. Anyway, if I could, I would like to see the body of the other woman. Before it becomes corrupted.'

Handy just nodded.

'It's at the local workhouse morgue,' he said. They were in the morgue of the London Hospital, as Jarman had insisted the body be taken there, promising Gresham it was a one-off visit and not a return to work. 'We can go now if you want?'

They took Jarman's brougham through the shadowy streets of Whitechapel. When they got there, a rather nasty surprise awaited them.

'What the flaming hell do you mean, "missing"?' thundered Handy at the morgue attendant. The man was a grubby individual with a pot belly, who stank of gin. His greasy hair, combed carefully over his balding pate, fell down to brush his dandruff-laden shoulder as Handy shook him roughly by the lapels of his jacket.

'I don't know, Mr Handy!' cried the attendant. 'I came in this morning as usual, and the body was gone. Honest to God!'

'Why didn't you get in touch?'

'I thought you must have known. I thought you'd given the word for it to be moved!'

'But you didn't check, did you?' roared Handy. 'You just sloped off for another quart of flaming gin, didn't you!'

The attendant flopped backwards and forwards in Handy's strong grip. It seemed like the Inspector was going to hit the man, so Jarman gently placed a hand on his arm.

'When did you see the body last?' he asked the shaken attendant.

'Last night, sir. She was tucked up, neat as you like, I promise. Then, this morning, she was gone. I swear it, Mr Handy,' he continued, turning back to the man who held him. 'I don't know where she went.'

'Did you notice any scars on the body?' Jarman continued. 'On the arms or legs? On the breasts?'

The morgue attendant just shrugged to the question. Handy glared at him for a second longer, then violently pushed him away. The attendant hit the wall and knocked over a large glass jar on a table, scrabbling to stand it upright again before its dubious contents spilled all over the floor.

'Well, she didn't get up and walk out,' growled Handy at the man. 'Somebody moved that body. And *you* are responsible.' He pointed a finger at the man. 'I'll have your bloody job for this.' He stalked out of the morgue.

Jarman caught up with him outside, in the grim courtyard. Groups of desultory, skeletal vagrants sat or stood around, eating the meagre meals they had earned from their work that morning. They looked at the two men with hollow eyes.

'Sorry, Dr Jarman,' said Handy, eventually. 'I hate this place at the best of times.'

He stared around the high brick walls and the thin figures in their rags. The two men could smell their filthy bodies from where they stood.

'These places are evil. Pure evil,' continued the Inspector, and Jarman realised he had just caught something of the man's past here.

They left the workhouse. In the carriage, they talked of what they should do.

'I'll get Frank onto it,' said Handy. 'See if he can find out what happened to the body, and I'll get in touch with Shafto, the surgeon who performed the autopsy. See if he asked for it to be moved, then we'll talk to the night watchman.'

'The question may not be *what* happened, Inspector. But rather, why.'

Handy frowned at him but said nothing.

With little more they could do about the mystery for the present, they returned to Leman Street and so into Handy's small office. Handy gave the autopsy photographs of the first body to Jarman, who went through each one slowly whilst Handy went to get Callow to see if he could find out where the body had disappeared to.

'Look at this, Curmudgeon,' said Jarman.

'I'd rather not,' said his man. 'I'm a servant, not a bloody detective.'

'Oh, you're a servant now, are you?' asked Jarman. 'Here was I remembering a man who said he had no master and never would.'

Curmudgeon pulled a face and took the photograph, grimacing as he did so.

'What am I supposed to be looking at?'

'The throat. Look at the throat.'

Curmudgeon forced himself to look at the wound, rather than the grimacing face it belonged to. He could not see what Jarman was getting at.

'What about the bloody throat?' he growled.

Jarman eyed him briefly over the ream of photographs he held in front of him like a pack of cards.

'There is a time and a place for your grumblings, sergeant,' he said, very softly. 'This is neither the time nor the place.'

Curmudgeon shifted uncomfortably in his seat. 'What about the throat, sir?' he asked in a subdued voice.

'That woman we saw this morning. Her throat was cut while she was still alive. This one suffered the same death.' He shrugged. 'At least it looks that way. Hard to tell without actually seeing the body.'

Curmudgeon looked at the photo again. 'So, what are you getting at?' he asked.

Jarman shrugged again. 'I'm not quite sure. I think…'

He was cut off as Handy returned, carrying four chipped mugs full of dark, police-strength tea. He was followed in by Callow. Introductions were made.

Handy plonked the teas down.

'She's been burned,' he said.

Jarman and Curmudgeon just looked at him, perplexed.

'The first woman, Eliza Cotton. Her body has been burned and her ashes have been raked into the workhouse grounds.'

'On whose orders?' asked Jarman, outraged.

'Nobody knows,' replied Handy, blowing on his tea. 'Apparently the order came in last night. This message was given to the night attendant at the morgue. Frank happened to be here when the attendant came in this morning on his way home to tell us it had all been done.'

He handed over a sheet of paper. It had the typed instructions for the destruction of the body on it and at the top was the emblem of the London Metropolitan Police. The message stated that, as the autopsy had been completed, and to avoid any incidence of disease arising, the corpse was to be burnt in the morgue's furnace forthwith. The clothes were to be similarly destroyed. There was no signature.

Jarman turned the note over and held it to the light. It was, to all intents and purposes, an official letter.

'Curious,' he said, eventually.

'It's more than curious, Jarman,' said Handy. 'It's dereliction of duty, that's what it is. Either that, or someone with access to official police documentation deliberately got rid of that body.' He sipped the tea. 'And any evidence you may have discovered on it.'

The four men looked at each other.

'Why would anyone do that?' asked Curmudgeon, eventually.

No one answered him; the question hung over them like a sword.

'Well, I don't believe I can be of any more help here, today,' said Jarman. 'If it's all right with you, Inspector, I shall go home and do some research there. I'll see if I can come up with anything that may help.'

Handy nodded and the four men shook hands. Jarman and Curmudgeon left the station and climbed aboard the brougham.

Across the road, leaning on a wall at the corner, stood the reporter Edward Ely. He watched the brougham leave and scribbled something down in his pocketbook. Then he casually sauntered off, smiling all the while.

\*

Edward Ely believed he was a good man. He believed he was bringing the truth to the masses with his reporting for the Evening Star newspaper. The truth, he always told himself, should never be hidden. For with the truth came knowledge, and Ely knew that with knowledge, came power. He intended to use that power to get what he wanted in life. And what he wanted was to be rich. He truly believed his reporting would one day make that happen.

At only twenty-four years old, he was still seen as a junior body in the newspaper office. Two years before, he had brought in the tea for the reporters working on the Ripper case. He had seen the letters signed *"From Hell"* and he had been thrilled to the bone by the whole affair.

In the two years since, he had been promoted and had spent his time divided between his work and his private obsession: The

Ripper.

Ely had always believed that the killer was still around, and it looked as if he had been proved right. The two murders in the last three days showed that. Ely was certain that the killer would strike again. He wanted to be ready for when that happened.

That man he had seen twice now: that morning as he had stood with the crowds in Church Street, and this afternoon outside the police station. He knew he had recognised him, and now, with a two-year-old front page in front of him, he remembered.

Doctor Carter "Jigsaw" Jarman. Abberline, the Inspector on the Ripper case, had brought him in towards the end of that awful, but eventful, autumn. He had obviously been thought of as useful, but the murders had stopped, so he had clearly not been *that* helpful.

And now the police had brought him back. Which meant Handy must think the Ripper had returned; why would he have enlisted Jarman's help again if he didn't?

Ely smiled as he dug into Jarman's past. He wanted to know everything about him. For with knowledge, comes power, and with power, comes status. And with status, Ely could make himself as rich as Croesus.

He pulled on his wire-rimmed spectacles and got down to work.

# Chapter Six

## Contemplation

Jarman sniffed and sat upright at his desk, pushing his fingers through his long hair. He picked up the cup of coffee Curmudgeon had plonked in front of him and pulled a face as the cold liquid touched his lips.

'Curmudgeon, could you make a fresh pot of coffee, please?' he called towards the kitchen door. For an answer, he heard Curmudgeon muttering and swearing and banging pots and pans around with unnecessary force. He turned back to the photographs.

Why the body of the first woman had been destroyed was a mystery, but it was a mystery for Handy, not for himself. He was here to try and help catch whoever it was had murdered the women. If indeed it was the same man. And Jarman thought it was.

But the way the women had been killed irritated him. It seemed clear from the notes of the autopsy carried out by Shafto that the woman had died from a single slice across her throat. She had been murdered and then cut upon, and the second woman had *definitely* died because of her sliced throat. Whoever did it must have been completely drenched in her blood on both occasions. And yet no one had seen anyone answering to that description wandering around either Bucks Row or Church Street. Of course, in the murky, gas-lit lanes, and with so many butchers' shops and abattoirs around, a man could have a perfectly good reason for being stained with blood. But this man must have been covered in gore, Jarman was sure of it.

He shook that particular problem away for the moment, and turned to the other problem: that of the way the two women's throats had been cut. The slices were the same. This was what he had been trying to tell Curmudgeon, but his ideas had not formed properly at the police station. They were both singular slices, going from right to left, or, from the killer's perspective, from left to right. His autopsy on the woman from Church Street showed that the cut had been deeper on the left side of the cut, which indicated that the killer had squatted above her, the knife in his right hand, and had cut her from that side: his left. From what he could make out from the photographs of the first woman, Eliza Cotton, the cut was the same, although without access to the corpse this would be difficult to prove.

But this was the problem that tugged at his mind.

Most of the five Ripper victims had several cuts to their throats: at least two. Therefore, if this killer was the same man, he had either become much more adept at his work, or he had become stronger, as it seemed to make sense that the huge gash he had made in the women's throats had taken someone of huge physical strength to do so in a single slice.

Jarman pondered this as Curmudgeon brought him fresh coffee. Jarman thanked him and leaned back in the chair, crossing his booted feet on the tabletop and lighting a cigarette.

He suddenly stood and went to a bookcase across the room, taking a file down and rifling through old newspaper cuttings and medical reports. He found the file on Annie Milwood and sat back down to read it.

The woman said she had been attacked on February 25th of 1888. She had been stabbed several times in what the newspapers had called the *"lower regions"* and had died several days later, probably from her wounds. Another victim of violence, Emma Smith, had been attacked in April of the same year. Something had been used to penetrate her and the poor woman had died from peritonitis, again a few days after her attack. In August, Martha Tabram was also found, with her throat and vaginal areas mutilated.

These three women, and others, had never been formally identified as Ripper attacks, but the way they were attacked led Jarman to believe they were by the same assailant. Although the five women who definitely were Ripper victims—Polly Nichols, Annie Chapman, Elizabeth Stride, Catherine Eddowes and Mary Kelly—were mutilated in ever worsening ways, the modus operandi was similar. From Annie Milwood in the February, to Mary Kelly in the November, each attack had got more horrific. As surgeon on the last case alongside Abberline, Jarman had seen the body of Mary Kelly, although he had not performed the actual autopsy. He had said then that the killer would not stop. But he had been wrong.

However, these latest cases were different. He didn't know what it was that made him sure of this, he just knew it. They were similar to—although obviously much worse than—the early Ripper attacks, but the slicing of the throats whilst the women were still conscious and trying to fight back was different to the Ripper cases. In those cases the women had seemingly been strangled into unconsciousness before the mutilations occurred.

The partial scalping of the latest victim could just be a new and horrific acceleration of the killer's mad desires. However, whether this killer was the same man who had killed the women the Ripper had come to be so infamous for, was, to Jarman, perhaps a different story. But then why had these new murders started on the exact anniversary of the murder of Polly Nichols, the first of those women the Ripper had definitely killed? Coincidence? Or something deeper?

He closed the file and placed it back in the shelf, closing the glass door. When he got back to his coffee, he found that this too had gone cold. Not wanting to irritate Curmudgeon any longer, Jarman instead allowed himself a small whisky. And he allowed Mary to enter his thoughts.

*

He awoke hours later, as he was being lifted into his bed by Curmudgeon. The whisky decanter was empty, something he was suddenly aware of. He felt the alcohol burning through his body and he felt the old remorse and pain burning through his soul.

He stared at Curmudgeon above him, his eyes blurry with unshed tears as the man tucked his sheets around him.

'Why did she leave me, Billy? Why did she leave me?'

Curmudgeon sighed and smiled down sadly at Jarman.

'She couldn't help it, Captain. She didn't want to go, but she couldn't help it.'

Jarman stared at him like a child, until his whisky-sodden brain closed down once more, and he slept. A single tear broke free and trickled down his cheek into the pillow.

Curmudgeon frowned. The tear on Jarman's cheek bothered him, and he wiped it from his face, then he blew out the lamp and closed the bedroom door behind him softly. He stood outside the bedroom for a long time, staring into nothing but the past. Then he squared his shoulders, sniffed, and took himself off to his own bed.

\*

Jonas Handy sat in the kitchen of his small, sparse, but comfortable house in Finsbury. On the table in front of him, the photographs of Eliza Cotton and Molly Harnath lay in all their grainy, horrific glory.

Handy and Callow had been walking the streets all day, building up a picture of what the dead woman had done in her last hours, and, more importantly, who she was.

They had eventually, with more luck than judgement, come across Janey Swann, who told them that Molly 'Thought she was better than the rest of us' Harnath, had been in the snug of *The Barrel* at ten the previous evening. They said she'd had a run in with a man in the street, and that she was later going to an appointment with a gentleman.

There was no description of either the man she had fought off or the man she had been planning on meeting up with, but Janey had been shown the dead woman's clothes and had sworn that they were Harnath's. Handy had not allowed her to see all the clothes because of the blood on them, or the body itself: that would have just caused mayhem in the streets if Swann then told everyone about it. But Harnath's hat had a bright red cloth poppy attached to it, and Janey had sworn that it was hers. A visit to the local dosshouses had then backed up the theory. The woman whose scalped and mutilated image lay in front of Handy on his table was Molly Harnath. But the question remained, of course. Who killed her?

Handy sipped a cup of tea, eventually standing and taking it with him into the only other room in the house, which contained a faded couch. He sank into it and sat with his eyes closed for a second, just letting the silence of his small kingdom sink into his bones.

The ownership of a house was a luxury that, when he was young, would not have been even a dream for him. Food enough to stop his stomach cramping with hunger had been a dream. Being clean had been a dream.

Handy had been born in Old Nichol's. He was the son of a prostitute, probably little different to the two women whose killer he now sought. His father was just another customer whom he had never known. His earliest memories were of him being turned out of the hovel they lived in so his mother could ply her trade in peace. He would wander, barefoot, around the cramped, dingy alleyways, trying to shelter his ragged little body from the elements, as, all around him, men and women grunted and rutted in the shadows. He would usually find a corner to sleep in, his dirty thumb in his mouth, until the day brightened the sky, when he would slink off home again, to crawl in beside his mother, who, although she stank of gin and semen, was at least warm.

He had been kicked and beaten on a few occasions as he

wandered the East End night, but the creatures of Spitalfields usually left him alone; immersed in their own privations as they were.

Until that morning he had returned home, jumping nimbly across the bricks the locals had thrown as a walkway into the shit that wallowed four inches deep in the filthy courtyard. To find his mother not warm, but as cold as marble and as still as the grave.

He had no idea what she had died from; he was only eight at the time. But there was vomit on the floor and on her lips and later, when things had changed, he realised she must have choked in her sleep on cheap gin.

He had hung around the freezing, greasy hovel for a day or two, fighting to keep the rats from his mother's body, until hunger forced him outside, where he stole a pie from a seller and was immediately caught. The pie man punched him in the face a couple of times, then caught sight of a police constable walking by, trying not to look.

''Ere,' he shouted to the constable. 'This little bleeder's been nicking my wares. You gonna do somethin' about it or not?'

The unenthusiastic constable had taken him away and deposited him in a police station. The desk sergeant had frowned at the boy's battered face and gave him a cup of tea and a hunk of bread, which he devoured immediately. The sergeant had left him sitting on a bench by the door; he probably wanted him to bugger off and not be in the way, but young Jonas reckoned that at least it was warm and dry in the station. Better than being outside.

He had spied a broom in the corner and started to sweep the floor. The sergeant, over the counter, saw this and smiled. When he was finished, the sergeant gave him another cup of tea and slice of bread, this time with a bit of cheese to go with it. To Jonas, the first time he had tasted such a delicacy, it was like manna from heaven.

Over the next few days and weeks, the sergeant—Handy, his name was—gave him other menial jobs to complete, and Jonas did them as quickly and as efficiently as he could, before standing in front of the desk and saluting when he received his rations. The sergeant had allowed him to sleep in one of the cells. Then, one day, he had taken him into the back office and told him to take his clothes off.

For a second, Jonas was terrified. Although he did not really understand, he knew what his mother did when she was naked, and he had heard of other boys in the area who had been taken into dark rooms by hungry-looking men who constantly licked their lips to engage in things he really did not want to know about. But there was a fire roaring in the grate, and a tin bath full of hot water in front of it. He did as he had been ordered and stripped off his filthy, threadbare trousers and shirt. They were the only clothes he possessed.

'In you get, then,' said Sergeant Handy, indicating to the bath, and Jonas climbed into something that was so wonderful, he could not think of the words to describe it. Since arriving at the station, he had not spoken to anyone, but as the water warmed itself into his bones, he sighed, contentedly.

'Thanks, mister,' he said.

Handy smiled at these first words he had heard the boy utter.

'Right,' he said. 'This here in my hand, is what you might call a bar of soap. This here soap shall be moved in a vigorous motion all across your body. Understand that?'

Jonas nodded.

'Then it shall be vigorously moved across your face,' continued the sergeant. 'Then we shall cut that mop of yours and get rid of the visitors you have living in it. Understand that?'

Jonas nodded again.

Handy returned half an hour later and stared at the now clean little boy in the filthy water of the tub. There was a strange look on his face as he did so. He carried a pile of clothes in his arms: a shirt, trousers, socks and boots, and a small jacket and cap.

He also had a towel, and he told Jonas to dry himself down. Then he took a pair of scissors and chopped Jonas' hair down to the scalp.

'That's got rid of them little buggers,' he said as he watched the last hunk of hair sizzle in the fire. 'You'll keep your hair short from now on. That way they won't come back. Understand that?'

Jonas nodded once again and climbed into the clothes he had been given. They fitted him perfectly.

Handy stared at him in the clothes for a long time, then stood and turned his back. Jonas saw his arm move, as if the sergeant was wiping something from his eye. Then the man turned back to him.

'If I let you go back out there,' he said. 'You'll be dead within a year. And if I can stop that from happening, I will. I've seen too much of it. How would you like to come home with me? I only have a small house, but it's empty now. Been empty for a while. And you don't take up too much space. We can keep each other company.'

And so young Jonas, against all the odds, found a house, with a portrait of a woman and a boy long since dead. He found a name. And he found a father. And like his father, when he was old enough, he joined the police. But unlike his father, Jonas Handy was an incredibly clever young man. His father had taught him how to read and write; now Handy showed him what it meant to be a real policeman. Although Handy senior had died seven years ago now, he had lived long enough to see his son promoted to Inspector. And the look on his face had shown Handy the love he had never known as a boy. The love he still felt for his father now.

He sat up in the couch, glancing at the portrait of the woman and boy he had never known and the photograph of the man he had come to love. Sergeant Handy had had little of value when he died, but he had left him the house and everything in it. Handy now had more than he would ever have imagined when his mother's corpse had been hauled off to be flung into its pauper's grave all those years ago.

With a sigh, he returned to the present time and the problem he had. Who the hell had authorised the removal and destruction of Eliza Cotton's body? This thought came again as he sipped his tea. He remembered reading about the mistakes the last time round: the clothes that were washed without being properly investigated, the words on the wall in Goulston Street the night Catherine Eddowes and Elizabeth Stride had been murdered: "*The Juwes are the men that will not be blamed for nothing*".

Even though that had likely been nothing more than an old piece of graffito, the fact it had been wiped away before any investigation into it could happen was problematic. Even the piece of petticoat that had been found there with the writing had disappeared later. Some of these things could be passed off as just bad police work, but sometimes it almost seemed to Handy as if someone had been trying to get in the way of the investigations. Was that same person, or persons, trying again now?

Handy stood up and made himself another cup of tea. Then he returned to the photographs and stared at them as his cuppa grew cold once more at his elbow.

# Chapter Seven

## Villiers

Callow knocked on his door early the next morning.

'We might have something,' he said, as Handy beckoned him in and gave him a cuppa.

'The last woman, Molly Harnath, from Church Street.' Callow gulped at his tea; he looked like he had been awake all night.

'What about her?'

'Well, I got back to Janey Swann, the dolly who identified her clothes, to see if I could get anything else out of her when she was sober, and she said something funny. She said, "She should have stayed in the other job". I asked what she meant and she said that up until a couple of months or so ago, Molly had worked in a match factory in Mile End. I thought it might be worth our while to go and ask some questions.'

Handy smiled, already pulling on his coat.

'You thought right, Frank. Well done. Let's get up there and see if we can find anything out.

They hailed a hansom cab and gave the driver the address.

The factory, *Villiers FireSticks*, was a huge affair. The wooden gates themselves were nearly twenty feet high, topped with iron spikes. Twin chimneys to either side of the main gates were spewing black coal smoke into the already sulphur-laden air. Carts were loading and unloading huge wooden racks and barrels of all shapes and sizes. Even standing outside the factory the two men could hear the noisy racket coming from within. The ground they stood on trembled with the ferocity of the machinery inside.

They stopped a man and showed him their police identification. Then they asked to see the owner and he led them into the factory.

The noise inside was incredible and the man had to shout to make himself heard.

'The offices are through the other side!' he bellowed. 'Quicker this way! If you could follow me, sirs!'

Callow and Handy followed the man past ranks of workers, most of them women, all engrossed in various labours. The place stank from ranks of open crates full of gritty residue: the chemicals used to make the match heads. It made both men feel slightly sick. The man they followed noticed Callow staring at one or two of the women who, although young, seemed to have not one tooth in their heads. He smiled grimly at the sergeant's naivety.

'It's for the Phossy Jaw, sir!' he shouted at him. 'It starts in the teeth and gums, so any woman complaining of toothache is carted off to the dentist fast as you like. Pull 'em all out so it don't get no worse!'

Callow mouthed something in disgust, which was lost in the cacophony of the machinery and belts that whizzed and whirled around the factory. The whole place looked bloody deadly to the sergeant, but the mostly female working body seemed immune to its inherent dangers.

Eventually they found themselves outside again and they both heaved a sigh of relief as the door closed on the terrible noise. The man pointed at a series of buildings to the rear of the main factory. A sign on the wall of one of the buildings pointed up a wrought iron stairway to what looked like an office door.

'That's the way there, sirs!' the man shouted, still at the top of his voice. Perhaps this was how he always communicated. Handy thanked him and they climbed up the stairway and knocked on the door.

A young man, a clerk by the look of him, opened the door and Handy explained who they were.

'Is the owner of the factory in?' he asked.

The man glanced behind him and the two officers caught sight of a woman sitting at a desk through a glass partition at the back of the room. The young man knocked on the door and spoke to her. The woman glanced at them as the man talked and then nodded. The young man returned to the door.

'Miss Villiers will see you, sirs,' he said, and opened the door wider, inviting them in. He led them past a couple of desks that were piled with papers stuck on spikes, receipts by the look of them, and ushered them into the back room.

The woman was standing by a roll-top desk near the back of the room, and she regarded them coolly as they entered.

She was a stocky woman of about five foot six inches in height and looked to be somewhere in her forties, a badger streak of grey along the side of her otherwise black hair. Her eyes were very dark; they too looked almost black, and they were set in an angular face that seemed very stern as she waited for the policemen to speak.

'Miss Villiers?' asked Handy, and she simply nodded.

'I'm Inspector Handy and this is Sergeant Callow, H Division CID. Are you the owner of this establishment?'

Miss Villiers seemed to smile coldly at the question in his voice.

'I do not own this factory, Inspector. My brother has that title. I, as a woman, am simply an employee.'

Handy nodded, uncertainly. The woman seemed very sure of herself and unconcerned by the fact that two coppers had turned up at the factory. She did not seem very interested in why they may have been there.

'Is your brother around?' Handy tried again.

'My brother is at home, Inspector. He tends to leave the day-to-day running of the factory to others. Me included.'

'I see,' said Handy. 'Well, we're here to ask him a few questions about one of his other employees.'

'I can certainly help you in that department, Inspector. Part of my role here is to hire and fire, as they say.'

'I'd still rather talk to Mr Villiers, if that's possible,' said Handy. 'It's a rather delicate subject matter for the ears of a lady.'

Miss Villiers barked a sarcastic laugh.

'Oh, I see. I should faint at the very thought of whatever you want to speak of, should I? We women are too fragile to contemplate anything other than lunch and clothes?'

*Suffragist,* thought Callow. *Bloody hell. That's all we need.*

'Not at all, Miss Villiers,' replied Handy, smoothly. 'It's just that I think the actual owner needs to be aware of a certain situation. Then he can tell me who is best to ask for more information.'

Miss Villiers eyed them both for a couple of more seconds, the disgust she felt for what she seemed to see as their boorish behaviour plain on her face.

'If it is about an employee, I can give you dates of when they started, et cetera,' she said. 'But if you need to speak to Thomas, I shall give you his address.' She picked up a printed card and handed it over, then she raised an eyebrow.

'The employee's name?' she asked.

Handy hesitated, then shrugged. Couldn't do any harm. He would be talking to this Villiers soon enough anyway and, if this was his sister, he'd no doubt be telling her what they had spoken of later.

'The name is Harnath,' he said. 'Molly Harnath.'

Miss Villiers turned away and rifled through a file she drew out which had a list of names in alphabetical order. She found the page she was looking for.

'Yes, we had a Molly Harnath working here for three months. From April until June of this year. She resigned.'

'Any reason?'

Miss Villiers shook her head.

'No reason is written down here. If I remember correctly, she just told us she no longer wanted to be part of our company. It happens quite a lot with the charity cases.'

'Charity cases?' asked Callow, and Miss Villiers smiled. It seemed an ill fit on that rather harsh face.

'Now that is my brother's role. Ask him about it.'

She closed the file with a snap and placed it back in its drawer, standing again to face the two men.

'Well,' said Handy, eventually. He lifted his hat. 'Thank you for your help, Miss Villiers. We'll see ourselves out.'

He and Callow left. It was not until they were back through the noisy factory and standing outside the main gates before either of them spoke.

'Bloody suffragists,' said Callow, returning to his previous thoughts. 'Always got a bloody bee in their bonnets. Always in a foul bloody mood. I feel sorry for that clerk having to work with her.'

Handy smiled. 'I've seen women accomplish things you would never dream of, Frank. They're a lot stronger than you think. Perhaps if they were given a chance to show their worth, they wouldn't complain so much. However, yes, she does seem to have a rather spikey temperament.'

Callow laughed and they hailed another cab. Handy gave the driver the address for Villiers's house.

*

Neither Jarman nor Curmudgeon mentioned anything about the previous night as Curmudgeon plonked his breakfast in front of him. This was what always happened when Jarman lapsed, as he sometimes did. Both men simply ignored it. This strategy seemed to work best for them.

Jarman had just finished his meal when the doorbell rang, and Curmudgeon muttered a complaint as he went to see who it was. A moment or two later, Handy was in his sitting room.

He explained about the lead Callow had gleaned about Villiers's factory and that he had dropped the sergeant off back at the station to continue with the investigation about who ordered the destruction of Eliza Cotton's body.

'I'm just on my way to Mr Villiers's house,' he said. 'You said the other day that you had some spare time from the hospital at the moment? I was wondering if you would like to accompany me.'

Jarman frowned. He was not sure why Handy would want him with him.

'I know a little of Thomas Villiers,' he said. 'He has several factories, the one in Mile End being the first and largest. Bit of a philanthropist, I believe. He tries to employ women who have fallen on hard times. Gives them a new start.'

'Charity cases,' muttered Handy, thoughtfully. Then he glanced again at Jarman.

'Look, I know you're not a police officer, but Fred Abberline swears by you, and I've seen how your brain works. Plus, a wealthy businessman will perhaps be less on his guard with you around than he may be with a lowly detective such as myself. I'd like you to come along to Mr Villiers's house and see what we can find out.'

Jarman smiled at the detective's words. He was indeed a clever man, was Jonas Handy.

'Of course, I'll come along,' he said. 'Any help, and all that.'

They arrived outside the Villiers's house half an hour later. On the driver's seat above them, Curmudgeon whistled softly to himself at the size of the place. He was a long way from his native Newbiggin here.

Jarman and Handy climbed out and stood on the steps in front of the grand, polished front door. Jarman glanced at Curmudgeon and his man nodded back at him. He climbed down from the brougham and stood, stroking Daisy's neck and trying to look inconspicuous.

The door opened under Handy's knock and a young woman stood there.

Jarman took the lead as Handy glanced at him and he smiled at the young girl, removing his hat.

'Good afternoon,' he said. 'Is Mr Villiers at home?'

'Can I take your names, sirs?' the girl asked.

'My name is Doctor Carter Jarman, and this is Inspector Handy of the Metropolitan police. We were wondering if we could talk to Mr Villiers.'

The girl seemed a little shocked, as well she may have been. The police did not usually come knocking on doors in this neighbourhood.

A female voice came from behind her. 'Who is it, Ellie?'

The girl turned and had a hurried conversation, then the door was opened further to reveal a woman standing there.

She was small and slim, with auburn hair and deep blue eyes. She wore a blue day dress that matched those eyes and her face was smooth and blemish-free. When she smiled, her teeth were straight and even.

'Good day, gentlemen,' she said. 'I apologise about Ellie. She's not used to opening doors but it's the maid's day off today and the rest of the staff are busy.'

She smiled encouragingly at the Ellie, and the girl curtsied to the two men. 'If you would like to follow me, gentlemen. Mrs Villiers will see you in the Drawing Room.'

Jarman watched as the woman, Mrs Villiers, presumably, smiled at the young girl again and then preceded the three of them into a grand drawing room. As the girl left, Handy winked at her and whispered, 'Well done, love.' Ellie seemed shocked at the words for a second, then she smiled and left the room.

The woman asked them to sit.

'My husband is out at the moment, but he did say he would be back by 2pm.' They all glanced at a wall clock and saw it was quarter to.

'Would you like a cup of tea?' asked Mrs Villiers.

While they waited, she asked if there was anything she could help with.

'We're simply here to ask your husband a few questions, Mrs Villiers.' Handy spoke for the first time. 'It's a rather morbid business, I'm afraid, but we merely wanted to know anything about a previous employee at his Mile End factory.'

'Morbid?' asked Mrs Villiers. Jarman, watching her closely, saw that there was no fear in her eyes, just curiosity, matched with something else. What was it? Alarm? Secrecy? He left it for the moment.

'Nothing for you or Mr Villiers to worry about, ma'am. We're just trying to find out what happened to a woman who used to work in the factory. We…'

He was interrupted by the door opening and a tall, dark-haired man striding into the room, followed almost immediately by Ellie with the tea tray. The man glanced at Jarman and Handy, then took off his hat and casually threw it onto a spare settee. There were plenty to choose from. He shook both men's hands.

'Good day, gentlemen. My name is Thomas Villiers. Ellie here tells me you're from the police? Have you found out about my guilty little secret at last?'

There was a moment's silence in the room before Villiers burst out laughing. The two men and his wife then copied him.

Villiers stood about six feet tall. Like his sister, his black hair had a streak of grey at his temple, and he was clean-shaven. His face was long and angular, with a rather cruel twist to his lips. He wore a dark suit that Jarman quickly worked out probably cost more than a year of Handy's wages, and he had a gold watch fob hanging from his waistcoat pocket. His boots were glossy, as if the London dust did not dare mar them. He sat down and was served tea by Ellie, who seemed to Jarman to be watching everyone carefully, and was definitely more subdued than she had been when only in Mrs Villiers's company. The girl served the tea, then left.

Villiers had sat next to his wife, and again Jarman noticed something. His wife made a slight movement away from him. Hardly noticed, more of a stiffening at his nearness, but there all the same. He made a mental note of this too.

There was a liquid silence as all four of them sipped their tea. Villiers then cleared his throat.

'I hope you don't mind, gentlemen, but I am a busy man. What can I do for you on this fine day?'

Handy put down his teacup, glancing at Mrs Villiers.

'Anything you have to say can be said in front of my wife, er, Inspector?'

Handy nodded, and Villiers continued.

'We have no secrets from each other, do we dear?'

He looked at his wife, and Jarman watched as she lowered her eyes.

'Of course not,' she said.

'Well then,' said Villiers, brightly, turning back to Handy and Jarman. 'Be so good as to enlighten me with what you've come to say, Inspector.'

'Very good, sir,' said Handy. 'Two nights ago, a body was found in Church Street…'

'Ah, yes,' said Villiers. 'I read about that. Terrible by the sound of it.'

'Yes, well, the reporter who wrote that story is universally known for embellishing his reports,' growled Handy. 'However, the basic tenets of the murder were correct. I shan't go into them here, of course.' He glanced again at Mrs Villiers.

'Of course not,' said Villiers, and Jarman noticed a twinkle in his eye. Was he amused by this situation? Although Handy had asked him along as he was of a closer class to Villiers than himself, Jarman had noticed that it was the Inspector himself who was doing much of the talking. He glanced at the Inspector and suddenly realised that he had been asked along for a completely different reason.

'We found out this morning, that the victim had been, until June of this year, employed in your match factory in Mile End,' continued Handy. 'Myself and Dr Jarman here were just wondering if you had any information on the woman. Molly Harnath was her name. Anything that might prove useful for bringing her killer to a swift justice?'

His pencil hovered above his notebook.

'Are you a member of the police force, Dr Jarman?' asked Villiers, ignoring Handy and staring at the surgeon with his coal-black eyes.

'I am not,' said Jarman. 'I am a surgeon at the London Hospital. Inspector Handy asked me to look at the victim of this crime and to see if I could help in any way possible to find the murderer.'

'Not really the job of a surgeon, is it?' asked Villiers.

'Dr Jarman is one of the foremost experts on the criminal mind,' interjected Handy. 'He has studied the process of murder for years, and he has helped the police on previous occasions.'

Villiers stared at Jarman for a second and then nodded. 'I thought I recognised the name,' he said, leaning forward and putting his empty cup and saucer on the table in front of him. 'You seem to have picked up an unusual sobriquet from the people of the East End, isn't that right? Jackdaw, or something, isn't it?'

He was now not smiling so much as leering at Jarman. The surgeon just widened his own smile however, not rising to this rich man's game.

'Jigsaw,' he corrected. He glanced at Mrs Villiers. 'I must admit, I rather like it.' He sipped his tea. Mrs Villiers smiled uncertainly at him and lowered her eyes again.

'Do you indeed,' muttered Villiers, seemingly annoyed that he hadn't upset the other man.

'A strange name,' said Mrs Villiers, quickly, seemingly to try and inject some warmth into the chilly atmosphere. Jarman turned his smile warm and saw a blush appear on those rather lovely cheeks.

'It has something to do with surgery on bones,' he explained. 'Some of my former patients started calling me that and it stuck.'

'And yet, unlocking the secrets of a killer's mind,' said Villiers, softly. 'One could compare that to the piecing together of a jigsaw, do you think?'

Once again, Jarman turned to him. And once again, his smile changed.

'Oh yes,' he said, quietly. 'It could indeed.'

The two men stared at each other, until Handy cleared his throat.

'As you've said, you're a busy man, sir. Is there anything you might know about Molly Harnath that may help us in this investigation?'

Villiers tore his gaze from Jarman, and the surgeon once again found himself staring at the man's wife. She blinked uncertainly and her head went down again.

'I know nothing of the name, Inspector,' said Villiers, with an irritated wave of his hand. 'I run a, well, a charity, really. Its aim is to help women who have fallen on hard times. To give them a, err, a *proper* job. I'm sure you know what I mean.' He glanced at his wife as he said this. He seemed not to want to say the word "prostitute" within her earshot.

'Lots of women have taken up the offer,' continued Villiers. 'Some decide later that it is not for them and return to the streets to ply whatever it is they ply there.' He appeared to have calmed himself down slightly after seemingly becoming agitated. 'It's my sister you really need to talk to,' he continued. 'I employ her to look after the staff.'

Handy nodded, putting away his notebook. He stood. 'As I suspected, sir. I didn't really think that a man such as yourself would know anything about this, but it's my job to look into any piece of information, no matter how thin that may be. I hope you can forgive Dr Jarman and I for spoiling your afternoon.'

Jarman stood, too, and the three men shook hands. Villiers held Jarman's hand and applied more force than was necessary. 'Good afternoon, *Jigsaw*,' he said.

Jarman squeezed the hand right back until he saw the other man flinch. 'Good afternoon,' he replied.

They saw themselves out. When the door closed behind them, Jarman let out a long breath. He heard Handy chuckle.

'He don't like you, does he? He don't like you at all. Why do think that was?'

When Jarman did not answer straight away the detective spoke again. 'What do you think of him?'

Jarman shook his head. 'I'm not sure. He seems very sure of himself, but then again, he's a rich man; he would.' Handy smiled at this, knowing he had been right to bring Jarman along.

'I get the distinctive feeling that there is a little bad feeling between him and his wife,' continued Jarman. 'Just a feeling, however.'

Handy smiled again. *Is that what you think, or what you hope?* he thought, but said nothing.

He placed his hat on his head and sauntered towards the waiting brougham. A movement behind Jarman made him turn, just in time to see the lace curtain fall back into place. He wondered why he was sure it was Mrs Villiers who had been looking out at him.

He joined Handy inside the brougham. 'Get anything, Curmudgeon?'

The driver's upside-down face grinned at him through the hatch.

'The girl, Ellie. She's Mrs Villiers ward. Been with her ever since she was orphaned ten years ago. Apparently, her and Mrs Villiers are very close. She said that Mr Villiers often has gentlemen friends over. She doesn't know any of them, but they all dress like they're rich. She also said that the staff don't stay in the house after ten, but a couple of the maids have told her that they've seen a few women with the men at times. And not their wives, if you know what I mean. And she says that Mrs Villiers is often away at the country house they have. That's when the men and the girls come over. She said she hasn't seen that happen though, as she always accompanies Mrs Villiers when she goes to the country.'

'Curious,' said Jarman, sounding like it wasn't curious at all.

Handy stared at Jarman for a second and then grinned again. It gave his ugly face an amazingly pleasant hue. He leant forward and prodded Curmudgeon's legs.

'You got all that from ten minutes with that girl? You should have joined the police.'

Curmudgeon straightened, tutted and clapped the reins. 'I'd rather stick pins in me eyes than join the bloody rozzers,' he muttered to himself.

# Chapter Eight

## The Bloody Yard

The weeks after Molly Harnath's death passed by quickly.
Frank Callow and Jonas Handy found nothing to
indicate who had ordered Eliza Cotton's body to be burned. The
dismembered corpse of the second woman, Molly Harnath, was
finally allowed a pauper's burial and she was soon forgotten by
most who had known her. Just another victim of the East End. The
detectives found out, however, that Eliza, like Molly, had worked
for a short while in Villiers's match factory.

This was interesting to Handy but, for the moment, nothing
to get too excited about. Almost three thousand women had come
and gone through the factory gates since the place had opened,
and two hundred of them had been working as prostitutes at
one point or the other. Villiers's "charity" cases made up a large
percentage of the workforce. The fact that two of them ended up
being murdered could have been nothing more than coincidence.

Jarman spent a lot of time in his house, reading through the
old Ripper cases, as well as consuming as much information as he
could about Thomas Villiers; whom, he discovered, he had been
correct in thinking was being talked about as a potential future
Knight of the Realm for his charity work.

However, something was telling Jarman that the man knew
more than he was showing, and this gnawed at his waking hours.
Curmudgeon fussed over him in his usual bad-humoured way. He
had already hidden the whisky decanter but Jarman, who knew

precisely where it had been secreted, kept away from it anyway. He wanted to keep a clear head. Curmudgeon did not complain as loudly as usual when another coffee was asked for, as anything was better than the whisky and the memories the whisky brought about. Jarman realised what Curmudgeon was doing and was grateful, but neither of them said a word about it. They just got on with their respective jobs.

*

Edward Ely sat by the light of a lamp in the offices of the Evening Star. He had known there was something off with this investigation. He had followed Jarman and Handy to Grosvenor Square, and he had got close enough to hear that ape of a servant say something to the girl about Villiers. He had looked into the name, and it had not taken him very long to find out everything there was to know.

But it didn't really help him. Villiers was seen as nothing less than *comme il faut* in society. His factories made a huge amount of money, and he had been fairly well-off even before they were built, as his father had left him a rich man. Villiers seemed to be a dead end.

His digging into Jarman's past had also brought up nothing more than he knew already. He was a surgeon—a very good one by all reports—and he seemed to be a bit of an adventurer, but nothing he could really use. There was that story about his wife, of course, but that was not too much out of the ordinary. That was simply bad luck.

He also had nothing that helped him uncover what had happened to the recent victims. More importantly, there was nothing that gave him the answer he wanted so much: who the killer was. That was what Edward Ely really wanted to know, for this would make his name and make his fortune. Who was Jack the Ripper?

He was in no doubt that it was the infamous killer who had murdered the two women, and his headline grabbing report of the murder of Molly Harnath had certainly helped sell lots of copies of *The Star*. His editor seemed pleased about the story, although he was as mealy-mouthed as usual when it came to taking it further. After some persuasion, however, he had finally given Ely the go ahead to find out whatever he could about the murderer, but things just did not seem to be coming together.

The weather in London worsened. Fog enveloped the mid-autumn streets from dusk until dawn. They became even darker, more secretive and more dangerous than they had been before.

As he sat at his desk, Ely found himself wishing something else would happen.

He would soon find that his wish would come true.

*

Jack Macken whistled quietly as he walked, as much to keep himself company in the eerie fog as to cover the annoying squeaking of one of the wheels of his cart. He was pushing it in front of him and the left wheel had begun to squeal soon after he had left his house. It was not yet 5am and still dark. Jack had a way to go to get to the yard where he collected from, and the squeaking was giving him the right hump. He stopped and kicked the offending wheel a couple of times and then set off again, but it continued to make its pointless noises. Jack sighed a long-suffering sigh. Trials of the job, he thought, squinting into the murk.

He squealed and whistled his way down Settles Street and turned right into Fordham Street as usual, and as he did so, a figure suddenly hurtled past him. All Jack got was a momentary impression: a flat cap pulled down low so only the bottom half of a white face showed. The figure had a moustache, though, and that moustache and the hair under the cap was fair: Jack would swear to this later. The man was of average height and wore black trousers and black jacket, a white scarf tied around his neck. He carried a bulky pack on his back.

'Oi! Watch where you're going, you bloody halfwit!' shouted

Jack to the departing figure, his sudden anger in response to the fright the figure had given him.

The man didn't answer but just kept running, turning right at the top of the street and disappearing into the foggy night.

Jack shook his head in disgust. Bloody idiots, running around at all times of day and night. Probably been with some dollymop and was running to get home to his poor missus. Jack tutted as he thought about the people he had to deal with on a daily basis. Lot of bloody animals, that's what they were. Bloody animals.

He set off again up Fordham Street and then turned left into Myrdle Street, where the carter's yard was situated. He reached the gates but then turned as he heard a small, soft noise coming from a dark gateway on the opposite side of the street. Jack peered blindly into the darkness of the open yard, listening carefully. Nothing.

And then he saw something.

It seemed to be water; black water in the black shadows. It reached the step of the yard entrance and then dripped thickly onto the cobbles of the street itself. As soon as he saw the water, Jack knew that this was the noise he had heard: water, dribbling and pooling and spilling over the hard-packed ground inside the yard.

Jack pulled out a pack of Villiers FireSticks and the match flared in the smoggy darkness. And he saw that it was not water that was now flowing over the step of the yard. It was not water at all.

Trembling, Jack pushed at the half-open gate and took a couple of steps inside the yard. He was full of trepidation at what he might find, and the match shook in his hands.

When he eventually summoned up the courage to take one more step into the darkness, and he saw what the light from his match showed, Jack screamed. He screamed and screamed and screamed.

# Chapter Nine

## A Flight Through the Streets

Handy, Callow and Jarman stood in a circle, staring down at the body. If, indeed, it could still be called a body.

The mutilations on the corpse were huge. Even worse than those inflicted on Molly Harnath. The throat had again been cut, but this time even more terrible and horrifying desecrations had been carried out.

The bones of both arms and legs were exposed to the smoky morning air. They had been excised, brutally, and the flesh hung in tattered strips from them like discarded, scarlet wrapping paper. The head had once again been scalped, but this time the soggy bundle of flesh and hair had been flung into a corner of the yard, as if in a terrible rage. Everything about the corpse was ripped, sliced and defiled. It looked more like the offcuts a butcher might throw into the street rather than a human being.

Jarman bent down beside the body, but almost immediately stood up again, shaking his head at what he saw. 'I need to look at this properly, back at the hospital,' he said to Handy. 'I can't do anything here.'

Handy nodded. 'We're just waiting for the photographer to come,' he said. 'Then we'll get her moved.' He stared at the horrific hunk of flesh. 'That poor woman,' he said to himself.

There was a scuffle near the gate and they both turned to see Edward Ely push himself into the yard.

'The public need to see what's going on!' he cried. 'You can't keep it hidden forever, Inspector Handy. The truth will out!'

Handy groaned as the bobbies tried to haul Ely back out again.

'The truth, Handy!' cried Ely. 'The people want the truth!'

Handy suddenly snapped. Jarman saw this and tried to grab him, but he was far too late. Handy's eyebrows clamped together and he paled. A grimace of anger spread across his face. He launched himself across the grimy yard and grabbed Ely by the lapels of his jacket.

'The truth, Ely?' he screamed in his face. 'You want the truth?'

He dragged the reporter across the yard and pushed his head towards the slaughtered cadaver.

'There's your truth, you rodent! There! Is that what you wanted to see? Make you happy, does it?'

Ely seemed transfixed by what his eyes showed him; they darted around the mess in front of him and they registered burst eyes, grinning, lipless teeth, hoisted clothes showing skinned legs, and a gaping hole where a stomach should be. His hand slowly covered his mouth and his spectacles slipped even further down his nose.

'God almighty,' he eventually breathed. 'God almighty.'

Handy hauled him upright and held him by the lapels. He pulled his face within an inch of the other man's.

'Someone is out there making mincemeat out of these women,' he hissed at him. 'We,' he indicated with his head in the general direction of the men in the yard, 'are trying to find him. We want to stop him. You talk about the truth? You care nothing for the truth, Ely. You're just a scaremonger, a scribbler. All you care about is a story.' He pulled Ely even closer to his face. 'You, Ely, are a parasite.'

He roughly pushed him away and the reporter stumbled then straightened, panting with fear and horror. He pulled his jacket straight and pushed his spectacles back into place, trying to regain some semblance of composure under the hard stares of the policemen in the yard.

'This can't be hidden, Inspector,' he whispered. 'He's back, isn't he. Jack. He's back.'

Handy was about to answer when a copper pushed through the two other policemen guarding the gate.

'Mr Handy, sir!' he wheezed.

Handy eventually tore his ice-blue gaze from Ely.

'What is it now?'

The constable held out a thin sheet of cheap paper.

'A young lad I know gave me this. He says there's already a crowd of about a hundred men on their way now.'

Handy glanced down at the sheet. It was a pamphlet, torn at one corner where someone, presumably the lad the constable had talked of, had ripped it from a wall. It had a crudely drawn illustration of a man bending over a dismembered body in a dark yard that looked nothing like the place in which they stood. He grinned and his knife was bloody. His face was swarthy and almost comically evil, with a huge black moustache. The words under the pamphlet screamed:

*"THE JEWISH MONSTER HAS RETURNED! NO WOMAN IS SAFE UNTIL THE ZIONISTS ARE BEGONE!"*

Handy grimaced, then shrugged.

'Only a matter of time, I suppose...' he started, but the copper shook his head. His face was pale.

'You don't understand, sir,' he said. 'They're shouting that the police are in on it. The lad told me that they're going to protect their own if police won't. He said they believe the police are behind it, and they've let Jack the Ripper out to kill again. They. Are. On. Their. Way. Here.' He spaced the last words out for emphasis.

Jarman cocked an ear. He thought he heard something; it sounded rather like the roaring of a rough sea heard from a distance. He realised what the noise was even before Curmudgeon barged his way into the yard.

'They're coming,' he said. 'And there's bloody hundreds of 'em.'

Callow tutted at this news. 'Well, they can bugger off,' he said. 'I'll go and have a word with them.'

But Handy had heard the noise too, knew what it was, and had noted that it was getting nearer. He had seen with his own eyes what could happen when a mob got itself worked into a frenzy. There would be no talking with them.

He placed a hand on Callow's shoulder to stop him, and then he turned to the three coppers, as well as Jarman, Curmudgeon, and Ely, who was glancing around warily, sensing the tension in the other men. Handy knew that, if they stayed, there was a good chance they would all end up as dead as the woman on the ground. The mob would use any excuse to get rid of some rozzers.

'It's too late for that, Frank.'

He faced the frightened men in front of him, making his decision.

'Follow me,' he said.

*

They ran.

Through cramped and narrow alleyways and side streets, sometimes having to turn sideways to scrape along their filthy, narrow embrace.

Jarman, running along with the Inspector, was almost immediately lost. All he could see around him were grimy, grey dwellings, some of them looking like they were just about ready to fall down. Every vista he looked at was the same, every alleyway was identical. Everywhere was puddles of sewage, dead dogs and broken, ragged skeletons who stared blankly at them in their flight. Every turn seemed to lead into the same street or tunnel, but Handy unerringly led the seven men through backyards and snickets; over fences and under them.

The men were soon smeared in all manner of filth as they slid and climbed and tumbled along the deadly streets; and behind them, getting nearer all the time, was the noise of the crowd. They sounded like demons from hell as they screamed and yelled. They were getting closer.

There was a cry from the rear as one of the coppers, the one who had brought the pamphlet, slipped in a pile of human faeces in the middle of the ally. He slammed to the ground and one of the other policemen went to his aid just as the crowd burst upon them from around the corner. The blue-uniformed figures disappeared immediately under the crush of what looked like a thousand screaming devils. In an instant, they were gone.

Handy grabbed Jarman by the shoulder and pulled him onwards. Both men could barely breathe: both from their flight and from the thick, odious atmosphere that prevailed in the cramped alleys. Jarman heeded him and pelted after the Inspector, knowing that the two policemen were gone. Curmudgeon, Ely and Callow were on their heels, followed by the remaining constable whose face was white with terror.

They came to what seemed like a dead end, but Handy didn't hesitate; he knew those streets like the back of his hand. Without pausing, he barged into a dwelling on the left. The place didn't even have a door—it had long since been burned for warmth—and he led the remaining men through the house. In one room, sitting in a hazy mix of smoke and collapsing plaster dust, was a ragged individual. It was hard to tell at first whether it was male or female, but it seemed to be holding a skeletal baby that resembled a skinned rabbit hanging from a sagging breast. The woman watched with blank eyes as the group of men crowded into her room. There was no furniture to be seen. Just a floor to sleep on and the woman and baby.

Handy led the men through a hole in the wall where a man sat on a low stool making what looked like boot uppers. A ragged boy sat on the floor with him. They barely glanced up from their work as the boots of the men dislodged yet more plaster dust from the crumbling walls. They pelted past the man and boy and out into a tiny backyard. Up and over the yard wall they went.

This led them into a narrow, black snicket, overgrown with weeds and strewn around with all sorts of detritus. Handy turned right and pelted along its length. Behind them, they heard outraged shouting from the inhabitants of the house as the crowd followed them through the dwelling and began climbing the yard wall too. The bricks, barely having any lime left to keep them together, collapsed under the weight of the crowd. The howling madmen picked themselves up and continued their pursuit. Glancing back, Jarman saw that they all held knives or staves or lengths of wood. A fair few of them had picked up bricks from the broken wall and they lobbed them at their quarry as they ran. The missiles banged and cracked and disintegrated against the walls of the snicket.

Handy turned left at the end, knowing exactly where this last alley led to, then he stopped in his tracks, not believing what his eyes showed him as the others crowded up against him. They all stood, staring in horror. Their escape route was blocked.

What had been just another alley now seemed completely impassable, full of bricks and wood that had at one time been a house but which had been pulled down at some point in the recent past. The rubble looked blackened in places, so perhaps the house had been demolished to stop the spread of a fire, but whatever the reason for its destruction it now completely filled the alleyway, blocking the men's route away from the mob.

Looking upwards, Handy immediately made up his mind and started climbing the mountain of debris that had once been a building. They had no choice. He knew that, at the end of this alley, was New Road. If they could make it there, then it was another run up Mount Street and so to the local police station. There they would be safe. He hoped.

He glanced back to make sure the others were following him. Ely was there of course, the slippery little bastard, right on his heels, and Jarman and Curmudgeon were starting to climb too. Callow and the constable made up the rear.

Handy had almost made it to the top of the precarious mound of rubble when Ely, heaving himself over in a fever of terror, found the brick he had been clinging to giving way. He fell backwards, tumbling and bouncing down the heap to sprawl in the filth at the bottom.

Jarman tried to catch him as he flew past, but missed. He immediately started to go down to Ely's assistance, but Handy grabbed him.

'No time!' he shouted. But then he saw Callow.

The sergeant slid and scrambled downwards, past a surprised looking Curmudgeon and the constable. Curmudgeon shrugged, grimaced, and then let go of the rubble and slid down to help and the constable followed. But they were far too late.

The crowd fell upon them just as Curmudgeon touched ground. In an instant, the constable was grabbed and hauled into the crowd, disappearing under the stomping feet.

Jarman immediately started clambering downwards as he saw Curmudgeon swing a sledgehammer of a blow that knocked one of the men in the crowd to the ground. This man too was stamped into oblivion by the mob in their desperation to get to the rest of them.

Curmudgeon grabbed Ely and physically threw him back onto the pile of rubble, up which the reporter started scrabbling once more, his eyes wide with terror, his spectacles long gone.

Jarman passed him on the way down, with Handy close behind him. The Inspector cried out a warning and he saw Callow pull out his truncheon and start laying about him. Curmudgeon was at his side, picking up debris from the pile and smashing it into faces. For a second, Jarman found himself on the plains of Afghanistan again, lying wounded as Sergeant Billy 'Curmudgeon' Cunningham stood above him, protecting him from the hordes of Afghan soldiers. Then his feet hit the ground beside Curmudgeon and he was fighting for his life. He pulled out the short leather cosh he always carried and belted it into the nearest face.

He smashed a clenched fist into the face of another pursuer, sending the man sprawling. Callow and Curmudgeon fought madly at his side, joined a second later by Handy who showed just what he could do in a fist fight.

The four men fought with a savagery born of fear. If they succumbed, they were dead. It was as simple as that. The faces of the crowd in front of them were like animals' faces. There was to be no reasoning with them. They snarled and howled and screamed. Luckily though, the narrowness of the alley helped the four men, as the crowd could not all get into it at once. Only four men abreast could come at them, and each rank fell as Handy, Callow, Curmudgeon and Jarman fought for their lives.

They may have all made it, if some bright spark had not climbed the rickety stairs of one of the remaining buildings above them and hurled the brick down. The piece of masonry was weighty. It had been carried from the collapsed yard wall and it still had a huge chunk of lime attached to it, with another half brick embedded into that. It was jagged and heavy and clumsy, but for the man who threw it, it was a lucky shot. It hit Frank Callow square on the top of his head and crushed his skull like an egg.

The sergeant fell without a sound and Curmudgeon, acting on an old impulse, immediately dragged him behind himself, trying to protect the inert body from the mob. He had by now picked up a piece of windowsill with a slice of jagged glass still attached to it, and he swung it like an axe, daring the crowd to come near him.

Jarman, his face cut and bleeding, stared desperately around him. They were doomed, he knew it. There was no way they could pause in their defence even for a second, because the mob would be upon them. He glanced at Curmudgeon and saw the same realisation in his eyes. They had both been in dangerous situations before, but never had the omens been so much against them.

Handy was trying to get to Callow, but the space in which they stood and fought madly was just too small. For every man they knocked down another appeared, spitting and screaming in hatred. They all knew they were done for.

Another brick thrown from the crowd walloped into the side of Handy's head and he fell to his knees, where the boot of an attacker cracked into his chin. He collapsed back onto the foot of the rubble, his world spinning. As he lay there, dazed, he began to feel a strange sense of karma descend upon him. He had been born in the gutter, and it seemed he was about to die in it.

He glanced at Callow and groaned at the unmoving, bleeding figure. Poor, poor Frank.

Then a movement above him caught his eye. At the top of the mound, a figure came bounding over. Then another.

Suddenly, there were dozens of blue-uniformed figures scrambling over the mound of rubble. Coming from the other side. A shot rang out, then another, and one of the attackers fell, clutching at his chest.

Abruptly, the crowd was running. Running from the police who clambered down towards them, revolvers firing at any of them that stood still. Within seconds it was as if the mob had never existed. Their footsteps and their howls vanished back into the labyrinth of death and decay from whence they had come, the echoes of their screaming disappearing as rapidly as they had appeared. A tideline of bodies lay where the men had fought, squashed like rotten fruit by the sheer weight of the people who had attacked them.

Handy, his head still spinning, struggled to his feet, helped by one of the coppers who had climbed down the rubble.

'Sergeant Harris, sir,' said the copper. 'Mount Street Station. Are you well?'

Handy ignored the man and stumbled over the rubble to Callow who lay unmoving on the ground, blood pouring copiously from his head. Jarman was already kneeling over him, with Curmudgeon standing by, panting like a dog.

'He's alive,' said Jarman to him. 'But barely. I need to get him into surgery.'

Handy nodded and barked instructions to the coppers who now crowded the ally. He would thank them later, but right now he needed to get Callow to the hospital.

A makeshift stretcher was organised, and they heaved Callow over the mound and onto the back of a cart they commandeered.

As soon as they got there, Jarman prepared to go to work.

# Chapter Ten

## From Hell

Over four hours later, Jarman emerged from the operating theatre. Although he had quickly cleaned up his face when he got to the hospital, it was still scratched and scraped all down one side. His clothes were stained and torn, and he was pale with exhaustion.

Callow's skull was badly fractured. When they got him onto the operating table his pulse was weak and intermittent, but Jarman had worked with his usual calm efficiency. He had patched the sergeant's head together and stitched up the resulting wounds.

Handy was back when Jarman came out, waiting for word about his sergeant. He had thanked Harris, and the sergeant had informed him that it was Ely who had raised the alarm by running into the nearest station. Harris had quickly ordered firearms to be issued and had instructed his men to get over the rubble of the fallen down house. Despite his dislike of the man, Handy had brusquely thanked Ely for his help and then promptly got rid of the bastard so he would not cause any more trouble. He knew the evening paper would be full of what had happened that morning, though.

He had then taken more armed men back into Myrdle Street, and there he discovered that the murdered woman's corpse was gone. Bloodstains surrounded the area where she had lain, but as to the whereabouts of the body, he had no idea. Maybe the crowd had taken it, but Handy doubted it. The policemen who had accompanied him back into the warren of streets quickly looked away when they saw the fury on his hard face. He had led them further into the streets and tried to find out who had been involved in the riot. He had interviewed some likely candidates who he knew were always up to no good: anarchists and communists and the like. They shrank away from him as he kicked open the doors of their poor dwellings, their previous righteous anger dissipated by gin and by the fact they were no longer a part of a huge mob. Handy and his men had cracked a few heads and had arrested some of them, but the Inspector believed that there had not been a leader as such. The riot had simply been another one of the frequent gatherings that happened in the area, where men, who had nothing in their lives and no way out of their terrible existences, had roared in impotent fury and had tried to take out some of their frustrations on easy targets. In this case, the Jewish community and the police they had found gathered around that torn body.

No, instead of a ringleader from within the streets, Handy believed that the crowd had been set against them by another. Someone with the knowledge and ability to wind a mob up, give it a target, and let it go. If he could only find out who that person was, he believed he would find out who was interfering in his investigation.

*

Jarman took him into his office when he saw him waiting and poured him a whisky. He himself, had a small sherry.

'I've done all I can for him,' he said. 'His skull was badly fractured. I've repaired it as best I can, but the next twenty-four to forty-eight hours are crucial. If he is still alive by then, he may have a chance of some recovery.'

Handy nodded but said nothing, staring down into his glass instead.

'Does he have a family?' asked Jarman. 'A wife? Children? What about the other policemen who died today?'

Handy shook his head. 'The body's gone,' he said as an answer.

He looked up into Jarman's eyes. 'The one from Myrdle Street, I mean. Somebody moved it. Took it away. It's gone.'

Jarman sat opposite him. He shook his head in disbelief. 'Who…?'

'The same person who authorised the removal of Eliza Cotton's body,' said Handy. 'The same person who probably had those bloody pamphlets stuck up all over the East End.'

He downed his whisky and stared at the surgeon.

'Someone,' he said, 'possibly high up in the police force, is trying to destroy my investigation. They're trying to stop me from discovering who this killer is. And this morning, I believe they tried to kill me. They killed three innocent men instead, and perhaps they even killed Frank Callow, poor fellow. Perhaps they even tried to kill you.' He stood and picked up the decanter. 'Do you mind?' he asked.

Jarman indicated for him to pour another, which he did.

'Do you have any idea who it may be?' he asked, and Handy shook his head again.

'Haven't a bloody clue. It may not even be anyone inside the force. It may be just someone pretending to be. I mean, why would anyone want to stop us finding Jack the Ripper? The whole idea is preposterous.'

Jarman regarded him for a moment, thinking about what he had said about mysterious people trying to kill them to stop them finding out the truth.

'Inspector, I don't believe that the man who killed those three women is the same man who killed the other five two years ago. I think it's a different person.'

Handy sat back down and stared at him. 'It has to be the same man,' he said. 'You can't tell me that two different people would do what they did to those women. It's…*obscene* what happened to them. It *must* be the same person. And they must be absolutely mad.'

'I agree that anyone who could do that to another person must be mad,' said Jarman, 'but there are too many differences between what we've seen in the last few weeks and what happened back in eighty-eight. I have been scrutinising the evidence, and there are differences between the killings. Enough to make me believe they were not committed by the same suspect.'

He put down his glass of untouched sherry.

'I've already spoken with you about the means of death. The Ripper always strangled his victims first and then mutilated the bodies. This happened neither to Eliza Cotton, nor Molly Harnath. They were both killed by *having* their throat cut and the mutilations—if we are to believe the blood patterns from Church Street, which is the only scene we had a chance to look at properly—happened while Harnath was still dying. The same cause of death was, I suspect, how the woman in Myrdle Street died, although of course that is going to be hard to prove now as the body has gone.'

Jarman stood and went to the window, looking down onto Whitechapel Road.

'I believe that what we have here, Inspector, is what we might call a copycat killer.'

'A what?'

'A killer who, for whatever reason, is copying the Ripper's murders. Although this time he has gone even further. The mutilations to the limbs, the scalping of the heads. It's as if he is trying to prove that he is even more monstrous than the original killer was. Unless they were privy to the post-mortems of the five Ripper victims, how would anyone know about the strangulation first? My premise is that they did not know, and they killed the three women by cutting their throats, as the newspapers of the time suggested. Whoever it is we are hunting, Inspector, I do not believe it is Jack the Ripper.'

Handy stared at him for a while, then his head sank again, remembering the men who had been killed that morning.

'Who is trying to stop us?' he mused to himself, turning to

something he may have had a chance of discovering rather than what Jarman had said.

Jarman picked the glass of sherry up and turned to him.

'Perhaps the real question you should be asking of course, Inspector, is once again, why?'

The question hung silently in the office. Still unanswered.

\*

Edward Ely looked at the headline he had constructed about that morning's horror. He shuddered as he remembered the terror he had felt when he saw that mob closing down on them. Christ, they were terrifying. They had wanted to kill them all, *would* have killed them if Handy had not led them through that rabbit warren of side streets and alleyways. Thank God for Jonas Handy and his knowledge of the streets because, if not for him, Ely would have been torn limb from limb, he was sure of it.

He put the newspaper aside and turned back to the other reports he had been digging into, and he soon forgot about the close encounter with death he had experienced that morning as he read through the notes again.

They were everything he had gleaned so far about Thomas Villiers: hearsay, rumours, so-called eyewitness accounts that would, at the moment, be laughed out of court. But Edward Ely believed in the old adage that there was no smoke without fire. There was something not right about Thomas Villiers.

Ely had spent many days poking about into Villiers's life since he had watched Handy and Jarman leave the man's house. He had been to the factory and had spoken to the carters and the loaders and the girls as they finished their shifts. One girl in particular seemed like she may be useful in the future. All he had to do was make her trust him, and he had been working on this for a while. The notes he had pieced together told him nothing that could prove anything at all about Villiers; but together they were an interesting, yet useless, set of information.

Yes, there was something odd about Thomas Villiers. He had tastes for certain things that could be described as exotic, if nothing else. There could be a link between him and the recent killings, although Ely was in no doubt he would have to keep this all secret for the moment. If anything got out and Villiers heard about it, he would destroy Ely. He would never work on a newspaper again, even if he managed to pay the massive fines Villiers would no doubt heap down upon him for defamation of character.

So. He had to be careful. Very careful. His digging would have to be a secret from everyone at the moment.

He took a key from his trouser pocket and opened a small, slim drawer in his desk. He placed the papers inside and locked it again, pocketing the key once more.

One by one, the employees finished for the day and the office emptied. Soon, Ely was left alone, apart from the doorman, who was looking at his pocket watch pointedly.

Ely took the hint and left the building, walking the mile or so to his small room in Clerkenwell, stopping to buy a loaf of bread for his supper. He climbed the stairs and fumbled the key into the lock. He closed the door behind him and put the bread on the shelf in the apartment. It was only when he had taken off his jacket and shirt collar that he noticed the envelope lying on the floor. It looked like it had been slipped under the door.

He picked it up and turned it over in his hand. No address. No writing on the envelope at all. It must have been delivered by hand. He opened it and, at the sight of the red, occasionally misspelled and grammatically incorrect words, his blood seemed to freeze in his veins.

*Dear Boss*

*I have heard but little of my latest japes I should think I would have had more news than has been heard of. Is this down to you. I hear you have been nosing around in names and places Ha Ha! You had better stop or the next ripping might be yourself and not a whore like the others. You know who I am referring to. V. You are on the wrong track there boss and I think you might be better off if you stop now. My knife is sharper than ever boss and it likes to rip. If that is whores or nosies I don't care. Take heed nosy boss. Keep away from things that you don't belong in. Otherwise I will take your scalp too just for jolly Keep away from V.*

*Yours truly,*

*Jack the Ripper*

*PS. I know where you live and I can get at you at the time I choose. Ha Ha! Wont that be a funny thing!*

The letter was shaking in Ely's hands as he stumbled to a chair and slumped into it.

He had been here! The Ripper had been at his house: right outside his house! He knew where he lived!

Ely moaned as he realised the door was unlocked and he jumped towards it, turning the lock and checking it was secure. He ran to the stairs at the back of the apartment and checked that the door to the yard was locked too. Then he checked each window, cupping his hands around his face, staring out and down into the street, the breath rasping in his throat.

Christ. The Ripper knew him! He knew him!

Ely eventually sat again and picked up the letter, reading through it once more. He remembered the letters, signed *From Hell* that had been posted to the Central News Agency in 1888. One letter had talked of snipping off an ear from his next victim, and then Catherine Eddowes had been found, minus an earlobe that had been cut off. Ely had only seen photographs of the letter, but from what he remembered, the writing style looked the same.

He was being warned off from digging into Villiers' past. It was obvious that was who the killer meant by the term '*V*'.

Although he was naturally terrified, Ely also felt a fierce surge of adrenalin as he realised that he had been right. Villiers was involved somehow. Was Villiers the killer? Had he sent this to stop Ely getting close to his terrible secret? It must be that.

With a strange mix of horror and excitement, Ely stared at his terrified face in the mirror over the fire.

He had found him.

He had found Jack the Ripper!

# Chapter Eleven

## A Rather Sad Affair

### London, 1879

*T*he dark man smiled indulgently at the artist as the young man proudly unveiled his latest masterpiece.

The gallery was awash with light from the huge candelabras shining down from the ornate ceiling high above the crowd. It was late summer in London. Outside the windows of the gallery, away from the men in their eveningwear and the women in their dresses of satin and silk, far removed from the quiet, comfortable opulence, the city went about its usual dirty business.

The gallery, on the Embankment not far from the newly constructed Houses of Parliament, was full of the great and the good of London society. Lords and ladies, MPs and businessmen. They mingled and smiled and drank champagne and, almost unconsciously it seemed, plotted against each other. It had ever been thus.

The dark man excused himself quietly from the crowd surrounding the young artist; he had suffered enough of his ego. One or two of the ladies present watched him leave, either surreptitiously or overtly, depending on their marital or societal status, for the dark-haired man was very handsome.

He was tall, six foot at least, and his waist, emphasised by his well-tailored garments, was narrow, his shoulders broad. He was clean-shaven and his chiselled jaw and dark eyes had already made many *a young lady blush as he smiled his perfect smile at them. He took his glass with him and moved out onto a balcony overlooking the Thames. His cologne failed somewhat to disguise the smell emanating from the river, although the view, on this summer evening, was a fine one.*

*This is the future, thought the man to himself, lighting a cigar and staring out over the city. London was at the centre of an industrial world, burying the agricultural past of Britain and reaching out to the very stars themselves. A bold and brilliant country at the centre of a bold and brilliant empire. And he was going to be part of that future. He was going to be a lord of that shining, metallic wonder.*

*He sipped his champagne and grinned into the warm night. He was young, he was strong, and he was rich. And his soul was as black as night. His grin widened at this thought. He liked it.*

*He turned at a rustle of material behind him. He recognised the woman instantly and knew her husband. Knew of him, anyway. Sir Duncan Mackeson, landowner and businessman. Rich, powerful and at least twenty-five years older than Erica, his young wife who now stood before him.*

*She was a picture of regal Victorian beauty. Small and petite, with blonde hair curled professionally around her face. Her gown was velvet and of a deep purple. The exquisite form of her neck and shoulders glowed from the light of the candelabras that shone around her like a halo. She held her fan in both hands in front of her as she smiled at the man.*

*'Good evening,' she said. Her voice was like liquid silk.*

*He lifted his hat.*

*'Good evening,' he replied, and his eyes flickered to her bust in the rather daringly low-cut gown.*

*He saw her smile slightly at this and he felt something shift within him. A twist of some emotion: a dark, wild emotion. An old emotion. Careful, he told himself, his eyes lifting to her face once again.*

*He knew all about Erica Mackeson. Her reputation preceded her. Her husband must surely have heard those rumours too, but it seemed the man was besotted by his young and beautiful wife. He must have known he was the subject of ridicule and derision in the circles of the gentlemen's clubs dotted around the genteel areas, but if he did, he ignored them. Perhaps he was well compensated for being a cuckold, thought the man, running his eyes over the woman's figure again.*

*Erica held out her hand and he took it and touched it to his lips. He felt that twist within his black soul again—anger, hatred—and he forced it down. The touch of her warm, soft hand almost made him gag and he released it as soon as he had kissed it.*

*They spoke for a while, the woman with an increasing anticipation. It seemed she lived for this sort of adventure. The rumours were that a veritable omnibus full of young lovers had been warmed by her ample charms. She seemed to be attempting to mark the dark man as her next trophy.*

*He felt the pent-up hatred pumping in waves inside him and beginning to leech out of him like a dark wave. Did she really think she could dominate him with her slim arms and her neck and her face? How could she think that anything like her fragile, clean, carefree body would prove attractive to him?*

*That anger was suddenly palpable. It was like bile in his throat. He could almost taste it. He wanted to do what he always did. He wanted to show this bitch what she was to him. That she was nothing to him. Nothing like the women he sought out. She did not smell. She was not filth. She was not polluted. He reached up and touched her hair, his fingers trembling as he rubbed it between them.*

*Erica pretended to be shocked at his presumption, but he could tell she was excited. He could tell straight away. Her breathing became faster, her face became flushed and her bosom heaved. He began to tug at her hair as the thought came to him that she was probably becoming damp at the thought of what they may do. The whore. The clean, sweet-smelling whore.*

*His other hand suddenly grasped her breast and she gasped and tried to pull away.*

*'Not here,' she breathed, but the man became more excited as he heard the fear in her voice.*

*'Whore,' he rasped, verbalising his thoughts and Amelia's eyes widened in alarm. The glowing party was just feet away from them,*

*but this man seemed to ignore all the people near them. She looked into his face and it was no longer handsome; it was twisted and hard and spiteful. His hand fastened around her hair, tugging some of it loose from its bonds. He tried to rub it between his fingers again, but Erica managed to pull away from him. She slapped him hard across the face.*

*'You are no gentleman,' she hissed at him. 'Why I would think...'*

*'Think what?' he asked, and his voice was course and harsh. 'That I would tup you just because you are pretty?'*

*Erica's face twisted itself, this time in disgust at his course language.*

*'I would rather cut out your heart than lie with a woman like you,' he whispered, hoarsely. 'I would rather cut out my own!'*

*He needed to be away from here, away from this place. He could feel the old putrid hatred exploding from him. He had to leave. He pushed past her, just as her elderly husband emerged onto the balcony, drink in hand, wondering no doubt, what his wife was up to now. The dark man ignored him and stormed out of the gallery, hundreds of eyes following him.*

*Outside, he took several deep breaths, forcing himself to calm down. A few pedestrians on the Embankment strolled by, enjoying the fine summer evening.*

*The dark man smiled when one of the pedestrians stopped beside him. He felt safer now. He always felt better when his Guardian was by his side. He hailed a hansom cab and they climbed in. The dark man gave the driver instructions.*

*As they drove, the dark man felt the impatience welling inside him, alongside the anger. It was bursting from him. He knew his Guardian felt the same and they shared a strange, secret smile.*

*Before long, they were in Whitechapel.*

\*

Jarman shook his head, sadly.

He and Handy were standing by the hospital bed in which Frank Callow lay. He was awake and staring, but his face seemed twisted with a strange palsy and he was unmoving. He just stared at whoever talked to him. It was Jarman's belief that he heard but did not understand.

Handy was holding Callow's hand, but he may as well have been holding the hand of a dressmaker's mannequin. Callow, the Callow he had known, was gone.

Jarman indicated with his head for Handy to follow him and once again took him up to his office on the first floor.

'The damage was just too much,' he said. 'His brain is irrevocably damaged. He suffered an attack of apoplexy shortly after waking, and he has had another since then. He is prone to fits now, too.'

Handy slumped into a chair, rubbing his head in his customary rough way.

'Poor Frank,' he said, finally. 'Poor, poor fellow. He didn't deserve this.'

Jarman nodded in silent agreement and sat opposite the Inspector.

'He is a brave man,' he said. 'He saved Ely's life that day.'

'Bloody Ely,' growled Handy, but was unable to vent his fury at the reporter too much. At least he had brought the back up just when they had needed it.

'There's a benevolent fund at the station,' he muttered. 'We pay for it ourselves, so it's not much. But it should be enough for him to be looked after.'

Jarman just nodded again and kept quiet about what he knew would happen. Callow was finished. The fits would continue and one of them, probably not long from now, would end his life. As awful as this reality was, the surgeon believed that a man like Callow would have preferred to go quickly rather than suffer interminably. The benevolent money would probably be better spent on buying a wreath.

'Did you find anything about who started the riot?' he asked.

Handy sighed. 'No. The pamphlets just seemed to appear overnight. They were all over the place, but were centred on the areas where Jewish settlers have moved into. Three Jewish men were killed the night before they came after us. The same night as the woman was killed.' Handy stared into the empty fire. 'Whoever it was, they knew where to strike the match. The whole place was ready to erupt. There has always been a hatred of the Jews in Whitechapel. The pamphlets just lit the fuse.'

'It was ever thus,' murmured Jarman.

'Somebody who knew how to organise a crowd,' continued Handy, 'and who knew we would be there, did this. And while those constables were being trampled to death and Frank Callow was being turned into a vegetable, that same somebody organised the removal of the body of that woman.'

He looked at Jarman, conspiratorially.

'It's someone high up in the force,' he said, almost whispering the words. 'It has to be. Someone, with power and influence, is trying to stop the investigations into these murders. And they're willing to kill to do it.'

Jarman said nothing for a while, and then opened the decanter on the table in the corner. He poured a whisky and gave the glass to Handy.

'But why would that be?' he asked. 'Why would someone in a position of authority be at all bothered about the murders of those unfortunates? Surely a senior police officer, if that is indeed what you are implying, would rather the killer be caught. Why go to all this bother to stop that from happening?'

Handy sipped his whisky and licked his lips. Jarman caught a whiff of liquor and decided to join him. He never even thought about the night Curmudgeon had to lift him into his bed. That was then, this was now. He was completely in charge here. It was only when he was alone that the occasional problems reared their ugly heads.

'It's my belief that whoever caused all this "bother" is involved in the murders,' said Handy. 'I think they might even be the murderer themselves.' He stared into a corner. 'As crazy as that seems.'

'Perhaps,' said Jarman, doubtfully.

They were quiet for a while, both deep in thought, then the

door to the office burst open, startling them both.

'Curmudgeon!' said Jarman, wiping the whisky from his trousers. 'For God's sake man, can't you ever just open a door without pulling the damn thing from its hinges?'

Curmudgeon frowned, confused. This was how he always entered a room. It was like everything he did. Noisy.

'There's been a bit of development,' he said, then turned to Handy. 'That reporter. The one who was with us down Myrdle Street?'

'Ely? What's he done now?' asked Handy.

Curmudgeon smiled, grimly. He hadn't liked Ely much either.

'He's gone and got himself killed.'

# Chapter Twelve

## Another Death

Earlier that day, Edward Ely had gone to work early. That was no problem for him as he had barely slept the night before. Every noise, every drip from the gutters, every shout from the paperboys or the late-night carousers outside his window had snatched him awake in the chair he slouched in, a poker gripped in his hand like a sword.

What little sleep he had managed to grasp was full of disjointed, nightmarish visions: of blood and steel and jagged flesh. When he finally woke on that, the last day of his life, he remembered he had dreamed about that woman in Myrdle Street. He had been in the yard with her. The gate was closed and locked behind him, and he stared down at her gutted and brutalised body. The yard was dark and damp and silent.

And then suddenly, the dead woman had sat up.

She had sat straight up, and her scalped and ruined head had turned slowly towards him. She had stared at him with her ruined eyes. She had grinned at him with her lipless teeth, and her savaged, open skull steamed in the cold air.

Ely had stared at her, aghast, his mouth open in terror, but unable to make a sound. He could not breathe and he could not move. He was frozen to the spot.

The corpse had struggled to its feet in front of his horrified gaze. Pieces of the flayed flesh of her thighs plopped to the wet ground around her, splashing into the puddles of water and blood.

Then she had stumbled towards him, her skeletal arms outstretched, her gaping throat still oozing blood even though her heart had long since stopped beating.

Ely had eventually managed to scream as the lumpish, inhuman figure staggered stiffly towards him. He screamed and screamed, blindly turning to the yard gate, pulling and beating at it frantically, but it would not budge an inch. He yanked and yanked at the handle, but the gate stayed irrevocably shut. Beyond the gate, outside in the street, he could hear that mob laughing at his plight. Behind him, he heard the gutted corpse splashing towards him through the puddles of its own blood.

He screamed once again when skinless fingers appeared on his shoulder. He heard a wet, bubbling cackle and smelt her fetid breath. She was right behind him.

The corpse pressed—*snuggled*—itself up against his back, her savaged arms sliding around his waist. He felt her mutilated face against his neck. He could not move.

'My knife is nice and sharp,' the thing hissed in his ear. 'Isn't that a jolly?'

The dead woman then yanked him around to face her. But it was not her who stood there, it was instead a black shadow. A faceless, fiendish thing with no form; nothing, except two red eyes, glowing in the blackness like the fires of hell.

'My knife is sharp, Edward!' the horror screamed. 'It's nice and sharp!'

Ely cried out as a glinting knife, a foot long, appeared in the claws of the monster in front of him. The knife tore into his stomach with a fury born of Hades.

Ely had thrown himself awake and lay where he had fallen from the chair, panting.

He had breakfasted on a cup of tea. He tried to eat some bread but the memory of that figure lying in the yard in Myrdle Street made him gag every time he swallowed. He gave it up as a bad job and dressed.

When he thought he was strong enough, he re-read the letter

he had received. He didn't know what to do. He should of course, hand it straight over to the police. It could be a vital clue as to the identity of the Ripper and, along with the notes on Villiers, it all seemed to point in the direction of that man as being the killer himself. Who else could the 'V' be, alongside the line about him sticking his nose in, if not? Villiers was the Ripper, and he somehow knew he had been digging into his past. He knew what Ely had found out about his little club.

But Ely was loathe to let the information go. Where would his fame, and more importantly his fortune, come from if he handed everything over to Handy and his pals?

No. What he needed was definitive proof. Then would come the headline of the century and the glory of the man who discovered Jack the Ripper! He could dine out on that for the rest of his life. Ely could see it all; he would write a book about how he had come to discover the truth about Villiers. He would be invited for after dinner speeches, interviews, perhaps even travel abroad to tell his story.

Despite the fear he had felt the previous night, and still felt now, Ely smiled. Just a little more digging and the world would be his!

He was the first one in the office and he sat quietly for a while, relishing the rare silence of the empty newsroom. He took the letter from his pocket and unlocked the slim drawer on his desk, placing it on top of the notes he had collected so far on Villiers. Then he closed and locked it safely once more.

James Lyon, his editor, came in and called a curt good morning, moving past Ely and his desk into his small office in the corner of the room.

*What to do?* thought Ely. He needed more information, yet he was bereft of the means to continue. He wanted to dig deeper into Villiers's background, but he needed money to do that. Potentially for travel, and for the odd bribe to Villiers's associates. The girl he had an appointment with would not cost him much, but others might ask a higher price. He glanced at Lyon who was now sitting, smoking a cigar in his office and reading the morning post.

Leaving his desk, Ely knocked and entered the office. Lyon looked at him quizzically.

'I may have something,' said Ely. 'Connected to the latest killings, and possibly to the Ripper killings too.'

Lyon indicated for him to sit. 'Tell me all,' he said, but Ely shook his head.

'I can't. All I can tell you is that I have some good but, at the moment, unprovable evidence about the possible identity of the killer.'

Lyon stared at him for a long time, and then sat forward. Ely saw the interest in his eyes. 'Who is it?'

This was the moment Ely had dreaded. He needed his editor to believe him so that he would give him the time and resources to really start digging into Villiers's secrets. But to do that, he would have to give him the name.

'Thomas Villiers,' he said, eventually.

Lyon continued to stare at him for a second longer and the interest in his eyes seemed to turn to something else, then he barked a disbelieving laugh. He sat back in his chair.

'Thomas Villiers,' he said, softly. 'The same Thomas Villiers who owns all those factories?'

Ely nodded, his mouth dry.

'The same Thomas Villiers who moves in circles so high *you* would break your neck just to gaze up at them?'

Ely began to feel his hopes sag at the tone of the man's voice.

'The same Thomas Villiers whom, it is said, will be receiving a knighthood later this year for his work with the poor?'

All Ely could do was nod again, feeling despair at the mistake he had made. He *knew* he should have kept quiet.

'Do you mean to say, the same Thomas Villiers who, if he ever heard about this conversation, could have this newspaper closed down within the hour, and you and I thrown into the street? That Thomas Villiers?'

He was not just incredulous now, he was furious.

'I know it sounds ridiculous…' started Ely.

'No!' shouted Lyon. '*You* sound ridiculous! How in God's name did you think I would entertain such foolishness? One word of such nonsense and this newspaper is finished!'

He stood and glared down at Ely, pointing his finger at him. 'You will never mention that man's name again within my office,' he said, quieter now but with no less venom. 'I will hear no more of it.'

'What if I have proof?' asked Ely.

'What proof?'

And it was here that Ely hesitated. What he had was not proof at all. Just random accounts that would be destroyed by the work of even the greenest lawyer in Chancery Lane without the man bothering to take his hands out of his pockets. He had nothing.

Lyon saw the realisation flit across his face and nodded grimly, a strange look of relief flitting across his face.

'You see the problem,' he said.

'Yes, sir,' said Ely, quietly. 'Of course. Forgive me. My impatience gets the better of me at times.'

He stood to leave and the editor coughed. He turned back.

'Not one word, Ely.'

He nodded again and left Lyon's office, feeling the unjust petulance of a small child.

Idiot. The man wouldn't recognise a story if it barked at him. He sat back down at his desk. He was right. He knew he was right, but he had no proof. Even though the letter mentioned '*V*', that could have meant anything; at least that would be what the high-priced barrister that Villiers would no doubt employ would say. And, of course, the judge would believe him. Those people all moved in the same circles. But he was right, all the same.

Ely rubbed his jaw. He needed more. He needed proof.

He waited until the newsroom filled up and then slipped out. He had one more lead and he was going to take it.

The editor watched him leave. Then he called for one of the news boys.

He had a message to send.

*

Jarman, Handy and Curmudgeon stared at the body of Ely.

The alabaster-faced corpse lay on its back on the broken down, rotting wharf where it had been dumped after being dragged from the Thames. It was a chilly day, foggy as usual, and the soaking wet figure was bone cold. There was silence, broken only by the puffing of a steamer on the river and the lonely cries of seagulls circling overhead, constantly on the lookout for food. The whole place stank of seaweed and sewage.

A docker on his way to work had noticed the body in the water, trapped by debris near the bank. He had alerted the police, who in turn had alerted the hospital where they knew Handy was.

Handy turned to the docker.

'He was near the bank?' he asked.

The docker nodded.

'This 'ere wharf ain't been used for long a year,' he said. 'I knew he weren't no docker when I saw 'is fancy suit. He was trapped by all that gubbage under the staves. Otherwise, I am quite sure he would have scooted all the way out to sea.'

The man chuckled, good-naturedly. This probably wasn't the first drowned corpse he had seen. Handy nodded, took the man's name and address and then let him go about his business.

Jarman had bent down by Ely and was looking at him intently.

'No bruises, no obvious wounds,' he said. 'It simply looks as if he drowned.' He continued his examination as the seagulls cried their lonely laments above him and the steamer hooted in the distance.

'Ah,' said Jarman, suddenly. He had lifted Ely's head and was feeling about underneath.

'Give me a hand, Curmudgeon,' he said. 'I want to look at the back of his head.'

Curmudgeon, with his usual mutterings and grumblings,

helped Jarman turn the body onto its front, drying his hands on his trousers when they were done. The surgeon parted Ely's sopping hair at the back of his head.

'You see, Inspector?' he said as Handy knelt beside him. 'The raised contusion? And the speckled dots around it? He either hit his head and fell into the river, or someone hit his head for him and he was then tossed in. This definitely happened before he died or the speckling would not have occurred. They are the beginnings of a bruise. If his heart was stopped, they would not have formed.'

'So, murder then?' asked Handy after a while. Ely's head had set him off thinking about Frank Callow again.

'Oh, I can't say that, Inspector. This could easily have been an accident. I'll need to study the body closer to confirm or deny anything. We need to get him to the hospital so I can have a good look.'

Handy nodded and started the arrangements to have the body removed. As they waited for the carriage to come and collect it, a familiar figure approached.

'Constable Rose,' said Jarman. 'How are you?'

Rose smiled with pride that Jarman had remembered him. He saluted.

'Very good, sir, very good.' He smiled at Curmudgeon, who just scowled at him. The young constable seemed disappointed, but then grinned when Curmudgeon gave him a wink.

'Anything, Rose?' asked Handy, and the constable nodded.

'We think we probably know who she was,' he replied.

Jarman raised his eyebrows at Handy, who explained.

'I sent young Rose here out into the streets to see if he could come up with anything about our missing woman, the one from Myrdle Street. As we have no body, an identification may at least help. He turned back to Rose. 'Go on,' he said.

'I talked to various dollies around town,' said Rose, taking out his notebook from his uniform pocket. 'Eventually I was pointed in the direction of a pub called the *Drunken Swan*, over on Brushfield Street.'

Handy nodded. He knew the tavern well.

'Anyways, I talked to the potman there and he put me in the direction of one of the barmaids. Elsie was her name.'

The lad smiled dreamily at the thought of Elsie. Then he seemed to rouse himself.

'So anyway, I talked with Elsie, and asked her about any regulars that hadn't been in for a couple of nights, and she told me about a woman called Hetty Kennedy. A regular: in and out every night, Elsie said. Up until the night before you found the body in Myrdle Street when she didn't show, not even at six when she usually stopped in for a, erm…'

He scanned his notebook for the beer the woman usually drank, but Handy interrupted.

'We don't need to know her tipple, lad. Just tell us what else you found out.'

'Well, she didn't come in at six, like I said, and she hasn't been seen since. I got a description. Five foot four, medium build, dark hair. Usually wearing a dark blue dress and a red scarf.'

Here Handy and Jarman looked at each other.

The description would help little; the body had barely looked human, but the mention of the red scarf took both men back to the morning they had discovered the body. The corpse had definitely been wearing such an item.

'Right. It's probably her, although Hetty could turn up at any time, I suppose. Did you find out anything about her?'

'Yes, Mr Handy. She lived on Butler Street. I went to the address and found it occupied by eight other people who lived there. They said they all shared the rent. And they all said they hadn't seen Hetty since Thursday evening. They did say that she had "sweetened herself up" though. Like she was going to meet someone special, although they didn't know who that might be.'

Handy nodded at the constable.

'Good work, lad. We'll make a detective out of you yet.'

Rose's fingers trembled with pleasure as he fastened his notebook away.

'We'll need interviews with all those others that lived with her,' he said. 'We'll get them down the station to do that. Rose, I'm putting you in charge of it. Get yourself off and get it sorted.'

'Yes, sir!' said Rose and dashed away.

The carriage came to collect the body of Edward Ely and they made their way to the hospital.

# Chapter Thirteen

## A Perusal of the Evidence

'Murdered then?' asked Handy, and Jarman nodded. They were back in the morgue of the London Hospital again, trying to keep away from Dr Gresham and the admonishing glances he would shoot at Jarman whenever he saw him.

'Definitely. Someone knocked him on the back of his head and then compressed his neck, strangling him while he was either unconscious or incapable of fighting back. See the mark at the base of the throat? That's where the killer pressed in their thumb, cutting off his breathing.'

Jarman straightened.

'Presumably he was then tossed into the river near that wharf. It's old and unused so there was little chance of anyone seeing anything untoward. It was only because the body snagged on the detritus under the staves that he wasn't swept completely away. The only thing I can say in his favour is that the poor fellow would not have felt much. It would have been quick.'

Handy sighed and rubbed at his head in his customary way.

'What the hell is going on around here?' he muttered. He looked at Jarman. 'Do you think it was just bad luck? That he was just the victim of a robbery? His watch was missing and there was no wallet in his pockets.'

Jarman shrugged.

'I have no idea, Inspector. Whoever did it could have easily taken those things to cover their tracks, but I believe that whoever killed him was a professional. I don't think your average bludger would have killed like this. This is more subtle. I think whoever did it is well versed indeed in the art of murder.'

Handy nodded, deep in thought.

'Well, I'm going to go to his place of work, see if I can find out anything there.' He looked at Jarman. 'You want to accompany me?'

They left the cold, dead body of Edward Ely to the tender mercies of the morgue staff. Jarman called on Curmudgeon, and they were in Fleet Street in no time.

They were pointed in the direction of the editor's office by a junior.

'That's Mr Lyon's office, sir,' he replied to Handy's enquiry. 'He's the editor.'

The boy then rushed off, his inky hands full of papers, while Handy and Jarman knocked on the door of the office.

They introduced themselves when they were inside and Handy broke the news of Ely's death.

Lyon just stared at them for a moment.

'But I just talked with him this morning,' he said, as if this could repudiate the reality of the news.

'What time was that, sir?' asked Handy, glancing at the clock on the wall behind the editor. It was almost five pm. Ely's body had been found at half-past one.

'It was early,' said Lyon. 'No one else was in, say about a quarter-past seven?'

'Was Mr Ely in the habit of coming in so early?'

'Not at all. If anything, he usually slipped in just before his hours started. He thought I never noticed, but, well. There we are.' He stopped his criticism of Ely as he remembered the man was dead.

'What did you talk about?'

'Sorry?' asked Lyon, coming back to the conversation.

'When you spoke this morning. Was it about anything in particular?'

'No. Nothing in particular.'

Jarman, watching carefully as he always did, noted the man's eyes slide away to the left.

'Well, what *did* you talk about?' asked Handy. 'Anything you can remember may be very important.'

'He just gave me a little run down of his adventures the other day,' said the editor, and it seemed to Jarman that he had suddenly remembered the events in Myrdle Street and was seizing upon them.

Handy nodded. Something told Jarman that he didn't believe the editor either.

'I see,' said the Inspector. 'Could you direct us to Mr Ely's desk?'

If the request surprised the editor, he did not show it. If anything, he seemed eager to get them out of his office.

He took them to Ely's desk and Handy smiled coldly at him.

'Thank you for your assistance, Mr Lyon. That will be all. For now.'

Lyon frowned at the tone of Handy's voice as much as the summary dismissal, but nodded and walked away.

'Well, he's keeping something back,' said Handy when the man was gone.

'Indeed, he is,' agreed Jarman. 'I wonder what that something is?'

They picked through the various papers on Ely's desk, and moved a cup that was destined never again to be touched by the reporter's hands. They opened drawers and lifted files. Nothing they found was the least bit useful.

It was Jarman who tried to open the slim drawer, hardly seen under the larger ones in the side of the desk.

'Locked,' he said. 'I wonder if Lyon has a key for it?'

'Bugger bloody Lyon,' muttered Handy. He reached into his pocket and pulled out a complicated-looking contraption.

'Picklock,' he said, grinning a toothy grin at Jarman, who could not help but smile back. 'You can take the lad out of the Nichols, but you can't take the Nichols out of the lad.'

He bent down and within half a minute the drawer was open and they were rifling through the papers. Their eyes widened when they read the files about Villiers. They widened even further when they saw the letter.

'What the bleedin' hell had Ely got himself into?' gasped Handy.

Jarman glanced up and saw Lyon at the window of his office, staring at them, white-faced.

'I suggest we get back to the station, Inspector, so we can look these over at our leisure.'

Handy looked towards where Jarman was staring, and he smiled grimly at the editor, waving the papers at him.

'I suggest you're right,' he said. They left the newsroom.

\*

Back at the station, with Curmudgeon ensconced beside them, happy with a mug of tea, they spread out the papers on Handy's desk.

'Mr Ely was certainly digging around Villiers, wasn't he?' murmured Handy.

'He was indeed,' answered Jarman, thoughtfully. He was re-reading the letter.

'And that,' said Handy. 'What do you think of it? Do you think it's real? Or do you reckon Ely wrote it and was going to send it to the paper? To try and stir the pot? I wouldn't put it past him.'

'Possibly,' said Jarman, frowning. 'You remember, of course, the letters that were received back in eighty-eight? The so-called "From Hell" letters?'

'Course I do, I saw them myself.'

'Then you should know if you think this one is the same,' said Jarman. 'I don't think it is.'

Handy took the letter from him and scanned it again.

'The handwriting seems very different if memory serves me correctly,' he said. 'You know, a few people, Fred Abberline included, thought that those letters were sent by someone connected to the press, just to drum up more newspaper sales. But this one is different. The originals were just gloating, but this... This is a warning. Ely was being warned not to dig into "V", whoever that is. Because we can't prove that it's Villiers they're talking about.'

'Agreed,' said Jarman. 'Although, circumstantially, the fact that this letter was in a locked drawer with documents about Villiers is curious, to say the least.'

'There's not really much, though, is there,' said Handy. 'All these documents show is that Villiers was part of some sort of private club, and that he and some pals engaged in what you might call nefarious parties with women. No doubt it's nothing his wife would want to read, but then again, there's nothing to show any connection with the three dead women.'

'Apart from the fact that we know two of them were part of Villiers's "charity" work,' said Jarman. 'It would be very interesting if we could find out whether the third woman, the one who went missing from Myrdle Street, was part of that charity too.'

Handy went through the papers again, shaking his head.

'Look, it's interesting, I'll give you that, but it proves nothing. Hundreds of women have been taken off the streets by Villiers and put to work in his factory. Just because two, or even three of them end up murdered can't, at the moment, be seen as anything other than coincidence.'

He looked up at Jarman.

'There are no names here, and nothing to show any connection at all with the murders. Only the assertion, gleaned from some very dubious witnesses by the looks of it, that Villiers was engaging in some sort of entertainment with friends of his. Immoral perhaps, if we read between the lines, but not illegal.'

Jarman nodded. 'We could deduce that Villiers's "friends" are from the same social circle as Villiers himself, would you agree?'

'I would have thought so.'

'Then it seems logical that we could also deduce that those friends would be very unwilling to have this information released into the hands of the media and therefore into the public domain.'

'Yes.'

'That they are the type of men who could easily, if they so wanted, hire a professional killer to get rid of someone who was, perhaps, getting a little close to the truth. The truth being that these men are engaging in what we can suppose to be sordid and disreputable activities with women *not* from their social circle, if you understand my point.'

'Dollymops,' said Curmudgeon, speaking for the first time.

'Quite, Curmudgeon. Although your vernacular lacks its usual decorum. Yes. Prostitutes. These men, if the reports in these papers are correct, have been engaging in what, being all men of the world here, we could possibly call "sex parties." The women were paid to have sex with these high-ranking gentlemen.'

'And you think Ely found this out and they got rid of him?' asked Handy. 'Seems a little far-fetched. Having a rumble with a dolly is one thing, but murder is quite another.'

'I have usually found, Inspector,' said Jarman, 'that the higher a man rises, the darker his soul becomes. I doubt any of the people alluded to here on these sheets would lose too much sleep over the death of a lowly reporter. Their reputation is usually their biggest concern.'

Handy frowned at him.

'You talk of these people as if they are singularly different because of their money. Surely you come from a similar background, and I know that you would never engage in criminal acts. You speak of these people as if they are a separate entity.'

Jarman glanced at Curmudgeon, who just stared back at him.

'I do indeed come from a comfortable background, Inspector, but I am afraid it did not last. I watched my mother being thrown out of her house because of the gambling debts of my father. A man who took his own life rather than face up to the catastrophe he had instilled upon his family. For a while my mother and I were forced into a life that was not how we had envisioned it would be. Unlike most of my brethren, I have known hunger. I have known shame. However, I took to medicine and then joined the army as a surgeon; and I ensured my mother enjoyed a pleasant, if moderate, end to her days in a cottage in Richmond.' He glanced up at Handy, and the Inspector saw the cold gleam in his eyes.

'I am nothing like these men,' he said.

Curmudgeon picked up his mug.

'I'll make us all another cuppa,' he said.

There was a silence in the room for a while.

'Well, what about the letter?' asked Handy, rather chastened by Jarman's words. 'What do you think of that? Is it real? Is it connected to these reports about Villiers?'

'It certainly seems to be a warning, does it not? But what it has to do with these terrible murders, I do not know. We can surmise, of course, several possibilities. It could have been Villiers himself who wrote it, warning Ely off. Or it could have been Ely, perhaps to print it to see how that rabbit would fly with Villiers. Or, of course, it could be from someone completely separate. A different killer entirely.'

Jarman frowned as he rubbed the paper between his fingers. He could not but help think that there was something strange about it. What was it?

'But that would mean a connection of some sort between Villiers and the Ripper,' said Handy, bringing Jarman back to the conversation. 'That would mean something a lot darker than a bunch of rich men enjoying themselves with a bit of low-class flesh. A lot darker even than hiring someone to kill a snooping reporter.'

Curmudgeon re-entered and handed them all a tea.

'Indeed, it would, Inspector,' Jarman said, taking the hot mug. 'Indeed, it would.'

The three men sat in silence again, drinking their tea.

# Chapter Fourteen

## A Visit to the Country

The next day, Jarman and Curmudgeon were back at the station with Handy to meet Rose, who had brought in the people who lived in the lodging house with Hetty Kennedy. He was accompanied by a man in his fifties who smiled nervously at everyone.

'Who's this?' asked Handy.

'The name's Jack Macken, sir,' said the man. 'I'm a carter. Work down Myrdle Street. I'm the one who found the body, sir.'

'Why didn't you come forward sooner?' growled Handy, and the man quailed in front of him.

'Well, I reported the body, but then there was that 'orrible riot, wasn't there,' he said. 'I made sure I stayed at home with me door locked. It wasn't until I saw the place was quiet again that I felt safe enough to come out. I saw the constable here and told him who I was.'

'Mr Macken said he saw someone, sir,' said Rose. 'The night the woman was killed.'

They took Jack straight into Handy's office.

They listened to Jack's account of what he had seen that night, and took down the description. Handy was ecstatic.

'At last,' he cried. 'We've got something, at least.' He turned to Rose. 'I want this description out everywhere, including the newspapers, understand? Everywhere. I want to get my hands on this fair-haired fellow.'

Rose nodded, then hesitated.

'What is it?'

'I'm quite a dab hand at drawing, sir,' said Rose, reddening. 'Perhaps I could take Mr Macken here and draw the person he saw that night from his description? Might jog a few people's memories?'

'Or give them false ones,' Handy said, doubtfully.

Jarman smiled at the frowning Handy.

'There's no harm in it, Inspector,' he said. 'Images often help in cases such as this.'

'All right,' said Handy, eventually. 'You go and do your drawing. While you're at it, why don't you get Jack here a bacon sandwich and a cup of tea.'

'Ooh, Gawd bless you, sir,' said Jack, looking like all his dreams had come true. They left the office.

'Right,' said Handy. 'Let's get talking to that lot out there.'

The people who had shared the house with Hetty Kennedy were a motley collection. Four of them were women who all said they were seamstresses, but Handy recognised an East End prostitute when he saw one, and he knew exactly what they did to cover their part of the rent. Three of the men were dockers: low-browed, slope-shouldered hulks who, it seemed, could barely string a sentence together. The last man was a fish porter at Billingsgate. One by one, they were interviewed and dismissed. Handy asked them all whether Hetty had ever worked at any factories around town, carefully not mentioning Villiers FireSticks, but they all just shrugged. They knew virtually nothing of their former housemate. They did not really know anything about each other. They shared a house simply as a means for each of them staying off the streets. It was just survival. One by one they shuffled out of the station and back to their dark and hopeless lives.

The days passed. Rose produced his drawing of the suspect and was rewarded with a smile and a slap on the back from Handy. The illustration, showing a blond man wearing a cap and a white scarf, running down the street with Jack Macken throwing up an arm in surprise beside him, was given to the newspapers, along with a description of the man. Plenty of people came forward to say they knew who the person was, but every time this led to nothing. Usually, the witnesses were disgruntled ex-wives or girlfriends who simply wanted to get their errant partners into trouble. Handy had two women arrested for wasting police time and the stream of vindictiveness slowed to a mere trickle. He had decided to withhold any mention of the letter from the press as both he and Jarman were unsure of its provenance and so decided to keep it under wraps until they could be sure whether Villiers was involved in anything other than extra-marital immorality.

Handy was also still engaged in trying to find out who had moved the dead bodies and determine who was involved in the riot they had been caught up in. One or two people were brought forward but Whitechapel had, as usual, closed ranks. Even a man with Handy's reputation found nothing but blank stares from people he could usually rely on to give him good information. The perpetrators, whoever they were, would probably never be brought to justice. This failure hung over Handy, and it was made worse when, on the day the image of the fair-haired man was printed, Frank Callow died after suffering another, final fit.

Handy and Jarman went to his funeral. Afterwards, Jarman tried to engage the Inspector in the small talk that was ever part of any healing process, but Handy did not respond. He stood by his sergeant's grave in the cold drizzle, his face drawn and harsh. Jarman knew he blamed himself for Callow's sad demise, as well as the death of the other constables.

Over those days, Jarman spent his time going over the papers they had found. Again and again, he held the letter in his hand. There was something about it that tugged at his mind, but for the life of him he could not fathom out what that something was. He turned again to the notes on Villiers.

He had known there was something not quite right about the man. Jarman had come to depend on his inner feelings, and Villiers had set numerous clanging alarms going in his head. When they had met so briefly in his house, Jarman had felt that there was something almost brooding about the man. Villiers was like the still, dark hours before a storm. It seemed that a violence was bubbling, just below the surface. The man was a domestic bully, he had deduced that straight away. His wife, Susannah, was too demure, too much the picture of perfect marital bliss.

He remembered when Villiers had sat next to her and she had stiffened at the closeness. Almost as if it was something she was unused to and disliked. Why would a wife feel that way towards her husband? Had they ever been close?

Making a decision, Jarman told Curmudgeon to ready Dusty and the brougham and made his way to Villiers's house once more. It was not the maid who opened the door, however. It was a young man: a groom, by the looks of him.

'I'm afraid Mr Villiers is at the factory today, sir,' said the groom. 'He said he would not be back until the evening.'

'And Mrs Villiers?'

'The mistress is at her country home for the weekend, sir.'

Jarman nodded.

'Thank you,' he said. 'You have been most useful.'

He turned to Curmudgeon, whom he had not failed to notice had brushed the dry mud from his greatcoat and combed his hair. He smiled at the man's obvious disappointment.

'Don't worry, Curmudgeon,' he said. 'I believe that a trip to the country is in order. Be so kind as to book rooms for us in Dorking, and two train tickets for said station.'

Curmudgeon frowned. 'Why Dorking?'

'Because that is where Mrs Villiers's country home is located, of course. Dene Manor. It has belonged in her family for over a hundred years. I have looked this information up, you know. That's where she is now. Probably with that girl: Ellie was her name?'

He watched as the desired effects of his words swept across Curmudgeon's battered face.

'I'll get right on to it,' he said, climbing into the driver's seat. 'Hurry up, then!' he cried, impatiently.

Jarman smiled and climbed in.

\*

They caught the noon train to Dorking and booked into the hotel. Jarman collected directions for Dene Manor from the hotel receptionist and, as the house was only two miles out of town, and as it was a fine, crisp autumn afternoon, they decided to walk to Mrs Villiers's house.

As they walked the grassy path, both of them savouring the cool, country air after the smog of London, Curmudgeon asked him what he thought he would accomplish going there to talk to Mrs Villiers.

'I'm not really sure, Curmudgeon,' answered Jarman. 'Truth be told, there was something about Villiers that didn't sit square with me. It's simply a feeling, nothing more, but I believe Mrs Villiers may know more about her husband than she has said so far, and I'm wondering if she will be more forthright when he is not around her. And if nothing else, you may even bump into Ellie, eh?'

'Don't know what you're talking about,' grumbled Curmudgeon, but Jarman saw the eagerness in his eyes.

'I simply want to ask the lady a few more questions, out of earshot of her husband, that's all,' said Jarman after a while.

Curmudgeon, swinging a stick at the passing flowers by the roadside, said nothing. But he knew Jarman. He just hoped the surgeon knew what he was doing by meeting up with the mysterious, and very pretty, Mrs Susannah Villiers again.

They soon came upon Dene Manor. It was large, but not too imposing: a square Georgian house with a trim, well-tended garden at the front, broken into separate areas by small, neat bushes. Upon first inspection, the place looked deserted but, as they approached, they saw a watering can and wheelbarrow by the corner. Signs of some life at least. They walked up to the front door.

To Curmudgeon's obvious delight, it was Ellie who opened the door. She curtsied to Jarman and then grinned at Curmudgeon, who swept off his battered hat and grinned back at her.

She showed Jarman to the drawing room, leaving Curmudgeon outside.

'Dr Jarman, ma'am,' she said.

Susannah Villiers was sitting on a window seat reading, and she looked up as Ellie introduced him. Surprise, and perhaps trepidation, chased themselves across her face, but Jarman was sure he saw pleasure too. She smiled uncertainly at him.

'Dr Jarman, what a pleasant surprise. I was not expecting you.'

Jarman bowed.

'My apologies, Mrs Villiers. I was in the area and thought I would call on the off chance you were available. I hope this is acceptable. I certainly do not wish to intrude on your time.'

'Not at all,' she replied. 'Please, sit down.'

Jarman did as he was asked, placing his hat beside him on the settee. Susannah sat opposite him, still by the window. She put her book down.

'Would you like some tea?' she asked.

'Thank you.'

Susannah nodded to Ellie, who curtsied and left to make the tea.

'My apologies for disturbing your respite,' said Jarman. 'I can see why you must love it here. It is very peaceful.'

Susannah smiled, and Jarman could not help but notice how much more relaxed she seemed in her own home. Or, perhaps, it was because her husband was not there with her. He glanced at the book.

'Edgar Allen Poe,' he said, surprised. 'Rather a dark subject matter for such a lovely day.'

Susannah smiled.

'I find Poe to possess elements I can relate to at times,' she replied. 'His prose can be exquisite, even though, as you have said, the subject matter can be bleak.'

Jarman nodded. He found himself just staring at the woman by the window, her auburn hair haloed by the golden light outside.

He believed he could spend a lot of time just looking at Susannah Villiers. With some effort, he managed to bring himself back to why he was at the house.

'I'm afraid I have not been totally truthful about my reasons for being here,' he continued, and a small resigned smile flickered across Susannah's face.

'I did not, for one second, believe that to be the case,' she said.

'Then, let us be frank,' he said. 'I would like to ask you a few questions, in my capacity as someone helping the police with their investigations. Would you accede to that?'

'It depends on what you ask,' she replied. 'I have come away from London to immerse myself in the countryside of my youth. I try to forget all about that city when I'm here.'

Jarman nodded.

'I can see why you would want to do that. London can be chaotic at times. I myself have always enjoyed the country air.'

'Are you from London?' she asked.

'Originally, I'm from Richmond,' he replied. 'But I left the area when still quite young. After qualifying as a doctor, I joined the army; looking for adventure, I suppose.'

'The army. My goodness. And did you find it?'

'Find what?'

'Adventure.' Susannah said this word softly, with a smile and in such a way that Jarman felt something warm and vital wash through his stomach. The woman was smiling at him in a way that a married woman should perhaps not smile at another man. He managed to return the smile, lopsidedly, but he could not deny the feeling of contentment he felt in her presence.

'I found a little too much of it, I'm afraid. So I left and re-joined the London Hospital.'

They stared at each other for a while, until Ellie knocked and entered with the tea. She raised an eyebrow at the atmosphere in the room and seemed to smile to herself as she poured the tea. She curtsied at Jarman again, then left.

'So,' said Susannah. 'You said you wanted to ask me some

questions?'

'I do,' said Jarman, putting down his cup.

'About my husband, I suppose,' she said, noting his reluctance to start.

'I wish no ill respect towards your husband,' he said. 'And the reason for my asking—the murders I have been involved with—I am sure have nothing at all to do with him personally. I simply wish to ask about his charity work. With those unfortunate women he takes in to help them with their futures.'

Susannah nodded, almost to herself, then she sighed and he sensed a change within her. Was it disappointment?

'What would you like to know, Doctor? I am simply my husband's wife. I have no knowledge at all of what goes on in his factories. I'm not sure how I can be of any help.' She sipped her tea, and Jarman, noticing everything as usual, saw that her fingers were trembling slightly.

'The charity side of the factory,' continued Jarman. 'When did he start with this commendable work?'

'I believe it was before he and I wed,' said Susannah. 'Which was in 1887. The factory was already up and running and he had started taking in those-those women, before that.'

Jarman nodded. 'Did he ever tell you why he decided on this worthy cause?'

Susannah smiled a rather sad smile.

'I once asked him that very question myself, when we were newlywed, and he said to me that God had made him great. And that it was his duty to help those that had not been blessed as he had been.'

'I see. And how many women have benefitted from his work?'

'I do not know the answer to that, I'm afraid. But I believe that it must be in the hundreds.'

'And he is to be knighted for it, I hear. You must be very proud of him.'

Susannah stared at him for such a long time that he began to feel uncomfortable. There was something about this woman.

Something so very *right* about her. Jarman knew that, if he was not careful, he would just believe every word she said, simply because it was her saying it. And that would help no one in this strange investigation he had been caught up in. For a second, Mary's smiling face floated into his mind and he blinked in surprise. It almost felt that the smile was a one of encouragement. He took a deep breath. What on earth was he thinking of? Back to the job in hand.

'It is a great honour,' she eventually said.

Jarman did not reply and they were silent again for a while, until Susannah frowned.

'Would you take a turn with me around the garden, Doctor Jarman? I feel a little warm.'

'Of course.'

They left the house at the rear where a large garden lay: woods to the back, hedges to the sides and a lawn with a fountain in the centre. Susannah led Jarman onto a gravel path that ran around the edges of the lawn. As they emerged from the house, they caught sight of Curmudgeon and Ellie sitting on a bench at the side of the house, deep in conversation. They both smiled at the rather fetching scene.

'You asked if you could be frank, Doctor,' she said as they strolled. 'I will endeavour to be the same. You are of the mind that my husband is somehow involved in those beastly murders.'

She held up a hand as he started to deny this.

'Please. Let us both speak freely. I am tired of circling the subject.'

They walked a little further, and Susannah glanced around her, making sure they would not be overheard, even though the garden was deserted.

'My husband is not a good man, Doctor, although if anyone ever said I had uttered those words I would bring the not unimpressive weight of my fortune down upon them. Do we understand each other?'

Jarman nodded. 'Of course.'

'He is my husband. As far as he is concerned, I am his property. Everything I have is his. A woman has little say in what goes on in her marital home, as you know.' She waved a hand around her. 'All of this. This was once mine, my dowry after my parents died. But it also belongs to him now since our marriage. Although it is my inheritance, he said his name should be added on the deeds. I am trapped, Doctor Jarman, and I must look to my own survival. So, nothing of what I am about to tell you must go beyond this garden. Are we clear about that?'

Jarman was silent for a while as they continued walking. Trapped, she had said. For a second, he just wanted to forget all about the reason for his visit. He just wanted to walk in the garden in the cool, clean country air and speak to Susannah Villiers about anything but her husband, and he cursed himself for his foolishness. She was a married woman. She was not free, as much as he suddenly wished that to be the case. Whatever notions he was beginning to feel, they could never be fulfilled. He thought about what she had said and, eventually, he shook his head.

'I am afraid I cannot give you that affirmation,' he said. 'If I believe that whatever you tell me will help with an investigation into murder, then I must divulge it to Inspector Handy, the man in charge of that investigation. I would have no option. My only caveat is that Inspector Handy is, in my opinion, one of the finest men I have ever met. His dedication to his duty is exemplary and I believe he would use any information only as far as it would help apprehend the vicious killer we are on the hunt for.'

Susannah seemed to consider what he had said for a while and kept walking, thinking carefully. She eventually stopped and turned to face him.

'Then I am afraid I must keep my peace, Doctor. I cannot have that information becoming public property. I am afraid of what will become of me if that happens.'

'Are you in danger?' he asked, suddenly fearful of what he may have dragged her into. 'Tell me the truth. Do you think you are in danger? Because your protection is paramount.'

'Above even a murder investigation?' she asked, looking deep into his eyes. She seemed to like what she saw, and for a moment he believed that she was about to say something they perhaps both wanted to hear, but then she sighed and turned away, walking back towards the house.

'I am not in danger the way you surmise, Doctor. At least, I don't think I am. My danger would be being left to fend for myself in a vicious world made by, and for, men. I cannot have that. I have more than myself to worry about.'

And with those words, Jarman felt a strange, terrible grief descend upon him. It seemed that in that moment, his hopes and dreams were shattered. They were silent as they re-entered the house, and then Jarman took his leave.

'If you change your mind, please contact me,' he said, quietly as he left. Susannah said nothing.

He and Curmudgeon were a mile down the road before either of them spoke.

'That Ellie is a fine girl,' said Curmudgeon, dreamily, swishing his stick at the flowers again. The sun was lowering and it cast a golden glow over the fields and the trees, glorious in their autumn foliage.

'I'm sure she is,' said Jarman, deep in thought. 'Did you find anything else out?'

'Only that Villiers himself has never set foot in Dene Manor,' replied Curmudgeon. 'Not once. It belonged to Mrs Villiers's father. Apparently, she comes out here a lot by herself while her husband stays in London. Ellie said that he preferred the dirt and the soot rather than the countryside. She says she's always happier when she and Mrs Villiers are here. She much prefers it to the city house.'

'Or, perhaps, what is in that house,' said Jarman.

He was still thinking about what Susannah had said, and what it meant. And how it stupidly made him feel.

*I have more than myself to worry about*, she had said.

The truth of that statement was unmistakable. And, for Jarman, it was like a nail in his heart.

Susannah Villiers was pregnant.

# Chapter Fifteen

## A Visitor in the Night

Jarman had, as he always did, left a covered candle burning by the bed. He liked to be able to see everything immediately if he woke in the night. It was a hard-learned habit he had acquired in Afghanistan.

It had taken him a long time to nod off and he had not dressed for bed, simply taking off his boots and laying on top of the covers. The knowledge that Susannah Villiers was with child haunted him for some reason, and he burned with a strange jealousy at the thought that such a fine woman had married such a cold, and possibly dangerous, man. It confused him until he thought of what she had said in the garden. That she was trapped. Like many other wives, she seemed to be entangled in a loveless marriage, carrying out her wifely duties whilst never feeling the happiness that true love can bring.

As he lay on the hard hotel bed, Jarman ruminated on how lucky he had been to find that love, and how its loss still tortured him now, six years since Mary had died.

They had first met in 1877, as he was just setting out as a doctor. He worked day and night at The London hospital as a junior, gaining an enviable reputation as an incredible surgeon. Mary, although from a middle-class background, had followed her calling and trained as a nurse, working at the hospital alongside him. From the moment he had set eyes on her, he was smitten.

As he began to doze on the bed, Jarman allowed himself a small, bitter smile as he thought about those years. The walks in the park, the brief illicit assignations in various empty offices dotted around the hospital. They were, he believed, the best years of his life.

But the need to ensure a steady income for his mother had led him to join the army as a surgeon, almost immediately being posted to Afghanistan. He often wished now that he had never embarked on that journey, that instead he had stayed with Mary. He would have had a few more precious years with her at least. However, he had gone, and when he returned to England two years later—leaner, quieter, haunted by what he had seen—it was Mary who had cured him. She still worked at the hospital and, with a position secured there, he had pursued her once again, delighted that she still reciprocated his feelings towards her. It seemed she had understood his reasons for leaving and they had married barely a year later. Because of this, Mary had to leave her work as a nurse. It was what neither of them wanted or thought was right, but it was the rules of the hospital. Mary had continued to assist him in his private work however, and her quick mind and skilful hands were loved by Jarman just as much as her ready wit and beautiful face. He was, he believed, in those few, short years, the happiest man who had ever lived.

He frowned as the old memories attacked him. He did not want to think about them, but he was on the verge of sleep and was no longer in control of his mind. It was showing him what it had shown him so many times in the past and there was nothing he could do about it.

That day reared again in his memory. That day when Mary had been snatched from him. That day when the young policeman, so very like Constable Rose, had led him into the morgue where his beloved wife lay dead, murdered for the meagre contents of her purse.

As the days after her funeral passed and the police found nothing, Jarman had turned his entire function over to finding the killer. Finding him and making him pay the price for the hell he had inflicted upon him.

Jarman had thrown himself into trying to understand the science of criminality, and into locating the man who killed his love. Using his incredible mind, as bleak and cold as it had become, on a dark, rainy January evening in 1887 he had eventually caught up with the murderer of his wife.

Jarman groaned in his half-sleep as that night slid open before him again. The killer, a homeless wreck named Henry Percy, was sitting, propped up against the wall in that filthy dark alleyway in Whitechapel, holding his stomach where a knife had torn into him, pleading for help. He had received none.

Percy was already dying by the time Jarman found him. Just another victim of a drunken East End brawl. He had been stabbed and left to die, just as he had stabbed Mary and left her to die. He gasped at Jarman, begged him to stem the blood, to call for help. Jarman had ignored those pleas and ignored the skills he possessed which might have saved the man. Instead, he had simply stood in the rain and watched as Percy died in front of him, watched as the horror and pain swept across the man's face as he went to his final judgement, watched as he became no more.

But when Jarman had turned and walked away from the corpse, he had felt nothing of the vindication he had thought he would have, nothing of the sense that justice had been restored. Instead, he had felt only the same clawing grief that Mary's death had left him with, magnified a thousand times over. Another vagrant had died on the streets of the East End, and Mary was still dead. And she would have been horrified by his actions.

He continued with his work, both as a surgeon and, very quickly, as an expert on the motives and minds of killers. He was desperate for something new to take from his mind the love he had lost, and through his investigations he found his purpose again. As a doctor he saved lives, he made things better; and as a criminologist he began to understand what had turned a young man like Henry Percy into a killer. He began to understand the poverty that had driven Percy to accidently kill an innocent woman. He began to understand the East End and its people. He threw himself into investigating and unravelling the minds of murderers, and this new purpose allowed him to start to live again. He had begun to heal himself as well as healing others.

Along with Curmudgeon, the hoary ex-sergeant whose life he would not give up on in Afghanistan, he had moved to his bachelor flat in Bond Street, allowing himself nothing except his surgery and his studies into the minds of killers. These things were all he had. They were all he wanted. His expertise had been the reason Frederick Abberline had sought him out when the Ripper cases were at their height and it was, of course, why he was helping Handy now. Only Curmudgeon knew of Mary and was, perhaps, the only man who even remotely understood him.

But, as Jarman eventually succumbed to sleep, it was not Mary he thought of. It was the beautiful, yet mysterious face of Mrs Susannah Villiers that slid into his consciousness. For the first time in six years, he felt an attraction to a woman, even though she was a woman who could never be his. To all intents and purposes, she was owned by Thomas Villiers. He tried to push the thought of her face away, but she would not leave him. And it was the thought of her that finally allowed him to sleep.

*

It was in the deep, silent hours of a country night that the attacker struck.

Jarman opened his eyes and searched the shadowy room, which was brightened only by the guttering candle under its glass canopy. Something had broken his sleep. He listened carefully for what that something might be.

There was nothing for a long time, and then a noise came to his ears and he realised that was what had woken him.

It was a scratching sound, and for a moment he thought it was a mouse, gnawing behind the skirting boards. But then there was a click and he realised the noise had been the sound of a knife or a jimmy scraping underneath the sash of his window. The click was the sound of the latch being turned.

He had closed the curtains before lying on the bed when he had retired, and he now watched them carefully, his hand moving across to the chair where he had left his coat. He fumbled inside it and gripped the object he sought.

His eyes had never left the curtain, and after two minutes of interminable silence he heard a slight shudder as the window was levered upwards, and the curtains stirred with the draught. He sat up.

The window opened further and when he saw a hand appear, carefully pulling aside the curtain, he moved.

With two quick strides he was across the room and he swept the curtains open. He saw a white blur of a face behind the glass, then he brought his small but heavy cudgel down onto the intruder's hand.

He heard the man gasp as the shot-filled leather implement crashed down, then he grabbed the bottom sash of the window and heaved it open.

But the man outside was too quick.

The window opened onto a sloped roof leading down into the garden of the hotel, and this was what the man stood on. He snatched his wounded hand back and ducked as Jarman swung the cudgel.

It whistled over the top of the man's head, and he was already moving. His other arm—his right arm, Jarman noted—moved, and Jarman was suddenly aware of a revolver drawing a bead on him. He threw himself over the bed just as a huge bang and a flash lit up the room. Jarman snatched a glance over his makeshift barricade in time to see the figure turn and jump from the roof to the lawn eight feet below. He heard a muffled curse and saw the man limping away into the night as fast as he could, holding his wounded hand.

The bedroom door burst open and Jarman whirled, for a second thinking another attacker was upon him, but it was only Curmudgeon, dressed in his long johns and his hair dishevelled.

'What the bloody hell was that?' shouted Curmudgeon. 'Sounded like a pistol shot!'

Jarman turned back and stared out into the blackness. The man was gone. Curmudgeon joined him.

'You all right?' he asked, and Jarman nodded.

Curmudgeon peered out the window. 'Should we go after them?' he asked, but Jarman shook his head.

'We'll never find him tonight. Whoever it was has a thousand hiding places in those woods.'

He closed the window and locked it again.

'Who do you think it was?' asked Curmudgeon

'I have no idea,' answered Jarman in a cool, calm voice. 'But if I had to guess, I would say it was the same man who killed Edward Ely the other day. They knew what they were doing, and they came armed. I don't think your average Dorking burglar would be taking on a job like that.'

Curmudgeon sat on Jarman's bed and they both turned as the hotel manager peered around the doorframe, holding a trembling candlestick.

'What on earth is happening?' he asked. 'What are you doing to my hotel?'

Curmudgeon wearily stood and went to the door.

'Mind your own business,' he snarled, and slammed the door in the man's face.

'So, what do we do now?' he asked.

Jarman shrugged, pulling his watch from its pocket and checking the time. 'Go back to sleep, I suppose,' he said.

They divided the four hours left of the night between them and at eight the next morning they left, ignoring the accusing and angry eyes of the manager.

They caught the morning train back to London.

*

On the same day that Jarman walked in the garden with Susannah

Villiers, Jonas Handy re-visited the factory of her husband.

He had been re-reading the notes from Ely's desk. Villiers was definitely up to something a little saucy, but whether it had anything to do with the murders was something else. He felt, like Jarman did, that Villiers's charity work was somehow connected to the deaths. He wanted to know whether Hetty Kennedy had ever been a part of this charity work and had decided that the only way of doing this was to look at whatever records there were of the women Villiers had "saved" from the streets.

He took along with him Constable Rose, and once again entered that hellish world of steam engines and belts and cacophony. Then they were through the factory itself and they went up the steps of the office and entered without knocking. Handy told the clerk to get Miss Villiers.

'I'm sorry to disturb your work once again, Miss Villiers,' he said when she emerged from the office, 'but I'd like to go over the records of Mr Villiers's charity work. In particular, any lists of names of the women who were part of it.'

Miss Villiers gazed at him for a while.

'I see,' she said. 'Can I ask why you require this information? My brother's work is well known. He has helped hundreds of women over the years. I'm sure you could ask him about it, he is here somewhere.'

'I might just do that,' replied Handy, returning her cool stare. 'But for the moment, the records will be fine.'

He kept his gaze on her until she turned and retreated into the office, returning with a thick ledger.

'All the names of the women are in there,' she said. 'Can I ask when I can expect it back?'

'Oh, for the moment I only want to go over it myself, Miss Villiers,' said Handy. 'We can look at it here if that's satisfactory with you. What about that desk?'

He pointed to an unused table in the corner. Miss Villiers simply sniffed and turned away, closing the door of her office behind her.

Handy and Rose sat and went through the ledger. Rose took

a couple of spare sheets of the receipt papers from the desk of the clerk to make notes on the various names. Both Eliza Cotton and Molly Harnath's names were written down, with both of them confirmed as "left" a couple of months or so before their deaths. Of Hetty Kennedy, there was no mention.

After half an hour or so, they returned the ledger to Miss Villiers.

'Is Mr Villiers still here?' asked Handy. 'I feel as if I should give him my regards.'

'No. He left while you were with the ledger,' said Miss Villiers. 'One of the factory managers told me.'

Handy vaguely remembered a man coming into the office while he and Rose had pored over the names in the book. He nodded.

'Thank you. I believe I have all I need for the moment. Good day, Miss Villiers.'

They left and once more walked through the factory, Rose wincing at the bellowing of the huge steam-driven piston that powered the belts.

They had left the gates of the factory itself before a young woman approached them hurriedly from inside. Handy recognised her from his previous visit with Callow. It was one of the women who had been forced to have her teeth pulled because of the Phossy jaw.

'Are you lookin' into what's going on here?' she asked, glancing around her.

'What do you think you know?' asked Handy.

'Those girls, the ones the Ripper took,' she hissed, her voice sibilant because of the missing teeth.

'What about them?'

'They all worked here. All of 'em. They were part of Villiers's work. And that's not all.' She glanced around herself again, nervously.

'Can you give me any names?' asked Handy. 'Any information?'

'Not here,' the girl said. 'I have names, but not here. Not now. I told the overseer I was just having a quick piss, so I don't have the time. I have to get back.'

Rose frowned at the woman's coarse words.

'Can you come to the station on Leman Street? Later today?' asked Handy.

She shook her head. 'I can try to get there tomorrow. Anything I can do to help those poor girls. It's not right what happened to them.'

She turned to go, but Handy caught her arm.

'Hetty Kennedy,' he said. 'Was she here too?'

The girl looked around her once more, and quickly nodded. Then she was gone, running back into the factory and swallowed up by the noise.

Rose turned to Handy.

'If that's true, then it means the ledger has been fiddled with, sir,' he said.

Handy smiled, grimly, scenting something like the truth.

'Yes, it does, Rose. Yes, it does.'

The two of them walked quickly away. They had more work to do.

# Chapter Sixteen

## A Riotous Assembly

Jarman paced Handy's office. On his return from Dorking, they had promised to meet up and discuss the various new questions that both their investigations had turned up.

Curmudgeon watched him, knowing the old signs. This investigation was becoming an obsession with his employer, and he believed that his meeting with Susannah Villiers had not helped his temperament. Curmudgeon was seeing something in Jarman that he thought he would never see again, and the change in the surgeon's demeanour was stark. Jarman was becoming interested in a woman.

There had been one or two female acquaintances who had warmed the cold apartment for brief periods, but they had never lasted. It was as if Jarman was determined never to open up his heart again. As if he feared what that might entail. Curmudgeon scowled as he realised that the surgeon was doing that now. And the idiot was doing it over a woman who could never be his.

He and Jarman turned as the office door opened and Handy and Rose entered, both of them looking pleased with themselves.

'You've found something?' asked Jarman.

'Perhaps,' said Handy. He briefly took them through what had occurred at the factory and the meeting with the toothless woman. Jarman sat and looked at the names Rose had scribbled down on the office paper.

'So. Two of the women who were killed have definitely been

part of Villiers's charity programme, and both left a month or two before they were killed,' Jarman said. 'The other woman, the one whose body went missing after the riot, is not mentioned. If the ledger is to be believed, then she was not a part of this work. But the girl you spoke with today indicated that she was.'

Handy nodded.

'Which leads us to two separate conclusions,' continued the surgeon. 'Either the girl is wrong, or is lying, or the ledger has been tampered with.'

They were quiet for a while as they each thought their own thoughts.

'Right,' said Handy eventually. 'We've got names, we need to talk the owners of them. Rose?'

'Sir?'

'I need you to start rounding those women up.'

'All of them, sir?' Rose was aghast. 'There's hundreds of them!'

'All the more reason to get started then,' said Handy. 'I'll organise a couple of other lads to help you, but you're in charge. Right?'

Rose nodded, pleased at the level of authority he was being given, but mortified by the task in hand. He saluted and left the room.

'So, what happened in Dorking then?' asked Handy, turning to Jarman. 'Did you get anything from Mrs Villiers?'

'She knows something, but she is afraid to divulge it,' said Jarman.

'About her husband?'

Jarman nodded. 'And there is something else.' He told Handy about the attack in the night.

'Blimey,' he said when Jarman had finished his tale.

'And there's no way it was just coincidence?' he asked 'Just a local seeing an opportunity to steal a watch or a wallet from a rich visitor?'

'Local thugs tend not to carry revolvers, Inspector. No, this man was a professional. He was coming to kill me. Luckily, I'm a light sleeper. And I always carry my little club about my person, especially when I'm out of town.'

Handy sighed. 'You think it was the same person who did Ely in? You said that killer knew what he was doing too.'

'I have no doubt at all, Inspector.'

'I think we should bring Villiers in,' said Handy. 'See what the bastard's been up to.'

Jarman shook his head, briefly. 'As much as I wish we could, there is still no real evidence of his hand in any of this. Villiers can and would hire the best defence possible. He'd have us both with our trousers down within thirty seconds.'

'But you said Mrs Villiers…' but Jarman interrupted him.

'She will say nothing about her husband. I think she possibly knows about the "parties" Villiers has been obviously participating in, but I think that is probably the end of her knowledge. And she has other things to protect, anyway.'

'What do you mean?'

'Mrs Villiers is with child, Inspector. She will do everything in her power to protect it and herself.'

'She'll bloody well do as the law tells her to!' said Handy. 'If she knows anything that can help this investigation, she must let us know.'

'I'm sure she will, in good time,' said Jarman. 'But at the moment, even we do not know what we're looking into. There is still nothing to link the murders and Thomas Villiers, apart from the fact two of the victims definitely worked at his factory. That is it. Everything else—the murders themselves, the missing bodies, the letter, Ely's death—none of those things can be proven to lie at Villiers's door. They could all be totally unconnected. And I would suggest that, until we find that connection, we are better off keeping our cards close to our chests. Mrs Villiers is frightened of her husband, yes, but I'm afraid she is not the only wife who feels that way. There are hundreds of them just outside the door of this station. From Whitechapel to Kensington. It is the way of the world, unfortunately.'

He stood to leave, indicating to Curmudgeon who stood, pulling a face at not being offered a cup of tea.

'The young girl, she said she would come tomorrow, did she not?'

Handy nodded, deflated again after his earlier exuberance.

'We'll come back then. See what she has to say.'

He and Curmudgeon took their leave.

Across the street, leaning on a corner, a man with a bandaged hand watched them. He was bulky and wore a cheap suit and bowler hat. His face was hard and flat and cold. As the brougham turned a corner, he eventually moved. He rubbed his bandaged hand ruefully, and then limped off into the throngs like a spectre.

*

The next day proved to be a wild one. Overnight a storm had developed. In a way this was beneficial, for the strong wind blew away the choking smog, but it also blew litter and rags and all sorts of detritus around the streets of Whitechapel. As Jarman jumped down from the brougham, the rain suddenly came down from the black skies like an avenging god. He ran inside the station, leaving Curmudgeon to find some sort of shelter for Daisy.

The station itself was heaving. It was full of women, each one of them haggard, down-trodden, dirty, damp and foul, and they all seemed to be talking raucously at once. They cackled as he came in with his hat almost blown from his head. Two or three constables were trying to sort them out and get names, but it was like herding cats. The women were having a jolly old time about it all. In their midst stood Constable Rose, red-faced and sweating as they good-humouredly berated him.

'Come on, sweetheart,' one of them cried. 'You're taking longer than a pissed up potman with brewer's droop!' The throng cackled again.

'Now that's enough of that,' said Rose, sternly, trying in vain to inject some authority into his voice. 'Just wait your turn and I'll get to you as quickly as I can.'

'Ooooh! Promises promises!'

Rose's face grew even redder.

Jarman left him to it and knocked on Handy's door, entering when there was no answer from inside.

'I'm telling you this is ridiculous!' shouted a uniformed officer who was sitting at Handy's desk in Handy's seat. Handy himself was standing to attention in front of the man, looking slightly sick.

'Well, sir, I thought it was best to interview the women, to see if they know anything.'

'Anything about what?' barked the man. 'There is nothing to know about!'

Jarman coughed politely and they both turned to him.

'And who are you?' asked the uniformed man. He was a short, neat man with a handlebar moustache and perfectly groomed hair, glistening with oil. He stared at Jarman with the sort of righteous indignation the surgeon had met many times before. It was the stare of an egotistical man who had been promoted to a rank of authority. He had met many like him in the army.

Handy quickly made the introductions.

'Sir, this is Doctor Carter Jarman. He's been assisting me with the investigation. Jarman, this is Assistant Commissioner Pence.'

Jarman nodded, but Pence just turned to Handy.

'So, this is the civilian you have been allowing to scrutinise police information, is it?'

He turned to Jarman.

'I believe your area of expertise is surgery, yes?'

Jarman nodded again, his face carefully blank.

'I don't see how a doctor can be of any use in a murder investigation,' said Pence. He turned again to Handy, picking up his cap from the desk.

'I want nothing more said about Thomas Villiers, Handy. The man has nothing—*nothing* at all— to do with these murders. The very idea is preposterous in the extreme. I've listened to your pathetic story of women connected to the factory, and I can hear them outside this very door right now. It sounds like a tavern out there! You've turned my police station into a bawdy pub!'

He strode to the door and put his cap on, adjusting it until it was perfect.

'Find out who killed those women, Inspector: *that* is your job. Not harassing innocent men who happen to be upstanding citizens of this city.'

He gave Jarman an up and down glare, then left without another word.

The women outside surrounded him and tried to take his cap, but the constables quickly moved in to get them out of his way. He strode outside to his carriage with the laughing of the women ringing in his ears. It got louder when the wind blew his cap off for him. His driver went running off down the street after it as Pence climbed stiffly into the carriage to wait. Jarman closed the door of the office softly.

'He seems pleasant,' he said, and Handy laughed, slumping into the seat Pence had vacated.

'Seems Mr Villiers is a member of the same club as our Assistant Commissioner Pence,' he said. 'Had a word with him. Asked him to tell me he would be pleased to help in any way he could with any police investigation, but then made it perfectly clear that he was bloody furious about it all.' Handy rubbed his head. 'God alive. What a bloody mess,' he muttered.

They were interrupted by a harassed-looking Rose, who slinked through the door, sideways.

'Gerroff!' he cried to one of the women, who was fondling his bottom. He closed the door behind him thankfully.

'All ready?' asked Handy, and Rose nodded.

'You're still going to interview them?' asked Jarman. 'After what Pence said?'

'Well, they're here now, aren't they?' said Handy with a sly smile. 'It would be churlish not to.'

They went out into the gang of women and Handy soon had them standing in silence. He called out a name and the woman came forward.

'You're first, darling,' he said, as he and Jarman followed the woman into the office.

He closed the door behind him.

# Chapter Seventeen

## The List of Names

### *London 1883*

*T*he dark man sat in his room. It was a late winter's night and yet there was no warming fire roaring, no lamps had been lit. He sat like a cold shadow amongst many shadows; a part of the darkness, still and silent. Only the glitter of his eyes could be discerned in the faint luminescence of the snow that billowed outside the window.

He was satiated. He had been out into the streets earlier, their filth covered by the snow, appearing clean and pure for once in their existence, although this was a fallacy. The dark man knew that, if he dug only an inch into the snow, he would find the usual dirt and decay. And, as always, he had. He sat in the shadows, a whisky in his hand and clean bandages covering the marks on his arms: the cuts he had given himself earlier. He smiled as he remembered the other cuts, the scarlet, ruby red cuts he had given to the woman he had persuaded to take part with him in his little games. He sighed, contentedly, sipping his drink.

He closed his eyes, listening to the wind whistling around the house and down the chimney. He thought of himself as that cold wind, blowing through the streets, cleansing them. Healing them.

He sighed as, for some unknown reason, he thought about his youth. He thought about The Father, yes; but now that he was at peace, if only for a while, he thought about The Mother too.

He barely remembered her. She remained in his memory only as a dark-haired phantom, a ghost who occasionally haunted his existence. He remembered her smell more than her face. He remembered the stench of death that fell upon him every time he was in her presence. The sweet, cloying smell of mortality as her days grew short and she wasted away before him. And that was the smell he always craved so much: the smell of putrefaction, the smell of skin and flesh melting into nothing. The smell of a body dead before its soul had followed it. That smell was what he searched for on his endless quest. The ripe, dirty smell. He had never found the exact fragrance, but the grim aroma of the women he sought out seemed to satisfy him for short periods of time. They were the closest he came to peace.

He remembered lying with The Mother, although the memories were just the shades of reality; he had been very young when she died. When she left him. He remembered resting his head against the crook of her shoulder, gazing up at her profile. She would stroke his hair, her eyes staring into the abyss of her coming demise, and he would do the same to her: rubbing the thinning locks between his fingers, the feeling of this warming his soul.

Sometimes he and The Mother would hear The Father roughly showing one of the serving girls how she should be treated, but they ignored it. When he was with The Mother he was safe, for The Father never entered her room. He seemed to fear what was within it. Only one other dared to enter The Mother's room apart from him.

The dark man stirred in his chair, his eyes turning to the storm outside, the smell of decay in his nostrils. It was not his fault he had those needs, those impulses. Not his fault at all.

It was only at times like these, when he had been satisfied, when his lusts had been fulfilled and his humours released and re-balanced by the cutting, that he thought of The Mother, and that he might somehow be different to other people. This sometimes brought a rising terror to his soul, and he would whisper prayers to God to save him from his wickedness.

But then he remembered The Mother's words as she stroked his hair and smiled her deathly, grimacing smile at him as he stroked hers.

'God has great plans for you,' she would whisper in a voice that *grew weaker every day. 'God has great plans for you.'*

*And the dark man would stop his prayers, as he once more realised that God was speaking to him, speaking through him, and everything he did, all the bestial thoughts that burned in his head, were the words of God. Why else would He have sent his Guardian if He did not have great plans for him? The dark man truly believed that he was creating God's Will on Earth.*

*He smiled at these comforting ideas as they stumbled and ran through his broken mind. He sipped the whisky and watched the storm.*

*Barely seen in the gloom, his silent Guardian sat with him. They both watched the storm outside grow stronger.*

\*

It was late into the evening by the time Handy and Jarman had talked to all of the women Rose had managed to find. Over eighty of them had been hauled in, but not one of them had anything to say about Thomas Villiers.

A lot of them still worked at the factory, although fifteen of them had left after a few months to go back to the streets to ply their bodies for pennies and gin.

They asked the girls why they had turned their backs on a job, on a way out of their sordid and hopeless pasts, but they just shrugged their shoulders and said they did not like to be told when and where they had to be at a certain time. They seemed to be of the mind that, although their work was hard and dangerous, at least it was up to them. At the factory, they said there were rules and regulations and overseers. They said they hadn't liked it, but Jarman believed that there was more to it than that.

They asked them about Villiers and whether they knew of his little parties. Some of them giggled at the mention of these parties, some of them became silent and still. None of them admitted to knowing anything about them. From past experience, Handy knew by halfway through the day that he would get nothing from them. They had closed ranks. However, he persisted until all the women had been spoken to.

One by one the women left, and the station eventually settled down to its usual quietness. Handy and Jarman sat with drinks in their hands; Handy had unbuttoned his shirt collar and it lay on his desk beside his hat and the reams of notes he had made. All the notes were useless. There was nothing in the women's statements that pointed a finger at anything untoward having happened at all, never mind who may have committed a crime.

'I think we're barking up the wrong tree,' he said, eventually. 'I think I've become so focused on Villiers that I'm not doing my job properly. I should be trying to find out who killed those girls, not chasing phantoms around a bloody match factory.'

Jarman observed him over the top of his glass. 'I believe the two things must be connected, Inspector. The fact that two bodies have gone missing tells us that someone does not want you to complete your work. That same someone must have resources above and beyond the ordinary. Enough, perhaps, to pay for the services of a professional assassin. If that girl you spoke with is correct, if Hetty Kennedy was also part of Villiers's work, then there is a superficial connection between them at the least.' He sipped his sherry. 'What do we know so far?' he asked.

Handy sighed and put his glass down, ticking off the facts on his fingers.

'We know three women have been murdered in the foulest of ways,' he said. 'We know that they were all working girls. We know that two of them, at some point, had worked at Villiers's factory. We have an eyewitness account of a fair-haired man running from the area of the last murder. We have one of those bodies being taken from the morgue and destroyed, apparently on police orders. We have the third body disappearing into the night like a bloody magician's assistant. We have a dead reporter who had some papers in his desk indicating, but not proving anything about Thomas Villiers. We have a letter, supposedly from Jack the Ripper, who no one has seen hide nor hair of in the last two years, also locked in said reporter's desk alongside the papers on Villiers. And we have a villain skulking around who either followed you to Dorking or was there waiting for you and tried to kill you. And we have four dead coppers, including a very good friend of mine. Have I missed anything?'

Jarman could hear the frustration and anger in Handy's voice. He understood it. He felt it himself.

'What we seem to be missing,' he said, 'is anything that can provide a link between any of these things. We are missing proof. And without proof, we are helpless.'

Handy picked up his drink and drained it. 'Welcome to my world,' he said.

At that moment, Rose knocked and entered. Handy looked at him with a jaundiced eye.

'That girl's here, Mr Handy,' said Rose. 'Her with all the missing teeth.'

Handy raised his eyebrows. 'Is she now,' he said. 'Send her straight in, Rose.'

The constable disappeared and, a second later, the girl entered the room.

The two men stood and Handy indicated to a chair. They all sat down.

'Right,' said Handy. 'Thank you for coming in. First things first. What's your name?'

'Grace Wright.'

'Age?'

'Twenty-four.'

Jarman shook his head to himself. The girl looked fifty if she was a day. The toothless mouth did not help, of course.

Handy continued with the opening questions, gaining the woman's address: a lodging dwelling on Fairclough Street.

'You said yesterday when we spoke that you had some information you wanted us to hear?'

Jarman noted that Handy was not giving her any crumbs. He wanted her to do all the telling without leading her in any way.

The girl was nervous. This was clear from the way she glanced at Jarman. From his clothes, he was obviously well off. Perhaps she had so little trust in wealthy men that she was afraid to speak in front of him.

'I can leave the room if you wish,' he said to the girl, with a smile. 'It is imperative you tell Inspector Handy everything you know, and if you would feel more comfortable with me not being here, then that's fine.'

The girl gave him a long, scrutinising glance and then seemed to come to a conclusion. She shook her head.

'It's all right, sir,' she said quietly. 'I don't mind if you stay.'

Handy sat with his pen in his hand. With a glance, he asked the girl to start.

'I was working the streets,' she began. 'This was November last year. I'd been on the streets for a good four or five years before then.'

Jarman sat back in his chair and closed his eyes, listening. The girl was saying she had been a prostitute since the age of eighteen or nineteen. And God alone knew what her life had been like before that.

'Anyway, last November, a man came up to me. It was during the day, so I didn't really think he wanted a f—' she paused and glanced at the handsome gentleman with the long hair in the chair with his eyes closed. 'I didn't think he wanted to buy my services,' she continued. 'However, he said he worked at a factory, and that the owner of that factory was looking for workers. He asked me all sorts of questions, mostly about my work as a dollymop.'

'Was this Thomas Villiers?' asked Handy, but the girl shook her head.

'No, it was Clinchy.'

'Clinchy?'

'Robert Clinch. He's a clerk at the factory. You must have seen him when you were in the office.'

Handy nodded, remembering the man who had been in the main office outside Amelia Villiers's room. He wrote the name down. 'Carry on,' he said.

146

'He said that the factory owner, he didn't mention no names at the time, would pay me a good wage, make sure I'd have plenty to eat and give me a place to live if I wanted. I was mightily suspicious as you can imagine, but Clinchy just gave me the address and told me that, if I wanted, to have a wander along to Mile End at some time and see what I thought.

'Well, November was cold, if you remember, so I took a walk and saw Clinchy, and before long I was part of the workforce. Clinchy was as good as his word. I got a hot meal, a bath and a job. I thought all my Sundays had come at once. At the beginning.'

Handy left that phrase for a second.

'Did you meet Mr Villiers at all?'

'Just at the start,' said Grace after a pause. 'He introduced himself to all of us new 'uns and then left everything to that harridan of a sister of his. She sorted us all out. It was her that sent me off to the dentist when I had a toothache, the bitch. I had no idea they were going to strip my bloody mouth. Couldn't go back to the streets now if I wanted to. Who the hell would want to poke something with this face?' She pointed to her haggard visage angrily.

'So. You simply worked at the factory.'

Here, Grace shuffled uncomfortably in her seat.

'At the start, yes,' she said. 'I did my job and got quite good at it, it's amazing how you can learn to do complicated things easily if you do it over and over, hundreds of times a day.

'Anyway, about March this year, this was before I lost all me teeth, Miss Villiers called for me and asked if I would be interested in making a little extra money. She said it would be "entertaining" for a few people. Well, I was very happy to do so. Any more money is always useful. So, me and a couple of other girls…'

'Names?' snapped Handy.

'I didn't know all of them. But Hetty was there, Molly Harnath, and another girl. There were four of us altogether.'

Handy nodded and indicated for her to continue.

'We all ended up at a house, up the West End. We went in through the back and found ourselves in a lovely big drawing room.

147

There was food and drink and Mr Villiers was there, along with some more gentlemen. At least we thought they were gentlemen.'

Grace lowered her eyes, took a deep breath, then continued.

'That first night wasn't too bad,' she said. 'It all ended up with the girls…seeing to the men, if you get my drift. However, we were all paid handsomely, and we all thought that would be that, that we knew the sort of man Thomas Villiers was. Him and his friends. But we knew nothing.

'I was at that house, Mr Villiers's house, on four more occasions. And each time it got worse.'

'What do you mean?' asked Handy. Jarman had opened his eyes and was staring at the girl.

The girl was staring out of the window, but Jarman believed she saw little of anything in the street beyond.

'They, those men, had…passions,' she said, eventually. 'They are twisted men. Dirty, obscene men. They started to do things you would never believe. Villiers himself was the worst, but all of them took part. They started to hurt us. They seemed to get excited about hitting us, cutting us while we…while we were servicing them.'

'Cutting you?' asked Jarman, appalled. He was thinking about Susannah and what she perhaps had wanted to tell him.

Grace nodded. With no embarrassment at all, she quickly untied the buttons on the front of her dress. All across the top of her breasts were white scars, the remains of what looked like several slices the girl had endured.

'Got more of those on my legs too,' said Grace, re-fastening her dress.

Handy seemed to bring himself back to the room.

'Do you have any names? Apart from Villiers?'

Grace paused. She seemed unsure, but she eventually nodded.

'After I'd had my teeth pulled, they didn't ask for me again,' she said. 'But the other girls went back a few times. Always when Mrs Villiers was away at her other house, apparently. Hetty told me they seemed to get worse. They would work themselves into a frenzy. But always, once everyone was cleaned up, they were given a pretty penny to keep quiet. Hetty left the factory after a while. Said she couldn't stand it anymore and would rather be back on the streets.

'They interviewed her before she left, her and the others. Hetty never said anything about what was said, but her face was as white as snow when she came out of the office. All she said was that they'd given her some money, but I think she was given a warning. Then I heard her and the others had all been killed by the Ripper.'

She looked pointedly at Handy, and the detective slumped in his chair, rubbing his head.

'I'll need those names you spoke of, Grace,' he said. 'And even then, I don't know if anything will come of it. You're talking about influential men. Powerful men.'

Grace nodded. 'I was going to tell all this to that reporter the other day. But he never showed up. Mustn't be that interested.'

Jarman and Handy glanced at each other.

'I know I can't go back to the factory,' she continued, missing the glance. 'I knew that when I said I would talk to you. If they find out I've said anything, I have a feeling I'll end up like Hetty and those other girls. But...'

Grace began to cry. Huge, silent tears that spoke of a life wasted, a life bereft of love.

'They didn't deserve that,' she gulped. 'They were dollies, I know that, same as me. But they were people, Inspector. People. They didn't deserve to be treated like that and they didn't deserve to die in the way they did. No one does.'

'Don't you worry about going back,' said Handy, standing and placing a hand on her shoulder. 'I'm going to put you somewhere safe, Grace. Somewhere they won't find you. And you, my girl, are going to give me those names.'

'I went into the office once,' she said. 'Clinchy took me in. It was when I got back from the dentist and I was upset about it all. He went to make me a cup of tea. There was a ledger on the desk and I leafed through it, to take the pain away I suppose. It was full of names. And they were all the men at those meetings at Mr Villiers's house. And there were signatures beside every one.'

Grace looked into his ice blue eyes, wondering if she could trust this man with the information.

'Clinchy closed the file and took it away, sharpish. Told me to forget I'd seen it, but I made sure I remembered them. Most of them, anyway.'

Handy nodded. He gave Grace his handkerchief to wipe her eyes.

Then he gave her a sheet of paper for the names.

# Chapter Eighteen

## The Realisation

Handy told Rose to come into the office and gave him some money.

'Take this girl to this address,' he told the constable, scribbling on a piece of paper. 'Don't let anyone know where she's gone. Come straight back here when you've seen her safely inside.'

Rose left with the girl.

'It's a lodging house out by the docks,' Handy explained to Jarman. 'I've used it before when I want to disappear, which I've had to on a couple of occasions. I know the owner. Ex-copper. Good bloke.'

He turned to the names she had written down on the sheet of paper and sighed.

'We're in a barrel full of bother here if she's telling the truth,' he said.

Jarman had to agree. The page contained some very illustrious names: mostly businessmen but some minor landed gentry too. The two names that jumped out at both the men, however, apart from Villiers himself, were James Lyon, the editor of the Evening Star, and one Montgomery Pence: Assistant Commissioner of the Metropolitan Police.

'I've never liked the bastard,' said Handy, taking out his cigarette case and offering one to Jarman. He inhaled deeply. 'I'm willing to believe he likes to have himself the odd good old time with a bunch of dollies, even that he's the sort to hurt people while he's doing it, but I can't believe he's up to anything as bad as murder. He's been in the force his entire life, for God's sake.'

'If we are to believe that the order to destroy the body of Eliza Cotton, as well as the mysterious manner in which the third body disappeared, came from someone in a position of authority, then why not Pence?' asked Jarman. 'Especially if his reputation was on the line. You saw the marks on that poor girl. God only knows what she went through. They were the same as the old scars we saw on the body of Molly Harnath, and we can assume that there were similar marks on the other dead girls, perhaps the main reason why the bodies were stolen in the first place. If you were Pence, would you want that news getting out?' Jarman ground out his unfinished cigarette into the ashtray. He was still angry about the scars he had seen on Grace.

'And of course,' he continued, 'someone ordered the death of Edward Ely. And tried to have me killed. I'm not saying that was Pence. But it may well have been another one of these men named on this sheet. Any one of them has more than enough money to hire a professional assassin, although Pence probably has more of the ability to do so, with his connections.'

'God alive,' muttered Handy. 'What are we to do? We could be talking about corruption and murder, right from the top. If these men have already killed to keep tongues quiet, there's no end to what they may still yet do. Those girls were ripped apart; butchered worse than cattle. And the people who are possibly responsible are some of the richest and most influential people in the city. Indeed, in England.'

Jarman was staring into space. 'Do you think there really is a dossier with all those names written in it?' he asked.

Handy pursed his lips and shrugged. 'It would make sense, if you think about it. From Villiers's point of view, I mean. A list of names would be a very good way of making sure everyone involved kept quiet.'

Jarman sighed and then stood up. He called for Curmudgeon, who had wandered off to look for tea.

'There's nothing more we can do tonight,' he said. 'I'm going home to see if I can think of anything else. I suggest you get some sleep, Inspector. You look done in.'

Handy smiled wanly and said goodbye. But, as he looked at the list of names again, he knew he would not get much rest that night.

\*

Jarman was sifting through the papers Ely had hidden in his little drawer. It was past midnight and the storm had burned itself out hours ago. The street outside was dark and silent. Curmudgeon had already retired, and Jarman was left alone with his thoughts.

Susannah Villiers slid into his head again, even though he had pushed her out several times already. Why did she have such an effect on him? He had hardly even glanced at another woman since Mary had died. Yes, there had been one or two women whom he had accompanied to the theatre or for a meal, but nothing more. There had not been even the slightest attraction towards them. Why, then, did Susannah Villiers play so much on his mind?

They were so very different, those two women. Mary had been blonde and vivacious and outgoing. She had sparkled like the sun itself. Until that day, of course, that awful day which should have been so happy for them both, but which had turned into the horror it had become. The day when Jarman had been left, standing alone, in a freshly decorated baby's room that would never be occupied, with nothing left. Only a dead wife and a child that would never be born.

Jarman sighed and rubbed his eyes, pleased that Curmudgeon was not there to see him weeping once again. His companion had seen too much of that in their years together. The allure of the whisky decanter called to him but he denied it, pushing the thoughts of Mary aside.

Susannah Villiers was completely different to his wife. Dark, serious, quiet. A woman with secrets. And, he reminded himself

153

for the thousandth time, a woman married to another man and expecting that man's baby. He should forget all about her apart from her perhaps being a missing piece in the strange puzzle he had become immersed in.

And yet, as he closed his eyes momentarily, it was not Mary's face who came to him. It was Susannah's.

With a grunt of annoyance, he stood and went back to the table where the papers were spread out. He had asked Handy if he could take them home to study further and the Inspector had readily agreed. It seemed he was perfectly happy with a civilian handling this evidence and Jarman allowed himself a small smile at the thought of the policeman. He was a good man; a man dragged up in the harshest of conditions, who could easily have slipped into the ever-awaiting arms of drunkenness, crime and early death like so many of his brethren had done. But he had turned away from that and instead had fought against it, using everything the law could bring him in his fight to see justice done. Yes, Handy was a good man indeed.

He picked through the papers in a desultory manner. He was tired, bone tired. Yet a strange uneasiness made it impossible for him to sleep. He knew that if he lay down, his mind would simply turn everything over, again and again, and he would wake up in a worse position in the morning than he was now. He picked up the letter Ely had kept in his desk. Was this really from the killer himself?

The way the women had been murdered still played upon his mind. There was a savagery that had obviously been apparent in the deaths two years before, especially the death of Mary Kelly. But these new killings were different. He knew they were different. He had nothing to prove his theory, but he was *sure* that the man who had murdered those five women back in 1888 was not the same man who had killed the three women over the last few weeks. The scalping of the last two victims and the way their throats had been cut especially played on his mind. Jarman was becoming more and more convinced that whoever had killed these latest victims was *not* the Ripper they all feared had returned.

Then there was all this about Villiers apparently supplying prostitutes for him and his high-ranking friends. The murder of Ely and the attack on himself. Were these things even connected at all? Or were he and Handy charging off down a corridor with nothing at the end of it but a brick wall?

He slumped into the chair by his table, still holding the letter that warned Ely off from "V".

He frowned as he once again had a feeling of recognition about the letter. What *was* it?

He picked up his magnifying glass and stared hard at the writing. He believed that whoever had written it was right-handed: the sloping of the uppercases easily led to that conclusion. This matched what he had seen of the wounds to the one corpse he had examined, but meant little. Most people were right-handed. That did not really help.

He noticed that the pressure the pen had used on the paper was uniform. There was no sign of extra compression anywhere in it. This was unusual, as his knowledge of the psychopathic brain told him that a broken mind usually led to ranting and raving in written form, and this in turn usually led to parts of confessions or tauntings being savagely scribbled. The results of a broken and twisted consciousness.

But this was written quietly; that is what he believed. The author had sat, calmly and quietly warning Edward Ely away, and said what he would do to him if he didn't. Grace, the girl from the factory, had said she was supposed to meet Ely. Had the killer found out and fulfilled their warning? Was this new Ripper that man? And was he the same man Jarman had seen as a shadow outside his hotel window in Dorking? Or again, were all these things not connected?

Jarman dropped the letter onto the table and rubbed his eyes again. He glanced at the clock on the mantlepiece. Almost one in the morning. Time for bed.

He retired and, unexpectedly, fell asleep almost immediately.

He did not dream. And it seemed that the relaxing of his mind into unconsciousness must have done something, must have pulled at some invisible lever that lifted a veil. It revealed to him what was familiar about that letter.

He awoke, instantly alert. He suddenly knew what had seemed so strange about the note.

He picked up the candle beside the bed and used it to light a lamp which he took into the study. He glanced at the clock on the wall, noting that it was almost four in the morning. He sat down and picked the letter up, rubbing it between his fingers. Then he nodded to himself.

He was right. It was not the *writing* that had pulled at his memory. It was the *paper* the writing was on!

Jarman grinned.

He suddenly knew where this paper had come from.

*

'Are you sure?' asked Handy.

'Absolutely,' Jarman replied. 'Look at the texture, the size. Compare it with the sheets you took from the factory. This is a very fine grain paper. It's been torn from a block of similar sheets. This is the kind of paper used for writing chits. And receipts.'

It was barely eight in the morning and Jarman was back with Handy in his office. Outside, the market was being set up and the street was bustling with traders all shouting and laughing with each other.

Jarman had woken Curmudgeon as soon as it began to get light, ignoring the swearing and grumbling as he had dressed and then went out to ready the brougham. They had called at Handy's house on the way and picked him up. Handy had climbed into the carriage still pulling up his braces and with a piece of toast gripped in his teeth. As soon as they arrived at the station, Curmudgeon had sloped off to find a mug of tea and they were left alone.

Handy took the letter from him and held it up to the light of the window, alongside one of the sheets that Rose had taken from the clerk's desk at the factory office. They were identical.

'I knew there was something strange about it when I first saw it,' said Jarman. 'I foolishly believed it was something to do with the writing, but of course it was the paper itself. It is not what one would usually write letters on. That was the problem. Then last night I realised I had seen other sheets just like it. The ones you took from the office to write the names of the girls down. It is the exact same paper as used by the clerk, Robert Clinch.'

Handy looked up as Curmudgeon entered holding mugs of tea.

'Right,' he said. 'Let's get going.'

He and Jarman left the room, leaving Curmudgeon with the tea.

'Curmudgeon!' called Jarman. 'Come along!'

Curmudgeon swore loudly and slammed the teas onto the desk. He'd never get any breakfast at this rate.

He followed them out of the station.

# Chapter Nineteen

## The Arrest

They pulled up at the factory twenty minutes later. Jarman told Curmudgeon to wait with the brougham, and he and Handy went inside. It was the first time Jarman had set foot in the factory, and to him it was hellishly noisy. Even Handy, used to it by now, grimaced as they made their way through it until they got to the other side where the office was housed. They climbed the wrought iron steps and entered the office.

It was empty apart from Clinch, who jumped at their entrance. He stood, putting down the cup he was holding.

Without a word, Jarman and Handy went to his desk and examined the receipts on the spike. Jarman held one of them up to the light, nodding at Handy. The Inspector turned to the clerk.

'Robert Clinch?'

'Yes?' The man was staring at them, white-faced.

'I'm arresting you on suspicion of murder,' continued Handy. The clerk stared at him, uncomprehending, until Handy was behind him, fastening his arms behind his back with handcuffs.

'What on earth are you talking about?' asked Clinch. 'Murder? What murder? Who?'

'We'll talk about that down at the station,' said Handy, then turned as the door was opened and Amelia Villiers entered. She took in the strange scene with a dispassionate face.

'Miss Villiers,' moaned the clerk. 'They're saying I'm to be arrested for murder! Tell them, Miss Villiers. Tell them I'm not a murderer!' His eyes glistened as the reality of his predicament started to infiltrate his brain.

Amelia Villiers turned and calmly removed her coat, hanging it up on a peg by the door. She unpinned her hat and placed it above the coat. Finally, she spoke.

'I hope you have good evidence about this murder Mr Clinch is being arrested for,' she said. 'As my brother's solicitor will be very anxious to speak with you as soon as he is made aware of this situation.'

'Mr Clinch is being taken to Leman Street Station,' said Handy, roughly. 'If Mr Villiers's solicitor wants to find out what's happening, he can come down there.'

Amelia continued to pin him with her haughty gaze, then simply nodded. She walked into the office and closed the door. She had said not one word to the trembling clerk, who just stared miserably after her.

'Come on,' said Handy.

They were back at the station before nine. Clinch sat in a chair in front of Handy's desk and the inspector at his seat opposite, with Jarman standing in a corner, watching.

'Where were you on the night of the thirty-first of August this year?' asked Handy. His intense blue eyes were like ice.

'Thirty-first of August?' asked Clinch. 'I don't know. I was probably at home.'

'At the address you gave us?'

Clinch nodded.

'And you live alone?'

Again, a nod.

'So, no one to back this up then?' asked Handy. He lit a cigarette. 'What about the second of September? The fifteenth of September? Where were you then?'

'I don't know,' moaned Clinch. 'How am I supposed to remember that?'

'It was only a few weeks ago, Clinch,' growled Handy, blowing out smoke. 'Surely you can remember that far back.' He changed tack. 'What sort of work do you do at the factory?'

'I'm a clerk,' said Clinch, moodily. 'What sort of work do you think I do?'

'Don't get saucy with me, lad. You'll find your head bouncing off my desk if you do.'

Clinch turned to Jarman for help but the surgeon just stared at him, his face impassive.

'I do the receipts, the paperwork for the factory,' he said shortly.

'Receipts for what?'

'For everything. Imports, exports. All the goods that come in and the matches that go out. Where they're sold, who to. That sort of thing.'

Handy nodded. He handed Clinch a sheet of paper.

'Could you write down your job description for me, please,' he ordered.

Clinch frowned, then did as he was told. Handy took the sheet from him after a couple of minutes.

'Hey, I wasn't finished,' said Clinch.

'This will do,' said Handy, placing the sheet to one side. 'Now then. What do you know of Mr Villiers? In particular, the little parties that he runs every now and then.'

Clinch paled at the mention of this. 'Don't know what you're talking about,' he muttered.

'You don't know anything about you wandering the streets of Whitechapel recruiting women to work at the factory?'

Clinch just stared at him.

'You don't know anything about some of those women, the women *you* recruited, who ended up at little parties at Villiers's house? You don't know what happens at those get togethers?'

Clinch stared at the floor, totally miserable now.

'What about a ledger? A ledger with names written in it, alongside a bunch of signatures and a description of what those signatures mean. Do you know anything about that?'

Clinch grew even whiter at the mention of the ledger. His lip trembled, but he kept quiet.

'I have not done anything wrong,' he whimpered, when Handy said nothing else. 'I'm not a murderer, for God's sake. I'm a clerk. I just push papers around, that's all. I don't murder people.'

He began to weep and Handy turned away, disgusted.

'What about cutting people?' he asked. 'Do you do that? Do you like to cut girls, Clinch? Like to watch them bleed? Is that what gets you excited?'

Clinch was frantic, his face wet with tears. 'That wasn't me!' he shouted. 'That was…'

He stopped himself at the look of triumph in Handy's eyes.

'Who was it?' asked the Inspector, quietly.

Clinch clamped his mouth shut.

'I ain't saying nothing more until Mr Villiers's solicitor gets here.'

Handy contemplated him for a second. Then he stood up and opened the door of the office.

'Rose!' he shouted. The constable appeared.

'Take this gentleman to one of our luxury suites, if you'd be so kind. I'll talk to him again later.'

'Luxury suites?' asked Rose, baffled.

'The cells, constable. Take this man to the cells.' He slammed the door behind them as they left.

He and Jarman gathered over his desk as Handy placed the letter Ely had received next to Clinch's half-completed job description. They both saw immediately that the writing was completely different.

'Bugger,' said Handy.

'This doesn't mean he's not involved,' said Jarman. 'Just that he didn't write the letter. But it definitely came from the office.'

Handy nodded. 'He certainly knows more than he's letting on, although no doubt Villiers will say that this sort of paper is used by factories all over the city. Would have been nice if it did match though.' He turned to Jarman. 'I want to go and find that ledger, if it's real. Would you like to visit that match factory with me again?'

*

Amelia Villiers was still in the office when they got there, alongside Villiers himself. They were in the partitioned office and they both looked up as the two men entered. Jarman thought he saw a quick, hard smile cross Villiers's face as he straightened from his sister's desk and they both came out into the main office. Jarman scanned the office they had emerged from, unconsciously noting every detail down; although there was not much to see, just Miss Villiers's desk, a small, empty fireplace and a well-used, faded couch, looking like it had seen better days. He turned his attention back to Villiers.

'Well now, Inspector. Doctor Jarman.' Villiers nodded at both men. 'I expect you have come here to offer me an explanation over your bizarre accusation of young Mr Clinch.'

He lifted his eyebrows, like a schoolmaster awaiting the answer from a feckless student.

'Mr Clinch is still under arrest and still at the station, Mr Villiers,' said Handy, unfazed by the taller man's obvious distaste for him. 'We are here to search these premises, based on something Mr Clinch said.'

'And what was that?' asked Amelia, when Villiers himself did not answer.

Jarman saw no worry in the eyes of the woman, but there was definitely a look of alarm on her brother's face.

'I'm afraid I can't say at the moment,' continued Handy. 'We'll know when we find what we're looking for.'

Brother and sister seemed unsure for a moment, and then Jarman saw their apprehension disappear as they both glanced over his shoulder. Jarman and Handy turned in time to see a figure enter the room, sweeping off his tall hat as he did so. He was a portly man of medium height, with a crown of magnificent white hair matched by a bushy white beard. He looked to be somewhere in his sixties, yet his back was straight and his eyes were clear and calculating. He wore a knee-length frock coat with matching trousers and waistcoat. He nodded briefly to Villiers and then turned his pale-eyed stare onto Handy.

'And what is the purpose of your visit to this factory?' he asked in a loud, clear, voice. A barrister's voice, thought Jarman.

'My name is Inspector Jonas Handy, sir. Can I enquire your name, as I am a policeman doing his duty?'

The man placed his cane on the desk beside the door and dropped his hat next to it.

'I would expect a policeman doing his duty would be accompanied by another policeman,' he said, finally. 'Rather than by a doctor who has no reason whatsoever to be here at this present time. My name is Grundy, Inspector Handy. Jedidiah Grundy, of Grundy, Lewes and Smeaton. I am Mr Villiers's lawyer. And I ask you again: what is the purpose of your visit here today?'

He was cool and calm and collected, and Handy knew at once that he would get nothing this day.

'The Inspector seems to want to search the office,' said Villiers, looking relieved and aloof once again. 'For what, I cannot begin to imagine.'

'I see,' said Grundy, eyeing Handy like a shark. 'And you will have had instructions and a warrant from your seniors for this search of course? From Assistant Commissioner Pence?'

Handy said nothing as both the Villiers grinned.

'Perhaps you have made a mistake, Inspector?' asked Grundy, still staring at Handy.

Handy sighed. He knew when it was time to stand and when to beat a retreat.

'I believe I'm not the only one,' he said, glancing at Villiers as he did so. He replaced his hat. 'My apologies, Mr Villiers, Miss Villiers. We'll let ourselves out.'

He and Jarman waited for Grundy to move out of the way and then left the office. Handy was furious.

'Bloody Grundy,' he growled. 'I've heard of him. He's the best lawyer available. If you have the money, that is.'

Jarman nodded. 'Yes. His reputation certainly precedes him.

There are many men walking around today thanks to his abilities, and a lot more who should be doing the same, lying in their graves.'

They found Curmudgeon standing beside Daisy, chatting up a pretty flower seller. He saw the looks on their faces and quickly climbed into the driver's seat.

Handy was still annoyed, but Jarman smiled, grimly.

'If nothing else, Inspector, we have riled him. And a riled man makes mistakes. He is definitely worried about that ledger, however, and I fear we will never see it. If I were him, I would destroy it forthwith.'

Handy agreed.

'And without that ledger, we have nothing. The links between Villiers and the dead girls are gone, as well as any proof that he had anything to do with the murder of Edward Ely.'

'We still have no proof about that at all.'

Handy slumped back into the seat of the rocking carriage.

'Pence is going to bloody eat me alive when he hears about this,' he said, gloomily.

They sat in silence for the rest of the journey.

# Chapter Twenty

## The Hanging Man

They got back to the station and huddled in Handy's office once again, thinking through their options. It always led back to the same thing.

'We need that ledger,' said Handy, stating the fact that was obvious to both of them. 'That, along with the signatures beside the names and the promise to keep their little secret, is at the centre of this. With that, we can perhaps get one or more of them to make a confession, and the threat of their participation in the parties at Villiers's house may be enough for them to give us more about Villiers and the murdered girls.'

He picked up the list of names that Grace had written down. 'We've also got Grace's account of what went on in that house. Although the word of a prostitute means little in the eyes of the law, I think that her testimony, along with the ledger, is the key to unlocking whatever madness Villiers has been up to. Enough to save more lives possibly.'

'We also have Clinch, of course,' said Jarman. 'He's not the killer, anyone with eyes can see that. He's no more capable of the horror that was inflicted on those poor girls than you or I, and he does not seem like the type of man who could professionally strangle a fit young reporter either. But he obviously knows something about what has been going on, and a confession from him, along with that of Grace and his knowledge of the whereabouts of the ledger, may be vital.'

He stood and paced across to the window, looking out at the filth and vitality of Leman Street.

'A swift confession from Clinch is your best bet, Inspector. With that, you get a testimony of whatever evil has been occurring at Villiers's house, you get the location of the ledger—if it still exists—and you get the grounds to pursue the investigation deeper. Not just at the factory, but at Villiers's house itself. With Clinch, you begin to start tugging at the thread that will unravel the whole garment. Pence could not stop that, even if he wanted to.'

Handy nodded, knowing he was right. 'Well, we'd better get it soon,' he muttered. 'Before Grundy gets here and Pence hands me my backside on a plate.'

He stood at the door and called over the nearest constable he saw, who happened to be young Rose.

'Get Clinch back up here. Quick' he said. Rose ran off.

Handy sat back at his desk and lit a cigarette with nervous fingers. He could feel his entire career in the police force teetering on the edge. If Pence was involved in whatever had been happening at Villiers's house, and if he didn't get some proof soon, then he might be sacked before the sun set. But what really burned in Handy was not this fear. It was that he would have failed to stop a killer. And he couldn't have that.

His reverie was destroyed when the office door burst open and Rose stood there, pale and sweating. The look on his face told Jarman and Handy that they had lost everything.

*

Clinch's body was lowered slowly, and the belt was unwrapped from around his neck. They laid the corpse on the thin cot.

Jarman stood after examining the body briefly. He shook his head at Handy.

The Inspector was furious. He could barely talk. For the first time in years, he felt the same impotent rage he had felt in the streets and alleyways of the Nichols as a child; the unfairness of a world in which some had so much, but in which he had to fight to survive in, every single day. Handy wanted to hit someone, to take out his frustration and, although he was loathe to admit it, his fear. His fear of where he was headed. It was not just his job, but the entire police force that was now under suspicion. The very organisation that had taken in that young, filthy, lost child and turned him into the man he was, seemed, at that moment, to be dark and leering and nasty. He took a deep breath and turned to the two men in front of him.

One of them was Rose, looking miserable and sick, although none of this was his fault. However, the constable still felt responsible. Clinch had killed himself under their very noses and he was part of that fault as he had been in the station all day.

The man standing beside him looked even more ill, as well he should. He was the sergeant in charge of the cells.

'When did you last see the prisoner alive?' asked Handy. His voice was low and dangerous.

'Half an hour ago, sir,' said the sergeant. 'I did the checks as I should.'

'And what was he doing?'

'He was just sitting on the cot, sir, quiet as you like. Looked miserable, like he had been crying.'

'So, one minute he's on his cot, and the next he's hanging from the bars,' muttered Handy. 'Why the hell did he have his belt?'

'I didn't know he did, sir. I checked him. Took his boots as I should have, and I swear he wasn't wearing a belt; I swear to God'

'Would you swear on your job?' roared Handy suddenly. The rage exploded from him and the sergeant quailed. His face was ashen at the implications of what Handy was saying to him.

Handy planted himself in front of the man and for a second it looked like he was going to hit him. Even Rose half lifted his hands as if to ward the Inspector off, but it was Jarman who quietly stopped him.

'Inspector,' he said. 'Would you take a look at this?'

Handy continued to glare at the sergeant, before releasing his pent-up breath.

'Get back upstairs,' he hissed. 'I'll be talking to you later. At length.'

The man scarpered, pleased to be away from the heat of Handy's rage. Handy turned to Jarman. 'What is it?'

Jarman eased Clinch's head back and Handy saw what he was showing him. The death in his cells suddenly seemed much, much worse than it had been. He looked at Jarman, not believing what he was looking at.

The small bruise, just below the Adam's apple, showed clear and new, under the savage marks of where the belt had gripped Clinch's throat. It was exactly the same as the mark Jarman had found on the body of Edward Ely.

'In my station?' whispered Handy. 'Murdered? In my station?' He slumped against the bars of the tiny cell, his fingers clenching and unclenching.

Jarman nodded.

'I'm afraid so. The signs are all too obvious. He was strangled, quickly and professionally, then he was hoisted up to hang from the belt to make it look like suicide.' Jarman gauged the height, quickly. 'Whoever did it is a most powerful man,' he mused. 'Although Mr Clinch, I would guess, is no more than ten stone, a dead weight is a dead weight. Especially when the body would have had to be held in place to buckle the belt around his neck.'

'The same killer as the one who murdered Ely?' asked Handy, already knowing the answer. Jarman nodded.

Handy turned to Rose. 'Anyone you can remember wandering around in the station you didn't recognise?' he asked.

Rose thought hard. 'Definitely not,' he said. 'I would have noticed anyone wandering in off the street and coming down here.'

'What if the person was wearing a police uniform?' asked Jarman. Handy and Rose both stared at him.

'Thank you, Rose,' said Handy. 'That will be all.'

Rose doubtfully saluted to Handy's back as the Inspector turned fully to Jarman.

'It makes sense,' said the surgeon when they were alone. 'A certain Assistant Commissioner could easily furnish a man with a uniform, could he not? And who would notice one more policeman wandering around a busy station?'

Jarman looked at the body, then at the clock on the wall near the bottom of the stairs that led into the cells.

'Whoever it was, they knew the times the cells were checked. Perhaps they had been given this information? Clinch was the only one down here. Somehow, the killer knew this too. Again, possibly from a source who was privy to this knowledge. They waited until the sergeant had completed his check, came down, murdered Clinch and then hanged him with a belt they themselves had brought with them. I believe your sergeant, Inspector. I do not believe Clinch was wearing a belt. Why would he? You can see he has braces buttons on his trousers.'

Jarman sat on the edge of the cot beside the cooling body.

'If we were ever in any doubt, this whole affair shows us that whoever killed this man, and probably Edward Ely too, is a professional. He is cool and calm and he is very good at his work. I believe this murder took less than ten minutes to complete. He was in, killed Clinch, and was out again before anyone even had a chance to notice a face they didn't recognise.'

He looked up at Handy.

'They're covering their traces,' he said, and saw the dawning horror on Handy's face. He felt that horror himself. He stood and they both uttered the same words at the same time.

'The girl!'

# Chapter Twenty-One

## The Girl in the Room

Grace Wright's body lay, still and silent, in a red puddle of its own making.

They had collected Curmudgeon and raced across to the boarding house when the knowledge of what was happening became so horribly clear to them, but they were far too late.

The door to the house was opened by Handy's friend, the ex-copper Wally Mathers. Handy, Jarman and Curmudgeon pushed past him without a word, barging up the stairs and into the room where Grace had been placed. She lay on the bed, her mouth gaping, the bedding sodden with her gore.

Jarman quickly checked the girl for any sign of life, finding none. Her toothless mouth yawned at him in a silent scream, and he frowned at the pathetic sight. He gently pressed her jaw closed. He checked her body, but there were no other signs of damage. She had been killed by a single well-placed stab to the heart, and she had probably died within seconds. Whoever did it may have only been in the room for a matter of moments.

As Jarman straightened from the corpse, he felt a breeze cross his face and stepped across to the grimy window that looked out over the black and filthy Thames. The window was slightly ajar, and he pulled it further open and looked out. It was only ten feet to the ground, and an old crate had been pushed from beside others piled against the wall of the house and placed under the window; Jarman could see the scrape marks in the oily mud where this had happened, and he realised instantly that any footprints would be useless in that muck. This, then, was how the killer had made his ingress and egress. He turned back to Handy and Curmudgeon, joined now by Mathers who stared in horror at what had happened in his house.

'That's that, then,' said Handy. 'This poor soul was the last chance we had of getting a conviction. And they knew it. So they killed her. We're finished.'

He turned to Mathers.

'Did you see anything, Wally?' he asked without hope.

Mather, still staring at the corpse, shook his head.

'I thought you said no one knew she was here,' he muttered.

'I didn't think they did,' replied Handy. 'There was only me, Doctor Jarman here and young Rose who knew where she was being kept. And don't start thinking of Rose as being the leak.' This was directed at Jarman. 'He's as straight as the day is long.'

Jarman nodded.

'He is. He had nothing to do with this. Why don't we talk downstairs?'

They all clumped back down the bare stair-boards to Mathers' kitchen, where Handy told the man to make himself scarce.

'I don't want you getting involved in all of this, Wally,' he explained. 'You're better off not knowing.'

Mathers nodded. 'I'll be off and report the murder in my house, then,' he said, heavily. 'Should take me about half an hour.'

Handy smiled at him and nodded. 'You do that, Wally. And no mention of seeing us here when you do.'

Wally pulled on a coat and limped out of the house. Handy turned to Jarman.

'I don't want Pence, or anyone else, knowing that we know about the girl, yet,' he explained. 'It's not much, but anything that keeps a few secrets from the murdering bastards who are doing this might be beneficial.'

Jarman sipped the tea that Mathers had deposited in front of him.

'So,' he said. 'Let us go over what we know. Villiers has been engaging in his horrible pastimes with the men on Grace's list, one of them being your Assistant Commissioner Pence.'

'He's not my Assistant Commissioner,' muttered Handy, but Jarman ignored him.

'Some of the women employed at these gatherings have been killed in the most heinous ways possible. They had all left the employment that Villiers had given them, probably because of what happened at his house. A reporter, investigating Villiers, has been murdered by a professional killer. The clerk, Clinch, who obviously knew something, has similarly been killed. And now that unfortunate girl upstairs also lies dead, probably by the same hand.'

'Why do you think it's the same man?' asked Handy. 'The other two were strangled, this girl was stabbed, and the three dollies were mutilated beyond recognition.'

Jarman sipped his tea, thinking.

'First of all, Inspector,' he said, 'I think we should not jump to the conclusion that the killer of the girls is the same man who killed Ely, Clinch and poor Grace. I believe them to be different people.'

'What? Why would you think that?'

'Whoever killed the prostitutes tore those poor women apart. The hair, the scalps, that has something to do with it. The killer is obsessed in a strange way with hair, and the women were murdered in a paroxysm of rage.'

'Do you think it's Villiers?'

Jarman stared at the Inspector. He nodded. 'I do.' He put down the mug of tea. It really was rather foul.

'However, if it was Villiers who is guilty of those crimes, I do not think it is he who is guilty of the deaths of Edward Ely, Robert Clinch and Grace Wright. Someone else killed them.'

Curmudgeon and Handy waited for an explanation.

'Those murders are just too…clean,' Jarman said, finally. 'They are the work of a professional. A cold-hearted and brutal professional, but a professional all the same. The quick dispatch of Clinch and Ely and the professional stabbing of Grace. They bear all the hallmarks of a man who makes his living from this sort of thing. The murderer of those three girls is the work of a sadistic beast, not a methodical killer.'

'But the Ripper strangled his victims before cutting them open,' said Handy. 'We know that Ely and Clinch were similarly killed. Why can't this be the same man?'

'Because the three women we have been investigating were killed by *having* their throats cut. Whoever the Ripper was, he enjoyed the action of the cutting: slowly and deliberately. And to do that he needed his victims dead. I've already told you that whoever it is we are hunting, it is not Jack the Ripper.

'I believe Villiers is the man who has killed those three women in such a hideous fashion. I believe he is a monster in human form. But I think the man who killed Ely and Clinch and Grace is someone different. Someone employed for his skills. Either by Villiers himself, or even by one of the other names on that list. Who do you think would have the connections to know where to hire a professional killer, Inspector? Who would have a knowledge of every criminal and ruffian in London? And who would know every safe house used by the Metropolitan police?'

Handy stared at him, wide-eyed.

'Then it has to be Pence,' he whispered.

'It makes more sense when we then think about the riot we were caught up in too,' continued Jarman. 'Who would know where to put up those rather inflammatory posters? Who knew just what levers to pull to make a community turn into a violent rabble? Who would have the knowledge, and the ability, to create that storm at the very time we were all in the vicinity? Who could supply a policeman's uniform? Who could easily have found out that I was going to Dorking? It all leads to a rather self-explanatory conclusion.'

Handy rubbed at his head.

'But it still makes no sense,' he said, exasperated. 'Why

would a man who has worked himself into position as Assistant Commissioner, a highly paid and highly thought of position, potentially throw it all away and engage in criminal behaviour?'

Jarman smiled at him, sadly.

'I've already explained this, Inspector. You have no concept of the utmost importance that social standing brings. It is everything. Above friends, above family, even above money, if you can believe that. Social standing is everything and, believe me, a man from that class will do anything he needs to do to protect his reputation. For every name on the list Grace gave us, their reputation is the most important thing in their lives. I believe there is little they would not do to keep it intact. These people buy themselves out of every problem. It is what they have always done. They're trying to do it now with the murders of Clinch and Ely and Grace.'

'Then why would Villiers kill those women in the way he did?' Curmudgeon spoke for the first time. 'Why would he risk getting the police involved?'

'That is simple, Curmudgeon,' said Jarman. 'It's because he is completely and utterly insane.'

He stood, picking up his hat from the table.

'What do we do now?' asked Handy. He seemed completely lost at the thought of his superior being involved in murder.

Jarman placed his hat on his head.

'We have absolutely no proof of anything,' he said. 'No proof that Villiers is the new Ripper, no proof that Pence is involved with these murders either. We need to find that proof.'

'And where do you propose we find it?' asked Handy as they left the house and climbed into the brougham.

'At the only avenue left open to us. With Mrs Susannah Villiers.'

Curmudgeon clicked his tongue and Daisy pulled out onto the road.

# Chapter Twenty-Two

## Susannah

## *London October 1887*

*T*he dark man paced the room, in obvious distress, eventually standing by the mirror and staring into it for the longest time, his dark eyes like pools of blackness. He was deep in thought.

He eventually sighed and turned away from the mirror. Downstairs he could hear the laughter of the men and the cackling of the whores with them. His need for his pleasures throbbed through him and he groaned, wrapping his arms around himself. He wanted to go down and join them, to see the flesh, to smell the scent of those gutter women, to see the blood smeared on their naked bodies and on his own. He wanted them to feel the pain and he wanted to feel it too.

But still, he hesitated. He really should not do that now. For the thousandth time he wondered why he had married that foolish creature who was, for the moment, thankfully absent from his house.

He was denied his visits to the filthy dens in the East End now. Denied entrance into the dark and dangerous world he loved so much. Denied everything he wanted since the clean one had entered his house. The one who did not smell. The one who did not grin with a toothless mouth. The one he wanted nothing to do with.

Oh, she had been willing to carry out her duties, that was for sure. She had almost begged him to bed her. And when he tried, when he really tried to do what she wanted, was it his fault that he found the *entire act horrifying? Was it his fault that he found no interest in her soft, unscarred, slim body and always left her as soon as the ghastly deed was over?*

*No. It was her fault. It was always her fault. She should do as he wished. She should stink and she should rut and she should be his whore!*

*But no. She would not succumb. She just stared at him with her stupid cow-like eyes and tried to understand what her husband wanted, when of course, she never could. Because she was not unclean. She was not what he desired.*

*The noise from the decadent party downstairs became louder as the bedroom door opened and a figure stood there, staring at him.*

*'I know,' he said. 'I know what you are thinking.'*

*The figure stepped inside and closed the bedroom door.*

*'Do you?' his Guardian asked. 'Do you honestly believe you know anything of what my mind holds?'*

*'You think I should not have married,' said the dark man. 'You think I should have passed that creature over.'*

*'And am I right?'*

*'I had to!' the dark man said, earnestly. 'It is expected.'*

*The Guardian said nothing.*

*'You said it was the right thing to do,' the dark man said, sullenly. 'This was your idea.'*

*The Guardian just stared at him.*

*'Go and enjoy your party,' the Guardian said at last. 'She is not here tonight. Tomorrow will look after itself.'*

*The door closed softly as the Guardian left.*

*The dark man took a deep breath. Looking into the mirror again, he sensed the feelings he never really understood seep through him. The feeling of remorse. Of doubt.*

*The sound of a cheer from downstairs, however, told him that the party was beginning to get interesting, and he smiled, forcing all human emotions from him.*

*Then he went downstairs.*

*To the flesh.*

*And the blood.*

\*

Curmudgeon parked a little way down the street under Handy's instructions.

'I don't want Villiers seeing the carriage out of the window and doing a runner,' he explained.

Jarman followed his lead, but he doubted Villiers would be at home. Something told him that the man would be off celebrating somewhere at the closing down of any truths they had tried to open.

They knocked and Ellie opened the door. She smiled over their shoulders at Curmudgeon, then showed them into the drawing room, where Susannah Villiers stood, as if she knew they would be coming and was waiting for them.

She asked them to sit down. Jarman noticed that she looked pale and drawn. Her eyes were shadowed by dark rings, and she seemed thinner than when he had seen her in Dorking. "Drained" was the word that sprang to his mind.

'I'm afraid my husband is not at home,' she replied to their enquiry. 'I have not seen him for the last few days.'

'Is that normal?' asked Handy.

'My husband's work sometimes keeps him from his home,' she replied. She emphasised the word "work" and neither man missed it.

'Mrs Villiers, I'm sorry to say that I believe your husband to be involved in something immoral, and possibly illegal,' continued Handy. The time for pulling punches was, it seemed now gone.

Susannah nodded. She did not seem surprised at Handy's words. She swallowed, unsure what to do or say.

Jarman leaned forward, his face earnest.

'Mrs Villiers. When we spoke in the garden of your house, you said you had things to say, but were afraid to say them. The time for silence has now passed. The Inspector and I have been engaged in an investigation that goes to the very heart of London society. That investigation includes assault and murder. Murder most foul. Your husband is at the centre of it. He is a monster, and I am prepared to stand in any court and repeat that accusation.'

Susannah stared at him, and her face, if that were possible, paled even more.

'And yet I would be laughed out of that court,' continued Jarman. 'We have no proof. Nothing. Every potential witness has met a grisly fate. They are all dead. Your husband and his friends are, we believe, responsible for those deaths. And we believe that your husband, especially, has committed acts so atrocious they are almost beyond words. We need your help, Mrs Villiers. Susannah. We need your help. We need you to do the right thing'

For a long time, Susannah just continued to stare at him, then her eyes passed to Handy. She stood and went to the window, looking out over the Square. She closed her eyes and sighed, fear plain on her face.

The sigh made Jarman want to go over to her and take her in his arms. To tell her everything was all right. To explain to her how he was starting to feel about her. But of course, he could not do any of that. She was another man's wife and she could not be with him, even if she wanted to be. She was a haunted beauty whom he genuinely wanted to help, but he had no idea what she felt about him. It could all be in his own head. Yet he was sure his feelings were reciprocated in some way. He was sure she viewed him as more than just a man investigating her husband. At least, he hoped this was so. More than that: he longed for it. He inwardly cursed himself for his stupidity. And his timing. Susannah eventually turned back to the two men and nodded.

Jarman stood and led her to a chair.

'I know this is not easy,' he said. 'I know you are frightened. But without your help, we believe more people may die, and die in the most gruesome manner. We are against the clock, because the murders we are talking about are not criminal as such. They are pathological. There is a *need* for the killer to strike again.'

'And you think Thomas is that killer?' asked Susannah.

Jarman nodded. 'I do. The Inspector and I need to know if there is anything about your husband that has struck you as strange. Anything you think he may be hiding, either physically or mentally. In short, Susannah, we need to know what you were going to tell me in Dorking. It may be you feel uneasy about disclosing these secrets, which are within the sanctity of your marriage, but please be aware that the Inspector and I are professional men. We have heard and seen just about everything life can throw at us. You need not be embarrassed or fearful. If nothing comes of it, your husband will never know you spoke, we promise. But anything that could help us prove what we believe him to be may keep another woman alive who might otherwise die in pain and horror.'

Susannah was silent for a long time, her eyes downcast. Handy gave Jarman a hopeless glance, but Jarman shook his head slightly, urging him to wait. Eventually, Susannah looked up at them.

'I know my husband is not a good man,' she began. 'Even before we were married, I sensed a difference to him. Something I could not quite put my finger on. I will be honest, gentlemen, as you have asked me to be: I did not want to marry Thomas Villiers.'

Handy was about to start asking questions but Jarman held up a hand, knowing that she must tell her story in her own time. In her own way.

'It was my father who insisted,' she went on. 'He believed the match to be right and proper. The dowry was good, and it would mean he would not have to worry about my future when he was gone. I thank God every day that both he and my mother were dead before they could discover what I had been married off to.'

She frowned at the memories.

'I want you to know that he has never hurt me. At least not physically. But our, our...contact, our marital contact...'

She stood and once again looked out of the window. This time her face was flushed pink. She continued to stare outside as she spoke.

'My husband and I have rarely ever been...intimate,' she

finished. 'And for that small blessing, I am relieved.' Jarman felt something seep slowly through his body. Was it shock that she spoke so poorly of her husband? Or relief?

'But at Dorking you said you had another to worry about. You said you had more than yourself to worry about.'

She turned to look at him and nodded.

'I do,' she said. 'I am pregnant with Thomas Villiers's child. My marriage has been a poor one, but it has resulted in the blessing of a child. And I must ensure that child is kept safe.'

She sighed and looked away from the men, plainly embarrassed by her confession. 'I am also worried about Ellie,' she said.

'Ellie?' asked Jarman. 'Your ward?'

Susannah nodded, taking a deep breath.

'My husband has been…forthright with his attentions towards Ellie. I have seen it with my own eyes and have always managed to diffuse the situation. But I feared for her safety if I were not with her. I feared what he would do. I believe I have become used to living in fear. It is draining me.'

Handy seemed satisfied with the answer, but Jarman barely heard it. He did not really know why the revelation that Susannah thought so little of her husband meant so much to him, except that it meant she was perhaps a step closer to being free somehow; free from the horror she had married. She had a child to think of, but she plainly felt no love towards Villiers. If anything, it seemed she hated him, and it suddenly felt to Jarman that a whole new future may have just opened up. One that he had been sure was closed to him before it had even begun.

'The parties, the gatherings at this house,' said Susannah. 'I found out about those very early on. As Thomas seemed to want so little to do with me, he craved the time with his friends. He never told me about what went on, of course. I believe he did not think I knew anything of them, or he believed I was so stupid that I would not be able to work out what was happening, but as I began to spend more and more time at Dene Manor, his get-togethers became more frequent. I heard that other women were involved, but I tried not to concern myself. By that point, I no longer cared what he did. Instead, I enjoyed my time away from here, safe in the knowledge that Ellie was with me and that we could both relax somewhat. But I heard the rumours of course. Women of the night wandering around the house. Who knows, perhaps even sleeping in my own bed.' She shuddered. 'I always had the maid change the bedding as soon as we got back.'

She came and sat in front of them again, seemingly more at ease. It seemed speaking about her plight was making her feel better.

'It would always happen in the same manner.' She continued. 'Thomas would grow more and more on edge. He would begin to eye Ellie in a dark and secret manner, until I could stand it no longer and I would suggest that I might like a weekend away at Dene Manor. He always seemed very eager for me to do so, and when I got back he would be relaxed and sanguine once again.' Her mouth twisted in distaste. 'As if he had been satiated.'

She lapsed into silence for a while, staring into nothing. The two men kept quiet.

'But I sometimes found things,' she eventually continued. 'Discarded pieces of clothing, forgotten behind chairs, under tables. Once, Ellie found a stocking with a speck of blood on it. It made me quite ill to think about what may have occurred. I had Ellie burn the stocking immediately.

'And then, two years ago, it all stopped,' she said. 'There were no more get-togethers with Thomas and his acquaintances. They just stopped.'

'Can you remember when this was?' asked Handy, and Susannah nodded, her face pale once more.

'It was in the early autumn of 1888,' she said, heavily. 'When the Ripper came to such horrible prominence.'

They were all silent. The revelation of what she had said was huge.

'During that time, Thomas came as close as he ever would to hurting me, I think,' she said. 'It was as if he had something *inside* him. Something dark and burning. Something wrong. His gatherings seemed to take the edge off that darkness but, with them no longer taking place, I watched, minute by minute, as he became more and more frustrated. More and more dangerous. One night, he came to my room—we had agreed on separate sleeping arrangements long before—and he… he had a knife in his hand. He used the knife…' Her breath caught in her throat and, instinctively, Jarman rose and sat beside her, taking her hand in his.

'What did he do?' he asked, his voice dangerously low. If Villiers had hurt this woman, he'd better hope that Handy got to him first, because he believed at that moment that if he caught up with him, he would kill him.

'Thomas used the knife to tear my clothes,' she said. 'Slowly. He just slowly sliced at them. His eyes were glazed and his mouth was slack. And all the time he had my hair in his hand. Rubbing it between his fingers…'

Susannah suddenly broke down and Jarman held her. It was only for a moment, but her body was quivering and warm and he wanted to stay there forever. She dabbed at her eyes and took a deep, quavering breath.

'But they eventually started again,' she said. 'The parties, the get-togethers, whatever they were, they started again. And he mostly left me alone again, thank God. Apart from a few, rare, occasions when he seemed to try and be the husband he should have been.'

For a moment Jarman just stared at her, a million different emotions flowing through him, then he eventually re-joined Handy. Susannah was once again by the window. She spoke without turning around.

'Is my husband Jack the Ripper?' she asked.

Jarman, at that moment, could not answer. He was consumed by emotions that he did not really understand, and it was Handy who spoke.

'We don't know, Mrs Villiers. We think he may be, though.'

He turned to Jarman, who was still staring at the back of Susannah Villiers, but the surgeon ignored him.

'Where is he now?' asked Jarman, a hot fury seeping through his body at the thought of what this woman had been through; the fear she had lived under for so long.

'I believe he is at his club, the Cardington,' said Susannah, looking more miserable than anyone ever has.

'We should leave,' said Handy to Jarman. 'We don't want to be here when he gets back. Keep Mrs Villiers out of it, eh?'

Jarman was silent for a second. Then he whirled around, and Handy—who had seen his fair share of men who wanted to kill him—took an involuntary step back from the fury in Jarman's eyes.

'He will never come near you again,' said Jarman to Susannah. 'I promise you.' Then he grabbed his hat and stormed out, Handy following him, hurriedly. They climbed aboard the brougham after Curmudgeon had quickly waved goodbye to Ellie.

'The Cardington Club!' shouted Jarman. And Curmudgeon, seeing the look on Jarman's face, simply turned and cracked Daisy into action.

\*

They had gone nearly a mile before either of them spoke. They were passing Whitehall, and Handy suddenly called for Curmudgeon to stop.

He closed the door of the carriage. 'I need to talk with Pence,' he said to Jarman through the open window. 'I want to see for myself how much he's involved in all of this, and I can only do that by looking in his eye.'

Jarman, still furious at what he had learned about Villiers and Susannah, nodded. 'Be careful,' he said.

Handy put on his hat.

'You too. Don't do anything stupid. We don't want this investigation to fall apart because of what you feel towards Susannah Villiers. Understand?'

Jarman took a deep breath, then nodded.

183

'I shall be the very model of decorum,' he replied.

Handy eyed him suspiciously for a second, then he stepped back. He watched the brougham roll away and then turned to the imposing building in front of him where Pence's office was located. He took a deep breath and crossed the busy road.

Jarman and Curmudgeon pulled up outside the Cardington Club ten minutes later. As was the norm for most of those very expensive establishments, the frontage was quite plain, with only the name of the club showing in plain brass above the door. Jarman rang the bell.

A butler opened the door and bowed. 'Can I help you, sir?' he asked.

'I believe that Mr Thomas Villiers is a member here,' said Jarman, not even bothering to remove his hat. 'I would like to see him.'

The butler frowned at the curt order, but remained courteous.

'I'm afraid Mr Villiers is not at the club at the present moment,' he said. 'Would you like to leave a card?' He held out his hand, expectantly.

Jarman eyed the doorway behind the butler and then up and at the windows above him, but could see nothing of the interior. He shook his head. 'No.'

He left the scowling servant and got back into the brougham.

'Where to?' asked Curmudgeon.

Jarman, his face hard and dark, thought for a second.

'The factory.'

They set off once again.

# Chapter Twenty-Three

## A Suspension of Duties

Handy sat outside the office of Montgomery Pence, shuffling uncomfortably in the hard seat.

He was nervous of what this meeting would bring about. He had nothing; no proof at all that Pence was involved in anything, except that his name was one of the names Grace had given them.

And the logic of Carter Jarman, of course. But he must be wrong, surely. Pence was an Assistant Commissioner of the Metropolitan Police. He was in charge of all criminal investigations in the Metropolitan area. Why on earth would he get himself involved in murder?

But then Handy remembered what Jarman had said: that these sorts would do anything to keep their faces clean, no matter how dirty they may really be under the public make-up. Was it really as simple as that? Would a man, *could* a man, order murder simply to save himself from embarrassment? Or was there more to it than this? Was his connection deeper than he and Jarman thought?

His musings were interrupted when the door to Pence's office opened and the small, neat man himself stood there. He did not look happy. He indicated to Handy to enter with a turn of his head and then went back inside, leaving the door open.

Handy entered, carrying his hat.

'Close the door, Handy,' barked Pence. He was sitting behind an impressive oak desk. On the green leather top was a reading lamp, an ashtray and a tray for correspondence. A gold pen lay at an exact right angle from the tray.

The room itself was magnificent. Oak-panelled, with glass-fronted cabinets containing books and folders and certificates of merit. A safe stood in the corner: a huge, green, cast-iron affair that Handy reckoned would take a weekend to break into. The window was behind Pence, and it looked out over Whitehall.

Handy licked his lips and spoke. 'It will surely be a shame when you move to the new building, sir,' he said.

Pence said nothing. New premises had recently opened on the Embankment as headquarters for the Metropolitan force, but Handy doubted they would be as nice as the one he was standing in.

'Why were you at the office of Mr Thomas Villiers this morning, Handy?' asked Pence, eventually. Handy tried to gauge what he saw in the other man's face, but failed. Pence was like a rock. Unlike most Assistant Commissioners, Pence did not have a military background. Instead, he had come up through the police ranks: a very impressive task. Very few made these heady heights, and to do so meant that Pence was now a very rich man who had learned long ago to conceal whatever was going on in his mind.

'I believe Mr Villiers to be involved in the murders I have been investigating,' he said, his mouth suddenly very dry. Pence was too composed. There was no fear at all on his face. Jarman had been wrong, and Handy suddenly felt like a damned fool. He had allowed a civilian unfettered access to a police investigation and he was about to face the music. He straightened.

'Evidence?' growled Pence.

'Nothing solid yet, sir…' began Handy, then paused. Was that relief he had suddenly seen cross his superior's face?

'Then why the hell are you hounding an innocent man?' Pence suddenly roared. He stood and came around the huge table. 'He's been here today! Him and his solicitor. They are to press charges, Inspector. Against you! And I see no reason why I should protect you from them. You accuse a man of crimes he didn't do, you and your *Jigsaw* Jarman. Oh, yes. I know all about him, Handy. I told you to get rid of him in your office the other day, but you blatantly ignored my orders. My orders!'

He screamed this last word at Handy, his face mottled and white with fury.

'By God, you have a nerve coming here today, sir!' he continued. 'You, of all people. A jumped-up jack-me-lad! A brat! An urchin from the streets! You were spawned from filth and you still revel in it. How dare you attack the good name of one of this city's most outstanding and upright characters? How dare you turn my police force into a freak show? Do you have even one inkling of how to do your job, man?'

Handy remained silent, but he could feel his anger beginning to boil. Spawned from filth? He gritted his teeth.

'You will apologise to Villiers, Handy. And you will do it today. Do you hear me?'

Handy shook his head, his own anger barely contained. 'I bloody well will not,' he said. He stared at Pence. He could feel his pent-up frustrations pouring out from him. The unsolved murders, those desecrated women, the three dead policemen. And Frank, of course. Poor Frank.

'You do know Frank Callow lost his life in the pursuit of this investigation, don't you!' he shouted back at Pence. 'You remember him, surely. My sergeant? My friend? He was killed along with three other innocent coppers by some bastard who caved his head in with a rock. He was fighting for his life in the filthy streets that I came from! And he was doing it because he was trying to do something right! Trying to solve one more murder in a city full of murderers. And Villiers, the man I believe to have committed those murders, wants me to apologise to *him*? You can tell Mr Villiers from me, Commissioner, that he can politely fuck off!'

Pence went very still. His moustache twitched as a smile snatched at his lips.

'You've done it now, Handy,' he whispered. 'I can't help you now.' He sniffed and sat back at his desk, picking up a sheet of paper from the ream in the tray. He quickly scribbled something down. He held the sheet to Handy.

'This is a note that I will be copying and officially stamping once you have left this office,' he said, quietly now. 'It is my order that Inspector Jonas Handy, *formerly* of H Division, is to be removed from his duties immediately, pending an enquiry into his behaviour. The suspension from duties is without pay. You can go back to the prostitutes and thieves in the grubby little streets you sprang from. Perhaps you'll find some siblings there.'

Handy stared down at the few words that meant the destruction of everything he had ever lived for. Everything he had held dear. For some reason his father's face came to him for a second, holding a bar of soap in his hand. '*You shall move this here soap vigorously across your body. Understand that?*'

'Good day,' said Pence. '*Mr* Handy.'

Handy looked at him as he began writing the second note. And he saw the bead of sweat sliding down his face. He suddenly smiled, and it was a smile that turned Pence's heart cold when he glanced up and saw it.

Handy bent over the desk and grabbed the hand Pence was writing with. He brought his face closer to the other man.

'I know you're involved, Pence,' he whispered. 'You know more about prostitutes than I ever will, don't you? I know all about you and Villiers and the girls at his house. I know what you like to do to them. How you like to watch them bleed. I know what a disgusting, wretched excuse for a man you really are.'

Pence's face was white once again, but this time it was with fear. More sweat dribbled from his carefully combed hair. He tried to pull his hand away but Handy was much too strong. His grip tightened.

'When I get that evidence,' he hissed, 'you will do well to be as far away from me as you can be. Because I also know that you've done worse than hurt innocent women. I know you've paid for people to be murdered. I think you ordered that riot as well. You remember that, don't you, Pence? When four policemen including my sergeant were killed?'

He grinned at the stricken look on Pence's face, knowing finally that he was correct.

'So, you've given me an order. In return, I will give you some advice. Get away while you still can. Because if I find out you were the one who caused Frank's death, I'll come back here and I'll bloody kill you myself.'

He shoved Pence away from him and straightened. He waited for the Commissioner to say something, but it seemed the man had become mute.

Handy crumpled his dismissal into a ball and dropped it onto the thick carpet, and without another glance at Pence, he stalked out of the office.

And out of his job.

# Chapter Twenty-Four

## A Little Spot of Burglary

Jarman and Curmudgeon stopped outside the factory. The night was drawing in and the last of the girls were leaving, wrapping their shawls around their shoulders. Every single one of them looked drained and weak and weary. They were like thin, nebulous ghosts, passing briefly through an ephemeral existence that was nothing except hard and brutal and hateful.

Jarman and Curmudgeon approached the factory door just as a foreman was locking up.

'Mr Villiers ain't here, sir,' he responded to Jarman's request. 'Left earlier this morning. He hasn't been in all day.'

'His sister?'

The foreman shook his head. 'She left hours ago.'

Jarman cursed, vehemently, and, in the opinion of the foreman, impressively. He and Curmudgeon returned to the brougham.

'Look, why don't you go home for the night,' said Curmudgeon. 'I know what you're like when you get riled up. Take a bit of time to think of the consequences.'

Jarman ignored him and climbed into the cabin. 'Villiers's solicitors, Curmudgeon,' he ordered. 'He may be there.'

Curmudgeon sighed and climbed up into the driver's seat. 'Bloody fool,' he allowed himself, quietly.

The visit to Grundy, Lewes and Smeaton, however, proved as fruitless as the visit to the factory. The door to the practice was locked and the windows were dark. Jarman kicked the polished door savagely, and Curmudgeon had to give a hard stare to a passer-by who was about to protest at the surgeon's rudeness. The man hurried away, averting his gaze.

Jarman climbed back into the brougham. He sat there, deep in thought. He did not answer Curmudgeon when he asked him where they were going now. After a while, Curmudgeon clicked his tongue at Daisy and turned in the direction of Bond Street.

Jarman was still silent when they pulled up outside Garretts Jewellers. He went straight up to the room without a word. Curmudgeon knew him enough to leave him well alone.

\*

If they had waited at the factory for another hour, Jarman and Curmudgeon would have been witness to a rather skilful burglary.

A lone figure, dressed in black, passed the locked gates and glanced briefly through the gap between the doors, seemingly out of distant curiosity, but in reality quickly checking for anyone inside. The figure then turned the corner and walked down the narrow alley that ran alongside the high, brick wall of the factory grounds before stopping at a barred side gate, which was also locked.

Jonas Handy, until very recently of the Metropolitan Police Force, checked the interior of the dark yard again and then dipped a hand into his pocket, pulling out the slim, complicated contraption he called his picklock. He selected one of the blades and, within seconds, he was inside the grounds. He closed the gate behind him, placing the padlock through the chain to make it look like the gate was still securely locked, before running along the inside of the wall, keeping to the shadows. He stopped and crouched, checked his surroundings carefully, and then pelted across the open ground to the foot of the metal steps. He padded quickly up and the picklock came out again. Within half a minute he was in the office.

He pulled out and lit a dark lamp and, with the eyes of a

professional thief, he quickly scanned the room for a likely hiding place for the object he sought.

He opened a few locked drawers and cabinets but found nothing. In one secure metal box he discovered over two hundred pounds in cash, but he replaced it all and moved on. That was not what he had come for.

He opened the door to Amelia Villiers's small, partitioned office, his dark lamp sweeping the room. Then he started searching again.

He found what he was looking for almost by accident. Searching shelves above the desk, his foot knocked against a tin bucket, used for discarded paper. He immediately crouched and grabbed the bin before it fell over. And there, under the desk, he spied something. He got down on all fours and peered closer, holding the dark lamp out in front of his face.

Under the desk, to the right and hidden by the innocent bin, was a thin door. It could barely be seen as it had been cleverly disguised as part of the wooden panelling that ran all around the office. But his burglar's eye had spotted it immediately. He felt around the door, his fingers locating a small hole, like a knot in the wood. He inserted his picklock and discovered that the latch behind the disguised blemish was a simple lever. He lifted the latch and pulled the door open.

He straightened. In his hands was a leather ledger, not unlike the one he had perused when looking at the names of the employees of the factory, but much smaller. It was barely bigger than a notebook and, from the writing on the first page, it just seemed to be another file belonging to the factory.

But Handy knew, as soon as he opened it, that this was what he had come for.

He left the factory as quietly as he had entered it, locking the gate behind him. He walked down towards the river and, when he thought he was far enough away, he caught a hansom to his house where he turned on the lights and sat with the ledger open in front of him. He licked his lips.

Half an hour later he was standing in his kitchen with a whisky in his hand.

He had everything he needed about what had been going on at Villiers's house. All the proof he needed was in that ledger. Every sordid little secret, every sordid little man, including Pence.

The ledger was in two parts. The first was a list of names; all the ones Grace had so bravely given him, but a couple more she had not written down but that he recognised. They were all citizens of supposedly high moral standing. Each one of them a high-ranking businessman or gentleman. Apart from Pence and Lyon, there were even a couple of backbench members of Parliament in there.

Each one had signed his name under a paragraph pledging them all to secrecy and laying out what the "club" they all belonged to got up to. That paragraph detailed some of what they had been engaged in at Villiers's house, and it was dated from February 1886 until one month previously, although there seemed to be a gap of several months in 1888: from September until the early months of the following year. Handy could, by now, guess why that might be. Every time the men had been to the house, they had signed this dossier, no doubt to ensure all of them would keep their filthy little habits secret. Some names were present every single time the parties took place, some were more intermittent, but they were proof that immoral behaviour had taken place there. Along with the evidence of Mrs Villiers, if she could be persuaded to testify, they would mean a public enquiry at the very least. It would be a start.

What they did not show, however, was anything to say that any of them had been engaged in murder, but as Handy sipped his whisky he believed it was definitely a start. Especially when he read the second part of the ledger.

This seemed to be a personalised account of what went on at the house by Villiers himself, as the writing matched the paragraph at the front of the document. Handy scanned it thoroughly, but the handwriting did not match the letter Ely had received, so that mystery remained. However, it also held some perplexing entries.

Apart from some rather sordid and sickening explanations of what had gone on at his house, Villiers also mentioned, more than once, someone he referred to as his "Guardian". Handy sat again and went through this section of the ledger, noting the dates. He knew them well.

*September 1st, 1888. The fool! What has he done? We now have proof that he was responsible for the others earlier in the year. My Guardian says that he must be stopped. What shall I do?! We have to stop for now. Have informed the others. They agree.*

*September 7th, 1888: Again! What is the idiot doing? We have talked to him once more but he still denies everything. What will become of me?*

*September 31st, 1888: Guardian has just told me of the other two. He must be stopped now. Have spoken with the others. We may have a man to help, although Guardian is unhappy.*

*November 10th, 1888: Another. My Guardian has made it clear that he needs to be stopped. The silent man has been dispatched.*

*December 3rd, 1888: Oh! Goodness prevails! My problem is no more! Thank you. Thank you! Perhaps soon, we can begin again!*

The gap between the gatherings lasted from September 1888 until March 1889, then continued again until August 1890. That was the last entry. Handy knew that each of the dates corresponded roughly with the murders that had occurred two years previously, starting from when the body of Polly Nichols was found, sparking the Ripper investigation. Could it be that he held in his hands proof that Villiers had murdered those women? And did it not, therefore, indicate that he was the Ripper himself? But if that were true then who was "the fool" whose actions corresponded to the days after Polly Nichols was murdered, and what did it mean when it said that he was responsible for the "others"? Handy remembered what Fred Abberline had said: 'I never really thought that Polly was the first one.' Was this an allusion to the three murders before Polly Nichols? Who, or what, was Villiers's "Guardian"? And who was the "silent man"? Handy sighed and put the ledger down. What the hell was going on?

More importantly, what was he to do about it? He was no longer an Inspector. He glanced at the photograph of his father as the reality of this thought soured within him once again. He had proof, proof that Pence and Villiers and all the rest of those men had been engaging in activities that would destroy their prestige but was not, as far as he could work out, illegal. Horrible, yes. Immoral, yes. But the girls took part willingly: at least that was the way the courts would look at it, and even with the cryptic messages along with the dates of the murders, Handy doubted he had anything more than a lever. It may be enough to wrangle his job back, but it would probably convict no one of the killings. Villiers would more than likely go free. Reduced in the eyes of society, perhaps, but still a free man. Handy closed the ledger. He still needed more.

A knock at the door caused him to freeze. He pulled out his pocket watch. Almost 8pm. Quietly, Handy stepped across to the dresser and pulled open a drawer, where he kept a quite illegal but perfectly serviceable police revolver. He was taking no chances.

He crept to the door. Another knock, and then an instantly recognisable voice called out.

'Are you in, sir?'

Handy opened the door, and there was Rose, wearing his uniform and cape and holding his Bulls Eye lamp.

'What the hell are you doing here?' growled Handy, indicating for the constable to enter.

Rose shuffled in, removing his helmet.

'I heard what happened over at Scotland Yard,' he muttered. 'I was just wondering if there was anything I could do? You know, I was just…'

He broke off and Handy smiled, feeling a wave of affection for this young man.

'You just came to see if I was all right, is that it?'

Rose reddened in righteous anger. 'I think it's diabolical, what's happened,' he said. 'You are the best, most upright man I have ever met, and I believe the AC has made a grave error. I know I'm just a lowly constable, sir, but you have given me responsibilities I never dreamed of.' He looked at Handy in the eyes for the first time. 'You are the policeman I wish to be, sir.'

Handy smiled again. 'Did you rehearse that little speech on the way here?' he asked, and Rose grinned, shyly, nodding.

'But I mean it, sir.'

Handy placed the revolver on the dresser as Rose pretended not to notice its presence, then he poured two whiskies. He lifted his glass.

'Thank you, George. Thank you.'

They drank.

*

Montgomery Pence nervously paced the floor of his office. The memory of that man Handy leaning over him and threatening him made his blood freeze just to think of it. He had to be stopped. *Had* to be stopped. He had thought that removing him from his job may have been enough to sort out the mess Villiers had got them all into again but, after the man had left, he had realised Handy was not the sort to just disappear. He would continue to stick his nose into things that did not concern him. Things that his sort had no right to interfere with. And so Pence had sent, as he had done on several occasions, for Bennet. He was due any moment, and Pence was in paroxysms of fear and guilt.

He paused in his pacing to look at the certificates on the wall of the office. His life. His entire life hung on the wall. Years of pounding the beat, of investigating, of mixing with the right people at the right time, of climbing the greasy pole to the heady heights of Assistant Commissioner. His sights were set even higher, on the Commissioner's role itself. But it would all come crashing down around him if even one word of his associations were made public.

Pence cursed himself for his stupidity in ever getting mixed up with Villiers. Not once, but twice! He cursed himself for his weakness. He cursed himself for his perversions. However, like all men of his ilk, those who are selfish and cruel and weak, Pence mostly cursed his luck.

It was not his fault that he attended those gatherings at Villiers's house. It was not his fault that he enjoyed the fruits: the scarlet, dripping fruits of his passions. It was not his fault he craved the feel of naked flesh, the warmth of sex, the aroma of sweat and blood. It was *them*. The women, the other men of his secret club. It was Villiers himself. *He* had got him caught up in this in the first place. *He* had introduced him to the gatherings at his house. Those conversations at the Cardington, when he had described what happened, how it would make Pence feel. How he could be free to indulge himself in every sordid little fantasy he wanted to. Pence never, not for one second, looked at himself truthfully and saw the monster he was. He simply enjoyed his pursuits. That it hurt others, or that it was as twisted and as cruel as he was, never even entered his head.

The knock on the door broke him from his reverie. He quickly opened it and found Bennet standing there, his cold, flat, hard face staring at him sardonically. Bennet knew what Pence was; he knew the perverse nature of his soul. But Bennet did not care. He had one thought and one thought only: how much money he could make from those who found themselves needing his particular skills.

Those skills had been honed by a lifetime of street-fighting and criminal activities. Bennet had always had to fight to get what he wanted in life and, as he had progressed from pugilist to enforcer to murderer, his skills had developed.

Pence had come across him years before. Bennet, his luck having finally deserted him, had been crouching in a cell, beaten bloody by the police who had dragged him there from the scene where two men had lain dead by his knife. Only the rope awaited him. He was finished. But Pence had seen the cold stare, he had read through the reports of the murders he had been arrested for, and for others he had not. He had listened to Bennet with interest when the man had replied to the question, 'Why did you do it?'

'For the money,' Bennet had answered, seemingly confused by the question. Why else would he have killed two innocent men? He had been paid to do so.

And so Pence had found another like him: completely amoral. He would do as he was asked as long as the price was right. He had used his influence to quietly spirit Bennet away from the cell, and he had become very useful to Pence in the intervening years. None more so than that time, two years before, when one of the club members had decided to start taking things into this own hands. When all the trouble had first started and the club had to shut down until it was over. Until the rogue member had been disposed of. Pence had suggested Bennet to the rest of the club and they had agreed, paid their money, and the problem had disappeared.

The club had decided that a small cessation of their activities was needed then but, being the men they all were, it had soon started up again. They could not help themselves. It was their nature.

And now it was all going wrong again. Lyon had tipped him off about that reporter, Ely, and Pence had thought that by setting Bennet onto him, that would have been an end to it all; but no. Handy and Jarman had started sticking their noses into the actions of their betters and Clinch had been taken. Bennet had got rid of him, and the girl too, the one who knew about the names, but it seemed that was still not enough.

God knows, Pence had tried. He had set the mob on Handy and Jarman, but had failed. He had tried to get rid of Jarman when he was in Dorking, but the man who stood before him had failed in that attempt too, gaining nothing from it but a broken hand. It seemed the pair led a charmed life.

If only those three women had not been killed in the way they had! Why had they been killed like that? And which member of the club had done it? He had got rid of the bodies to hide the marks of the club's work, but still Handy and his surgeon friend would not give up. Once again, Pence cursed Villiers and his twisted, monstrous nature, but the man had promised that it would be all over once Bennet had completed his tasks. He just had to hope this was true.

Bennet continued to simply stare at him, with blank eyes that saw the blackness of Pence's soul and did not care. He waited for his instructions.

Pence wrote down an address and handed it to Bennet.

'You'll need help for this one, I should think. You're down to one hand and Handy is formidable.'

'Handy is the same as everyone else,' replied Bennet in a voice as flat an unresponsive as his face. 'He can die.' He took the sheet of paper. 'The usual fee?'

Pence nodded. 'With a little extra for your hired help, should you feel you need it.'

Bennet turned and walked out the door without another word.

Pence sat back at his desk.

One more death, he thought. One more death and he would be able to breathe once again.

He poured himself a drink and waited for news of Handy's murder.

Then everything, finally, would be right again.

# Chapter Twenty-Five

## An Incident in Two Houses

### *London. December 1888.*

*It had all gone wrong. Everything had gone so, so wrong.*

*The dark man sat in his drawing room. The Wife was absent once again; absent and unmissed. He was alone in his great house. Apart, of course, from his Guardian, who never left his side. Outside, a drizzly dawn was beginning to break the sky.*

*The Guardian stood in the corner, watching him but also watching out of the window for the news that would soon come. The Guardian smiled at him, comfortingly, but the dark man still worried.*

*It had been so wonderful! Especially as The Wife was spending so much time away from London now. The girls, the music. The flesh, the blood. So, so wonderful. He believed he had never been as happy. He was saving those girls, saving them from the very thing he and his friends wanted, the very thing they craved. And they were grateful, in their callow, stupid ways. They took their money and they bandaged each other's wounds and they limped out. And every single one of them always thanked him when they left.*

*They were his children. The children The Wife had so far not provided. How could she? How could she give him that when her very presence disgusted him? Her pretty, pretty face. Her slim, white body. Her foulness! It was a wonder they had managed to couple on the few occasions they had. The very thought of her made him shiver in disgust.*

*The dark man sighed, standing and joining the Guardian at the window. And now his joy and his wants had been stopped. Because of him! Because he could not keep to the agreement. Because the fool had started enjoying himself on his own, dragging them all down with him. Putting them all in jeopardy because of his wantonness and his stupidity! Getting the police involved, sending his stupid letters to the papers! The idiot!*

*'Soon,' the Guardian soothed. 'Soon. It will all be better soon.'*

*They watched from the window.*

*For hours they waited, as the day grew brighter, as the dustmen collected the bins from the backyards, as the postman delivered his letters. They waited.*

*Until suddenly, he was there. The hired man. The silent man who hid his wares about his body. Who took his money without a smile, without thanks. The dark man could not remember hearing the hired man ever uttering a word. Not that he was bothered of course. He just wanted it to be over.*

*The hired man stopped across the road. His face, as usual, was flat and cold and hard. He simply nodded, once, in the direction of the window they stood at. Then he sauntered casually off. Across the rainswept Square. Gone.*

*The dark man turned excitedly to the Guardian.*

*'Is that it?' he asked. 'Am I safe now?'*

*His Guardian nodded.*

*'You are safe. He has been stopped. Although I still think you should have let me do it.'*

*The Guardian turned and left the drawing room, leaving the dark man alone. He sank into a chair, suddenly exhausted by his night-long vigil.*

*Safe. His secrets safe. Thank God, his secrets safe.*

*The dark man looked across the room to the table, where a leather-bound ledger lay. The Guardian had been right in telling him to extract the signatures of his associates. It had come in very handy in ensuring they all took collective responsibility for hiring the silent man and ensuring their continuing silence. He stood and went over to the ledger, picking it up and stroking it. He sighed, a tired sigh.*

*He had better find somewhere safe to keep this. Who knew, he might need it again someday.*

*Villiers retired.*

\*

'This ledger,' said Handy, holding up the file, 'contains information about some of the most influential and important men in this city. I believe those men have been involved in sexual deviancy, prostitution and murder. I need to get this to Mr Jarman to look over. I need his brain. However, Rose, it contains things that may have already led to the deaths of several people. The fact that it is in my possession means that I may be in danger too. I want to go to Bond Street to see Jarman. I am no longer an Inspector, I'm just a civilian, but I may be a civilian in the utmost danger and I would be most grateful if you would accompany me to Bond Street and to protect me, as is the duty you have sworn to undertake.'

Rose put his drink down and straightened, his face grave. Handy held up his hand.

'Before you agree to help me, George, you must know that I acquired this ledger tonight through nefarious means. By which, I mean I burgled Villiers's factory and half-inched it.' Rose blanched. 'As an officer of the Metropolitan Police, you have every right to arrest me and take me into custody. If you do, I believe I will be dead before the sun comes up tomorrow, just like Robert Clinch. So, I won't come quietly. Do you understand what I am saying to you?'

Rose took this information in, his face paler than it had already been when he came in.

'Of course, sir,' he said.

'Then what's your answer?'

'Sir, I will help you in any way I can.' A sly look fell upon him. 'Anyway, how do I know you've been sacked? How would I have heard about Pence doing that? I came here on your orders and followed your instructions believing you still to be my Inspector. Didn't I.'

A smile spread across the likeable, craggy face of Jonas Handy.

'Rose,' he said. 'You are going to make a fine detective one day.'

They toasted each other and drank.

Then the door crashed open in a welter of splintering wood, and three men rushed into the house.

*

Villiers screamed aloud in anger. Anger and fear. He tore off his hat and held his mortified face in his hands. He and his Guardian were in the office at the factory. And they had discovered something terrible.

Villiers had been so happy only that afternoon. Those men, those awful men Handy and Jarman; they were finished. They had nothing. Grundy had told him, over a very pleasant late lunch that the men had nowhere to go with the investigation. Pence had even sacked Handy! The man was finished, as he deserved. How dare he go to his house. How dare he talk to The Wife!

Villiers wondered what The Wife had said to them, his lips curling into a sneer of contempt. What had she said to Jarman? He had seen the looks between them when they first met. He knew the man had visited the house in Dorking. What had they got up to there? Being the man he was, Villiers imagined all sorts of things.

However, it no longer mattered. Everything was fine. The club would perhaps have to close its doors again for a while, as it had after the last little problem, but that was all. His reputation was spared yet again. God was once more shining down His merciful and golden smile upon him.

Villiers had called on the Guardian, and together they had agreed that his plan was for the best. They must destroy the ledger; it was too dangerous now. Yes, it possibly left him a little more exposed, but there was no other choice. The time had come. Villiers had smiled happily at his Guardian as they rode to the

203

factory. The so-called evidence that Ely had acquired would never see the light of day, Lyon would see to that. And Bennet, Pence's useful man, had already stopped Ely, Clinch and that toothless hag from ever speaking again. Pence had also made sure the bodies of those women had disappeared.

Now all he needed was the assurance from his Guardian that it would end. No more torn women. No more warning letters. He had looked deep into the eyes of his blond Guardian.

'You promise?' he asked. 'No more? You will do no more?'

The blond man smiled back at him.

'No more,' he lied.

Villiers smiled, happily. He had the promise. His Guardian had made mistakes, but there would be no more, and this time he would protect his Guardian as his Guardian had protected him so many times in the past. He could not be angry for what had happened. Even as the killings were taking place, the Guardian had sent the letter to warn Ely off when the reporter believed he was the killer. His Guardian always tried to protect him.

The others would never know the real truth. None of them even cared, so long as their reputations were left untouched. Everything would be fine because he had the promise. His Guardian had always told him the truth. He smiled again at the blond man, and he smiled back at him.

Then he had strode into the office and bent down to take the ledger from its secret space.

And everything had changed.

He screamed his frustration.

'It's gone!' he wailed. The public Villiers—the upright, outstanding philanthropist—disappeared in an instant. Gone was the calm, collected man of business, and only a fearful, tearful boy remained.

His Guardian quickly checked the locker, and then they both searched the rest of the office frantically, from top to bottom. It was no use. The ledger was gone.

It was the blond man who took the lead. Hadn't he always?

'Don't worry,' he soothed. 'Don't worry. I will fix it. Have I not always fixed it for you?'

Villiers nodded, weeping like a petulant child.

'Then let me handle it as I've always handled it.'

He gently lifted his head and Villiers saw the eagerness in his eyes.

'Let me fix it,' his Guardian begged.

And Villiers nodded his consent.

\*

Handy dived towards the dresser he had laid the revolver on. He grabbed it and turned as one of the men who had just kicked down his door fired his own weapon. The bullet tore into the shelf of the dresser an inch above Handy's head, blasting splinters into his face. He snatched a shot at the man who had fired, but saw his own bullet instead miss its mark and crack into the wall. The man ducked and Handy dived under the kitchen table and immediately fired again, shooting the man in the shin. The attacker screamed and fell to the kitchen floor in front of him, and Handy fired twice more into the prone body. The attacker stretched his arms wide with a moan, as if he were waking from a restful sleep, and then lay still.

Rose, meanwhile, had grabbed another of the attackers and was trying to wrestle the revolver from the man's hands. The interloper was much bigger and stronger than the constable, however, and Handy, scrambling to his feet, could see he was losing the battle. Rose had both hands grasped around the man's wrist, but the barrel was slowly coming down towards his face. Handy lifted the revolver and was about to shoot when he caught something scything towards him out of the corner of his eye, and ducked just as a knife flashed over his head.

He stumbled backwards from his attacker, but the man advanced quickly, the knife hissing through the air in a whirl of steel and death.

Handy lurched across a chair that had been knocked over by the sudden bedlam in his kitchen and slammed to the stone floor, the wind going out of him in a great whoosh of air.

Bennet allowed himself a rare grin as he saw Handy crash to the floor. He reversed his grip on the knife in his hand and dropped down heavily onto Handy's body, his knee slamming into the Inspector's stomach. His bandaged left hand reached for the gun in Handy's grasp and the knife in his right hand came down.

He was suddenly knocked flying as the other attacker crashed into him. More by luck than judgement, Rose had managed to wrap a foot around his assailant's leg and pushed him over. The man smashed into Bennet and the two of them floundered in a cursing tangle of arms and legs on top of Handy, who suddenly found his gun arm free and a head right in front of him. He lowered his revolver and fired.

The bullet punched clear through the top of the assailant's skull, blasting his lower jaw away so that it hung for a second, like a door with a broken hinge. He grunted once then slumped, his blood soaking both Handy and Bennet, who now managed to kick himself away from the corpse.

Rose was on him in an instant, grasping his knife hand and fumbling for the truncheon in his belt. Bennet backhanded him, a hard punch in the face, and Rose's head rocked back. Handy, still trying to extricate himself from the dead man on top of him, aimed again and fired the last round in his chamber. He completely missed the head he was aiming at, but the bullet drilled a neat hole through the already bandaged palm of Bennet's left hand, causing him to yelp like a kicked dog.

Bennet cradled his ruptured hand, taking in his chances in an instant.

Rose was clambering upright, his nose bleeding and a look of murder in his young eyes. He was again trying to pull out the truncheon stuck in his belt. Handy had reversed the revolver and swung it at Bennet's leg, but he jumped backwards quickly. It was over. He knew he could not win here today. His two compatriots were dead, he was wounded, and he faced two burly professional policemen who would be onto him in another second. Handy was already heaving himself out from under the corpse of the man he had shot. There was only one option.

Bennet ran.

He vaulted the still kneeling Rose and pelted out of the broken doorway into the night.

Handy shouted at Rose, 'Get after him!'

Rose hauled himself to his feet and ran out of the door after Bennet, wiping his bleeding nose on his sleeve. Handy eventually hauled the corpse off him and yanked open the drawer of the dresser, grabbing a box of ammunition. Then he was off and out the door too.

He saw Rose pelting down the street and sprinted after him. He quickly caught up with him and they saw Bennet disappear around the corner.

They ran after him, as fast as their legs could carry them.

*

Susannah Villiers heard the outside door open and a demure greeting from Ellie. It must be her husband, returning at last.

She steeled herself for the confrontation, as she always did when he came home, but especially this day. Did Thomas know she had spoken to Inspector Handy and Dr Jarman? What would he do to her if he did?

Susannah hated to be in his presence. She could barely believe that once she had been excited when he called. When her father had told her that he had asked for her hand in marriage, she had been as giddy as any young girl could have been by the attentions of a tall, handsome, rich suitor.

How those feeling had changed so quickly. How the dream had soured.

He had never been warm towards her. Right from the start, right from the time she first entered their marital home, she had felt nothing but an icy resignation from him, as if she were in his way somehow. As if she were just something he had to put up with. As if she were simply a possession that he thought he should have owned to try and show he was normal. She had asked him once, when it had become obvious what he was, why he had pursued her in the first place. Why had he wanted to marry her?

He had answered by telling her that it was because it was the right thing to do. She knew then that he did not love her. He had simply married her because she had been available and because it was what society expected. She was merely a disguise, hiding his true nature from the world.

Perhaps this would have been all right, but the awful, callow advances he had occasionally made towards her were a long way from what she had envisioned as a young girl reading novels of handsome lords and dainty wives.

He had seemed to want to get these fumbling advances out of the way as quickly as possible, and of course, on those two or three occasions, she had seen what her presence meant to him. As soon as the act was over, he had slinked from her presence. As if she disgusted him.

After that, it had been the razor blades and the knives. He seemed to enjoy watching the fear in her eyes as he moved the blades across her nightdress, to finally leave her, physically unmarked but with her attire in rags and her naked body curled away from his leering eyes.

Susannah shuddered. At least those occasions had seemed to satisfy him, for he usually left her alone after that, retreating back into the cool aloofness he usually held her in. And for this at least, she was thankful. The retreats to Dene Manor had become a lifeline for her, and for her young ward, Ellie, whom she knew was also a target of her husband's strange vices and whom she had sworn to herself she would protect from him. It was all she could really do.

She knew he was doing similar things with the women he and his friends brought back to his house when she was not there; the discarded, torn clothes she had sometimes found lying around proved that. But Susannah had simply come to believe that this was perhaps what love really was. It was women doing what men told them to do. She really had no say in the matter. The disgust she felt towards her husband, she also felt for herself. For a long time she had truly believed that her husband's coldness was her fault and that all men must be the same. When she had found out she was pregnant, she had felt nothing of the joy she should have. Instead, the news was like another door closing her in her cage. She would never be free of him.

And then Doctor Carter Jarman had appeared in her life. She had seen the look on his face when he had spoken to her so briefly, she knew he felt something towards her, for she was not a stupid woman. More importantly, however, she also knew what *she* felt when she was in his presence. He was so different from the man fate had joined her with. He was warm and caring and he genuinely seemed to care for her. Care *about* her. The smile on his face was sincere, not the mask Thomas Villiers used to cover his own dark soul. Jarman was a good man. Something she had started to believe did not exist. She wondered what being *his* wife would be like.

She was broken from her reverie by a strange sound. It was a muted thump, coming from just behind the drawing room door. She frowned.

'Ellie?' she called. No answer. Outside the lamp-lit room, the street was dark and her reflection stared back at her. It suddenly looked very frightened.

'Thomas?' she asked, quieter now. The silence that greeted this was ominous. It seemed to press against her body, tightening her chest, making it difficult for her to breathe.

'Who's there?' she whispered.

The door slowly opened, and Susannah saw the crumpled body of Ellie, lying motionless in the hall.

And the man standing over her.

# Chapter Twenty-Six

## A Startling Revelation

Carter Jarman sat with his eyes closed, his fingers steepled under his chin. The study was lit by a single lamp that hissed quietly beside him and the shades were drawn against the night outside. A casual viewer may have assumed he was sleeping, so still was he, but a line of concentration marred his forehead. Jarman was indeed awake. Awake and thinking.

He turned everything over and over in his head, trying to store away the anger and horror he felt for what Susannah Villiers had gone through at the hands of her husband, the years she must have spent tiptoeing around her house in fear of the creature she had married, the wasted years of her youth.

Instead, he ticked everything off that he had encountered over the last few weeks, the unspeakable horror of those murdered women, which spoke of a mind unhinged. The person who had committed those murders was a soul from hell. He was evil.

Was Villiers that man? He certainly fitted the bill. A man who enjoyed pain, who enjoyed seeing blood; indeed, who took sexual gratification from causing that pain and injury.

Then there were the other murders, and in Jarman's mind they were completely separate. The killing of Edward Ely, Robert Clinch and Grace Wright were the actions of evil, yes, but of a cold and calculating evil: a professional killer who did his heinous work for a fee rather than for personal gratification.

The letter Ely had received. The paper it was written on linked it to the murders, but was it from the Ripper? And if it was, was it the Ripper who had killed the three prostitutes in such a vicious way? Or was it merely a ruse by the cold assassin, using the Ripper's shadow to stop Ely from digging into Villiers's affairs even further?

He sighed quietly to himself as he thought the matter through, but Susannah Villiers kept pushing her way into his thoughts, mixed up with images of Mary, both of them swirling in a confused, twisting kaleidoscope of images of butchered corpses and dark, festering brick-walled alleyways. His breathing deepened as sleep began to overtake him. He thought again of when he had met Susannah Villiers.

And his eyes snapped open.

He remembered walking in the garden at Dene Manor and asking Susannah how long her husband had been saving the women from the streets by giving them jobs at the match factory.

'Since before we were married, I believe,' she had answered. 'Which was in 1887.'

Jarman stood and took a cigarette from his case, lighting it and standing by the table.

Jarman and Susannah were married three years ago. The parties had no doubt been going on since at least then, probably longer. A year after they married, the Ripper had struck in his autumn of terror, and then he had disappeared, seemingly back to hell where he had no doubt sprung from.

Any of those men on Grace's list could be the killer. Any of them.

Had he been on the wrong trail all along? Had his dislike of Villiers blinded him to the truth that Villiers associated with men just as evil, just as twisted as himself? Wealthy men? Men who could pay large amounts of money to put right a mistake one of them made? That they all signed their names to?

Jarman put out the stub of his cigarette and immediately lit another.

Had Jack the Ripper been an original member of Villiers's club? And had the club then taken matters into their own hands to hide their filthy secret when he started to fulfil his twisted fantasies away from the safety of Villiers's house?

Is that why the Ripper had never been caught? Was it because he could never have *been* caught? Had the Ripper been murdered himself?

This thought was incredible, but it seemed to Jarman to make perfect sense. The way the murders had escalated, the growing brutality leading to the horror he had witnessed in Millers Court. And then the sudden cessation, the Ripper seemingly disappearing into the mists of London, never to be seen again. Jarman remembered saying to Abberline that the murders would continue until the man was caught, but he had been wrong. The murders had simply stopped. Did they stop because the Ripper himself had been killed? Murdered to protect the men of Villiers's club?

It was an intriguing thought, but more importantly, however, was had it happened again? Were the horrifying new murders the work of another one of Villiers's associates? Another sick, twisted individual who found that he could not keep within the constraints of the club? And were the rest of the members of that club trying, once again, to put right their mistakes by paying a professional to do away with both the killer himself and anyone who knew anything about him?

If he was right, and if they had not completed their mission yet, then there was a psychopath on the loose who knew Thomas Villiers, knew where he lived, and, possibly, knew that he had put a price on his head. What would a man like that do?

Jarman threw the cigarette into the ashtray and grabbed his coat.

'Curmudgeon!' he roared.

And he prayed he was not too late.

*

Susannah awoke to a strange rocking motion. There was an awful, noxious aroma in her nose and she gagged at its smell and the dry, nauseous taste in her mouth.

As consciousness slowly came back to her in waves, Susannah found herself lying on a wooden floor that seemed to be moving and bouncing and jarring her about. She tried to put out her hands to shift her weight, as the floor was banging painfully against her hip, but she found she could not move her arms. With a thrill of terror she realised that her hands were tied in front of her. A huge jolt smacked the floor against her cheek, and she suddenly grasped that she was lying on the flat bed of a cart, covered by what felt like a thick, heavy sheet of tarpaulin.

She tried to open her mouth to scream and wondered why she could not, finally understanding that there was a gag covering her mouth: the reason, perhaps, why that horrible taste was so strong in her mouth. At the same time, she realised that the taste was the after-effects of chloroform. She had once sniffed the anaesthetic at the house of one of her husband's friends in the early years of her marriage, when she still believed she was in love with Villiers. She remembered that the man had laughed at what he believed to be her silly womanly ways as she had wrinkled her nose at the smell. She had time to wonder whether that friend was a member of Thomas's horrible club.

She managed to roll onto her back, the effects of the chloroform drifting away like nebulous smoke. She thought, perhaps, to throw herself from the cart, to run from whoever that man was who had entered her house. She groaned when she remembered the prone body of Ellie, lying in the hallway. Was she dead? Had she failed to keep the girl safe, the one thing she had promised herself she would do?

Susannah tried to kick away the tarpaulin, but it seemed to be weighted down around her. She could not move it. She was trapped in its tight, dark embrace; by a man who had perhaps murdered Ellie and who was now taking her to God-knew-where. For the first time, Susannah felt a paralyzing terror seep through her body. Where was he taking her? And what would he do to her when he got there?

She tried to find some way to work out where she was, listening carefully. The clop of the horse's hooves were ringing on what sounded like stones, and Susannah was sure she could make out a slight echo; perhaps the sound rebounding from houses on either side. She was on a road then, probably still within the confines of London. It all depended, of course, on how long she had been unconscious.

Susannah heaved at the tarpaulin over her body, but whatever was weighing down the edges would not give an inch. Either that or she was still weakened from the effects of the chloroform. Whatever the reason, she could do nothing but lie there, banging and bouncing from the wheels of the cart on the uneven flagstones. She tried instead to work at the covering around her mouth, but it was tight and secure. She could not move and she could not scream. She was trapped.

After what seemed an eternity, she sensed the sound had changed; it grew much louder for a moment and then disappeared, as if the cart had entered a tunnel and was now in an open space. Then it stopped.

She heard someone jump down from the driver's seat at the front, and then footsteps approaching the rear of the cart. Something heavy was pushed to one side and suddenly the tarpaulin was wrenched aside. She found herself staring at the man she had seen standing over Ellie's body.

His face was shadowed by the oversized cap he wore, but in the dim light coming from distant gas lamps, Susannah could make out fair hair and a thick, drooping moustache. The man was of medium height and build. He wore a dark, rough, workman's jacket and trousers with a black waistcoat and a white scarf tied around his neck. As Susannah stared at him, her eyes huge in her terror, the man grinned at her.

'Time to get out,' he said.

*

214

The brougham stopped outside Villiers's house and Jarman leapt out, running up the steps and banging on the door. Curmudgeon joined him a second later. There was no answer and Jarman banged again.

'Mrs Villiers!' he shouted through the letterbox. 'Susannah!'

Curmudgeon stood on his tiptoes and peered into the window. 'No one in the drawing room,' he said.

Jarman tried to open the door but found it locked. He smashed his shoulder against it, ineffectually.

'You'll break your arm before you break that door down,' said Curmudgeon.

'The rear,' said Jarman and sprinted off, turning down a narrow snicket between the row of huge houses. Curmudgeon followed him and they soon found themselves in the large rear yard of the building. A door stood to their right and Jarman tried the handle. It opened in silence on well-oiled hinges. The door led straight into a shadowy kitchen, but Jarman could see light, presumably coming from the hallway through the crack of another door. He quickly checked that the kitchen he was in was free of potential dangers, then stepped lightly across to the half-open door where the light was shining. He peered cautiously around the doorjamb.

He felt Curmudgeon close up against his back and he knew he was facing the way they had come, protecting them from attack from the rear. Without even thinking about it, they had slipped back into their old army habits. Habits that had saved their lives on many occasions in the past. Jarman took a step forward into the hall, pulling his leather, shot-filled cosh from his pocket as he did so, wishing he had a revolver instead. Curmudgeon came with him, still back-to-back, both of them peering around for any signs of ambush.

The hallway was empty, but the house was far too quiet for Jarman's liking. The hallway was well lit and empty and, as Jarman peered into the drawing room, he saw a dwindling fire in the grate, indicating that someone had been there relatively recently. He scanned the drawing room quickly, seeing nothing amiss, and then continued on his way down the hall, his eyes twisting up the large stairway for any attacker that may have lurked there.

They both jumped when they heard the groan. It did not sound human. It was a gurgling, whining moan that set Jarman's teeth on edge, but he was off like a hare as soon as he had located where it had come from.

The first room near the front door, a room he had not entered on either of his last visits, was a front parlour. Inside was a table covered in green lace, a tall lamp, and a settee. The mantelpiece was decorated with figurines. And on the rich Oriental rug in the centre of the room, Ellie lay, crumpled in a heap. The rug was half rolled up under her body, as if she had been dragged there. She moaned again, and then suddenly vomited, loudly and copiously, coughing and gagging at the suddenness of her sickness.

Jarman ran over to her and knelt down, quickly clearing the sick from her throat. Over the stench of the vomit, the sweet, cloying smell of chloroform wafted from the girl's gasping mouth.

Curmudgeon was staring in obvious distress at the sight of the girl.

'Curmudgeon,' said Jarman, but he didn't reply. He was just staring at Ellie, his face white.

'Billy,' said Jarman, gently, and Curmudgeon slowly turned his scarred face towards him.

'Get her some water,' said Jarman and Curmudgeon nodded, running back towards the kitchen.

Jarman raised the girl gently and propped her against the foot of the settee. He stroked her head gently until Curmudgeon came back. He handed the water to Ellie.

'Small sips,' he said. 'Rinse your mouth out carefully and spit the first mouthful out. Then drink.'

Ellie did as she was told, glancing at Jarman with a full mouth. He nodded—the rug was ruined by vomit anyway—and she spat the discoloured water out onto it, seemingly a little pleased at the small act of rebellion, as shocked and confused as she still evidently was.

Jarman quickly checked her over, making sure she was breathing properly, then he held her face in hands.

'Ellie. What happened? Where is Mrs Villiers?'

Ellie coughed and then grimaced at the taste in her mouth. She glanced around the room, seemingly disorientated.

'Ellie,' said Jarman again. 'What happened?'

'There was a knock at the door,' said Ellie, eventually, her voice made husky from the anaesthetic. 'It was a man standing there. He asked for Mrs Villiers. Said he was a friend of Mr Villiers, but I didn't like the look of him. He was in workmen's clothes, and I didn't think Mr Villiers would know many people like that.'

She coughed again, harshly and then retched, expelling air in a jerky fashion. Jarman slapped her on the back until she had regained her breath.

'What did he look like?' asked Jarman.

'He wore a dark suit, a workman's suit, as I said,' said Ellie. 'His cap was pulled down over his face, but he had a moustache and a white scarf.'

'A white scarf?' asked Jarman, remembering the eye-witness account by Jack Macken. 'Ellie, this is very important. What colour was the moustache?'

'Blond,' said Ellie, striking a cold nail through Jarman's heart. 'He was a fair-haired man. I told him to wait at the door and went to get Mrs Villiers, and then…'

'And then you woke up just now,' finished Jarman. Ellie nodded.

Jarman glanced at Curmudgeon and then stood close to the man.

'Go to the station. Tell Mr Handy what has happened, and tell him I think Mrs Villiers has been kidnapped. Tell him to meet me at the factory.'

'The factory?' asked Curmudgeon. 'Why the factory?'

'I believe that is where the man has gone. I think he's looking for Villiers and it's the only place he may be. The factory is where we will find all the answers to our questions.'

Jarman glanced down at the rapidly recovering girl.

'I just hope we're not too late,' he continued. 'I'm taking the brougham. Find a cab and get Handy. Quick as you can.'

He made to leave but Curmudgeon grabbed his arm.

'Hang on,' he said. 'If you're going to the factory then I'm coming with you.'

Jarman shook his arm free.

'I need Handy and the police,' he hissed. 'And I need them now. If I'm right, the man who murdered those women in that despicable manner has got Susannah. If we're not quick, she could end up just like them.'

He glanced down at Ellie and then back at Curmudgeon.

'Get Handy, and get to the factory. I'll meet you there. And tell him to come armed.'

With that, he was gone. Curmudgeon heard the brougham rattle away. He turned to Ellie and lifted her gently, sitting her on the settee.

'Lock all the doors and windows,' he said. 'And I'll get back to you as soon as I can. All right, love?'

He touched her cheek gently and made to leave.

'Mrs Villiers will be all right, won't she?' asked Ellie, fearfully.

Curmudgeon nodded reassuringly at her as he left.

But he really was not sure.

# Chapter Twenty-Seven

## The Factory

Handy stumbled, gasping, to a halt, one hand on the wall of the corner he stood at, the other on his knee as he sucked in huge lungfuls of air. Beside him, leaning against the wall, was Rose. Although younger and fitter than Handy, he too was breathing hard, and he snatched off his helmet and wiped a sleeve over his face that was wet with sweat and smeared with dried blood.

'Where the hell has he disappeared to?' panted Handy, staring about him.

The corner of the narrow street led into the much wider avenue of Mile End Road. At nearly nine at night the road was getting quiet, with only a few pedestrians wandering its dark length.

Rose trotted across to the other side and peered down the road where it gently curved.

'There,' he shouted, pointing.

He pelted off again after the dwindling figure. With a groan, Handy hauled himself after him, his legs shaking and his chest burning.

They continued their pursuit: two red-faced coppers wheezing their way along the thoroughfare, ignoring the astonished looks they received from the odd passers-by.

For a while, the only noise was their laboured panting and the slapping of their boots on the pavement. The assassin was still a good way ahead of them. He must have been a fit man, but he had been wounded and Handy could see he was tiring too.

He reckoned they had run about two miles now. They had seen no other coppers on the whole of their journey, and so they had simply continued to chase down the man who had tried to kill them both. By the time they were halfway up Mile End Road they had all slowed to little more than a brisk walk. Handy gripped the newly reloaded revolver in his pocket and just wished the man would give up. Then he could shoot the bastard and they could all have a rest.

They saw the assassin disappear around another corner up ahead and, despite their exhaustion, they re-doubled their efforts. When they turned the corner, however, Handy realised where the man was heading. It made perfect sense.

Up ahead, showing as a black silhouette in front of the newly risen moon, Villiers's factory loomed like a haunted house in a ghost story.

Handy stopped again, getting his breath back now that he knew where the man was going.

He was running to get paid. It was obviously Villiers who had set him onto Handy. Villiers and Pence, of course. And now the killer was wanting his fee and probably had his thoughts set on nothing more than jumping on the first ship out of England. That was what Handy would do in his situation.

When his breathing had got down to something resembling normal, he walked up to the factory entrance, staring up at the huge, locked wooden gates.

Rose joined him.

'Do you think he's in there, sir?' asked Rose.

'I do. The question is, though, how did he get in?'

He set off around the corner and down the narrow alley he had gone down earlier, stopping by the side gate. He had re-locked it when he had left earlier, and the bars of the gate fitted snugly into the wall which was at least twenty feet high, so they could not simply climb over it. Handy patted his waistcoat pocket, realising he had left his picklock at home along with his jacket and his hat. He'd left the broken door to his house wide open too. Probably been burgled by now. He sighed.

'We need another way in,' he said.

They circled the outside of the factory, walking all the way round the enclosing brick wall, but the only other gates they found at the rear of the factory were as high as the ones at the front. They soon found themselves back where they started.

'He must have had a key,' said Handy. 'It's the only way he can be inside.' He peered up at the spikes on the top of the main gates and then turned back to the constable. He quickly sized up Rose.

'How tall are you?'

He grinned at Rose as it dawned on the constable what he meant.

\*

The blond-haired man pushed Susannah ahead of him. The cart had been parked at the rear of the building, accessed through an archway from the lane behind the factory, the gates of which were now bolted closed. The door that the man told her to go through opened into the factory. Susannah had only been there a couple of times, as she had never liked the place. She stared around her, awed by its vast scale.

Just in front of her stood the huge steam piston that powered the belts and the machinery, brooding in its silence. It was twenty feet of heavy, oily iron. Susannah looked down over the rail and into the pit where the knuckle of the piston pumped up and down, and shuddered. The sight of that dark hole and the thought of the piston charging down into it made her feel slightly sick.

The man pushed her again and told her to climb the metal staircase that led to a maintenance office above the factory floor. The staircase opened onto a narrow metal gangway with chain guardrails that led to the office. Similar gangways radiated out from the maintenance office, which sat like the centre of a spider's web above the pit of the machinery. As the man pushed Susannah along the swaying, terrifying gangplank, she spied the spider himself. She should have known her husband was behind her kidnapping, but the reality of her new situation caused another flash of ice to flood through her body.

Villiers sat on a chair beside the solitary card table in the middle of the room. His face was pale and drawn, and he stood when Susannah was pushed into the office. The blond man closed the door behind him.

'Susannah,' murmured Villiers, after a pause.

Susannah tried to gauge what emotions, if any, were showing on her husband's face but she found it was impossible. They changed constantly. He seemed to be one moment on the verge of a grin, the next about to weep, then he would flush scarlet and looked to be on the threshold of an incendiary rage. And all the time his black eyes danced around the room, never still for an instant. Susannah had often thought her husband to be mad. This night, she was in no doubt. Thomas Villiers was completely deranged.

'Won't you sit down?' he asked, those mad eyes jumping all over, and his face twitching. Susannah saw that sweat was beaded on his face, dripping down from his jaw. She managed to shake her head at him.

'Sit!' he screamed at her and she jumped. Tears of terror were in her eyes and her heart felt as if it were trying to break out of her chest. The blond man grabbed her shoulders and pushed her into the seat Villiers had vacated.

Villiers tried to smile, but it came out as a crooked broken sneer.

'Where is it?' he asked mildly, although his voice was trembling in some sort of supressed, violent emotion.

Susannah tried to speak, but her voice caught in her throat. She tried again.

'Where is what?'

Villiers was breathing hard. He licked his lips as he stared at her. He seemed to be trying very hard to keep himself under control.

'Why, the ledger, darling,' he said.

'Thomas, I don't…'

Susannah yelped as he leant forward and slapped her hard

across the face. Her head was then yanked back to face him as he grabbed her jaw. He held a finger up in warning.

'Don't,' he said. 'Don't lie. I do not have the time. I want to know where the ledger is. The one your lover persuaded you to steal from me.'

Susannah's head was spinning from the blow. What was he talking about? What ledger? What lover?

'Thomas, I would tell you everything, if I knew what you wanted. I have no knowledge of any ledger, and I certainly do not have a lover. I do not know what you want from me.'

The last words were a moan of fear and incomprehension and Villiers's face twisted with sadistic rage again. He raised his hand once more, this time with his fingers curled into a fist, but managed to stop himself, seemingly with great effort. He took a deep breath and turned away from her, staring out at the huge, dark space of the factory.

'I took you away from that country hovel,' he said. 'I gave you money. I gave you status. I gave you everything a gentleman could give, and you turn away from me for a surgeon. A common surgeon.'

'Jarman?' asked Susannah, confused. 'You think Carter Jarman and I are lovers?' Despite her predicament, Susannah was starting to feel the first touch of anger. 'You did not take me away from anything, and you are certainly not a gentleman. I have money of my own. I have a house of my own. You know this to be true. I have not taken a lover, Thomas, although, as God is my witness, we both know I have the right to do so after the way you have treated me! You are a fiend! You were never a husband. You are a monster, Thomas. A monster!'

Villiers turned and looked at her, and Susannah suddenly knew he was going to kill her. She would die, there, in a dirty office in a match factory in Mile End. And she would die at the hands of the man she had once, long ago, loved. Susannah shrank away from his demonic glare.

Then a voice spoke behind her. She had almost forgotten about the man who had brought her here, so engrossed had she been in talking to her mad husband, but the voice brought about a fresh wave of terror. A terror that threatened her very sanity.

'Let me do it,' the voice said.

Because it was not the same voice the man had used when he had ordered her out of the cart.

Susannah turned and stared as the man removed his cap, revealing his face. Then he slowly pulled at the blond moustache, and it came away in his hand. Finally, he pulled off a blond wig, revealing long, pinned-up hair as black as Villiers's, stained with its familiar—terrifyingly familiar—streak of grey.

Where the blond man had stood, Amelia Villiers now stared at Susannah. And her black eyes were as mad as her brother's.

'Let me do it,' she repeated.

# Chapter Twenty-Eight

## The Revelation

### London
### August 31ˢᵗ 1890

*The room stank of sweat and unwashed clothes. The small, single-paned window was grimed and cracked and weary yellow light fought to enter it, leaving the room awash with shadows. From beyond that window came the tinkle of piano music and the sound of coarse laughing and shouting. Occasionally there was the sound of a glass or bottle being dropped and the sudden roar of an energetic crowd as another fistfight started. Villiers, who lay on the lumpy, stinking bed, smiled to himself. He was home.*

*The room that he lay in was bare and cold and less than eight-foot square. It contained only the bed on which he lolled, naked, and a scarred and faded dresser, in front of which sat a woman brushing her hair, peering at her reflection in the cheap, fly-blown mirror.*

*The shadows of the room meant that Villiers could make out only a silhouette: thick, tangled hair that hung down the woman's back, and the rounded shape of her shoulders. Like the man, the woman was naked, and he stared at her flattened buttocks as she sat on the hard, cold stool.*

*In the filtered light from the lamp outside, the woman's body was softened and smoothed, but Villiers knew better. He knew that her breasts were as flat as her nose that had been broken by someone many years ago. He knew her stomach was furrowed and puckered with the scars of the dead children she had produced. He knew her breath stank like a sewer. Yes. He knew Eliza Cotton.*

*And this was what he wanted. What he required. The parties, the get-togethers, the men who came to indulge in their little fantasies. They would never know his reality. They would never feel what he felt, because they were not like him. The women they used at his house were washed and cleaned, for the men who formed his little club did not want what the dark man wanted. They did not know the pleasures of the filth as Villiers did.*

*Sometimes, just sometimes, he found himself needing his old hunting grounds. And the dank pleasures they provided. And this particular woman would be easier to persuade. She had already partaken in his vices before at his house.*

*Eliza eventually turned from the mirror and smiled an ugly smile at him, her teeth even more yellow than usual because of the lamp light. She went to the bed and stood over him, bending so her thick but greasy hair brushed against his stomach. Her smile became wider when she saw the effect this had on his body.*

*'Closer,' he whispered, and she did as she was asked. He had paid her for the night and she was in a good mood. She would be in gin for a fortnight after tonight. Even though she had left the factory when she had been to a few of the parties, the unexpected arrival of Villiers and the money he had shown her had persuaded her to allow him his twisted fantasies once more. At least she knew what to expect now.*

*His left hand touched and stroked the woman's hair for a while as it caressed his naked stomach, before gently lifting her head. His other hand moved to the pocket of his jacket, folded neatly on the dusty floor. His fingers closed around the object he sought and he slowly lifted it into his and Eliza's line of sight.*

*She gazed at the knife with a sudden trepidation. He grinned at her.*

*'Sometimes, one needs an extra experience,' he said, quietly. 'Sometimes, one needs something more. But of course, you know that already.'*

*With this, he placed the blade of the small but razor-sharp knife onto his forearm. He drew it slowly across as the woman watched, blearily, still half addled by her earlier drinking session.*

*Villiers sighed as the old, familiar pain came to him, and his eyes gleamed as he watched the blood trickle down his arm, over the old wounds. He drew the knife across his arm again. His left hand still rubbed her hair between his fingers.*

*With a jerk of his head, Eliza did as she was asked, straddling the man and mounting him professionally. She began to move backwards and forwards, for Villiers had made it clear he wanted things to be slow, not rushed like her usual customers who could not wait to finish their business and then get themselves back to wherever it was they came from.*

*Villiers drew the knife across his arm a third time as Eliza moved above him, hissing with the pleasure only pain could bring him. He showed his bleeding arm to the woman and smiled as she peered at it closely in the gloom.*

*'Sergeant's stripes,' he said to her, grinning.*

*Eliza grimaced at what she knew was coming and rode him harder. She went about her business, wanting this night to simply be over now.*

*'Your turn,' said Villiers, and Eliza suddenly stopped, her eyes turning fearful.*

*'You said no more than three,' she said. 'I already have your marks upon me. Only three.'*

*His smile widened.*

*'No more than three. We can be sergeants together. Just like at the house. Don't stop.'*

*Frightened now, the woman resumed her movements and the pain, when it did come, was not as bad as she feared. He made a line across her dirty thigh, just above a few similar, older marks, and it stung, but the cut was not deep. Just like the last times. Two more to go.*

*Unseen to both of them, the door to the room slowly opened and a shadowy figure peered inside.*

*Eliza began to move faster, hoping to get it over with, but the man seemed to have a huge stamina. He cut her again, this time across the other thigh, and again the pain was slight. The woman closed her eyes. Come on, she thought. Do the last one. Get it over with.*

*Villiers' eyes suddenly bulged as he felt himself building to climax, and then something came into his line of vision. It was a black shape in the gloomy room and it rose up behind the writhing woman atop him. Villiers saw the glint of metal in the lamplight. He saw the figure grab the woman by the hair and yank her head back. He saw the blade flash down and across.*

*The knife was so sharp it sliced through Eliza's throat with barely a tremble. She gasped and bucked above him, and the blood spurted everywhere.*

*The blood sprayed all around him and over him. Eliza grasped at her torn throat and stared at him with horror as her gore flowed through her fingers. He was still inside her when those eyes faded and she was a corpse, and he was enveloped in scarlet. Everything became silent. The blood dripped and pooled.*

*For a second, Villiers just stared at the dead woman above him. He began to whine in terror when she hit the floor with a thump and the dark figure who had murdered her gasped aloud. Villiers jumped from the bed, catching sight of a blood-soaked monster in the mirror over the dresser, eyes wide and staring from a vermilion visage.*

*He stared at the face of Eliza's killer and he collapsed to his knees, collecting more of the woman's blood from the huge puddle where it still poured from her neck.*

*'What have you done?' he whispered. 'Oh God, what have you done?'*

*Villiers felt nothing for the poor, poverty-stricken woman he had just seen murdered. He thought not at all about what life had brought her, for her to die in blood-soaked savagery in a broken-down rented room in Whitechapel having sex with a stranger for money. His thoughts were only for himself.*

*'Why did you do that?' he asked, his voice a shocked croak. 'Why?'*

*His sister licked her lips, a look of almost sexual pleasure on her white face. She grinned at Villiers.*

*'Because I need to,' she replied.*

\*

'What the hell are you talking about?' roared Curmudgeon.

The desk sergeant blanched at the huge man's fury, but held his ground. He tried to assert his authority but quailed beneath the look on Curmudgeons battered face.

'It's what I heard,' he repeated. 'Inspector Handy is no longer, erm, an Inspector. One of the lads came in from Scotland Yard and said it was all over the place. Apparently, Jonas walked out of Pence's office with a face like thunder. No one's seen him since.'

Curmudgeon treated the sergeant to a varied and choice stream of army-learned curses and then turned away. He went outside and stared around the black streets. The place was already full of the night people: the pickpockets, the drunkards, the dollymops. Whitechapel was readying itself for another night of debauchery. Curmudgeon cursed again, loudly and fluently, earning an admiring cheer from a passing prostitute. He pulled out his watch. Twenty-five past nine. He couldn't wait. Jarman had gone to the factory and Handy was nowhere to be found, so he had no choice. He hailed a passing hansom and climbed in.

'Mile End,' he growled to the driver.

\*

Jarman arrived at the factory gates just in time to find Rose clambering dangerously from Handy's shoulders, one leg half over the spiked tops of the gates, straining and trembling. Handy was giving him encouragement from the safety of the ground. Jarman pulled the brougham over and jumped down, running over to Handy.

'Where's Curmudgeon?' he asked.

'He's not here. What's happened?'

Jarman quickly explained. 'The killer has Susannah,' he said.

Handy cursed.

'Me and young Rose had some visitors tonight,' he said. 'Two of them are still at my house and the other one came here. The two at my house won't be going anywhere. Pence sacked me, by the way.'

'What?'

Handy nodded.

'So I came here earlier this evening and found this.' Handy pulled out the small ledger from his trouser pocket.

Jarman quickly skimmed through it, grimacing at some of the descriptions.

'Look at the back,' said Handy.

Jarman did as he was asked and nodded to himself. He then flicked through the rest of the ledger and, with just a glance at one of the other pages, his faced paled in the moonlight. He suddenly realised he had been wrong. He had been so, so wrong.

'Oh my God,' he whispered.

'What?' asked Handy. 'What is it?'

Jarman wordlessly handed over the ledger, pointing to the page where Villiers had entered his private thoughts.

'We already knew that we were looking for two killers, and the one who killed the women is here somewhere, I'm sure of it. They took Susannah. The other killer is one of those men who attacked you tonight.'

'I don't see what you mean,' said Handy.

'They're covering their tracks, as I said earlier,' said Jarman, glancing up at the balancing Rose, who had managed to get his leg over the spikes at the top of the gates. With a grunt of relief, he managed to get the other one fully over, lessening the chance of doing himself a mischief.

'But I was wrong, Handy. I've been an idiot. All along, I thought that the murderer of those women was Villiers. I thought he killed those three girls because whatever was going on at the house was no longer enough for his deranged mind.'

Jarman shook his head at the moon.

'But I then deduced that it might have been another member.

They're all as mad as each other as far as I can tell. I think that was what happened the last time; I think I was right about that,' he continued, still shaking his head in disbelief. 'The man who killed Ely and the others: he was hired by the club to stop this rogue agent then. Two years ago.'

Handy stared at him.

'The Ripper?' he asked. 'You think they killed off the Ripper?'

Jarman nodded as Rose eventually disappeared behind the huge wooden gates. They heard his feet hit the floor on the other side.

'I do. And I believe they were successful. That was why the Ripper just vanished. Pence's man killed him. They got rid of any evidence that connected the Ripper, their former club associate, with them and their twisted ways.'

Jarman stared at the gates as they heard Rose's muffled curses as he tried to open them.

'But I was wrong about these new killings,' he said. 'I'm a fool. A damned fool. And my stupidity may just have got Susannah Villiers killed. This new killer; it's not someone from the club. But it is someone who knows about it. Villiers's "Guardian". She is the one who killed the three girls.'

'She?' asked Handy. 'What the hell are you talking about?'

Jarman once more pointed to the ledger, and to the front cover. Handy had seen it when he had read the ledger at his house, but the importance of it had not registered. His eyes widened now when he saw what Jarman meant.

The handwritten words simply stated that the ledger belonged to the factory. They read, *Property of Villiers FireSticks. Employment Records for the use of Miss Amelia Villiers.*

But it was not what they said that made Handy's eyes widen. It was the writing itself. It matched exactly the writing on the "Ripper note" left in Edward Ely's workplace. He stared at Jarman.

'Amelia Villiers is this "Guardian" he writes about?' he asked, aghast. '*She* is the new Ripper?'

'Yes,' said Jarman, grimly, still waiting impatiently for the gates to open. 'That's why I have been a fool. I allowed myself to believe what all men stupidly believe. That women are somehow a weaker sex than men; that a woman could not harbour the hatred and spite and madness that a man can. I have indeed been an idiot.'

'But the description that Jack Macken gave us…' started Handy.

'A disguise in all likelihood,' replied Jarman. 'Ellie, Susannah's ward, gave the same description: "A man of about five foot six".'

He turned back to Handy.

'How tall do you think Amelia Villiers is?'

'But the strength to do what she did to those women,' said Handy, unwilling to believe a woman could do so much damage to another human being. 'No woman could do that.'

'That is where we were both wrong, Handy,' said Jarman. 'Madness can give anyone, man or woman, almost preternatural strength.' Jarman turned back to the gates as they heard a cry of success from Rose, and the gates were pulled inwards.

'Amelia Villiers is mad,' he continued. 'Completely and utterly. And her brother is too. And with Susannah caught between the two of them, I do not hold out much hope for her survival.'

Rose pulled the gate open wider.

'Don't forget that other one is here as well,' Handy reminded them as they started running across the yard. 'The one who killed Ely and the other two. God knows what he will do about it all.'

Jarman didn't answer, and they were halfway across the wide yard when a rumbling, squealing noise caused them to pause. The noise grew louder and a trembling began under their feet.

Handy and Jarman turned to each other.

'The engine,' said Handy.

They ran towards the factory doors.

\*

Susannah almost fainted as Amelia Villiers unveiled herself in place of the man who had kidnapped her. However, there was a part of her that was not surprised. She had always suspected that the woman was as deranged as her brother, and she had been proved right. But why dress like a man? Why bring her here? What catastrophe had her connection to this strange family got her into?

Amelia took off the scarf and pulled at a corset that had flattened her bust and given her the shape of a man. She still wore the shirt and trousers, and she grinned at Susannah as she unloosened her hair.

'Surprise,' she taunted, quietly.

Susannah turned to Villiers for an explanation, utterly bewildered by what was going on, but he was just smiling at his sister.

'My angel,' he said. 'My Guardian Angel.'

Susannah frowned at him. It seemed like she had been dropped into the evil madness of one of the Poe novels she had recently been reading. She was totally and utterly confused by what was going on around her.

'All my life, I have relied on one person,' explained Villiers to her, dreamily. 'All my life I have *had* only one person. The person who has looked after me. The person who fixes my silly little mistakes. The only person in the world who loves me. My sister. My Guardian Angel.'

Villiers sat on the desk near Susannah, who strained against the bonds tying her hands. Villiers had undergone another transformation; his previous obsession with some mysterious ledger was gone now as if it had never existed. Instead, his demeanour was pitiful and pious. He gazed at his sister as if she were a golden goddess come down to earth.

'Did I ever tell you about The Father?' he asked Susannah, who managed to shake her head, fearfully.

'Oh, he was a great man. A great man. But like all great men, he had his little pleasures in life, and sometimes he had to put right the mistakes of his family. Especially me. I am afraid I made lots of mistakes.'

Villiers grinned down at her, but his eyes were blank and his voice was dull as he seemed to stare into the past.

'I was lustful, you see,' he continued. 'I lusted constantly. So

The Father punished me. He showed me what my lustfulness meant. He showed those girls, those stupid, fat, callow *bitches* who served his family what it meant to be the master of the house. He made me watch. And I learned. I learned so much. How to be cruel. How to be decisive. How the sting of the cut can heighten the emotions, make the blood run hot. Just how good pain and terror can feel. He taught me everything he knew.'

Villiers suddenly barked a harsh laugh.

'But always, afterwards, it was my Guardian who came to me. Who looked after me. Our mother was dead, you see, but I can still remember my Guardian and myself lying with her, both of us stroking her hair; how she loved it when we did that. But then of course, she abandoned us. She died. As everything dies. As The Father himself died.'

He laughed again and glanced at Amelia who was smiling too.

'Do you remember when he died?'

She nodded.

'Of course, you do. We were together, were we not, and he was hurting me again. I deserved it, no doubt. But he was in a foul temper that day, even more so than usual. He beat me and beat me and beat me, until I could barely see straight.'

He laughed, humourlessly at this memory, and Susannah frowned in disgust and horror at a silver thread of drool that slinked from his lips. His eyes glittered with malevolence.

'I saw my Guardian, though,' he continued. 'She swept into the room, and within a minute The Father was dead at our feet. I remember standing in his blood. It was warm.'

Villiers licked the line of drool away.

'It was decided that The Father had committed suicide; the knife was still lodged in the side of his throat, you see, and my Guardian had wrapped his dead fingers around the handle before we screamed for help. She always knew what to do. And two small children could never have been involved in anything so awful as murder, could they? My Guardian stayed with me as we moved around and I built up my fortune. And she stayed with me as I

234

enjoyed all the things The Father had shown me. She was always there, in the shadows. Watching and protecting.'

He seemed to suddenly remember who he was speaking to, and he shrugged.

'I won't go into every detail, my darling wife. But my Guardian has looked out for me all through the years, as she will look after me tonight. She helped me find the right girls for my needs, paid them what they wanted, warned them what would happen to them if they ever spoke of it. She has always been there for me. And if lately she has made her own mistakes, then who am I to blame her for that. Her needs are… complex.'

Susannah swallowed, her fear like a physical presence in her chest. Amelia stared at her like a cat eyeing a mouse.

'Mistakes?' she asked, breathlessly.

Villiers frowned at her, shaking his head in disgust.

'You know what I mean!' he snarled, his anger returning. 'The three trollop's your *Jigsaw Jarman* has been sticking his nose into.' He spoke Jarman's name with a sneer of derision. 'My Guardian's appetites are not for you or he to judge. She kills because she needs the world to understand. Understand that the streets and the alleyways are not safe. Those loathsome women need to know their place! She showed them their place!'

He stopped suddenly, breathing deeply. His face turned thoughtful.

'Anyway, it's all over now. She has promised, haven't you?' He said this to Amelia, who just stared at him.

'That other fool was a bigger problem than anything my Guardian might do,' he continued. He shook his head. 'The idiot. Only my angel here could see what that man really wanted. She tried to warn me and the others but we would not listen. We were all too caught up in the excitement.'

He took Amelia's hand.

'I am so sorry, my angel. I should have listened to you. We all should have listened to you. However, you gave us all the right instructions and we eventually did as you suggested, and just like all the other times, the problem went away. The Ripper disappeared forever. Thank God for you and for Bennet, eh?' He laughed, softly. 'You put everything right and we started our gatherings again. But those new women began to get above their stations, didn't they?'

Amelia nodded.

'History repeating itself,' continued Villiers. 'Sometimes my Guardian feels the need to correct them, those women being the filthy, dirty sluts they are. Sometimes, she feels they need putting back into their place.'

Villiers frowned.

'She made a mistake. That first one, it was all just a mistake, but she couldn't help herself. It is her nature. And afterwards, my Guardian picked up her knife and donned her peculiar clothing and took to the streets of Whitechapel. And she killed them, ripped them apart, as they all deserve. And they are gone now. All of them, and we can soon start afresh once more. It will happen no more. She has promised.'

Susannah could not quite believe the revelations Villiers was telling her. It had not been him who had killed those women, as she had thought. It had been his crazy sister, and he really seemed to think that Amelia was going to keep to the promise she had made. Looking into the black pools of madness that were Amelia Villiers's eyes, Susannah knew that he was fooling no one but himself. His sister was even more inhuman than he was, and Susannah knew that she would kill again. She would never stop.

The distant smile on Villiers's face fell away, and he was back to the cold, inhuman being he had been when Susannah had been brought into the room.

'And now, I have some bad news, my love,' he said to her, the corners of his mouth twitching into a sad smile. 'There are people who know about my little club and I need to get rid of as much evidence as I can. I'm afraid you have become a liability. I know you have guessed something of what went on at the house while you were in the countryside, and I know you have told what you know to the charming Dr Jarman and you obviously now know about my Guardian. But without evidence, and without your gabbling mouth, there is little Jarman can do. Bennet will see to him in good time. Jarman will be dead, Handy is already probably dead, and all will be good with the world again.' He smiled at the distraught face of his wife. 'Once you are gone,' he said.

He turned to Amelia.

'I'm afraid we have to make it look like an accident,' he said. 'No knives tonight. You know what to do.'

Amelia grinned and left the office.

Susannah tried to plead with her husband. She promised she would not say a word, but he just stood, silent and immobile, not even looking at her. It was as if she were not even in the room with him.

Eventually, Susannah asked the question she did not want to hear the answer to.

'What are you going to do with me?'

As if in answer, the great steam engine barked into life.

# Chapter Twenty-Nine

## The Blond Man

The hansom dropped Curmudgeon off at the factory. He ran across to the open gates and frowned. The rumbling under his feet and the noise coming from the building itself could mean only one thing. The factory was running for some reason.

He slipped inside the yard and ran across to the doors. He had just reached out a hand to pull them open when a figure emerged from the other side of them.

He appeared only as a shadow, and before Curmudgeon could react the man was upon him. He grabbed Curmudgeon by the collar and head-butted him hard in the face, knocking the bigger man backwards.

Curmudgeon shook his head, droplets of blood already spraying from his nose, and he saw the man coming towards him, a knife glinting in his hand.

Instinct kicked in immediately. Within half a second, Curmudgeon had weighed up his opponent and had honed in on any weak spots. He threw up an arm and blocked the knife thrust to his face, then with the same arm he grabbed the man's sleeve and moved closer to him, pinning the knife by his side. Then he grabbed the blood-soaked bandage on the man's other hand and squeezed his thumb into it with all his might.

Bennet screamed as the pain in his hand, already huge because of the damage done to it, blossomed into agony. He tried to squirm away from Curmudgeon, but the other man was much too strong.

Curmudgeon, still pinning the knife arm and still squeezing the bullet wound, drew back his head and returned the compliment Bennet had given him. Bennet's nose erupted in blood and broken bones as Curmudgeon head-butted him with all the strength in his great body.

Bennet immediately buckled, his world spinning. His legs gave way and the knife clattered to the yard floor as his nerveless fingers opened. Curmudgeon, however, was not finished yet. He had learned never to stop fighting until he was sure his opponent was either unconscious or dead. That way, they couldn't do any more damage. He hauled the half-conscious form of Bennet higher and punched him rapidly three more times on the jaw. Bennet collapsed to the ground, immobile.

Curmudgeon bent down and picked up the knife, tucking it into his belt, then he quickly and efficiently went through Bennet's clothes, looking for more weapons, but finding nothing else. He sliced through one of Bennet's braces and used them to tie his hands to a nearby iron guttering pipe, then he left the snoring assassin covered in his own blood, dead to the world.

Opening the door again, he stepped into the factory. The noise was huge, and belts and pulleys of all shapes and sizes were whizzing all around. He looked around, seeing if he could see Jarman.

He spied someone moving up ahead and ducked behind some crates. Peeking out again, he recognised Rose. As he moved into view, Curmudgeon saw the familiar and comforting forms of Handy and Jarman. He jogged over to them.

Jarman saw him and his face became immediately concerned.

'What happened to you?' he shouted over the noise.

'Bloke outside. Attacked me with a knife.'

'Probably the man we were after,' said Handy. 'What happened?'

'I persuaded him to have a little lie down and think over his life choices,' replied Curmudgeon. 'He's outside, tied up.'

Handy turned to Rose.

'Outside, constable. Check he's safe and sound and then get back in here, sharpish.'

Rose ran off.

Jarman, Handy and Curmudgeon scanned the factory. It was huge.

'They have to be in here somewhere,' said Jarman to the others. 'We can't hear a thing in this noise. We need to turn the engine off.'

With this he led them towards the huge engine that battered away at the far side of the factory, the massive, glistening piston shunting up and down at an alarming pace. They were halfway there when Handy happened to look up and saw a shadowy figure moving behind the frosted glass of the maintenance room above them. He grabbed Jarman's shoulder and pointed upwards.

'You get that bloody machine turned off,' he shouted in his ear. 'I don't have a clue how to do it. I'll have a poke around up there and see what's happening.'

Jarman hesitated for a second.

'I'm the one with the gun,' Handy reminded him.

Jarman saw the sense in what Handy had said. 'Take Curmudgeon with you,' he said. 'It may just be a maintenance worker, or it may not be and there may be more than one person, in which case you'll need him.'

Handy nodded and he and Curmudgeon ran off to find the steps that led upwards. Jarman crept through the deserted factory towards the engine, keeping to the shadows as much as possible. Handy had said he had no idea how to work the huge machine, and Jarman believed he had no more knowledge than the Inspector, but he had seen these things being turned off and on before. There would be a lever somewhere to do the work, so it should be fairly simple. He hoped. He kept walking, trying to look all around himself at the same time.

Just along the shop floor, Amelia Villiers hid behind the racks and the stacks of crates and barrels, watching Jarman move closer towards her.

She had been returning to take that bitch to her fate at the bottom of the engine pit when she had seen the three figures as they emerged from behind some crates, and she had dived into cover just in time. She watched as the policeman and that servant of Jarman's had run off, and she licked her lips as the surgeon himself got closer. Her hand tightened on the butcher's knife in her grasp. The knife she had used so many times before. She grinned to herself at the thought of what she would do to Jarman when she had him at her mercy.

Amelia Villiers had always loved the sight of blood. Ever since she was a little child. She would often cut marks into her skin, just to watch the trickles of blood, and feel the sting, the pure, righteous sting of her very own flagellant's wounds stirring feelings within her that she could not explain.

The Mother had tried to stop her doing these things when she had found out about her actions. She had held her and stroked her hair and had told her she need not do it. Neither of them understood why the little Amelia committed these acts. The Mother blamed herself and so Amelia had blamed her too. When she had moved on from hurting herself to hurting other things, it had seemed to break The Mother, already weakened from the disease that was slowly killing her.

Everything became a target for Amelia. From flies, to frogs, and on to cats and dogs. She cut and sliced, and The Mother would find the desecrated corpses dotted around the garden and she began to fear more and more for her daughter. And for her son who was three years her junior. Would Amelia try to do the same thing to him?

Of course, this was nonsensical to Amelia. She could not hurt her brother. She was his angel, his guardian angel. She protected him. From everything. From the fists of The Father, and from the reality of The Mother's suicide when Thomas was only four years old. The Mother had cut her own throat rather than linger any more from the slow, inevitable march of her disease. And, of course, to free herself from the demented household The Father had made for them all: a violent and abusive husband, and a seemingly mad and dangerous daughter.

When Amelia had finally moved from killing animals and had added The Father to her long list of shredded corpses, she had become a surrogate mother for young Thomas. Through various different orphanages, as they grew, as they waited for Thomas to reach maturity and collect the inheritance that was his, she had taught him the ways of the knife. She had shown him how to cut, how to make the pain become a friend. She had turned him into what he was destined to be.

Amelia bore the marks made by her own hand all over her body. No one had ever seen them, not even Thomas. Amelia showed her body to no one but herself; as she sat in her room, naked, in front of the mirror, watching another red line appear on her arms, her legs, her stomach, her breasts. In between her legs. Underneath the man's shirt she wore, Amelia's body was criss-crossed with long, thin scars, each one showing her devotion to her skills. Her devotion to the pain.

Amelia had dedicated her life to her brother. She had learned very early on that, as a woman, she could never hold the power she craved. But she could teach Thomas to lend her that power. She had taught him the beauty of pain and blood, and he had taken it even further than she could have imagined. She had always been near him, watching through the keyhole as The Father raped and abused the servants, making the boy watch as he did so. She was there, following in the shadows, when he first embarked on his excursions into the East End. Protecting him. Encouraging him. She had watched, proud of him, as he cut himself and cut the filthy whores he seemed to prefer. And as she watched, shrouded by the darkness, she added more red lines to her own body.

This had been enough until that night she had found herself gazing through the dirty window as Thomas had cut that whore in the room in Whitechapel. She had felt the old excitement course through her, and she could not help herself. She had charged into the room, her knife ready, her only wish to take control of what that bitch was doing. To make her choke on her own foul blood. And it had been magnificent! The feeling of utter power over another life, especially a life as pathetic as that filthy harridan's, was a taste she devoured. To watch the light fade from the woman's eyes, to see the blood drain from her foul body like a gutted calf! Amelia had known, right then and there, that this was why she had been placed on the earth. She was no longer a Guardian Angel, she was now an Avenging Angel, and she would never stop until those women were gone!

And the best thing, of course, was how they had disposed of the body. The fateful date of the murder had given her everything she needed. God had sent it as a sign. Thomas had been persuaded, as he was always persuaded. They had dressed the body and loaded it onto a cart to be deposited in the fishmongers in Buck's Row, and Amelia had carved into the woman's stomach and revelled in what she found there, while Thomas looked on, his face pale and frightened.

So of course, the police all thought that the Ripper had returned. The place, the date. How she and Thomas had laughed at their stupidity when they got back home. But, once started, Amelia knew she could not now stop. She had donned the workman's suit and the disguise of the moustache and wig. She soon found those other women, the ones who begged for money at the house, and she had gasped with sensual pleasure as she had driven the knife into their throats, and into the area where they made their money from. The desecrations to their bodies made her squirm and squeal with delight. In a strange way, Amelia Villiers took the same sexual pleasure from these murders as her brother did at his parties. Or The Father had done, all those years ago.

How she had rejoiced when she gutted them. How she had wallowed in their pain and their blood. What galled her, though, was that the murders were blamed on Jack the Ripper. Blamed on that fool, that interloper. Amelia hated the thought that *he* was getting the credit for *her* work. Why was it always men who got the glory? However, it meant that she was allowed her pleasures, and the police would waste their time hunting a phantom who could never be found, because he was already dead.

Amelia smiled at the memories of the blood and the flesh in those black yards and alleyways.

Thomas had made her promise to stop when he found out about her night-time adventures, and she had said she would. But that was a promise as hollow as her soul. She could not stop now, not now she had tasted the pleasure of the kill, not even for her brother.

But the end was in sight. It would soon be all right again. All she needed to do was get rid of Jarman, and then watch as that bitch her brother had married was ground into mincemeat under the piston in the factory *'A terrible, terrible accident, officer,'* she would weep. *'Yes. She was truly like my own sister.'* Ha!

Yes. Get rid of Jarman, get rid of the bitch, and that was that. She and her brother would be safe again. And one day, one day soon, Amelia would don her workman's garb again and set out into the streets. Amelia grinned at the thought of what her future might bring.

As she watched Jarman come nearer, the knife twisted in her grip. This could not be the same as those three women, unfortunately; there would be no time for mutilations here. Jarman needed to die, to shut him up. He had gone against her and her brother, and he knew too much. She could not have that.

Jarman was almost level with her now. The stupid man still had no idea his killer was within inches of him.

Amelia moved.

\*

Rose made it outside and blew out a breath of relief as the damned noise of that factory receded behind the closed door.

His eyes scanned the shadowy yard quickly, looking for the man Curmudgeon said he had tied up. It was very dark and he could see nothing, so he unhooked his lamp and shone it around.

He was at the front of the factory and could see nothing of the man. He frowned. Where the hell had Curmudgeon left him?

He walked along the factory wall, searching for where the assassin might be. He muttered a scolding to himself for not getting an exact location from Curmudgeon, and as he did so his foot suddenly struck something that bounced and clattered across the ground of the yard.

Rose located the object and picked it up. It was a piece of cast iron guttering; a downpipe by the looks of it. The end of the pipe was shiny and new where it had been recently snapped.

Frowning, Rose went back to the wall where the downpipe must have come from and quickly located the rest of it, still attached. Lying on the ground beside the broken pipe, the edges frayed where they had been presumably sliced by the sharp edge of the downpipe itself, lay what looked like a length of elastic braces.

Rose blanched as he realised what he had discovered. He dropped the pipe and ran straight back into the factory.

He saw Handy and Curmudgeon at the bottom of the steps and ran towards them, trying to gain their attention above the din of the engine, but they did not hear him. He shouted again and Curmudgeon turned towards him, tapping Handy on the shoulder.

Rose had time to wonder why a look of shock and despair descended over Handy's face, before something walloped into the back of his head, and everything disappeared.

# Chapter Thirty

## The Confession

Jarman caught the movement out of the corner of his eye and managed to throw up an arm, saving himself from the knife that hissed towards his throat. The attacker immediately snatched back their knife arm and thrust again, making Jarman jump backwards to avoid being stabbed in the stomach. He looked into the face of his attacker, and finally, he saw the real Amelia Villiers. The real Ripper.

He was looking into a face that grinned maniacally at him. Black hair with its streak of grey hung loose and lank around her face, giving her a wild, demented appearance.

But it was her eyes that froze Jarman's blood. Those eyes were like black holes; seemingly completely dark and glazed with a madness that mirrored the glittering madness within the woman's soul. Amelia laughed harshly at the expression of utter shock on Jarman's face.

'You thought you were oh, so clever, did you not?' she hissed, barely heard above the rumbling and squealing of the huge steam engine near where they stood. 'You thought you had worked everything out. You thought, because you are a man, that the Ripper had to be a man too.'

She laughed again, spittle flying from the slash of her mouth.

'You believed that only a man could do what I did, didn't you? You could never believe that my hatred, my strength would be enough.'

She was trying to circle around him as she spoke, her eyes flickering and dancing all around; ever alert to any advantage she could achieve. Jarman watched her carefully, seeing this woman dressed in a man's clothes with the huge, glittering knife in her hand, knowing she was right. As he had confessed to Handy earlier, he had indeed been a fool.

When he had first seen that brutalised body in Church Street, he had believed that it was definitely a man who had committed the murder. The thought that it may have been a woman had not even entered his head. He had believed that the murders had been sexual in origin and in perpetration, and that had been because of the wounds to the dead women's sexual organs. He had thought, as all his training had shown him, that those wounds were because of some crazed sexual frustration on the part of the killer. He had thought the murderer had been taking some form of twisted revenge. Never, not once, had he entertained that there may have been another motive. Simpler and yet, in its own way, just as horrific.

He grabbed the cosh from his pocket, and she laughed when she saw it. She indicated to the knife in her hand.

'Good luck with that,' she said.

She suddenly stamped forward and lunged again, and Jarman just managed to knock her arm away with the cosh. Amelia laughed once again, more hair falling from their pins and framing her face in unkempt tresses.

'So,' she said. 'Jigsaw Jarman, the criminal expert.' Here she laughed derisively. 'You are completely and utterly baffled that a woman could do what I have done, aren't you? You ask yourself the question: why did I kill them? Why did I butcher them as they deserved, the filthy whores? Why did I slice them up while they were still alive and laugh as I did it? How could a woman do such things?'

Jarman was trying to edge closer to her. He needed to get close enough to try and overpower her somehow, because Amelia was the key. The killer stood before him, but unless he could get her to confess in a court of law, he doubted any gentleman of the bench would ever believe him, even with the ledger. Especially after they had seen the photographs of the bodies. They would never believe that a gentlewoman such as Amelia Villiers could ever be as brutal and as monstrous as she was. He talked, both for his own curiosity as well as trying to keep this mad woman occupied on his words.

'You killed them because they were prostitutes?' he asked, still trying to edge nearer.

Amelia shook her head at his stupidity, still grinning.

'My brother has his passions and I have mine. His are menial. He cut their skin. I, however, cut their throats and I sliced their bodies, and I loved it.'

Amelia laughed once more at the disgust and horror that fell across Jarman's face.

'Yes!' she cried. 'There is your reason. Simple and satisfying. I loved it, and I craved more. That fool: that so-called friend of Thomas's. He went out and indulged in his own fantasies away from the house. Why couldn't I?'

'The Ripper,' said Jarman, taking another tiny step towards her.

Amelia nodded.

'When we found out who it was, I told them I would get rid of him, but Thomas would not hear of it and so eventually I told him to hire a professional, which they did.' A sneer of contempt fell across her face. 'He thought I was probably quite capable of killing women, but not men. He should have remembered The Father. I have no problems killing men.'

Suddenly she lunged again, and Jarman once more threw up an arm. She was ready for this, though, and turned the knife so it scythed across his upper arm, only his thick frock coat stopping any major damage. But it had cut him badly; he felt the dull ache that bespoke a deep wound. He took a couple of steps back from her, hissing at the pain.

'Why did you do what you did to those women?' he asked, trying to keep her occupied. He hoped that Handy or Curmudgeon might come soon, looking for him. 'Why did you debase their bodies so?'

Amelia howled a demonic cackle.

'You call yourself an expert on the behaviour of killers? You are pathetic,' she hissed. 'It is very, very simple, Doctor Jarman. I carved their bodies because it makes me feel alive! They were nothing but filthy whores and they deserved nothing more than I gave them. I enjoyed it, and in a way, I set them free from their evil lives, don't you think?' She scowled. 'I still do not understand why my brother and his brethren enjoyed those women. The smell of their bodies! I had to throw the sheets away sometimes rather than just wash them.'

She seemed to slump, slightly, lost in thought for a second, and Jarman managed to take a couple of steps towards her.

'They were vile. All of them. Vile. And those men desired them! Desired them and their flesh and their blood.' She shook her head. 'I have never understood why. However, it did not matter. I was going to show them what I thought about them and their cunnies. And I did.'

Jarman, despite his horror at the creature in front of him, was engrossed. Here was a mass murderer, a killer who revelled in the blood and the gore she caused. Revelled in the terror she had unleashed upon the city. But there was one more question he burned to know the answer to.

'Who was Jack the Ripper?' he asked.

Amelia's face twisted into the face of a demon. It was an expression of utter hatred and vitriol.

'Who cares?' she screamed at him. '*He* takes all the glory. *He* takes all the fame! Why is *he* the one everyone fears? Why is it not me?'

She seemed to be almost begging him to ask her questions about what she had done, and Jarman nodded, knowing that he had to keep her occupied if he was to have a chance of disarming her.

'You're right, of course,' he said, straightening from the crouch he had been in. He smiled at her.

'What?' she asked, her eyes wide and maleficent. 'What do you mean?'

'I mean, what difference does it really make? He's gone, yes? You got rid of him with your hired killer? So, yes, you're right. Who cares about him? He failed. I want to know more about you, Amelia. I want to know about the three girls you killed.'

She was staring at him, wide mouthed, panting like a dog. Even if she had not just confessed to the horrific murders of the women, Jarman would have known she was completely psychotic just from a glance in her direction. This woman was totally mad. But he needed that knife.

He indicated at her clothes. 'You disguised yourself as a man?'

She nodded, slowly, frowning, but, it seemed, willing and indeed, eager to talk about the killings.

'And a blond moustache and wig, no doubt.'

Another nod.

Jarman frowned.

'But what about the blood?' He saw her eyes light up with this word. 'I know you cut their throats whilst they were still alive. How were you not covered in their blood?'

Amelia suddenly laughed and straightened too.

'Because I thought about it, unlike that other idiot. I worked out what was needed before I even took to the streets. I used my brain. I had a pack on my back, you see. A simple pack. It contained everything I needed; my dress to change into, a bag, but also a simple hood and apron that covered my face and body. I cut, the blood sprayed onto my hood and apron, and then I took the hood off and packed it neatly away. Then, when I was finished with my... my alterations, I found a suitable place and changed. Everything went into the pack, which itself disappeared into the lady's bag. And off I would trot, an innocent woman going about her business, straight back to the factory where I would wash everything and then have a lovely little sleep on the comfortable couch in my office.'

Jarman shook his head. 'My God,' he muttered in astonishment.

Amelia smiled.

'Simple really,' she said. 'But only a woman could make it work.'

Without warning, she took a series of short steps towards him, the knife hissing through the air, only inches from his face. Jarman staggered backwards under the onslaught until he backed into an open, wooden crate. His hands, grasping behind him to keep him upright, fell into the crate, and his fingers clutched around some sort of powdery grit. He had no idea what it might be, but he was in no position to wonder. He grabbed a handful of the stuff and threw it into the face of Amelia.

She howled as the phosphorus powder burned into her eyes, and she staggered away from him, wiping at her face. He jumped and swung the cosh and, more by luck than judgement, it struck her knife hand. She yelped, and the knife clattered away across the factory floor, disappearing underneath the racks.

He moved towards her again, but she had managed to dislodge some of the burning grit from her face and she glared at him, her eyes red and streaming. She searched, still half-blinded, for the knife for a moment, and then, when she could not locate it, she turned and pelted up a nearby metal stairway that led up onto the web of criss-crossing walkways.

Wiping his hand on his trousers, Jarman sprinted up after her.

*

Curmudgeon and Handy saw Bennet loom out of the shadows behind Rose and hit him with a large spanner. They were already running towards him as he hit the ground, senseless.

Bennet had either not seen Handy and Curmudgeon when he attacked the constable—or he had seen them but was not thinking straight after his beating—but whatever the reason, he belatedly noticed the two men now, and he ran too. Curmudgeon pelted after him as Handy skidded to a halt and bent over the constable. He checked he was still breathing, memories of Callow tumbling through his mind, and looked at his head, which was bleeding profusely from a cut four inches long. He was knocked out cold and Handy knew he could do nothing for him at the minute, so he gently laid his head back down and leapt to his feet, running off after Curmudgeon and the assassin.

Curmudgeon was onto Bennet within ten feet, as the assassin was still sluggish from the previous assault on him. Curmudgeon dived at the man's legs, and they went down in a heap. By this time, Handy was there too, and he had timed it perfectly. He immediately gave Bennet a huge kick in the side of the head, and for the second time that night, the assassin was battered into unconsciousness.

Handy turned to Curmudgeon.

'Tie him up with something. And for God's sake make sure he can't get free this time. We can't have him jumping up and down like a bloody Jack-in-the-box every five minutes.'

He turned and ran back to Rose, who he was pleased to see was slowly coming round. Curmudgeon pulled Bennet's remaining braces from him and tied his hands tightly. Then he slapped the man's face to help him recover from Handy's boot.

'On your feet,' he growled, dragging the stunned man upwards.

He pulled him along as he joined Handy and Rose, who had by now struggled to his feet. Rose glared at Bennet.

'Bastard,' he muttered.

Bennet, as mad in his own way as Villiers and his sister was, just grinned at him and spat a bloody globule onto the factory floor.

Handy turned back to the maintenance office. 'Right, let us try to see if we can move more than ten yards before someone else gets knocked on the bloody head!'

They moved towards the bottom of the metal stairs.

# Chapter Thirty-One

## The Pit

Susannah watched as Villiers just stood, immobile, staring out of the frosted window of the office. It seemed he was staring at nothing, but as she craned her neck upwards she saw shadowy figures outside, walking along the gantry towards the office.

'Thomas,' she begged. 'It's time to give up. It's time to stop now. It is all over.'

Villiers eventually turned to her, and his face had changed again. Gone was the spitting madman, and instead he seemed resigned to his fate. Susannah was cheered by this expression, until Villiers reached inside his coat and pulled out a long, wicked-looking knife. His eyes gleamed as he stared at it.

'I've always thought that a knife is a rather beautiful weapon, don't you?' he asked her. 'Beautiful and useful.' He grinned at her and Susannah licked her lips, her mouth suddenly very dry.

Villiers changed once again and sighed, as if he were extremely sad, but even through her terror, Susannah could see that this expression was like every other that had ever appeared on his face. It was just a mask: a shield, hiding the reality of his selfish and damaged soul.

'I will still fix this, you know,' he said, slyly. 'I can kill you and still retain my reputation. Do you really think my friends in the courts, my special friends who have enjoyed all I have given them at my house, will convict me of anything? Are you really so naïve that you believe your death, and the death of those men about to enter this room, will really change my fate?'

Susannah stared at him, knowing there was nothing she could say that would break through his deranged mind. He was living in a dream world, and he possibly had been for his entire life. He really, truly could not comprehend anything else other than simply leaving this factory and going back to the life he had lived before.

'You must know you cannot go on,' urged Susannah. 'Those men coming here are almost certainly policemen. Jarman is most likely with them. They will not just let you go.'

'They will do what all their kind do when they see me!' he suddenly roared, making her jump again. 'They will cower before my greatness! They will tug their forelocks and do as they are told! They at least know their place. Unlike you!'

Susannah cowered as he screamed at her. Then she played the last card she had.

'Thomas,' she said. 'I am pregnant.'

The door to the office was kicked open and Handy entered, his revolver in his hand. Rose and Curmudgeon crowded in behind him, Curmudgeon dragging in the battered Bennet.

Villiers immediately moved behind Susannah, the knife in his hand close to her throat. His face was even more ashen by what his wife had just uttered. His gaze moved from Handy to the top of Susannah's head and back again.

'Put it down,' said Handy. 'Put it down now or I'll shoot you where you stand.'

Villiers, holding the knife close to Susannah's neck, shook his head as he tried to collect his thoughts.

'Pregnant?' he asked.

Susannah managed to nod, turning to look him in the eye.

'Your child, Thomas. I am carrying your child. If you kill me, you will kill our baby. Please, Thomas, please give it up. For your child, Thomas. For your child.'

Once again, several emotions seemed to be fighting on his stern, dark features. A child! She was carrying a child. His child!

'Why did you not tell me?' he asked, still ignoring the men in the room with them. 'You should have told me.'

'How could I, Thomas?' she asked. 'When I knew what sort of man you truly are?'

Villiers stared at her; pale, trembling, sweat coating his upper lip and brow. And he knew she was right. He once again thought of The Father, the man who had beat him and chastised him and made him watch what he did. Would he be a man like that? A father like that?

He slowly turned back to Handy as the Inspector shouted at him once again to lower the knife.

'I think not,' he eventually answered. It seemed his personality could change in an instant. He turned back to Susannah, and she saw a new emotion on his face now. It was a strange look of resignation.

'So, you are carrying Jarman's child, are you?'

Susannah's mouth opened in stupefaction. '*What?*' she asked.

'You've obviously been seeing a lot more of him than I first thought,' he responded, nodding to himself as if he believed his own lies. 'And now you think you can use that man's bastard against me?' He turned away from Susannah's horrified face and spoke to Handy. He had heard what his wife had said, but he had fooled himself in his own reality for so long that her confession had instantly been turned into something against her. Simply one more reason why she should die.

'I think what you should do is remember your place,' he said to Handy. 'Put your weapon on the floor and back away from it. And do it right now. Otherwise, I shall cut a hole in the lovely throat of my lying, cheating wife here.' He stared at Handy with his dark, glittering mad eyes.

Handy shook his head.

'No,' he said, simply.

'Do it!' roared Villiers. 'Otherwise, I shall cut her throat right now and you will all watch her die!'

With a grimace on his face, Handy threw the revolver to the floor, knowing he had no choice.

Villiers frowned at Handy, changing once again. 'How are you still alive?' he asked, irritated. Then he sighed and turned back to Susannah. 'It seems we are at a stand-off,' he muttered. The knife was pricking the skin of Susannah's skin, trembling with the rapid pulse of her throat.

'What will you do, Thomas?' asked Susannah, suddenly.

'What?'

'What will you do after you have murdered me and your unborn baby and the police have just let you walk away? Where will you go to?'

Villiers frowned at her, as if the question was completely mad.

'Jarman's baby,' he chided her, as if reminding her of his truth. 'And I shall go home, of course. Back to my golden life,' he added, dreamily.

Susannah shook her head at him.

'That cannot happen, Thomas,' she said, as if she were explaining something to a small child. 'Even if you kill every person in this room, which I doubt you can achieve, then your life is over, you must see that, surely. How can you go back home? How will you explain what has happened tonight? Your friends have helped you so far, Thomas, but I doubt they will help you anymore. In fact, I would not be surprised if they had not already hired another like this creature here to get rid of *you*. You have become a liability, I think. I presume that is this man Bennet you talked of.'

Villiers glanced at Bennet in a silent confirmation. Bennet, in return, just stared back at him, flatly.

'It is over, Thomas,' repeated Susannah, insistently. 'You are a murderer. You will hang for it. Hang like a common criminal. And I and your child will be the better for it.'

Villiers stared at her with a growing horror at what she had said. Then his eyes caught sight of something out of the large window behind her, and they widened even further. Unlike the rest of the smaller windows in the office, this was a viewing window, and it looked out over the whole factory. Susannah and the other men in the room also turned to look.

And saw the two figures standing on the gantry, right above the huge, pumping steam engine.

\*

The foot-wide gangway that Amelia had run along at the top of the steps trembled as soon as Jarman stood on it. He licked his lips and stared down into the deep pit where the huge knuckle of the single steam piston disappeared and re-emerged in its manic, thumping cycle. The gangway was right above that yawning chasm.

He looked up towards the end of the gangway, to where Amelia crouched with nowhere to go.

The gangway ran past where Jarman stood, past the top of the metal stairway he had just ascended and beyond, disappearing into the shadows of the factory's roof. But at the other end, where Amelia stared at him like a cornered animal, the gantry simply ended, bolted onto the bricks of the factory's outer wall. Amelia, half-cloaked in shadow, glared at him, her hair wild and tossed from the passage of air by the motion of the engine below.

She looked, to Jarman, like a crazed witch: strange and eerie in her male clothing, and with her unbound hair twisting and writhing in that column of air. Her eyes were red rimmed from the compound he had thrown into her face, and the powder had smeared into her skin, giving her a wild, ragged appearance. Jarman took a step forward, onto the narrow gantry that had nothing but a thin chain barrier running along the side of it between them both and the pit of the moving engine.

'It's over, Amelia,' he said to her, unknowingly echoing what Susannah had said to her husband. He said this loudly over the noise of the engine even though, thanks to the acoustics of the space, it was actually quieter up there above the machine then it had been standing beside it.

'You have come to the end,' he urged. 'Give it up now. Too many people have already been hurt. Too many have been killed. It is time to stop.'

Amelia continued to glare at him. Then she barked an arrogant laugh.

'Time to stop?' she asked. 'And then what? A hanging? Public humiliation?' She shook her head. 'You misunderstand the person I am, Jarman. I will never stop.'

And Jarman knew she was right. He suddenly realised that he would have to physically drag her down from that gantry, or one of them would die. He swallowed and took another decisive step towards her.

'There is one other thing I would like to know,' he called to her, taking another step. The gantry swayed again, and he saw a puff of brick dust appear near one of the bolts holding it to the wall next to Amelia. She either did not hear the noise or ignored it. He paused, waiting for the gangplank to settle.

'What do you want now?' she growled at him, as if he were an irritating student and she were his teacher.

'Why the date?' he asked. 'The first killing. Bucks Row, August thirty-first. Why did you make it the same date and place as the first Ripper killing? Was that part of your plan? To make a connection between your killings and that of the Ripper?' He took another step. Amelia was less than ten feet from him now, pressed up against the wall, but the gantry gave another squeal and even she turned to look at the bolt next to her head. It had been pulled an inch out of the brick and seemed very loose. She turned back to Jarman and gave him a strange, lopsided grin.

'That was when I knew God had placed me on this earth to carry out his work. He had arranged everything for me. It was fate.'

Jarman frowned at those whispered words but took another step, the gangplank creaking again. It was seemingly not built for more than one person at a time. Yet another example of a lack of money spent by the rich on those things that did not matter: the lives of the factory workers whose jobs took them up there.

'Amelia, it has to stop now,' he urged. 'You cannot hope to escape. I am here with the police. They have probably arrested your brother already. Your time has ended. The Ripper is finished.'

Amelia laughed, harshly.

'The Ripper will never be gone,' she said, scathingly. 'You know that. I may die, the original Ripper died, but as long as there are the wealthy and the poor, another Ripper will always be ready to take up their knife. It is part of human nature, Jarman. Something you know to be true. It is the law of the jungle. Just because the jungle is now made of bricks and iron does not mean human nature can be quelled. Somewhere, deep in the heart of humanity, is a roaring wolf that cannot be tamed. Dig hard enough for it, and it will rear up and tear your body to shreds.'

She suddenly sprang at him and battered him down, causing him to fall on his back onto the gantry's narrow footway. The breath went out of Jarman with a huge blast and he lay winded for a moment until Amelia fell upon him and her hands wrapped themselves around his throat.

Her strength was incredible, and Jarman realised now how she had sliced through those women's throats with such ease. Her madness had given her a power immeasurable. The gantry banged and bucked like a live thing beneath him as she crushed him down, and he suddenly, horribly, felt the whole structure lean to one side. He knew, without even looking, that the loose bolt had snapped free. Only one more bolt was stopping them both from falling into the pit below.

He grabbed Amelia's wrists, his head feeling like it was going to explode. He could not believe the enormous power he felt in those hands that were choking off his life, and he heaved uselessly at her arms, knowing that if he did not relieve the pressure soon, he would quickly black out.

He heaved and heaved, but the hands stayed firmly around his throat. Amelia was hissing demonically at him, and her spittle sprayed onto his face. He felt his lungs fluttering uselessly, saw a greyness appearing around the edges of his vision and he realised he had only one choice left.

He lifted his legs and wrapped them tightly around Amalia's waist as she lay on top of him. He squeezed them, tightly, just as she was squeezing his throat. They lay, silent and trembling for a moment, two quivering figures on a quivering, skeletal gangway; a horrible parody of a lovers embrace.

Eventually, as the greyness around him was turning black and his face was becoming mottled and strained, he felt one of her hands leave his throat, and she started punching at his thigh in an effort to get his legs off her waist.

The pain was immense, but he ignored it. Amelia had pushed herself up, using the one hand still around his throat, and this was all Jarman needed. With an immense effort, he suddenly curled his legs under her, his feet on her stomach, and he pushed with all his might.

Amelia flew backwards, her fingernails raking skin from Jarman's neck as she did so.

She did not go far—Jarman was too weak from his strangulation, and she was much too powerful—but it was enough for the remaining bolt holding the gantry to the wall. With a snap, it broke, and instantly, with a hideous squeal of metal, the whole gantry fell from the wall and collapsed downwards, bending like a hinge just above where Jarman lay. He felt himself sliding down the ruptured gangway, and he scrambled frantically for some sort of hand hold. He managed to jab his fingers into the interlacing grids of the gangway floor and watched, aghast, as Amelia tumbled down the broken section, her own hands scrabbling for purchase. He could do nothing to help her as her body slid towards the edge.

It suddenly seemed completely silent as Jarman stared down the length of his body at Amelia, rolling and bouncing down towards the gaping maw of the engine pit. He glanced up and saw that the gantry had bent just where his hands were, and the metal was slowly tearing itself apart with the weight of Amelia at the bottom of it. The gantry seemed to buck suddenly, and bent even more, the gangway floor splitting like a burst sack just beyond him. He looked down once again.

And saw that Amelia had found purchase. Her scrabbling hand had suddenly found a grip. She hung from that one hand, her fingers digging through the lacing of the metal floor, just as Jarman hung above her. But unlike Jarman, Amelia had nothing to push against. She dangled, with nothing but fifteen feet of empty air between her and the pumping piston of the steam engine.

'Amelia,' he gasped. 'Grab my foot. For God's sake, grab my foot!' He waggled his outstretched leg at her, as if to make the point. Amelia did not move. She just hung there by one, immensely powerful hand, as Jarman tried to stretch his leg towards her.

She looked down into the pit of the thumping engine, then she slowly turned her head back to Jarman. Her hair was twisting and turning around her head. He looked deep into her glittering, mad eyes, and for a second, a split second, he thought he witnessed fear. Then she seemed to grin at him in a strange, mocking admonishment.

She opened her hand.

And disappeared into the churning pit below.

# Chapter Thirty-Two

## The Room of Blood

Jarman pulled at the large lever, slowing the piston down, down, until it stopped with a clank and a wheeze. The silence wrapped itself around him like a cloak. He paused for a second and then walked around to the front of the pit. He looked down.

The mashed and flattened corpse of Amelia Villiers lay like a stain in the shadows at the bottom of the pit, and the raised—now motionless—piston was smeared with blood and gore where it had smashed into her again and again, crushing her out of existence. She no longer resembled a human, if indeed that was what she had ever been. Her head and torso were merely flattened shapes, smears painted onto the bricks of the pit floor. Jarman stared at the pulp that had once been a woman and for some strange reason, the shape the body had been pulverised into reminded him of a single portion of a jigsaw puzzle. A puzzle that had, finally, been pieced together.

With a grimace, Jarman turned away from the gruesome sight and looked up towards the maintenance office. There, he could see Susannah's pale face staring out desperately at him. And beyond her, the still, open-mouthed form of Thomas Villiers. And he was holding a knife to Susannah's throat.

Jarman was off and running as soon as he saw this, his heart, which had only just got back to normal, suddenly racing again at the thought of what might happen to Susannah. He prayed he would get there before Villiers could gather his thoughts after the death of his sister.

He pelted across the now eerily silent factory, and sprinted up the staircase leading to the office, bursting into a scene of strange stillness. He stood panting in the doorway.

Villiers was still staring at the huge, silent piston where his sister had died. He seemed to be in complete shock. Susannah had turned her head and was looking at him in terror and relief that he was alive after what she had just witnessed. Handy, Rose, Curmudgeon and Bennet were standing silently.

Curmudgeon was the first one to speak.

'And you say I enter a room noisily.'

Jarman ignored him, staring instead at the weapon in Villiers's hand, still held menacingly close to Susannah's throat. Villiers slowly seemed to come to his senses and turned to him.

'What have you done?' he asked, in a shocked whisper. 'What have you done?'

Jarman did not answer, and it was Susannah who spoke.

'She is gone, Thomas. Put down the knife before you are gone too.'

Handy, eying the revolver on the floor, nodded.

'She's right, Villiers. It's all over now. Nowhere for you to go. No way out of this. Put down the weapon and we can still sort this all out.'

Villiers tore his gaze from Jarman and turned to Handy. His face was the face of a man who had lost everything. A man who had lost his soul.

The room was silent, only Jarman's heavy breathing breaking the hush. Villiers was seemingly unable to process what he had just witnessed. It seemed as if he could not speak. As if he could take no action. Then his black, empty eyes seemed to clear.

'You killed Amelia,' he whispered, hoarsely. 'You killed my angel.'

He was like a man completely abandoned, and Jarman took a couple of quick steps towards Susannah. Villiers barely seemed to notice,

'It seems there is no one to save you this time, Villiers,' said Jarman. 'Your Guardian can no longer help you and she can no longer hurt anyone else. Come on, man. Put down the weapon. You can see your cause is lost. There has been too much death. Let your sister's demise be an end to it.'

Villiers was still holding the knife in his hand, but the surgeon could see something changing in the man's eyes. It was as if he were retreating into himself, retreating into his mad, broken soul.

Villiers seemed to think about what Jarman had said as his eyes glazed over. He saw, perhaps, a public trial: a vengeful public that cheered and bayed for his blood, his name splashed all over the newspapers. And those newspapers would be on every table at the Cardington Club, on every train seat in and out of London. His name, his face, and his reputation would be smeared and sold and laughed at, and he would have nothing left, and nothing to look forward to except a long drop in Newgate Prison yard, dressed like a common criminal and stared at by common prison staff. And perhaps, in what was left of his humanity, he saw a child staring at a photograph of the father they had never known, but with the knowledge of what that father had been. He could not face that ignominy. He seemed to nod to himself, and Jarman belatedly realised what was going through his mind. He made a move towards him, but he was too slow.

Villiers turned the knife. He stared intently at it for a moment. He saw his distorted reflection in the gleaming blade. And the reflection spoke to him. It told him to do what must be done. Jarman was right. Without his Guardian, he was nothing. Without his Guardian, there *was* nothing.

He seemed to smile down at Susannah as his hand tightened on the handle of the knife, but it could have been a sneer of hatred.

'A beautiful weapon,' he whispered once again. With a sudden jerk of his arm, he pulled the razor-sharp blade deeply through his throat.

He coughed and gagged as Jarman grabbed Susannah and pulled her towards him. She screamed, as Villiers sagged to his knees, as his blood gushed and spurted from the huge wound. His eyes never left Susannah's, even as he collapsed to lie on the floor on his side, even as they dulled as death came for him and he went to face his judgement. His eyes, his accusing eyes, stared at Susannah, and they seemed to blame her for his downfall. For the death of Amelia. For the death of himself.

There was a leaden silence in the room as Villiers's corpse trembled and jerked its way out of existence. Jarman held Susannah tightly, Rose and Curmudgeon stared in horror, and Handy shook his head in shock at what he had just witnessed. Nobody seemed able to move.

Apart from Bennet.

He saw his chance, and being the man he was, he took it.

With his hands still tied in front of him, he swung his fists upwards and to the side, smacking into the already bleeding head of Rose, who staggered backwards. Before anyone else could move, he had snatched the revolver from the floor and turned.

Later, no one could really say what they thought was going through his mind. Perhaps he was still concussed from his beatings and was not thinking straight. Perhaps he thought to shoot his way out, to escape his crimes as he had escaped from so many others. Perhaps, he simply wanted revenge.

But it was Curmudgeon who stopped him.

Bennet had no sooner grabbed the gun before Curmudgeon had recovered enough to understand what was going on. He was already moving when Bennet fired, grabbing the knife that he had tucked into his belt earlier and launching it in one smooth motion. Bennet was thrown backwards as the knife pierced his chest, such was the force behind it, and Curmudgeon, taking no chances as usual, stepped forward and booted him in the face. With a gurgle, the assassin collapsed on his back, staring up at Curmudgeon with an almost aggrieved expression. Then his eyes glazed over and he emitted one last, bubbling breath. He lay motionless, and his blood mingled and pooled with that of Villiers.

The room was once again silent for a second as they all tried to take in what had just happened Jarman turned to Susannah, whose body he had thrown himself across when Bennet had fired.

'Are you hurt?' he asked. 'Susannah, are you all right?' He took her hands in his, and she nodded, shock and horror still in her eyes by all she had seen and witnessed. She was beginning to tremble, violently.

Then her eyes widened even further, as she saw blood spreading rapidly in a thick, scarlet stain on Jarman's waistcoat.

Jarman blinked at her, wondering why her face was fading in and out of focus. *This seems very odd*, he thought, drunkenly. Then he took a staggering step backwards.

Jarman collapsed to the floor and stared up at the ceiling of the office.

He registered Susannah's face in front of him as she knelt over him. She seemed to be saying something to him, tears streaming from her eyes, but he could not hear her properly. Then Handy appeared, Rose, and finally, the terrified face of Curmudgeon.

Then everything went black.

# Chapter Thirty-Three

## A Final Meeting

The next day found Handy and Frederick Abberline standing outside the office of Assistant Commissioner Montgomery Pence.

Handy's unshaven face was strained, and black marks ringed his eyes. He had been awake for over thirty hours, but there was no way he was going to miss out on this. Abberline saw the wolfish look and placed a warning hand on his arm. Handy glanced at him and nodded. He knew what Abberline meant by the touch. He was just a civilian. He, Handy, had no jurisdiction, and it was only because Abberline allowed it that he was able to accompany the Inspector. But it felt good to be there.

Once they had got out of that factory, Handy had called on Abberline, who had met him at Leman Street Station as soon as he got the message. Handy had no authority since Pence had sacked him, but he knew Fred and he knew he would listen to his story.

Abberline had listened to what Handy said, looked at the ledger, and then accompanied Handy back to the factory where he saw the bodies of Villiers and Bennet, and took a grimacing glance at the mess that was left of Amelia Villiers. He put the wheels in motion straight away, allowing Handy to accompany him as they began to round up every single name on the list.

It did not take long for most of the named men to understand what they needed to do; and after a little persuasion, which took the form of Handy showing them the ledger with their names in it and telling them that he'd see them all in prison or hanged if they didn't give him something, a couple of them told him what they knew. Only a few of them had actually clubbed together to pay for Bennet, and those names were now in custody. And there was no doubt in Handy's mind that they would swing for what they had done.

Lyon had tried to bluster his way out of it, but soon crumbled when he realised the game was up. Handy explained that he knew exactly who had killed Ely, and that he knew Lyon had been a regular at Villiers's house. He showed him his signature and the dates, and said that he also knew that he had tipped off Pence, who in turn had got Bennet to murder Ely. Lyon had had his solicitor with him when Handy and Abberline arrived, but when the man saw the evidence against the editor, he just sat back in his chair, crossed his arms and told Lyon that he was on his own. So Lyon had given a written confession stating that he had sent a message to Pence, and that Pence was the one who had hired Bennet, therefore inciting them both in a murder plot. He told Handy and Abberline that it was Pence, through Bennet, who had started the riot that got Frank Callow and the other constables killed, and that Pence had acquired the uniform for Bennet to get into the station where he had murdered Clinch. Bennet had also killed Grace Wright; Pence had given him the address of the safe house.

So now the two men stood outside Pence's door with a warrant for his arrest in their hands and, in Handy's heart anyway, an almost physical lust for revenge. Abberline nodded at the two officers who were guarding the office to stop Pence making his escape, and knocked on the office door softly.

There was no answer, and without bothering to try again, Handy impatiently barged his way in. Abberline closed the door softly behind him as he followed.

Pence was standing behind his desk and a decanter of scotch, half full or half empty, depending on how long the man had been at it, stood on the green leather desk top.

His uniform jacket was slumped over the back of his chair and he was in his shirtsleeves. His previously perfectly groomed hair was sticking up in clumps, as if he had been pulling at it, and his eyes were red and puffy from weeping. He obviously knew the game was up. He smiled crookedly at the two men and saluted them with his glass, which he drained quickly when he saw the look in Handy's ice blue eyes.

'Whatever you want to say to me, I do not want to hear it,' he slurred. He glared at Handy. 'Filth from the gutter,' he muttered, repeating what he had said the last time they had met. He barked a laugh, re-filling his glass and gulping at it again.

'Jumped up Jack-me-lad, that's what I called you, and that's what you are. Nothing but scum, Handy. Nothing but scum.'

He stepped back hastily, his face suddenly terrified, as Handy moved towards him.

'Don't you dare touch me, Handy. You do not have the right to touch me. I am your superior!'

He screamed suddenly as Handy grabbed at the decanter on his desk and launched it at him, managing to duck as it whistled over his head and smashed against a wall. The room was suddenly thick with the smell of alcohol.

'My superior?' repeated Handy in a low, menacing voice, moving slowly around the desk. 'You think you're superior to me? I know what you've been doing, Pence, you filthy bastard. I know you hired Bennet to kill Ely and Clinch and Grace, and I know you did it before, when you got rid of the Ripper.'

Pence had backed into the corner now, away from Handy's advance. His glass of whisky shook in his hands and he stared at Handy with terrified eyes. It seemed he had lost the ability to speak.

'Murder is murder, Pence,' said Handy. 'You'll swing for it.'

He grinned at the sudden stricken look on Pence's face. He stepped right up to the Assistant Commissioner, his face within inches of the smaller man. He could smell the scotch on his breath.

'But do you know what's worse than that?' he asked the petrified Pence. 'Worse than ordering the deaths of those three people? Worse than killing four policemen? Worse even than killing Frank Callow, my friend? Do you know why I really hate you, you pathetic piece of shit?'

Pence just stared at him, his eyes brimming with more self-centred tears.

'Answer me!' Handy suddenly roared, and Pence dropped his glass, moaning in terror. Handy grabbed him by the throat and slammed him onto his expensive desk, staring down into his white, terrified face.

'It's what you did to those poor girls,' he said. 'That's what really angers me, Pence. You took those women, those women who have *nothing*, and you forced them into doing things no human being should ever do. You used your power in society to indulge in your sick little fantasies and you never, not *once*, had even one thought of what they were going through!' He banged Pence's head on the desk to emphasise his point.

'You were supposed to *protect the innocent.* That's what your job was. That's what the police do. But, instead, you used your rank to simply take what you wanted, what you desired. And those poor bloody girls had no choice. 'Cos that's what life is, isn't it? It's bastards like you riding rough shod over everybody else because you bloody well can, and those girls just took what you dished out because they didn't have a choice. They've *never* had a choice; from the minute they were born they've never had a choice. Never known any sort of comfort or love and all they ever had to look forward to was to service you and others like you to earn the few pennies you deemed to throw at them.'

Handy shook his head in disgust.

'The Ripper may have killed those girls' bodies, but you and people like you, you killed their souls a long time ago. *You*, Pence, are the scum.'

He reached into his pocket and pulled out a sheet of paper.

'Now, this here in my hand, is what you might call a warrant for your arrest. Understand that?'

Pence managed to nod when Handy knocked his head on the

desk again.

'You shall take this here warrant, and it shall be served. Understand that?'

This time, Pence nodded straight away.

Handy stared at him, glaring, wanting nothing more than to kick Pence's pathetic body all around his plush office. He fought against the impulse for a second or two and instead crumpled the paper into a ball and shoved it roughly into Pence's mouth.

Pence whined as Handy's knuckles mashed his lips, but Handy stopped the noise by slapping his face and then pushed him away, wiping Pence's saliva from his hand onto the man's jacket.

'And I, Pence,' he finished with, 'like my father before me, am a policeman. Unlike you. Understand that?'

And Pence, his career in tatters, his future ruined and his mouth full of a warrant for his arrest, wailed at what he knew to be true. He slid slowly down to the luxurious rug under the desk, where he curled himself into a ball and wept like a child.

Handy stared at him in disgust for another second, then he spat onto the rug beside him and stalked from the office.

Abberline, a smile on his face, knew better than to try and stop him.

*

A fortnight after the arrest of Pence and the other names on the list, Handy stepped outside the courthouse and was immediately swamped by the noise of the crowd that awaited him. The trial had been huge news, and reporters from all over the city threw question after question to him, but he ignored the lot of them, pushing his way through the raucous throng and climbing into the hansom waiting for him.

As the cab made its way through the busy streets, Handy took off his hat and rubbed his head, roughly. Then he lit a cigarette and turned to look out of the cab's window at the streets of Whitechapel, just trying to let his brain have two minutes of peace before it all started again.

The cab dropped him at Leman Street and he sauntered in, returning the salute of a constable just coming out on the start of his shift.

'You be careful out there,' he said, and the man saluted again and sauntered off.

Handy went inside and waved a greeting to the desk sergeant. Then he went into his office and sat down.

A constable came in and gave him a cup of tea. Handy thanked him and the man left. It was very quiet in the office. Handy sipped his tea and just revelled in the fact that he was in the office at all. He picked up the file in front of him, and read through it once again, his mind going back over the two weeks since that night in the factory. The night of blood and murder and mystery.

However, it was a mystery no longer. The crimes had been wrapped up, the murders solved and the case closed.

He picked up his cuppa and sipped it.

He thought of Carter Jarman.

Two weeks since the events at Villiers's factory, and still Jarman had not recovered. He had survived the wound—just—but infection had begun to boil its way through his system. There was little the doctors could do except keep the wound clean with carbolic and hope he was strong enough to recover.

However, he still fought. Weaker, paler, thinner every day. But he would not give up. He fought for every breath, and the infection seemed to be a permanent feature now. Handy had spoken to one doctor, an associate of Jarman's called Gresham, who sadly seemed to think that the infection would be the undoing of Jarman. But Handy could not give in to that thought. He knew the strength of the man who had stood by him throughout those hectic and violent weeks. He refused to believe a man such as him could perish because of a few germs.

He had just finished his tea when Rose burst into the room, noisily.

'Bloody hell, constable,' growled Handy. 'You're getting just like Curmudgeon.'

Rose grinned. 'Hope so, sir.'

Handy spread his hands in a gesture of enquiry. 'Well? What do you want?'

'It's Mr Jarman, sir.'

Handy felt a terrible weight descend upon him.

'What about him?' he finally asked, not wanting to hear the answer.

'He's woken up, sir. And he wants you to go right on over to the hospital to see him. Apparently, he wants to know what happened after we left the factory. He can't remember a thing. The porter down the hospital...'

He stopped talking when he realised Handy had left the office.

He stepped into the main station and saw Handy just climbing into a hansom outside. He turned to Rose.

'Come on, then!' he cried, impatiently.

Rose hurried to catch him up.

\*

Jarman groaned as he reached for the glass of water by his bedside. It seemed to be situated miles away from him and yet was only inches. His entire body ached.

He knew all the signs, even if Gresham had not told him. His fellow doctor had just left his side and had explained to Jarman how he had been in a fever since they had removed the bullet from his chest. The wound itself had almost done the job on its own; he was lucky to have survived it. But the infection was worse. It had reduced him to a shivering, delirious wreck. Every day, Gresham told him, he had waited for the news of his demise, and every day he had lived. As the weeks went on, Gresham realised that those days, those living days, meant a greater and greater chance of recovery. And so it had happened. That morning he had opened his eyes, and his mind was clear, his body cool. The infection had run its course.

He now waited impatiently for Handy. He was weakened, he was in dreadful pain, but he was desperate to know the outcome of the enquiry that must have already occurred. He wanted to know what had happened to Susannah. He wanted to know that she was all right.

The door opened and Handy appeared, grinning his toothy grin as he saw Jarman awake. He swept off his hat and stepped forward quickly to his bedside, shaking his hand vigorously, not seeing the wince on Jarman's face.

He spied a stool and dragged it across to sit by the bed, still grinning at Jarman.

'It really does my soul good to see you awake and recovering,' he said, enthusiastically. 'We all thought you were off to meet your maker for a long while, and that's for sure.'

'Thank you,' said Jarman, smiling back at him. His voice was thin, and he licked his cracked lips. 'Would you mind?' He indicated to the jug and a glass beside the bed. Handy poured the water into the glass and held it to him, helping him grip it as his fingers trembled. Jarman drank, deeply, then sighed.

'Thank you,' he said again as Handy put the glass back down. He eyed the file under Handy's arm.

'Is that an official document I spy?' he asked.

Handy nodded. 'It is.'

'Then…?'

Handy nodded again, hardly able to stop the grin from spreading on his face.

'Reinstated,' he said. 'You are once again looking at *Inspector* Jonas Handy. Inspector First Class, as well.'

'My dear fellow,' said Jarman. 'Allow me to congratulate you on that. The police force would be a weaker body of enforcement without your input.'

Handy's grin grew wider at the compliment. 'Thank'ee,' he said. 'Thank'ee kindly.'

'Now then,' said Jarman. 'What happened? What have I missed since I began my enforced recuperation?'

Handy blew out his cheeks and rubbed at his head. 'I'm not really sure where to start,' he said.

'I remember nothing after Bennet shot me,' said Jarman. 'Why don't you start from there?'

Handy got himself comfortable. 'Well,' he began. 'We—me and Curmudgeon and Rose, I mean—we got you into a cart outside the factory. It was Mrs Villiers who alerted us to the cart; she said it was how Amelia Villiers, disguised as the blond man, had taken her there in the first place.'

He paused as he saw the interest in Jarman's face at the mention of Susannah.

'I'll come back to Mrs Villiers later,' he said.

Jarman nodded, pretending that it did not matter, and Handy smiled again.

'So, we got you to the hospital; Curmudgeon drove, and I don't think that horse will be recovered yet. I've never ridden so fast in my life as I did that night. He just put his head down and—Whoosh!—off we went. Anyway, at the hospital, we quickly explained what had happened to you and they took you off for your surgery. We left Curmudgeon waiting, and I think he's hardly left your side since, by the way. He seems to blame himself for what happened to you, poor fellow. Anyway, me and Rose went back to the factory, via Leman Street. We got some help. I called on Fred Abberline, who came down too. I didn't have no authority, you see? Seeing as Pence had sacked me, the bastard.'

Handy then quickly recounted what had happened. How they had rounded up the names and how he had finally confronted Pence. Jarman listened, agog, as the tale was told.

'Anyway, there was a hell of a stink, as you can imagine,' continued Handy after he had recounted everything. 'The high-ups in the Met were apoplectic about Pence, apparently. They put someone in temporary position of acting Assistant Commissioner, a fellow named Boyce: good bloke. Knows his stuff, does old Boycie. He was the one who formally reinstated me as Inspector and gave me the promotion.'

'What's happening to those convicted?' asked Jarman.

'Just came from the inquiry today,' replied Handy. 'Most of the people at the parties have got away with it; those who did not directly have anything to do with the killings. Villiers is already dead, obviously, and we know the new Ripper will strike no more as his sister is now residing in just about the flattest coffin you will ever see.' He chuckled at the poor joke.

'Lyon is for the rope,' he continued. 'He thought he wouldn't swing by giving us all the information about Pence, but the court saw things different. Pence himself was due to hang too, but the slippery bastard had his sentence commuted to life imprisonment because of his former work in the force. I was angry about that at first but of course, what it means is that he will have a hell of a time of it until some bludger sticks him with a shank. To be honest, he'd be better off following Lyon and taking the long drop, but somehow the thought of *ex*-Assistant Commissioner Pence tip-toeing his way around Newgate Prison trying to keep out of everyone's way warms the cockles of my heart. It could not have happened to a nicer fellow.'

He chuckled again.

'It's been a strange few weeks,' he continued. 'I never thought, for an instant, that a woman could have committed those crimes. Goes to show something I should have learned a long time ago. Never trust anyone.'

He looked at Jarman, shrewdly.

'We have all the loose ends tied up for this case,' he said. 'But not for the case two years ago. Fred was mightily unimpressed that I could not give him a name for those awful crimes committed in '88. Did Amelia Villiers say anything about it, when you were doing your trapeze act in the factory roof?'

'About the identity of Jack the Ripper?'

Handy nodded.

Jarman shook his head. 'I'm afraid she said nothing about that killer. She seemed annoyed when I mentioned him.' Jarman raised his eyebrows at the Inspector. 'But I suspect you have something to say on that matter?'

Handy laughed, briefly. 'You read me like a book, Dr Jarman. Read me like a book, you do. Or should I say,' here he opened the folder under his arm, 'like a file. Now, we will never know for sure, as Bennet was obviously a very competent man. Jack the Ripper is dead. But once everything was sorted, it struck me that there may have been an easy way to check, to give us at least a tantalising clue as to that man's identity.'

'Go on,' said Jarman, smiling. He knew exactly what Handy was getting at.

'I thought to myself, everything that wonderfully erudite Dr Jarman said has come true. And then I thought, if the Ripper was part of the group, and the killings happened in the autumn of 1888, when the group closed its doors for such a short time, then perhaps a perusal of the names that were in the ledger before that date, and the ones who came back when everything had been fixed, may have been illuminating.'

Jarman sat straighter in his bed; his pain forgotten. 'And?'

Handy handed him a sheet of paper. Ironically enough he recognised the sheet as one of the receipt sheets from the factory. There were three names on it, written in the Inspector's own hand. Two of the names had been crossed out.

Jarman stared at the name, and then slowly looked back to Handy.

Handy nodded.

'Each of those three men were part of the club in the months leading up to the autumn of 1888,' he said. 'And none of them returned when it opened again. The two that are crossed out are still wandering around, and cannot be convicted of anything. Nothing to prove that they were engaging in anything other than extra-marital shenanigans, as twisted as they were. One of them at least, will be one of the many divorces we shall probably be soon perusing in the papers. I would imagine that the wives of all those club members will not be best pleased with their husbands and what they've been up to.'

He leaned forward and plonked a stubby finger onto the remaining name.

'He, however, as you will well remember, as it was all over the news at the time, disappeared in early December 1888. His body was found floating in the Thames. He had apparently committed suicide.'

'Like Edward Ely,' said Jarman, and Handy smiled, grimly.

'Like Edward Ely.'

Jarman looked at the name again.

'My God,' he muttered. 'Who would ever have believed that *he* could be that infamous killer.'

Handy took the sheet from him and tucked it back into the ledger.

'Not that we will ever prove anything now, which is why I never mentioned this to Fred. The family would kick up a hell of a noise if this came out, so I'm doing him a favour by keeping it quiet. I believe Jack the Ripper will probably remain anonymous forever. And perhaps that's for the best. Perhaps that way, people will soon forget all about him.'

He patted the folder. 'I'll keep this, though,' he said. 'And when I'm old and grey, I shall sometimes take it out of the secret place I shall hide it in, and I'll pour myself a drink, and I'll show it to me dad, and I'll tell him that his son solved the mystery of Jack the Ripper. He'd like that.'

They were interrupted by a knock on the door, and Rose poked his head around the frame, grinning when he saw Jarman awake.

'Rose,' said Jarman. 'How are you?'

Rose entered. His face was green and yellow with healing bruises and Jarman saw that he was wearing a cheap but smart suit, a bowler hat in his hand.

Handy saw the look on Jarman's face and grinned.

'I've taken on *Detective* Constable Rose. He's too good a copper to be slouching around in ill-fitting police uniforms. Don't he look sweet in his suit?'

Jarman grinned and gave his hearty congratulations to the

blushing DC.

'We've got a call, guv,' he said to Handy, eventually. 'Been a murder. Down on the New Road. Someone shot the owner of a tavern. Mr Boyce sent a messenger.'

Handy sighed and stood up. He held out his hand to Jarman.

Jarman gripped it, and the men shook.

'Thank you for all your help. Jigsaw,' said Handy, and Jarman laughed.

'You are more than welcome. Jonas. If you ever need me again, you know where I'll be.'

Handy nodded, and the two men left.

Jarman belatedly remembered that Handy was going to tell him about Susannah, but Rose's appearance had cut their chat short. He was desperate for news about her, but it seemed he would have to wait. He sipped his water and sighed into a silence that was abruptly destroyed by the manic entrance of Curmudgeon.

'You're awake,' he said.

'Your powers of observation have not deserted you in the last fortnight,' replied Jarman, wiping at the water he had spilled on the blanket when Curmudgeon had barged in.

Curmudgeon just stood there, grinning stupidly. He tried to speak, his eyes sparkling for some strange reason, but could not seem to find the words.

'I know, Curmudgeon,' said Jarman, softly. 'I know.'

Curmudgeon sat and they talked about nothing for a while. Curmudgeon kept trying to apologise for not protecting him in that factory, but Jarman would have none of it, so they talked about nothing again, until Curmudgeon stood abruptly.

'Well, now that you're feeling better, I can perhaps get back to some sort of life without having to hang around here day and night like a bloody hospital porter.'

'You are looking decidedly clean, Curmudgeon,' Jarman noted, taking in for the first time the newly shined boots, clean greatcoat and freshly brushed hair. 'Are you off somewhere?'

'Me and Ellie are off to the theatre, I'll have you know,' said

Curmudgeon, glancing at his pocket watch. 'I should be going, actually'

'Ellie?' asked Jarman. 'Mrs Villiers's ward?'

Curmudgeon nodded.

'I've been seeing quite a lot of her, as we've both spent most of the last two weeks sat outside your room.'

'Why has Ellie been outside my room?'

Curmudgeon shook his head at this. 'Ellie goes where Mrs Villiers goes.' He saw the frown on Jarman's face. 'She hardly left your side, Jarman. Not until today, when she realised you were going to be all right.'

He handed Jarman a letter.

'She left this with Ellie.'

Curmudgeon looked at him with a glance that seemed suspiciously like pity, then he was gone. Jarman sat with the letter in his hand, not knowing what to think. Eventually, he tore it open and read what she had to say.

*"My dearest Carter,*

*My apologies for this use of your given name, but I have been alone with you so many times now, with you sleeping and dreaming and twisting in your bed, that I believe I have quite forgotten we are virtual strangers. I really do not know where to start with this correspondence. You saved my life, Carter, my life and my child's life, and you did that by almost throwing away your own. Thank you. For everything, a thousand times over. Thank you.*

*Because of your actions, I and my child have everything we need. I have everything back. Everything that was once mine is now mine again. My dowry, Dene Manor. Everything. I have even taken my maiden name again. I want nothing more to do with that despicable family. All of my husbands' wealth, everything he accrued, the London house, the factories. I have decided to donate them all to charities. Charities that help the weak and the powerless of society. Those people need it more than I, and it is fitting that everything he tried to take from them is returned. As I have already said. I have everything I need.*

280

*I do not begin to know what you must think of me, Carter, and I cannot bring myself to face you, because I fear what I may see in your eyes. I fear you will be disappointed. As society obliges me, I am in my time of mourning, but instead, I feel free. Free of that awful man and everything he stood for. I had almost given up hope that there were good men left in this world. You showed me that there are. You are, indeed, the best of men.*

*My hope is that one day, we can meet as friends. I want to enjoy the company of a man I know to be good and true. And one day, soon, when time has passed, I would like to find out where that friendship may lead.*

*But I am a widow, carrying my dead husband's child, so please know that I would never ask this of you. It is simply a wish of mine. A wish I know may never be fulfilled. I need some time to come to terms with my new freedom, to fully appreciate the peace and the beauty of my home in the country. To understand where my future may lie. I hope and know you will understand why I was not there when you recovered. I hope you can forgive me for that. And I hope that one day, we will meet again. To talk of the future perhaps?*

*Whatever that future may bring, please, please know, Carter, that the sacrifices you have made, both for myself and my baby, will never be forgotten.*

*I shall forever be in your debt.*

*I shall forever be your friend.*

*Thank you again, Carter. May your life be as rich and fulfilling as you deserve.*

*Sincerely and gratefully yours,*
*Susannah Dene.*"

Jarman read the letter twice through, a strange melancholy flowing through him. He felt deflated, used up. Useless. He had started out on this horrifying adventure as a man alone, with only Curmudgeon keeping him from his own demons. Now, after all the blood, the corruption, the horror. Now he was a different man. He still had Curmudgeon, yes, but he also had new friends: Jonas Handy and

George Rose. However, it seemed the friend he really wanted was out of his reach. She was only a few miles outside of the sprawling, filthy, crime-laden city called London, but she may as well have been on another planet. It seemed she somehow blamed herself for the madness of her husband and her sister-in-law, and needed time alone to come to terms with what had happened to her. He could not blame her for that.

However, he also recognised that the letter gave him some hope. He knew that he was not going to give up on her, and he also knew that, when she was ready, he would be waiting. Then they could both, perhaps, see where that may lead.

Jarman put the letter back into its envelope and turned to stare out of the window at the city. Out there, at this very moment, the three children of London; Deprivation, Crime and Horror, were hiding their despicable faces from the sun. But when the moon rose tonight, and the fog rolled along the dirty, dangerous streets, those white, inhuman faces would grin up into the night.

And Jigsaw Jarman, a man with new friends, but a man still alone, vowed he would be there to do his best to stop them.

# The End

# Did You Enjoy This Book?

If so, you can make a HUGE difference.

For any author, the single most important way we have of getting our books noticed is a really simple one—and one which you can help with.

Yes, you.

Us indie authors and publishers don't have the financial muscle of the big guys to take out full-page ads in the newspaper or put posters on the subway.

But we do have something much more powerful and effective than that, and it's something that those big publishers would kill to get their hands on.

A committed and loyal bunch of readers.

Honest reviews of our books help bring them to the attention of other readers.

If you've enjoyed this book I would be really grateful if you could spend just a couple of minutes leaving a review (it can be as short as you like) on this book's page on your favourite store and website.

# Historical Note

This is NOT a story about Jack the Ripper. That story has been told many, many times, and there are many, many experts on the subject. I am not one of them, and I trust that anyone who knows anything about it will forgive any mistakes I may have made. Let us, instead, put those mistakes down to artistic licence. However, it is set within the world the Ripper inhabited, so the reader is entitled to know what is fact and what is fiction.

All the characters in this novel, apart from Frederick Abberline, are fictitious. The names of the Ripper's victims are real, as are the names of the women who were killed before the so-called 'canonical five' were murdered. The only other real name that is mentioned is constable John Neil, who was one of the first men to stumble across the body of "Polly" Nichols: the Ripper's first victim. Every other character sprang from my own imagination. The streets of London mentioned are obviously real, although some of them have changed names over the intervening years, and could, with a bit of imagination, have easily been the scenes of the murders described in this story.

There were match factories situated in Mile End; however, the chances of them having a huge steam engine powering them are, unfortunately, very remote. Most match factories consisted of working by hand; "piece work"; i.e. the workers were paid for what they produced, and in most cases they had to buy for themselves the raw materials they needed to produce the matches. There was a match girl strike in 1888 against the terrible working conditions that these women had to endure. But I wanted someone to get squashed in a Victorian steam engine, and I needed a female workforce, and so *Villiers FireSticks* was created. Again; artistic licence.

*Phossy Jaw* was a real, and horrible disease, brought on by close contact with the awful chemicals used in these establishments, and it sometimes resulted in women having to have their entire lower jaw removed. By 1890, however, it was, thankfully, a little better known about, and therefore not so prevalent as it had once been. It is also true that workers sometimes had all their teeth pulled if they showed any signs of toothache. This happened at the Bryant and May factory (unrelated I believe from the modern company which bears the same name.) I have no idea whether the phosphorus was stored in gritty form in crates, but I thought that would be good to chuck in Amelia's face, so, once again, I fell back on artistic licence.

Which leads us to the conditions I have described of the streets of Whitechapel. Although I have, as is my want, defined these streets as filthy and dangerous, the reality was that they were probably just as bad, if not worse. Jack London's *The people of the abyss* is a good start to find out what life was really like in the East End. And he was there in 1902; twelve years after this novel is set. The area of Old Nichols, for example, where Jonas Handy hails from, was a place teeming with disease and abject poverty. If the reader would like to know more about this, then I recommend *The Blackest Streets* by Sarah Wise (Vintage Books, 2009). It truly shows just how horrific life could be in the East End, and it tells an engaging, yet extremely disturbing account of life in that particular slum. On a similar note, and although it sounds incredible, there are accounts of upper-class families who did, indeed, visit these slums to stare in horror and appreciation of what they themselves were lucky enough to have. A sort of day trip of deprivation.

As I have previously said, this is not a story about the Ripper. However, I needed some background about that killer, and so, for this background, I mainly delved into two other books. *The Five* by Hallie Rubenhold (Doubleday, 2019) is an engrossing look into the lives of those five murder victims, who have become so famous only because of how they died. It shows how each one lived, and gives reasons why they ended up as they did. If nothing else, it turns on its head the idea that all these women were slovenly slatterns, and gives the real reasons why they ended their days under the Ripper's knife. It also shines a light as a sad indictment to Victorian society, which could indeed be cruel and dark if one was unfortunate enough not to be born into wealth. For the sake of simplicity, I made all the victims in this novel drunken prostitutes, but the real reasons why women ended up like this is far more complicated. And far sadder. I thank my daughter Lizzie for buying this book for me.

The other book I used was a gloriously graphic account of the killings: *The Complete Jack the Ripper* by Donald Rumbelow (Penguin, 1988). This book not only gives an almost blow by blow account of the murders, but also gives an excellent account of everyday life and death in Whitechapel. On this note, I will give a special thanks here to one of my oldest friends: Darren Brown. He gave me this book to read a while ago, and he also supplied me with various old maps of 19th Century London while I was writing, on which I could plot the scenes of this novel. He has a lot of things like this about the Ripper. Because he's weird.

The awful way the Ripper killed his victims means that there are one or two descriptions in this novel that are graphic in nature. I apologise to anyone offended by this, but, as in all things, a quick skim through the reports on Mary Kelly, or a glance at the photographs of her murder, show that fiction can never be as horrific as real life.

A note about the three killings that happened before the murders of the canonical five. Two of these women died a few days after the attacks on them (one of them mentioning a blond man) the third died at the scene. There were even a couple of murders that happened *after* the five were killed. The strangulation of the victims also needs discussing. It's generally believed that at least four of the five canonical victims were strangled into unconsciousness before the Ripper began his grisly work. In order to not muddy the waters too much, I have smoothed those details somewhat by saying that they were all strangled beforehand to give Jarman something to hang his hat on when looking for differences between Jack and Amelia. I trust Ripperologists will forgive me.

Researching this novel also gave me a chance to delve into the fascinating world of the history of the Metropolitan police. I have tried to get things as close as possible to what was going on in the police force at the time (e.g. when Handy mentions to Pence that he would be moving soon, the headquarters of the Met moved from Old Scotland Yard to the Embankment in 1890, so I thought I would add that little detail in.) Policing those streets must have been awful, and the police themselves were underpaid and overworked and it was a dangerous and thankless task. In July of 1890, some constables even tried to organise a strike for better pay and pensions. As Jarman himself might perhaps say, 'It was ever thus.' Pence, as Assistant Commissioner, would have been on a not unimpressive salary: £800-£1000 a year, the equivalent of around £200,000 (roughly) in today's money, and AC's were, unlike the upper echelons of other forces, usually from a military background. Some men did work their way up through the ranks, however, so Pence's success is not outside the realms of possibility.

I made Jarman a surgeon because I was looking for a character who was not a policeman but rather an enthusiastic and intelligent amateur. I suppose I was looking for a sort of Sherlock Holmes persona, except Holmes is a very cold and odd fish. I wanted my main character to be a man of action, but also a man of science and goodness. And surgery was certainly becoming much more of a science by this time; the publication of Pasteur's Germ Theory in 1861 and the advances in anaesthetics and disinfectants forwarded by the likes of Simpson and Lister meant that, by the turn of the Twentieth Century, hospitals would be a lot more familiar in structure to the modern reader than they would have been only fifteen or twenty years previously. Therefore, Jarman is a man of science and humanity. Just as I wanted him to be. As a little aside here, I am aware that although Jarman uses the phrases 'serial killer' and 'copycat killer', these were not generally used at the time the novel is set. I thought Jarman should have that honour, however, and I trust any experts will allow my indiscretion to stand.

Handy is obviously a different kettle of fish. A man dragged up in the harshest of conditions who, through luck and intellect, becomes an incredible detective. In his own way, he is as focused on the truth as Jarman is. These two men, from totally different backgrounds, form the backbone of this novel.

The Villiers siblings are, of course, as horrible as I could make them. They bare no correlation with any people I know about, either dead or alive. I wanted them to be evil, but not in the archaic, moustache-twiddling, villainous ways we often associate with Victorian melodramas. I have tried to give them a reason for their horrifying pursuits, but again, I remind the reader that this is a work of fiction. And every book needs its baddie(s).

As far as this story goes, I am hoping to soon expand on the Victorian world of the main characters. Jarman now has a group of acquaintances that he trusts and understands. They have become his friends.

Therefore, Jigsaw Jarman, Jonas Handy, George Rose and the redoubtable Curmudgeon will return. And, who knows? Perhaps Susannah Dene may well be there alongside them.

# Glossary of Victorian Slang Words

There are one or two slang words used in this story that were used at the time. I thought I would place them here in a short glossary for reference.

Dolly/Dollymop: A prostitute or woman of low repute. (One of many different words for this profession.)

Jack: A detective

Bludger: Could mean a pimp, but in this context, a mugger, thief or murderer

Tallywag: A man's private parts

Cock Lane/Cunny/Quim: A woman's private parts

Dairies: A woman's breasts

Cully: A prostitute's customer

# Acknowledgements

I need to thank a few people. Firstly, as always, to my family. I love you all. Also, a massive thank you to the beta readers (Andreas Rausch, Ami Agner, Dan Elford, Justine Gilbert, Joyce and David Oxley, Elizabeth Shipp, Andrew McCairn and Catherine Goodwin) who took this book on when it was in a pretty raw state and whose advice and ideas turned it into something a lot better. To the advance readers who also took the time out to read and comment. To Pete and Si at Burning Chair: thank you for your continued patience with me and my work and for your help, support and advice.

A special mention must be made here to the author Steven Saylor. Many years ago, I became captivated by the character of Gordianus the Finder in Saylor's Roma sub-Rosa series of mystery novels, set in Ancient Rome. Once I became hooked on these, I think the idea of writing my own historical crime novel one day began sneaking around my brain. Eventually (after many years of getting round to it) that day has dawned, but instead of having one protagonist, like Gordianus, I ended up with two in the form of Jarman and Handy. Who would have believed it?

Finally, to you, the reader of this book. Thanks for taking a chance on it. I know you didn't need to, and I really can't thank you enough for giving it a go.

Richard Ayre
Newcastle upon Tyne
September 2021

# About the Author

Richard Ayre was born in Northumberland, too many years ago now to remember. He has had a variety of jobs including roofer, milkman and factory worker. Tiring of this, Richard studied for a degree with the Open University and now teaches History for a living.

At an impressionable age he fell in love with new wave Heavy Metal and rock music and at about the same time read his first James Herbert novel. The combination of these two magnificent things led him to write his first novel, Minstrel's Bargain, a tale of music and horror. He now lives in Newcastle upon Tyne where he continues to write whenever he can. When not writing, or putting children on detention, he can be found pottering around the Northumberland landscape on his motorcycle, Tanya.

You can contact Richard via Facebook, Twitter, or through his website: https://richardayre1.wixsite.com/richard-ayre-author

# About Burning Chair

Burning Chair is an independent publishing company based in the UK, but covering readers and authors around the globe. We are passionate about both writing and reading books and, at our core, we just want to get great books out to the world.

Our aim is to offer something exciting; something innovative; something that puts the author and their book first. From first class editing to cutting edge marketing and promotion, we provide the care and attention that makes sure every book fulfils its potential.

We are:
- Different
- Passionate
- Nimble and cutting edge
- Invested in our authors' success

If you're an author and would like to know more about our submissions requirements and receive our free guide to book publishing, visit:

www.burningchairpublishing.com

If you're a reader and are interested in hearing more about our books, being the first to hear about our new releases or great offers, or becoming a beta reader for us, again please visit:

www.burningchairpublishing.com

# Other Books by Burning Chair Publishing

**A Life Eternal**, by Richard Ayre

**Point of Contact**, by Richard Ayre

**The Fall of the House of Thomas Weir**, by Andrew Neil Macleod

**The Curse of Becton Manor**, by Patricia Ayling

The Brodick Cold War Series, by John Fullerton
**Spy Game**
**Spy Dragon**

**Near Death**, by Richard Wall

**Blue Bird**, by Trish Finnegan

The Tom Novak series, by Neil Lancaster
**Going Dark**
**Going Rogue**
**Going Back**

**10:59**, by N R Baker

**Love Is Dead(ly)**, by Gene Kendall

**Haven Wakes**, by Fi Phillips

**Beyond**, by Georgia Springate

**Burning, An Anthology of Short Thrillers**, edited by Simon Finnie and Peter Oxley

The Infernal Aether series, by Peter Oxley
**The Infernal Aether**
**A Christmas Aether**
**The Demon Inside**
**Beyond the Aether**
**The Old Lady of the Skies: 1: Plague**

**The Wedding Speech Manual: The Complete Guide to Preparing, Writing and Performing Your Wedding Speech,** by Peter Oxley

**www.burningchairpublishing.com**

Printed in Great Britain
by Amazon